Nocturne by K.G. Bolingbroke

Published by Aura Creative Collective, LLC

First printing, 2025

Front Cover Design by K.G. Bolingbroke

Back Cover Design by Svetlana Perovic

Cover painting *Princess Tarakanova* by Konstantin Flavitsky

Title Page, *Prologue* and *Epilogue* Graphics by Black Bird Designs

ISBN:979-8-9921871-0-6 (Paperback)

979-8-9921871-1-3 (Hardcover)

Author's Note

This work contains some themes and depictions that might be sensitive to certain readers. It is also not recommended for young readers as it contains adult content and is highly suggested for mature audiences only.

NOCTURNE

K.G. BOLINGBROKE

To Mr. Bolingbroke
Ours is an eternal union

PROLOGUE

"*I* HAVE TRAVELED THOUSANDS *of miles and hundreds of years,*" *the woman dressed in all black said so softly it was nearly a whisper. "I do not intend to turn back now because of your fear." Her voice transformed from a murmur to a snarl, tinged with a timeless dialect that sounded from nowhere yet everywhere at once. The man stood still, waiting.*

She occupied his favorite armchair by the window of his bedroom. It sat in the corner of the dimly-lit room, illuminated by a single candle and the dying flames in the fireplace. Her face was shrouded by the hood of the cloak she wore and on her lap, her hands cradled an object that was difficult to discern. She clutched at it more defensively as his gaze flicked towards it again, seeing it glitter. Was that an urn?

"I will not do it," he replied, his voice braver than he felt, although he was unable to withhold it from trembling still. "It is against the will of God. A perversion to all that is holy."

She sneered. "You will. Otherwise, you will suffer the same fate as your father and that of his father before him."

"You are her, aren't you?" he stammered, taking a half step back and wiping the sweat dripping from his brow.

"Her?" she repeated, amusement seeping from her voice.

"The daughter of Lilith, the spawn of the Devil... you seek to restore—"

"Enough!" she interrupted. "You know what I have come here for. If I am cursed to walk this Earth eternally, I do not wish to walk it alone."

Had he not been so frightened, he might have been touched by this hint of humanity, but it was odd coming from her. His heart pounded in his ears and sweat now dripped into his eyes.

"And if I do it, will you lift the curse you have bestowed on my family for centuries?"

"I will. You and your descendants will never see the likes of me or my kind ever again."

"You will never harass us, follow us, threaten, or murder us ever again?"

"You have my word."

His usually comfortable bedroom felt small and stifling, like the walls were closing in around him, trapping him, warning him that he had no other choice but to comply. "Very well. I will need remnants of the deceased."

She rose to her feet sharply and he stumbled back to create more distance between them. The room felt even more like a prison suddenly; he was like a caged hare and a wolf had just been set loose into the enclosure. She continued to clutch what he had confirmed was an urn, holding it close to her.

"I have them here, but should you make any attempt to tamper with or destroy them, you can rest assured your death will come

to you swiftly and violently. Your death and the death of your family."

"Spare my family and you have my word." He was surprised at how brave he sounded when he felt nothing close to the sort.

"I stand by my promise. Do what you need to prepare and only I will handle the remains."

He took a deep breath, searching for any courage he could muster, and began to back up towards his bed, keeping his eyes on the woman. She did not move but he could feel his flesh prickle as her eyes remained fixed upon him. Slowly, he lowered to his knees and began to pull a chest out from under his bed. He opened it, still eyeing her warily, and removed objects out of it one by one—various jars, feathers, and then finally, a worn book bound in black leather.

Straightening to his full height, he opened the ancient book passed down to him from his father, flipping through the pages until settling on the page he was looking for. He then lowered cautiously to his knees once more and took a piece of chalk from the chest, drawing a five-point star on the floorboards and enclosing it with a circle. He carefully placed an object from the chest at each point of the star one by one: a black feather, a small skull having once belonged to some indiscernible animal, and a withered severed finger.

"The remains, madam," he asked, reaching for her urn. She did not relinquish it. Instead, she placed it down at the point of the star nearest her, ignoring his request. She loomed over him, making sure that no harm would come to the contents of the urn.

"Then finally, I need—" Before he could finish, she procured a vial from somewhere beneath her voluminous cloak and handed it to him. Their fingers touched briefly as he took the vial from her and he shivered at how cool her fingers were. Not quite as cold as the dead but neither the warm touch of the living.

"*The blood of the living, Madam?*" *he asked.*

"*Yes, the blood was drawn from a willing participant,*" *she confirmed,* "*who is still living.*"

He opened the vial and smeared some of its contents on the star's final point. Then, with the rest, he smeared it on his forehead, chin, and then finally his chest after he had removed his waistcoat and shirt. Before he continued, he threw another log on the fire and stoked the flames, coaxing them to grow mightier. When the room was better lit, he cast a cautious look at the face of the woman. The hood still shielded her features but from what he could see, he reckoned she was exquisite with the soft curve of her chin and her plump lips that arched slightly upward. He also caught a flash of her long pale neck.

"*Remain focused,*" *she chided him, and he was ashamed that she could seemingly read his thoughts.*

Clearing his mind not only to spare any further embarrassment but to focus on the task at hand, he began to read aloud from the timeworn leather-bound book. His eyes began to cloud over as the words on the page began to take hold of him and he slipped into a stupor. The words were all he could sense, feel, and even smell. The words of perverted Latin incantations of summoning, calling, and gathering. Words of fear, unholiness, and darkness.

He remained in this stupor for an immeasurable amount of time, whispering the incantations from the black book. His companion sat completely still, only rising to renew the log in the fire or relight the candles. She said nothing the entire time, not that he would have noticed if she had, so consumed as he was in this nocturnal text, never meant to see the light of day. The words it carried bore the fruit of a condemnable craft, of dark powers that had been passed down to him from his father who learned them from his father and so on.

Suddenly, he began to convulse, eyes rolling back in his head as he was thrown from the book. His enigmatic companion caught him swifter than a flash of lightning, cradling his head before it reached the floorboards. She needed him alive to complete the task that only he could perform. Few remained who carried this dark power.

The words consumed him still, despite the convulsions. He could hear them reverberating in his head as froth began to spill from his lips. The flames from the candles turned blue and the flames from the fireplace turned black before they flickered and extinguished entirely. An animalistic groan echoed from some place. Was it from his own lips or from somewhere beyond this room?

The woman's hood was thrown back as she leaned over him, dabbing his forehead with a cloth. As the delirium halted for a brief moment, he saw large round eyes bearing into his, and they were encased in the thickest fringe of eyelashes he had ever seen. He was captivated, clinging to that as his delirium returned and his body continued to convulse for an eternity. Then, just as suddenly as they came, the convulsions stopped, and he was pinned to the floor. The groan sounded again. The urn near his feet shuddered, then crashed, its contents spilling.

Ashes.

His companion rose to her feet, her features somewhat disguised by the pale blue flames illuminating the room. As he remained pinned to the floor, he could finally begin to make out her face.

She was the most beautiful woman he had ever seen.

She pulled a short blade from the depths of her cloak, now ignoring him entirely, and she raised it over their heads. He winced in anticipation, envisioning the blade plunging into his heart, but that is not what happened. She threw back her cloak to reveal the pale top of her breast swelling from the bodice of her gown. She pressed the blade to her skin, slicing her flesh along the swell. There was a trickle of blood, the blackest color he had ever seen.

She knelt down and grasped at the ashes that had spilled from the urn, taking a handful in her small delicate hand, her long fingers enclosing around them protectively. With her other hand, she pressed on her wound, causing more blood to spill and trickle onto the ashes.

After a few drops, she blew the ashes towards the pentagram on the floor and the candles flickered. The ashes then quivered and began to move, taking shape. That was his cue. While still pinned to the floor, he continued his incantations, struggling through the sweat and weariness beginning to take hold of him. The ashes continued to tremble, move, and shift until they formed the silhouette of a man. The groan sounded again, deafening this time, causing him to begin to convulse again but he did not let that stop him from whispering the words of the leather-bound black book.

Then it stopped and all was still.

His convulsions had stopped, but he was still pinned to the ground and therefore unable to see what was occurring. It wasn't until he heard soft whimpering that he had some semblance of what was going on. His eyes were beginning to droop and the corners of his vision were starting to grow black. He fought against the current of shadows threatening to overcome him, wanting to see the fruits of his labor after all this time, but it was difficult to resist as it was taking a strong hold on him.

Then, he heard a sudden intake of breath of someone who had just emerged from a body of water after nearly drowning.

The whimpering took the shape of a gasp which then morphed into soft crying.

Then he heard a man's voice.

The newcomer spoke hoarsely, with a deep voice that had remained unused for some time. Though he spoke tenderly.

Guided by the woman, the newcomer rose unsteadily to his feet where the ashes had once lain. The necromancer, pinned to the floor, could no longer force his eyes open and he succumbed to the darkness enveloping him.

"Thank you, Herr Van Helsing," was the last thing he heard before the darkness consumed him.

I

OCTOBER 1495

"THIS COLD IS GOING to be the death of me," Helene muttered under her breath. A hacking cough further emphasized her displeasure.

"It is going to take a lot more than a chill to bring you down," I assured her. "Besides, this chill is nothing. We have this all the time back at home."

"It's different here," she croaked before clearing the phlegm that had risen to her throat. "The air, it's thicker. Not at all like the air in Austria."

It was no use rebuking her, she was in one of her moods today, antsy I am sure, after having been cooped up for so long. Instead of challenging her, I extended my legs, stretching them in the carriage carrying me to my new home, Romania. As I was the eldest child of the Holy Roman Emperor, Maximilian—and a daughter at that—I had the unfortunate privilege of marrying a lesser ruler east of the Holy Roman Empire. One would think that being the eldest daughter, I would be married to a French or Spanish prince, princes of more progressive and powerful courts, but that privilege was being given to my younger sister, Margaret.

When I was a child, I came across a rumor that had been spread about me when I was born. It was said that I was cursed; that I carry my curse in my raven-colored hair—the color of a gypsy's—suggesting that I am not my father's daughter.

The night I was born, a raven flew into the birthing chamber and became disoriented, crashing into items, throwing them about, and causing chaos. The midwives screamed as they flapped their own arms, trying to catch it and expel it from the chamber while my mother remained helpless on the bed with birthing pains coursing through her body. This was seen as a bad omen. Then, when they saw I was born with an inky thatch of hair, the suspicious midwives began to whisper. The raven crashing into the room was a curse from my real father, cursing my mother for having forsaken him for Maximilian. My mother was fair-haired, and my father was redheaded, so when I was born, my dark hair was quite a shock, I was told. My birth also did not match up with the date that my parents were married. I was born in secrecy a few months before they officially wed. So the whispers grew louder, and it was believed that one day my real father would come to claim me as his heir to rule the gypsies.

I remember hearing this rumor when I was about eight or so. I was devastated as I had heard it from a group of children at my father's court—children of his various nobles—on a day they felt they needed to be particularly cruel. I came crying to Helene, throwing myself into her lap and telling her

I didn't want to be kidnapped by the Gypsy King. Of course, she assured me that no such thing would happen, but it was also then that she began to school me in the ways of politics.

Helene has been my nurse since birth, and she confirmed that Maximilian the First was my true father as she was the one who had provided cover for my parents during their premarital rendezvous. My step-grandmother, who was a large influence in arranging the marriage of my parents, also reassured me as I grew up, telling me that my grandfather, too, had very dark hair. Even still, that never quite quelled my insecurity about my hair, feeling dark, odd, and ugly among the other bright and pretty girls at court. Despite their reassurances, the rumors continued to fester, and my existence became a thorn in my father's side when I was constantly overlooked by potential suitors. My brother, Philip, had been betrothed to Juana of Castile and the negotiations of Margaret's betrothal to Prince Juan of Spain began before the negotiations of my marriage to this Romanian prince even started. My brother was to marry next year, and my sister the year after that, though their contracts had been set and sealed long before mine. Out of courtesy, and to spare me any further embarrassment, my father requested that those marriages wait until mine was completed.

Finally, an ambassador from the Prince of Romania came, solving my father's political woes. So now, at the ripe old age of eighteen, I was traveling with Helene and an escort to be married.

I wasn't thrilled at the prospect of leaving my home and the life I knew before, especially when I knew so very little about my soon-to-be husband. But my father expected me to do my duty as the daughter of an emperor, so I found myself torn between my sense of duty and my own personal desires, which were to remain home with my family and continue my passions of music and painting.

All I knew about my betrothed was that he had recently inherited the throne as a result of his uncle passing away of old age, but negotiations of our marriage had started some time before his uncle's health grew worse and it became clear he would inherit the throne.

Despite no other marriage prospects, my father would not agree to such a marriage unless he was certain this Romanian prince had a throne to sit upon.

I also understood that I was not to be his first wife, but instead his second. His first wife had passed away under mysterious circumstances several years ago. I was shocked when I first heard this, for I assumed my betrothed would be around my age, but instead he was about a decade older than me. It was not uncommon for royal women to acquire husbands much older than them, but I suppose I had been rather naive thinking that I could escape that fate. Now I had spent the last couple of weeks during our travels wondering what my new husband would look like, as he seemed so old already, our age difference feeling like a wide chasm that I wasn't sure we would be able to overcome.

When I was not daydreaming about what he would look like, I was busy studying Romanian, my new language, while the carriage rattled on towards this new country. While I wouldn't consider myself a quick study of languages, I could speak French and Latin just as well as my native German, and found Romanian somewhat easy as it was rooted in Latin just as French was. I hoped I would be fluent by the time we arrived.

In addition to studying this new language, I had a lot of time to think on this journey. As I pushed the curtains aside to look out the carriage window, the ring on my right hand caught my eye, and my thoughts drifted once again to my last day in Austria.

I had been packing my last few belongings—the ones I insisted to my chambermaids that I handle, as they were near and dear to me. I held my paint brushes in my hand, wrapping them carefully and placing them gently in the trunk while Margaret watched me curiously, draped on the stripped mattress of my bed.

"Why don't you let the chambermaids do that?" Margaret had a tendency to be nosy. Most found it endearing, but as her older sister, I did not. Everyone found everything Margaret did to be endearing, and she seemed utterly faultless—whereas I was always regarded with suspicion and dubiousness. I regarded her for a moment, putting my hands on my hips in thought.

A few years younger than me, Margaret wasn't a beauty, but nor was she unattractive, falling somewhere in between. She did have large chestnut eyes, and they were very becoming, but between them was a nose that started out thin and grew a bit bulbous and thick at the bottom. Under the thick bottom half of her nose were wide full lips that pursed rather perfectly. Under her headdress, she had thick abundant fair hair, like our mother, but with a tint of red that came from our father.

"Because I want to make sure that I have everything and there is no oversight," I responded. "It's a long journey from Austria to Romania, and I can't very well have any items that were missed sent to me very quickly, can I?"

What was ultimately striking about Margaret was how clever and witty she was, traits similar to our father that even I found myself compelled towards. She was well-read and educated, having spent ten years at the French court after our mother's accident.

Our mother's horse had tripped and fallen on top of her during a falcon hunt, breaking her back. When she succumbed to her injuries, Father was devastated, but had hardly any time to grieve her. I saw very little of him during that time, but I came to understand later that Mother's death had forced him to protect her lands from the French king, who had hoped to seize control of them despite them being my brother's birthright. To appease the French king, Father sent my sister to France at the age of two, where she was eventually to marry the dauphin. His attempt to keep the peace through marriage was rebuked, though. The dauphin married someone else. My poor sister was sent back home to Austria and my father was forced to quash revolts instigated by the French king in Flanders. The revolts continued until three years ago when Father was able to finally repress them. Then shortly after the revolts ended, when my father ascended as the Holy Roman Emperor following my grandfather's passing, he relinquished these lands to my brother, Philip.

"No, I suppose not," she conceded. Then she sighed. "I will miss you very much."

I smiled. Despite Margaret being the most advantageous between us sisters, I knew she could not control any of it and that she bore no ill will towards me. I held nothing against her as well. When she was sent to France, I was only five years old, so we didn't grow up together. When she moved back home, her chambers were assigned near mine and we grew close.

"I will miss you too," I replied, my tone warm as I meant it genuinely. "It's a shame that we grew up without one another only to reunite and then be separated again. However, this time it is me that is to depart."

Margaret sighed again. "I suppose this is the price we pay for being the children of an emperor."

She stared at one of the gowns I had pulled out and began to finger the hem. I could practically hear her thinking from where I stood.

I reached over and took her hand in mine. "We will see each other again."

"But you will be in Romania and I will be in Spain. They are on completely opposite sides of one another."

"We will find a way," I assured her, giving her hand a gentle little squeeze. "Especially when we are on our thrones, there will be no one to prevent us from meeting again. Perhaps we can meet halfway and reunite here in Austria. I am sure Father would not mind."

A gentle rap at the door interrupted us. "Come in," I called.

The giant maple door opened and a chambermaid came in. "His Majesty requests your presence, Your Highness." Her eyes remained lowered as she curtsied.

Margaret flashed me a look of encouragement and I nodded slightly, only for her to see, then I followed the chambermaid. As she led me to my father's chambers, my stomach began to flip at the realization that this would be the last time I would travel through these great imperial halls with their high ceilings and immaculate paintings of our ancestors decorating the walls. As I inched closer to my father's chambers, paintings of my mother in various styles became more frequent. It would be obvious to anyone that my father still missed her.

At last, I reached his chamber and saw the fireplace had been lit, crackling merrily and roaring with a hearty flame.

Sitting before it was my father's familiar figure, leaning towards the light while reading a parchment. Even leaning, one could see his impressive height as one of his legs was extended before him, and the flickering flames emphasized his prominent jaw and rather large nose that hooked at the bridge.

"The Archduchess, Your Majesty," the steward announced with a bow.

My father's attention turned towards me immediately and he broke out in a warm smile. While he wasn't traditionally handsome, his pleasant and optimistic demeanor was appealing to nearly everyone. I had seen people melt at his feet time and time again and it wasn't merely because he oversaw a vast empire, but because of his charm.

I curtsied as he acknowledged me. "Your Majesty."

He held his hand out to me and I reached for it to kiss his ring, but he stopped me with a slight gesture of his other hand. "No need for that this evening, my daughter, we are alone. Come and sit with me by the fire."

He took my hand while I did as he asked and he regarded me for a moment or two in silence. As he did so, I refrained from shifting in the chair beneath me from discomfort. I always hated when people stared at me.

"You truly are very beautiful," my father said softly, almost as if he was saying it to himself. "Even more beautiful than your mother, I daresay. Those other suitors truly missed out on obtaining such an exquisite wife."

I lowered my eyes as I felt my cheeks burn at the compliment for I had never felt beautiful, instead always thinking myself rather uncomely.

"Do not lower your eyes. There is nothing to be ashamed of. The rumor isn't true and I should know. I was there when you were made."

I couldn't help but laugh at his crass remark, despite not wanting to imagine my parents... well...

"I think this marriage will do well and it certainly will benefit the empire," my father continued. "Your future husband is a very intelligent man and comes from a ferocious lineage. A line of *dragons*, I have heard. '*The Dragon*' is what they called his grandfather. And his father, '*Son of the Dragon*.' His family history with the Ottoman Empire is a turbulent one, but an alliance will serve us well. Your husband gets an alliance with an even more formidable empire, and I get to keep an eye on both Hungary *and* the Ottomans, as you will serve as my eyes and ears in the east. King Wladislas, that Hungarian bastard, will feel the pressure of being in the middle of us should he decide to betray the terms of the treaty we established after those long five years of war. If he does, your husband has agreed to come to my aid, forming a front on both of the Hungarian borders should conflict arise. Yes, it will be a useful alliance. But that kind of talk is not why I summoned you to my chamber this evening. I know you leave in the morning so I wanted to grant you one last gift in addition to your dowry."

He rose and I moved to do the same when he again gestured slightly with his hand, preventing me from rising. His smile glittered at me once more as he turned toward his bedchamber, located behind the door on the opposite side of the sitting room. He was gone momentarily but returned with a small wooden box in his hand. He returned to the chair opposite me near the fireplace and he leaned towards me, propping his elbows on his knees, holding the box out.

"Come look," he invited with a smile. I felt a smile creep across my own lips as I leaned forward, feeling like I was about to be let in on a delightful secret.

He opened the box and inside was a small delicate ring with a gold band and a seal bearing a coat of arms I did not immediately recognize. "Out of all my children, I understand that you have been overlooked despite being my eldest. Therefore, I would like to grant you the title of Countess of Hainaut, a title that once belonged to your mother."

My breath caught as a lump began to grow within my throat. I stared at the ring, unable to move. I could only stare in awe. My father then took the ring from the box and pushed it gently onto the smallest finger of my right hand. I continued to stare at the four lions stacked over one another in two columns, facing left. While it couldn't be carried over onto a small ring, I remembered the lions as being black and red, alternating in their colors from left to right over a gold background, a banner I had seen once or twice before when my mother was being honored.

"I do apologize for the lack of a grand ceremony, but I had to wrestle your brother from part of his inherited lands, so I'm afraid this will have to do. However, it was imperative that before your long journey to Romania, you know that you always have a home within this empire."

I stared in disbelief at the ring on my little finger. As I looked closer at it, I could see that it was indeed the seal of the County of Hainaut. "Thank you, Father. This is more than I could have asked for."

The lump tightening in my throat brought me back to the confines of the carriage, pulling me out of my memory and reminding me of my current situation.

"At least the landscape is beautiful," I offered to Helene, swallowing the lump in my throat and reclining back in my seat. I didn't want to weep in front of Helene, especially since I was fulfilling my role as a daughter of the Holy Roman Emperor. This is what I was born to do, what was required of me, and I wanted to do my father proud by meeting my duty with bravery instead of tears. Instead, I continued admiring the endless landscapes we encountered while traveling through both Hungary and now Romania.

The recent peace with Hungary allowed us to travel through unscathed, and I welcomed the beauty Hungary had to offer and, due to the extensive plains, it was easy to navigate through. However, our travel began to grow difficult as we reached Romania—the terrain became much more uneven, even mountainous at times. Accompanying this mountainous terrain were thick swathes of forests that stretched beyond where the eyes could see. It became particularly treacherous as the sun went down and, because of the forests, darkness seemed to envelop us far quicker.

Admittedly, I became uneasy the further we traveled into Romania, as the reality of my situation was really beginning to settle in. The trees and landscapes were beautiful, but my compliments of them were portrayed with more confidence than I actually held, and I didn't feel as though it was just the nerves of getting married. It was more than that, and I was very unsettled—as if I was descending into a cave dense with shadows, never to return and see the light of day again. As the feeling began to escalate, I reached for the red rosary that had once been my mother's, holding it between my fingertips, seeking comfort by caressing the soft beads made with pressed rose petals.

Helene continued her grumbling. I chose to ignore her and instead prayed silently, wondering what fate my father had thrust me into.

II

"**M**y Lady."

I heard a voice gently calling me. Deep, but pleasant. A man's voice. Someone whom I did not recognize. The sensation of smooth velvet washed over me. Yes, it was though his voice was made of the softest velvet. And it caressed me in a way I had never felt before. Awakening my senses as if they had been long asleep. I was more aware than I ever had been.

"My Lady."

My body warmed, tingling pleasantly as if I had just slipped into a warm bath. I was overcome as this sensation began in my scalp and traced slowly down my body, ending at the soles of my feet.

"My Lady." I heard it again, but this time the velvety baritone voice was gone, replaced with something familiar. A woman's voice. I felt the sensation of suddenly and forcefully landing on the ground, my breath being knocked out of me. It was very much akin to the time I was climbing a tall oak tree as a child with my brother and had fallen out.

"My Lady!" The woman's voice repeated, more insistent. My eyes fluttered open and I was met with Helene grinning at me, something I hadn't seen since before we left Austria.

"What is it?" I growled, perturbed that Helene's shrill voice had interrupted my dream of the lovely male voice calling to me.

"Look," she said breathlessly, which was then succeeded with a round of coughing. Once she regained her composure, I leaned over and peered out the window opposite mine.

I was met with a startling sight and a little gasp escaped me.

Embedded in the thick blanket of the forest's foliage were red-bricked turrets piercing the gray sky. The turrets sloped into beautiful sand-colored stone walls surrounded by thick, imposing pine trees creating an overlay, covering the rest of them.

The backdrop only added to the beauty of the castle I was beholding, nourishing this spectacular sight as the castle was encased by rolling hills and mountains behind it, brimming with trees whose leaves fully embraced autumn, greeting me with brilliant gold and auburn. Austria had many breathtaking sights, but a semblance of mystery shrouded this castle which I presumed I would be calling home. I knew so little about this country and its prince, which only further emphasized its wonder, making it all the more titillating. This majestic sight was situated on top of a tall hill overlooking a small village. We were too far away for me to tell details of the village, but I could see the roofs of homes that paled in comparison to the splendor of the castle stronghold that overlooked them.

"Bran Castle, Your Highness," Helene announced, still grinning. "A gift from your future husband. He purchased it from King Wladislas with the persuasion of your father, as part of the negotiations for your hand."

"It is lovely. Helene, we have many wondrous sights in Austria, but this is magnificent." I remained breathless, unable to take my eyes from the castle cradled by forests and mountains. "I don't know that I will ever tire of the sight of it."

"Good, because I understand we may be spending a lot of our time here. His Highness also has a residence in Târgoviște, where his father used to hold court, though I do not know if that is where His Highness will continue to reside since purchasing this castle."

"He would not live with me?"

"It all depends, my dear, though do not expect it. We have discussed this before, your sole purpose is to provide an heir and serve your father's empire by being his eyes and ears in Eastern Europe. You must expect your husband to take mistresses, and perhaps to even bear illegitimate children. And you must turn a blind eye to it at all times. You must endure it and rise above any humiliation that it may bring. While your father was madly in love with your mother, he had every right to take on mistresses. Had that happened, I'm certain your mother would have borne it in great stride."

I barely remembered my mother. My memories of her were fragmented. The most prominent of those memories were of her fair hair and her gentle, musical voice. And she always insisted on holding me, never passing me over to a wet nurse, even well up until she passed away when I was five years of age.

Helene regaled me of what a strong and imperative figure my mother was in her own right. It was she who chose my father as her spouse, and when they did marry, she did not step down from ruling her lands. Instead of taking them over, my father remained co-ruler. Nor did her lands go directly to my father after her passing, instead passing to my brother. My father only remained regent until my brother was of age.

My father lovingly allowed my mother's independence. As Helene reemphasized, my parents were madly in love, even going so far as to share a bedroom and sleeping in the same bed together each night. To me, this seemed perfectly normal growing up, but it wasn't until later in my life that I learned this was a rare occurrence in other royal families. In fact, my father's parents couldn't have been more opposite and spent very little time together. I hoped my own marriage would take the shape of my parents', but it would more realistically take the shape of my grandparents'. Perhaps that was for the best, for I found the idea of sleeping beside a complete stranger to be rather unsettling. Besides, if we did spend little time together, then I would at least be left alone to pursue my artistic endeavors.

"Well," I replied, "I guess we will have to see then." Even if it was a loveless marriage, this beautiful castle ahead of me would be enough, for I was already in love with it.

A stinging sensation burst from my lip and I realized then how hard I was biting down in anticipation of arriving in Brașov, the town outside of Bran Castle. I had been mistaken before in thinking it was merely a village, the trees shrouded many of the buildings, and as we came closer I recognized it was a beautiful town instead.

"On the contrary, Brașov is hardly a village, Your Highness," Avram Ionescu, the Romanian ambassador who had negotiated my marriage to the Romanian prince, informed me. When Bran Castle grew closer, he fell back, walking his horse beside my carriage. I remarked how I had been mistaken in the town's size. "It is a thriving town housing all sorts of people. There is a hearty Saxon population that still resides here as well."

"I see," I replied. "So, in addition to having a relationship with the Holy Roman Emperor, your prince thought an Austrian wife would increase his popularity with the Saxons that remain."

Ambassador Ionescu grinned. "Her Highness is very keen." Then his face fell a little bit and I swore a shadow flickered across it. "The prince's—or rather, *Voivode's*—family has had a strained relationship with the Saxons that still occupy the area. So, yes, it does not hurt to appease them by taking on an Austrian wife."

"It always boils down to politics," I retorted.

"I think you will enjoy the town," he continued, his sunlit-beam of a smile returning. "It is brimming with trade and craftsmen. Should there be anything Your Highness requires as you make your home at Bran Castle, I am certain it could be easily found in Brașov."

"Well, we shall see. I hope to not only win the popularity of the Saxons but of the Romanians as well."

"I am certain that all that lay their eyes on you will fall in love with you."

I regarded him for a moment, my brow raising at his effortless flattery. Ambassador Ionescu was not particularly attractive. He was stout in stature and a bit thick around the middle. He had a patch of dark hair that grayed at the temples which extended out to a mustache that covered his upper lip almost entirely. Despite his rather mediocre appearance, he was a pleasure to be around, as his demeanor was always jolly and he was rarely in a sour mood.

"Such flattery, ambassador," I chided him lightly. "Something I haven't come across from you before."

His grin managed to grow wider. "Maybe it's just the joy of being home, Your Highness, though I do not speak any untruths."

Home. Hearing that word caused a sudden pang in the center of my chest. I instantly envied Ambassador Ionescu, a man who could come and go as he pleased, whereas I would be bound to remain in Romania for the rest of my days. The home I had known before was long gone, and after experiencing this arduous journey, I did not know whether it was possible for me to ever return.

"You must be delighted to be home, ambassador," I replied, masking any sadness I was suddenly feeling. "And after traveling through Romania, I can see why. The country is beautiful."

"There is nowhere else in the world like it," he agreed. "I will ride ahead, Your Highness, to make sure that all is ready for your arrival."

With that, he tapped the stirrups of his saddle and was off before I could manage a reply. Meanwhile, our line was slowing as we entered the town, receiving entry to the town's fortified walls. I suppose with the Ottomans at the southern border, one could not be too careful. I pushed aside the curtains of the carriage and watched as we entered, immediately met with the familiar sounds of a bustling town. It almost reminded me of Innsbruck, my father's chosen capital and where we lived together at the imperial palace. My heart leapt at the sound of it and while I wasn't met with the sight of the Alps looming over the town, the mountains of Romania were similar, so it wasn't terribly different. The homes tucked together in close proximity shared an unexpected familiarity, with similar half-timbered architecture which I had been accustomed to seeing my whole life. Even the cobblestone road on which we traveled didn't appear dissimilar to the one in Innsbruck.

Our arrival had caused quite a stir because—in some sort of strange phenomenon—the town seemed to grow quiet for a moment or two, but then there was an uproar of sound, people calling out and chattering at once. They began to line the streets to meet their Princess Consort, a title I learned from Ambassador Ionescu I would be receiving. I leaned out of the window to wave and greet them after Helene managed to stuff me into a nice clean gown specifically set aside for this occasion. It was a lovely red Milanese gown with slashed sleeves that revealed my white long-sleeved chemise underneath. A black panel adorned the front, and the bodice laces were loosely tied to allow the panel to show through. My hands traced the red skirt trimmed with black velvet along the hem, absent-mindedly grazing along the vines and leaves embroidered with gold thread as I eagerly watched the crowd for signs of their approval. Helene thrust my long black hair into a gold-netted caul, as that was easiest to arrange in the small confines of the carriage, and I had hoped it was enough to contain my unruly locks as I passed by the gathering people.

As we continued down the cobblestone streets, it dawned on me that Brașov's similarities to Innsbruck ended with the town's architecture. With every passing second, I was bombarded with cascades of color from the finely woven embroidered clothing worn by the townspeople. Admittedly, it was exquisite. Their garments seemed to be transported from an older time, but the embroidery on the fabric was unlike anything I had ever seen—incredibly detailed and just as colorful. Both the men and women wore the colorful and intricate designs on their loose-fitting cotton shirts. Then, for some of the women, it continued onto their skirts and head scarves.

I was met with plenty of waves and smiles, though there were some that regarded me sternly under their bushy eyebrows or furry caps. As we continued through the town, I began to notice people dressed rather well and more modernly, with their elaborate gowns and doublets made of expensive fabrics; wealthy people, I assumed. They waved at me energetically, whistling or cheering at times.

"The Saxons of Brașov, I presume," I said to Helene while continuing to wave.

"I understand the Saxons tend to be merchants and the nobility," Helene replied. She also peered out the window as even she could not contain her curiosity.

While I do not mean to be vain, I could only imagine what a sight we must have been. Our line stretched down the street as far as one could see with fully dressed and armored knights of the Holy Roman Empire, bearing the Emperor's golden imperial banner of the black two-headed eagle, talons outstretched, each of its heads looking off to the side with the combined arms of Austria and Burgundy on its chest. I was thrilled, excitement and curiosity getting the best of me as we traveled through the streets. I loved seeing the people smile and wave at me. In the distance, I could smell meat roasting somewhere and I wondered if perhaps we were close to the marketplace.

As we rambled closer to the castle, children began to run alongside my carriage, waving and laughing. One young boy managed to catch up and press a bouquet of wildflowers towards me. I took them from him and passed him my hand-kerchief, a souvenir he could bring back to his family. Any nerves rattled by my arrival were soothed by the overwhelm-ingly warm welcome I received from the people of Brașov.

Finally, I heard the call of the captain to the guards and the carriage shuddered to a stop. My heart began to thud in my ears and nervousness welled up in my throat.

"It will be quite all right, Your Highness," Helene insisted, as if she sensed my nervousness. "I will see what I can do about getting you something to eat, as well as a bath. It is imperative that we wash the dirt of the road away before meeting your betrothed. He has waited this long, but I am certain he can wait a bit longer to meet you."

"Your Highness," the captain of the guards said after opening the carriage door with a bow. He extended his hand and I took it, allowing him to assist me out of the carriage. It felt good to stand and stretch after sitting for so long. He re-leased my hand and turned to assist Helene out. Meanwhile, I took a moment to view the castle up close.

It was just as impressive up close as it was from afar. Though not nearly as large as the imperial palace in Inns-bruck, it was still lovely. What I had not seen from afar was the exquisite stone base of the castle, specifically near the entrance. The castle was built quite literally on a hill and partially into a rocky crag. I knew that if I was to go to the tallest of its many towers, I would be able to see all of Brașov below. It was absolutely breathtaking.

"Your Highness," I heard a familiar voice say.

I looked to the entrance of the castle, and at the top of the steep staircase leading up to the front door was Ambassador Ionescu. His usual jovial countenance was replaced with a furrowed brow.

"What is it, ambassador?" I called to him, my voice swept up by the chilly wind trailing up the hill. I clutched my fur cloak closer to my neck. Behind me, my guards were dismounting and the captain was overseeing the care of the chest that held my dowry.

Ambassador Ionescu stumped down the steps more swiftly than I thought him capable. "Your Highness, I am afraid I have something to tell you." I waited for him to meet me at the bottom of the stairs and catch his breath before he continued.

"What is it?" I asked, trying my best to keep agitation from escaping my voice. After all, I was craving a bath, a meal, and perhaps even a nap more than anything.

"I am sorry to say that you will not be meeting the Voivode, for he is not here."

"Not here?" My brows furrowed at the news and I turned to Helene with my confusion.

Her eyes rounded as she overheard. "Not *here*?!" she repeated. "What can you possibly mean?"

"Exactly that. His Highness is not here, I was just notified by the Chief of Staff. He informed me that His Highness' arrival has been delayed."

"Delayed? How?" I inquired, my confusion taking the shape of annoyance as well as disappointment.

"Yes, how? It is not as though our arrival is a surprise," Helene added with a scoff.

"My best understanding is that he was involved in a raid. A skirmish with the Ottomans near the border."

"A skirmish? Is he unharmed?" The sound of my heart thudding in my ears resumed.

"I believe he is. I received a short letter written in his hand. Here."

He handed me a small piece of parchment and as I brought it closer to my face, Helene leaned over my shoulder to read as well.

"Ambassador,

Forgive my absence. I was called to answer a raid of Ottomans as Bayezid was sending his men to terrorize our people, hoping to instigate the rivalry of our fathers. I will not be there in time for the arrival of the Archduchess. See to it that she settles in and informs the staff I have hired that they are to be at her call should she be in need of anything. I will be there as soon as I can to honor the terms of the marriage contract agreed upon between myself and the Emperor. Signed, *His Highness, Prince Vlad V."*

I read it twice more, somewhat in disbelief and in partial agitation. I understood that the border had been attacked, but could he not have sent other men and stayed behind? After all, as he stated in his letter, he had a marriage agreement to fulfill. I traveled all this way, therefore I had assisted in completing my father's end of the bargain. He needed to meet his. I felt rather insulted. Furthermore, he gave no indication in his letter of when he anticipated to arrive. Was I to wait endlessly for him to decide when he would like to marry me?

"This is an insult to the Holy Roman Emperor!" Helene cried out, almost as if she had read my thoughts. "Her Highness did not travel all of this way only to be slighted in this manner."

"My apologies, madam," Ambassador Ionescu said, lowering his head. "I am certain no insult is meant by His Highness. He is a very passionate man, you see, and his feud with the Ottomans goes back from before his grandfather—"

"None of that is our concern!" Helene interrupted.

"It will be after the Archduchess' marriage! It is the concern of all of the Western world, Christianity itself is at stake..."

I tuned out their bickering as I thought for a moment, trying to swallow my own pride and agitation. Yes, this was an insult, but on the other side of the coin, I could not blame him for overseeing the care and keeping of his lands; my father would do the same had the roles been reversed. Sometimes it was better to take matters into one's own hands than rely on someone else, especially in such a dire situation. Besides, I really craved a bath and was longing to see if the inside of this castle matched the beauty of its outside.

"Enough!" My voice echoed through the trees bordering the hill that the castle was perched upon. Helene and Ambassador Ionescu stopped their bickering immediately and looked at me with wide eyes. "Three weeks," I continued, "we will give the prince three weeks to return. And if he does not, then we will return to Austria, dowry and all. Three weeks and then we can consider the marriage contract null and void. Now, Ambassador Ionescu, I long for a bath. Please, escort Helene and me inside so that I may tidy myself."

III

M Y TEETH CHATTERED AS Helene combed my hair. I finally had a bath, and it was chilly in my new bedchamber. The fireplace had been lit but it had not been burning long enough to have the room entirely warmed, the coldness seemingly swallowing any bit of the heat. My bath water was not terribly hot, either. I felt as though I was never going to get warm.

Helene's hands were gentle as they ran the comb through my long hair. They had always been gentle, ever since I was a child. She had been taking care of me for as long as I could remember, the closest thing I had to a mother now. I was grateful to have her with me, I thought to myself as I relished her hands working through my hair. Very grateful, indeed, as I remained in this foreign land for maybe three weeks, or maybe for the rest of my life.

Even after all this way, my fate was murky and covered in uncertainty.

When Helene was done and had left me alone to tidy things, I sat on my bed staring once again at the ring my father had gifted me the evening before I left... *know that you always have a home within this empire.*

Countess of Hainaut.

I had never been there before, so I had not the slightest idea what Hainaut looked like. All I knew was that it was not far from the sea, northwest of France, so I assumed it was beautiful, but regardless, I liked the sound of my new title. Archduchess of Austria *and* Countess of Hainaut. That is, of course, if Prince Vlad followed through with his end of the contract. If not, then perhaps I could return to my father's empire and just live happily as a countess, not being a thorn in my father's side anymore, and serving his empire in other ways. Perhaps I could even marry who I wanted—surely my father's alliances with Spain were enough, as powerful as that country was.

I sighed, lowering my hand and looking at my bedchamber, recalling how I had done the same in my bedchamber at my father's palace for what I understood was the last time. On the day I had to depart for Romania, I had marveled at the high ceiling with the wooden beams, then grimaced as I gazed at the tall windows whose sill hosted my favorite reading spot. My gaze trailed from the windows to my extensive armoire emptied of all of its contents, either given to my sister or packed away. I recalled how I looked at the beautiful and massive canopy bed that I had occupied all of my life. Dread had pooled in the pits of my stomach. Everything had suddenly seemed so real. Deep down, I had always known this day would come—as children of the Holy Roman

Emperor, it was expected, but it had felt far away, details of someone else's life. Now, it had all come crashing down and it was real, standing right before me.

As I sat memorizing my bedchamber at the imperial palace in Innsbruck, my thoughts had been interrupted by a gentle knock at the door, announcing Helene's arrival, followed by Margaret.

"Come now, there is no time for dawdling anymore," Helene had hooted. "The carriages are packed, the dowry safely tucked away, and the escort is gathering in their respective places. You don't want to keep everyone waiting."

"No, I do not," I had replied, my voice sounding far away as I continued to fixate on the dread pooling in my stomach.

Margaret said very little, but there was an expression fixed on her face that only added to my unease. Usually she had a pleasant and mirthful demeanor, but at that moment she appeared not only as though she was about to cry, but that she had seen something unsettling. I met her gaze and tried to read her thoughts by looking into her eyes, but Helene was ushering us both out, grating on us to get moving, and I was unable to ask Margaret if she was well.

Helene ushered me out of my room, past my receiving chambers, and out into the corridor, clucking behind me with Margaret trailing behind her. As we approached the doors leading out into the courtyard, the stewards opened the doors for us and I was met with the sight of my escort prepared to depart. It was clear my father spared no expense for my vast escort to Romania, but a daughter of the Holy Roman Emperor would serve well as a hostage, especially as we traveled closer and closer to the Ottoman Empire. There were murmurs of the Ottomans kidnapping brides and nobles in order to receive generous ransoms—a fate I prayed would not befall me. As we were also traveling with my dowry, and between it and myself, any kidnapper would become a very wealthy man, indeed.

"My daughter." I heard a warm voice behind me. I turned and saw my father reaching out to me. I allowed myself to be enveloped in his wonderful embrace, returning with my own. I feared it would be the last time I would.

"Father," I murmured. I desired to tell him that I would miss him greatly, but I refrained from doing so. After all, this was my destiny, to further serve his great empire. Instead, I squeezed him tightly, not caring about protocol or perception. Again, I feared this would be my last chance to embrace my father, so I did not care if it was uncouth.

"My child," he replied, "it will be sad to see you go, but remember that I am so proud of you and grateful for your service." His arms tightened around me, and my heart warmed. He did not care about perception, either. Then he pulled away and I noticed my brother and step-grandmother standing beside him, both of whom had come from Burgundy just to see me off.

My step-grandmother was incredibly tall, even without the outdated headdresses she wore. She stooped down for her own embrace, enveloping me in her slight arms. "Things are going to go magnificently," she told me softly in my ear. "I know you shall do us all proud."

She was not my blood-related grandmother, of course, but she may as well have been. She became my grandfather's second wife after my grandmother passed away from sickness, becoming like a mother to my own.

I regarded my brother, Philip, last, realization dawning on me that this may be the last time I would see him, too. I took a moment to memorize his features. He was tall, like our father, and very slim. His hair color was similar to that of my sister's, fair with a reddish tint. He had certainly inherited our father's charm, but instead of pointing any of that charm in my direction, he had liked to tease and taunt me throughout our childhood. He certainly had a cruel streak in him. That day, however, he was kind and gentle, a side I had rarely been the recipient of.

"Sister," he said kindly, enveloping me. "I will miss you greatly. It's strange to think that this day has already come."

"You need not tell me twice," I said wryly, choking back tears at the prospect of leaving my family. "I will miss you greatly as well. My departure allows too much room for you to deceive people into thinking that you were the superior tree climber when we were children, when in fact it was me that surpassed you every time."

He chuckled good-naturedly and replied, "You had best believe that is what I will do the moment you are gone. I will make sure that fact is written in the history books. After all, history is declared by the winners."

"'Winner', ha! I don't recall you being so witty, little brother. When did that happen?" I couldn't help but laugh, his humor delaying any developing sadness.

"I have always been witty, big sister. Surely you remember that, unless you have fallen out of too many trees."

"All right you two, that's enough," my father inserted, bearing his good-natured grin. "It is clear my wit has carried onto the next generation."

"Surely this wit is a trait that carries on through Mother's line, Father," Philip replied mischievously, "for it is stubbornness and ambition that runs through yours."

Father let out a hearty laugh. "Now, now, that is enough. Wish your sister farewell for she is already falling behind. She has a long journey ahead of her."

My brother embraced me once more and whispered softly in my ear, "It is true that I will miss you. Please come home to us one day, as soon as you can."

"The soonest I can," I replied, squeezing him gently and fighting back tears.

He pulled away and Margaret reappeared before me. Her countenance seemed more at ease, but not enough to reassure me that all was well.

We reached for one another to embrace and I whispered in her ear, "Is all well, dear sister?"

"All is well enough. Focus on the journey ahead of you, dear sister, and I will continue to pray for you."

I grimaced at her grim and foreboding words, but before I could inquire further, my father reached for me once more. "Do not forget, you are a daughter of the Habsburg dynasty and I know you will make us proud. Travel safe, dear daughter, and Godspeed."

He planted a kiss on my forehead and Helene took that as her cue to place her hand gently on my elbow and lead me towards the carriage that would be my home for the next several weeks.

I stepped inside, rearranging my skirts as I took my seat on the bench, and I clasped my cloak around me with my sister's words echoing in my head. A sense of dread began to blossom once more in the pit of my stomach. When the carriage began to lurch forward, the last thing I saw was my family standing there, waving, and the further we moved ahead, the smaller and smaller they appeared.

Tears welled in my eyes and began to spill as the memory of my last day in Austria faded and I came back to the unfamiliar bedchamber I was now in, loneliness looming over me. However, I quickly brushed the tears from my eyes when Helene re-entered the chamber to dress me.

I would be having dinner with the ambassador, after which he promised me a tour. I had not seen the entirety of the castle since I had been ushered away upstairs quickly so I could bathe. From what I had seen, it was beautiful, but rather empty. My new quarters, which were on the second floor towards the south of the castle, contained nothing but a bed, an empty armoire, and a trunk containing only some of my clothes at the moment. The rest would be brought up tomorrow and put in place by Helene. The four-poster bed was made up, at least, and admittedly, I was eager to climb into it for it would be the first time I had slept in a bed in weeks. The floors were all dark wood, the walls a creamy white, and then the ceilings had dark wood panels with beams to support the ceiling. The floor was bare, and would definitely need a rug before winter came.

"His Highness, the Voivode, wanted to leave the complete furnishing of the castle in your hands," Ambassador Ionescu had explained upon our arrival. "After all, this castle was a gift to you as part of your nuptials."

That is, if I was staying, of course, I thought as he explained that to me, but I did not say those thoughts out loud. Instead, I just nodded and smiled, admittedly delighted that I would be the one able to furnish a home for once. *If* I would be staying.

Helene took the time to pleat my hair in a simple braid. Once my hair was done, she dressed me in a plain gown in a deep green color. Then she escorted me downstairs to the dining room.

Ambassador Ionescu rose from his seat to bow when I entered the chamber. The dining room, too, was rather empty, containing a long table with eight places, three on each side and two at each of the heads. Ambassador Ionescu had been seated at one of the side chairs, reserving the head seats for royalty. Once he completed his bow, he reached for my hand and led me to the head of the table at the other side. He pulled my chair out and then pushed it in for me as I sat down. Before barely the blink of an eye, a servant had appeared and was pouring me a glass of wine. Helene curtsied and left me alone with the ambassador to resume unpacking my things, no doubt. She had plenty of work ahead of her and it would definitely take a couple of days.

"Is Your Highness feeling refreshed after your bath?" Ambassador Ionescu asked kindly, resuming his seat.

"I am, thank you. It was much needed after such a long journey."

"It indeed was a long journey, but we are here at last. It will only be a light dinner, I'm afraid, of pheasant and dates. I hope you will find that acceptable."

"That will be just fine, ambassador. I understand the timing of our arrival was hard to determine and I am just happy to be out of the carriage and walking around again." I took a sip of wine and found it to be utterly delicious. My tongue was instantly overcome with a burst of berries and spices, followed by a dense smokiness. "This wine is marvelous—I hope there will be more."

"There will be if that's what Your Highness desires. That is a good Romanian wine, so there is more where that came from."

"I would like that very much. Even if it's to take back home with us."

Ambassador Ionescu's face fell for a brief moment but then he rearranged it to look more presentable when speaking to an archduchess. "The Voivode *will* be here, Your Highness. He is not one to back out on his word. Besides, that correspondence was days old. He may be nearly here already."

I took another sip of the wine, a deeper one this time. "Perhaps. But the breaking of our betrothal would not be the first my father has encountered. If you do recall, my sister was meant to be married to the French prince instead of the Spanish one. We are all aware of how that panned out."

He then grinned. "How about if the Voivode is not here in *two* weeks, I personally will pay for a cask of that wine for you to take back?"

Unable to help myself, I grinned. "Very well. I accept your terms."

He held his cup to me in a salute and I returned it. Together we took a sip just as two servants appeared with our dinner.

The castle was remarkably quiet, I noticed, as Ambassador Ionescu gave me and Helene a tour of what could potentially be my new home. I was used to a bustling staff and someone escorting me everywhere I went, whether it be stewards or a maid accompanied by Helene. During this tour, it was only the ambassador, Helene, and me. I wasn't sure if I was unsettled by the quietness or in appreciation of it. Though the more I thought about it, the more I believed I could very well get used to it.

The castle itself was just as beautiful on the inside as it was the outside. There were many, many rooms. The exterior was quite deceiving, as from the outside, it didn't look like there were many rooms at all. There were four floors, more than I would have guessed. The number of rooms per floor decreased as one ascended the stairs leading into the castle's towers, most of which faced southwest, while the watch-tower stood on the northeast section of the castle.

The dark wood floors and ceilings were common through-out; every room had them. Some rooms had grand wooden beams meeting the floor and ceiling, usually the larger rooms had these beams for extra support, and all of the walls of the rooms were coated with a warm cream color. The windows in each room weren't terribly large, but fitting nonetheless, and they all were capped with an arch. The fourth floor boasted a terrace and I noted that detail so I could explore it and perhaps set up my easel there to paint the scenery it overlooked. Finally, I was told that there was a large un-derground floor, which contained the cellar as well as the dungeon, but Ambassador Ionescu did not think it suitable to show me that space.

We were reaching the end of the tour when I thought I saw something in the corner of my eye shifting in the shadows of the corridor leading to the foyer. I stood still, my heart beginning to pound.

"As I had mentioned before, it is His Highness' wish that you undertake the furnishing of it in any way that you desire. He wants you to feel at home here," Ambassador Ionescu had said without noticing that I had stopped. "What is it, Your Highness?"

Helene, too, turned to me, questioningly. "Nothing, I thought I saw something—" Just then, a large rat the size of a kitten came skittering past my feet and brushing against my skirt. My body seized and I screamed. My scream then caused Helene to cry out as we jerked back, pressing ourselves against the wall. The rat disappeared back into the shadows. Helene glared at Ambassador Ionescu whose cheeks grew red. Having been a recipient of Helene's glares before, I understood the embarrassment he felt.

"There is a lovely, *lovely* courtyard nestled between the walls of the castle," he continued, pushing through the embarrassment of how things had been turning out since we arrived. "Seeing as it is dark and chilly outside, I will take you for a tour there tomorrow and show you the courtyard as well as the kitchen and servants' quarters. I imagine Your Highness is quite tired."

By now, I had gathered that a small handful of servants had only recently taken up residence here in preparation for my arrival, hired by the Voivode.

"Is the Voivode going to reside here as well?" I asked. Helene shifted uncomfortably beside me, no doubt thinking that we had discussed this matter before, but if I was expected to furnish this castle, I needed to know who was going to reside in it.

"Of that, I am uncertain, Your Highness. His capital remains the same as his father's, at Târgoviște, which is south of here." Ambassador Ionescu's gaze shifted.

"No need to look so uncomfortable, ambassador," I replied lightly, "I only ask in order to prepare, if I am to furnish this place as my home. In any case, it is getting late. Come, Helene, let us retire to bed. We shall meet you in the morning for breakfast, ambassador, and then for a tour of the courtyard afterwards."

He smiled and bowed. "Goodnight, Your Highness."

Helene took me back to my room on the second floor where she dressed me for bed. "First the prince's delayed arrival and now rats? We will definitely have to get rid of those rats..." she muttered angrily under her breath. As she did so, I noticed she had emptied the trunk of my clothes that was brought up and put the items in the armoire.

When I remarked upon it, she replied, "It should be enough clothes for three weeks. I will not finish unpacking until we know for certain the prince is going to stay true to his word." I noticed the malice that dripped in her tone. "In the meantime, three weeks is a long time to stand around and do nothing, so I retrieved some of your books as well as your painting supplies. I noticed that the terrace would be a lovely place to sit and paint. In the very least, a landscape by your hand would be well worth taking back to Austria."

"Helene, it is almost as if you had stepped into my mind," I said to her, unable to contain my smile, "for it was the first thing I thought of, as well, when I saw the terrace."

IV

"**M**y Lady."

The voice had returned. Whispering in my ear. Awakening my senses.

"My Lady."

I twisted at the sound of it, trying to climb through the layers of sleep to wakefulness.

Wanting to awaken. Wanting to see the face to whom the voice belonged. The voice that stirred sensations within me that I had never encountered before.

"I am coming for you."

I thrust awake, bolting upright, covered in sweat and panting as fear coursed through me.

The voice.

I could have sworn it whispered right in my ear and I could feel breath upon the side of my face. Accompanying the breath, I swore I had felt someone's fingers trailing down my neck to the side of my breast.

I was covered in darkness.

I thrust my hands out, trying to reach for someone there.

My hand was met with nothing but a bunch of fabric. I continued to pant, my heart racing.

Pulling aside the curtain that enclosed me into the four-poster bed, I blinked rapidly, disoriented, trying to push away any traces of sleep that lingered.

No one was there. Instead of a voice, Helene's gentle breathing drifted up from the pallet on the floor at the foot of my bed where she slept. There were naught but embers in the fireplace on the opposite side of the room.

My breathing slowed.

A dream. It was just a dream. But the breath on my ear seemed so real. As did the fingers trailing down my neck to my... A dream, that's all it was. No one was there. No one but Helene, asleep on the floor, the embers in the fireplace, and the light of the moon that beamed through the windows.

I released the curtain, allowing it to flutter back to its place, and I laid back down, lying awake until eventually sleep took over and I succumbed to it.

The servants were lined up as Ambassador Ionescu led me to the kitchen. There were only five of them, including the chief of staff who also served as the cook. When the ambassador introduced him to me, I complimented him on last night's dinner as well as this morning's breakfast, testing out my halting Romanian and seeking practice when I could. I felt as though it was a rough start, but the chief of staff gave no inclination of it, maintaining a pleasant and kind demeanor as I stumbled my way through the language. He was the only one who spoke to me as we discussed the preparation of the prince's arrival and the possibility of hiring more staff. The other four—three men and one woman—remained silent with their eyes lowered.

Afterwards, we stepped out of the kitchen to the courtyard and I saw what Ambassador Ionescu meant when he said it was lovely. It *was* very charming. It was encircled by the castle walls and I noticed that there were multiple doorways framed by arches leading out to this courtyard. It was not very large but the ground was fashioned by stones, then there was a short retaining wall that held up a small landing. At the top of that landing was the opening of a well. Looking up, I saw that overlooks bordered the walls on the second and third floor, and the overlooks allowed one to see down into the courtyard. The terrace overlooked this courtyard as well.

"This is lovely," I agreed. "Is that well still functional?"

"It is, Your Highness. All of the castle's water needs will be supplied by that very well."

"This castle continues to surprise me," I replied.

Perhaps my father would be willing to let me keep this place should the marriage contract fall through, and I could continue to live here. I would stay out of the way and my father wouldn't have to worry about any more betrothals. Between my brother and my sister, that should be enough to serve his empire.

"Has there been any further correspondence from the prince?" I asked.

"None, I'm afraid."

I did not reply immediately. Of course there hadn't been. At this point, at the very least, the prince could have sent some follow-up correspondence. His silence was aggravating.

"What a shame," I finally said. "You are dismissed, ambassador. I am certain you have some family you wish to visit or some other affairs to attend to. It seems as though there is nothing more we can do but wait."

And wait we did.

I spent my days on the terrace after Helene had set up my easel there, and I started with a painting of the courtyard, an area I knew I had to capture on canvas. It was chilly outside as autumn worked its way towards departure and winter ushered in. During breaks from my painting sessions, I also took a moment to write a lengthy letter to my father, explaining the situation and informing him of my decision. I had it delivered as soon as possible so as to have the letter reach his hands at least by the time we departed.

Helene had also taken over as chief of staff during this time, a role the cook was happy to hand over. She organized the stocking of the kitchen and then between her and the other servants, they did a deep scrubbing of the interior of the castle. Finally, she oversaw the care and keeping of my father's guards, most of whom had set up lodgings on the grounds at the bottom of the hill. There were a handful of guards along with the captain of the guard that took up lodgings in the round tower to ensure my security. Ambassador Ionescu remained, insisting on doing so to make sure to intercept any potential correspondence from the prince that might have come, though none did. Eventually, the two-week mark came and the day after, a large wine cask was delivered.

By then, I had finished my painting of the courtyard and had begun work on trying to capture the castle as I had first seen it on the road traveling towards it, cradled in the forest canopy. When my courtyard painting had been completed, I had my easel moved into the room next to mine so as to stay out of the cold air. I was working on said painting when Helene came with Ambassador Ionescu, admitting him in.

"As promised, Your Highness," he said, his usual jolly demeanor rather subdued again today, "the cask of Romanian wine has been delivered. My gift to you."

"Thank you, ambassador," I replied, feeling a bit smug at the arrival of my cask of wine. "I cannot wait to dive into it."

He emitted a grimace that was meant to be a smile and then he changed the subject, looking at my painting of the courtyard propped up against the wall. "It is an exact likeness! Your Highness has exceptional skill."

"Yes, I thought I would take the time to capture some scenes to bring back home to Austria so that I could one day look upon and recall the Romanian landscapes with fondness."

The ambassador did not address this remark, instead replying with, "You were able to capture the lighting perfectly. How astonishing!"

"My father is a great investor and admirer of the arts. He saw to it that his children took up a form of art or two in their studies."

"I recall your skill on the harpsichord, but I did not know you were so skilled with a brush. It is a shame we do not have a harpsichord here for you to play. It would bring some much-needed life into this house."

"It is a shame, for I would not mind another pastime to keep me occupied while we continue to wait. I do miss the sound of music, something I also did not lack in Austria."

I caught Helene side-eyeing me with a smirk playing on her lips. Poor ambassador, to be in a room with such harpies. But at this rate, it seemed a certainty that the prince was not coming, and I could not contain my ire any longer; this rejection was not something I could tolerate. Arriving back in Innsbruck was going to be utterly embarrassing.

Unable to reply, Ambassador Ionescu bowed. "Your Highness..." he murmured and retreated from the room.

"Do you think I was a bit harsh?" I asked Helene, wiping my brush clean of the paint to prevent it from drying. I selected a new one, then chose a lovely auburn to capture the color of the leaves surrounding us.

"Not at all, Your Highness. This whole event is utterly shameful and insulting. If anything, I think you have been particularly patient and kind." She then released a loud barking cough.

"Perhaps you need to see someone about that cough, Helene. It has lingered for weeks now."

"It's no use fretting over me, I will be fine. It's just this weather."

I stopped painting for a moment and studied her as she tidied the room. A strand of hair escaped her kerchief and I noticed how faded and nearly gray it was, wondering how I didn't notice that before. She had once been fair-haired but it seemed like it had suddenly changed overnight. The creases around her eyes looked to have multiplied as well, something I was also noticing for the first time. Her sleeves were pushed up revealing her forearms and the exposed skin looked a bit more creased and loose than it had before.

Shame washed over me as I became vividly aware of how quickly time had passed. Helene was no longer the young, lovely woman who had stepped into the role of my mother when I was only five years old. Had doing so aged her more rapidly? I mean, she was in charge of an archduchess of the Holy Roman Empire and had been since I was born, but her duties had only increased since the passing of my mother.

She must have felt me staring at her for she stopped and her sharp hazel eyes leveled with mine, something she was able to do when it was just the two of us. When there were others present, the protocol had to return.

"What is it?" she asked after a moment.

I felt an urge to tell her that I loved her, to express my gratitude for raising me in place of my mother, but it felt scary and foreign to do so. Maybe it wasn't allowable due to protocol? Was this something I *was* allowed to do?

I swallowed the urge and instead replied, "Nothing. Just curious to see what it is you are doing. Not packing already, surely?"

"No, not yet, though His Highness only has a couple more days before I direct the guards to prepare for departure. He may have six days left, but it will take at least three to get prepared to depart again and that would be with employing all of the guards!" She then sighed. "I am very sorry it is turning out like this. You have done all you could and it is no reflection on you, Your Highness."

I wasn't sure how to reply. After all, the prince was the last of the suitors. There was no one else. My return to Austria would be absolutely humiliating, and the rumors of my legitimacy would almost certainly erupt again. My father would be undoubtedly furious, but I do not know what he would do in response to our humiliation. Perhaps he would just relent and let me take up my residence in Hainaut. I wouldn't even have to return to the imperial palace, I could just go directly there to spare him any embarrassment. Yes, I too would be embarrassed, but at least it would relieve me of having to marry a stranger. Though, on the other hand, my father could force me into a nunnery where I would take up the habit. I considered myself a devout Catholic, attending Mass daily and confession regularly, but the idea of being forced into a convent unsettled me. To me, a convent would be a cage, for I did not think I would be able to pursue my music and my independence to come and go as I pleased. It would further my humiliation by emphasizing my undesirability. Realizing the possibility of this outcome made me wish that the prince *would* honor his end of the contract.

Helene was finishing up and would soon leave me alone with my thoughts. I freshened my brush and continued to paint, trying to not imagine what my life would be like in a convent. She was just about to leave the room but then turned back to me.

"I had forgotten to inform you that I discovered that book among your things, wrapped in one of your chemises. Did you put that there?"

I peered at the item she was referring to. She had placed the small, thin, brown book on the table that housed my paints. "No, I have never seen that book before in my life. What an odd place to store it. Do you think it was maybe one of the maids at the imperial palace?"

"Perhaps. I did not look inside of it, but perhaps it contains lewd things and your departure was a convenient way to get rid of it on a moment's notice. Shall I dispose of it?"

"No, no. I will take a look at it later."

Helene's eyebrow shot up. "And if there *are* lewd contents in there?"

I laughed. "We do not know that to be the case, Helene. That is merely a conclusion *you* jumped to. After all, it was wrapped in one of my chemises, so now I am curious to see what it holds. Leave it there and I will look at it some time later."

V

Tʜᴇ ᴛʜɪɴ ʙʀᴏᴡɴ ʙᴏᴏᴋ had piqued my curiosity but I did not allow myself to peruse its contents until nightfall when everyone was asleep. Once nighttime cloaked the castle in clandestine darkness, I slipped out of bed, padding across the chilly floor to the table, past where Helene slept to where the book had been left behind. By the time I reached the book, I was humming with anticipation. Helene even seemed to have forgotten about it, succumbing to sleep immediately after laying her head down.

If we were to stay, I would have to insist that she get a room of her own near mine. The castle had plenty of rooms to spare. She was far too advanced in age to be laying on a pallet on the floor of my room anymore. I worried that her doing so any longer would worsen that cough, at the very least. I told myself that I would discuss it with her in the morning. Then

I laid back on my pillows and leaned towards the oil lamp to better see the contents of the book.

Inside the front cover, I noticed some very small and neat handwriting. Tracing the tiny, looping script, a pang of recognition hit me.

"*My dear sister,*" it began, "*I found this inadvertently while looking for another book in Father's library. As it would happen, I pulled out my selection and this fell out of the bookshelf and landed open. I nearly thought nothing of it until I studied the page it had opened up to a bit closer. I read it and thought you should be aware of its contents. It has to do with your fate after all. I'm so sorry, dear sister, forgive me. Your ever-loving sister, Margaret.*"

My brows knit together as I read Margaret's note, utterly confused but unable to ignore the churning in my belly. I hurried to open the book, though it was so thin and contained so few pages, it was more of a pamphlet, really. The title read "*The Wickedness of the Eastern Devil*", which did little to calm the sensations in my stomach which had traveled to my heart, galloping steadily in my ears. I scrambled to turn the next page and began to read eagerly.

As I read, the pounding of my heart grew and my head began to swim. A chill began to settle in my veins. I was mortified. What I held before me was unlike anything I had ever read or could even imagine in my wildest thoughts and in the blackest recesses of my mind. In my naivety, I did not realize people could produce such cruelty. At one point, I had to stop reading because I thought I was going to be sick. *The Wickedness of the Eastern Devil* spoke of a man so evil, so wicked, that one would think he was the Devil himself.

And that man was the father of my betrothed.

This pamphlet told violent tales of this man, this dev-il—Vlad the Impaler—who executed not only his enemies but his people, by driving a stake through the lower ends of their bodies and forcing them through their mouths. Then, once they were properly impaled, the large wooden stakes would be forced into the ground, and if they did not die immediately from shock or the impalement itself, they would be left to die as their own weight dragged them down the stake, penetrating their innards. The pamphlet spoke of how he impaled two monks in order to assist them to Heaven more quickly, simply for the sake of being cruel. Another anecdote described him boiling people alive in a large copper cauldron. Finally, as if the initial stories weren't enough to send me into a complete state of distress, there was one account that described how he had mothers and their babies impaled together, on the same stake, having cut the women's breasts off and placing the babies head-first into the wounds prior to impaling them. It sent my hand flying to my throat, stifling a scream.

The room was spinning and bile rose to my throat. I felt as though I was going to be sick. Never in my life had I read of such evil, such cruelty, and now I was to be married to the devil's spawn. Was he just as cruel as his father? Is this why he was shrouded in such mystery? Keeping his tendency for evil a secret so that he could rub shoulders with the most powerful ruler in Europe by marrying his daughter? Did my father know of this? I could not help but feel betrayed.

My head pounded with so many questions as I struggled to keep myself from being sick. Had I gotten up, there was no doubt Helene would be alarmed, and no one else should know of what I had just read. No. I had to get a hold of myself. *Breathe, just breathe.* One breath. One more. I closed my eyes to stop the room from spinning. If I displeased my husband, would he have my breasts cut off and insert a stake through my body? Was that to become my fate?

A memory flashed before my eyes—Margaret's face the day I departed Austria. She was so distressed. At last I understood why. She had tried to tell me but was unable to get a moment alone with me to tell me in private. But realistically, she was as powerless as I to change anything. Whether my father knew about this or not, it did not matter. We had a purpose, and that was to serve our father's empire. Regardless, she had to let me know somehow, but I wasn't sure if she had done me any favors by stowing the book away in my things. Perhaps ignorance was bliss and I would have been better off not knowing as there was nothing I could do to change it.

My breathing began to slow as I regained my composure. Finally, the room stopped swirling and my heart began to quiet, though the churning in my stomach had not left entirely. A brazen thought leapt to my mind. Was there a face to match this cruelty? I dared to scan through the pamphlet once again, unable to control myself, and sure enough, there was a woodcut image depicting Vlad the Impaler.

The face I beheld before me was not what I would have expected. A finely dressed man appeared before me wearing a cap and staring away, far away, at a three-quarter turn. Beneath his cap was long, waved hair hanging past his shoulders that at times curled around his face. His jaw was strong and angled, his chin sharp, and his lips were covered with a thick mustache. Meeting his mustache was a long, thin nose capped by high, sharp, arching cheekbones, two thick eyebrows above them. The cruelty lay beneath those eyebrows. In his eyes—round, almond-shaped, and heavily lidded. Eyes that carried suspicion and staunch determination, but were also cold and held what appeared to be intense, vengeful anger.

I stared at his likeness for a long moment, taking in his appearance, memorizing it. All the while, I couldn't believe what it was that I had just read, and the fact that I now resided in the lands where such cruelty and evil existed. I was to marry his son and be bound to him forever. I would forever have to endure the fear that I might be subjected to such cruelty, too.

I turned the page, intending to close the book and be done with it once and for all, for I had endured enough of the horrendous contents contained within, but I had not noticed that there was one page left. My stomach gave a great lurch. Blindly, I flung my legs over the side of the bed, pitching the book aside and reaching for the chamber pot beneath my bed. In less than a second, my stomach heaved its remaining contents into the chamber pot. The room was once again spinning as I heaved not once, but twice. It wasn't until I was done that I noticed Helene was at my side, murmuring into my ear and rubbing my back.

"Dinner must not have agreed with me," I mumbled in a lame attempt to divert her attention from the book containing such horror.

"It would appear so." Her eyes held great concern as she pushed back my hair from the filth. "Lay back in bed and rest. Tomorrow, you shall remain in bed and you will have nothing but broth, then perhaps some bread if you are up to it. I shall see to it that you are not disturbed."

As she took the chamber pot from me and disappeared to empty it, I crammed the book under the pillows. I wanted to cast it into the fire, but I did not have the energy to get up. Neither were the flames large enough to consume it swiftly to avoid drawing Helene's attention to it. I almost wished it contained lewd items versus the horrendous, horrific, and demonic contents it did contain.

When Helene returned, I was leaning back against the pillows. It was almost as though knowing the book was beneath me was scorching a hole in my back. She remarked at how pale I looked as she tucked the bedcovers under my chin and pushed my hair from my face. She stoked the fire to get it going again and insisted she would remain awake until I fell asleep. Then she closed the curtains of the four-poster bed, imprisoning me with this vile thing until I could get the chance to dispose of it.

I couldn't get the image out of my head. The woodcut image of people impaled on tall wooden stakes, their eyes wide and mouths agape like fish that had been torn from the water only to suffocate on land. The bodies being mutilated, cut into pieces. Then, finally, of Vlad the Impaler seated at a table, watching all of this unfold in delight while feasting on an elaborate banquet, dipping his bread into the blood of the tortured.

VI

I DO NOT KNOW when I had fallen asleep. That image remained burned into my eyes for what felt like an eternity. Closing my eyes didn't banish the nightmarish scene, nor did keeping them open as I was enclosed in darkness, the book burning into the pillows beneath me. I was unable to prevent myself from conjuring the scene. There were times throughout the evening when I cursed Margaret for exposing me to such a thing, and then other times I silently thanked her. Then, I would toss and turn as I imagined what those poor souls went through as the wooden stake penetrated their bodies. I could not fathom how painful that must have been. It was little wonder why the Saxons—those remaining, anyhow—hated my betrothed and his family. I had read that Vlad the Impaler's victims were often Saxon merchants and their families. It was also no wonder why the Voivode desired an Austrian archduchess——he needed to strengthen his rule with ties to the Holy Roman Empire and keep the remaining Saxon inhabitants happy. Voivodes were elected to their thrones by the nobles, or *boyars,* as they were called. Therefore, a voivode's reign was not guaranteed, so they were forced to immerse themselves in politics and strengthen ties with allies to ensure they remained on the throne. With our arranged marriage, there was no doubt that my betrothed was doing just that. With all of these thoughts and images coursing through my head, I did not sleep very much. I didn't even realize I had fallen asleep until I awoke some time in the afternoon, dazed and confused by how low the sun was sitting in the sky through my bedroom windows.

As Helene had promised, she made sure no one had disturbed me. She sat near the door mending an article of clothing as I slept, something I noticed after I jerked awake, disoriented, confused as to what time it was and why I was asleep.

"Good afternoon, Your Highness," she said merrily. "You have slept a long time, but I am glad as you so clearly needed it after last night's event."

"What time is it?" I croaked, my dry throat hoarse from being sick the evening before. Helene indicated to the tankard of watered-down ale next to my bed and I reached for it, drinking greedily to assuage my sore throat.

"It is well into the afternoon," she replied, "sunset is only a few hours away. Now that you are awake, I shall fetch you some broth and perhaps some bread. How are you feeling now?"

The scene of bodies dangling on large pikes, rotting in the sun flickered in my mind. "Better," I lied, taking another sip of ale.

"That is good. You don't seem to have a fever," she murmured, pressing her hand against my forehead. "Perhaps it was last night's dinner; perhaps it was a bit undercooked. Lay back and continue to rest while I fetch you something to eat." In a swift swirl of skirts, she was gone.

Lying back and resting was the last thing I wanted to do. I wanted to throw myself out of the bed, urge Helene to start packing immediately—doing it myself if need be—gather all of my father's soldiers, and flee from this cursed place. I would gladly enter a convent if this was to be my fate. If not that, then I would get up and continue walking until I could no longer. Anything to get those images out of my head. But, I was trapped and couldn't do either lest I draw unwanted attention to myself and to that horrid book. I once again recalled Margaret's face on the day I left Austria and was reminded of how powerless the both of us were in our father's game of politics.

Helene returned and I feigned a smile, presenting eagerness to eat and indicating that I was feeling better when I, in fact, was not. For the rest of the afternoon and into the evening I was confined to my bed while Helene read to me to pass the time. My focus wavered in and out while she read. I tried so hard to imagine the events unfolding in the novels she read out loud, but more often than not, they were conquered by the images I had stumbled across in that little brown book. The villains of Helene's stories took on the menacing face of Vlad the Impaler, with his round, angry eyes and thick mustache.

Night fell and I asked that Helene read to me until I fell asleep. If my request bore any suspicion, she did not let it on, instead doing as I asked. I didn't want to be alone with my thoughts and while her reading didn't drive them away entirely, it distracted me well enough. Soon, the words lulled me and my breathing slowed. I eased down on my pillows, letting my eyes flutter closed and allowing the flickering of the flames in the fireplace to underscore the soothing tones of Helene's voice.

The fog was thick, so thick it nearly suffocated me. I found myself in a dense forest, surrounded by trees. I was barefoot, my feet cold against the bed of leaves that had fallen from the trees surrounding me. I knew not where I was; this was no forest I was familiar with. Or perhaps it was, the fog being so thick, it was too disorienting. It rolled and swirled around me as I walked tentatively, throwing my arms out in front of me lest I walk into one of the stark trees. Occasionally, I did touch a trunk of one of the trees and its bark was so cold beneath my fingertips, a sensation of unwelcome accompanied it. I was not welcome here. I glanced down at the ground below me again before moving onward and saw I was in my nightgown. Last thing I remembered was Helene reading to me. How did I get here?

I heard rustling. I was not alone. "Is anyone there?" I called out, my voice a pathetic whimper.

I pressed myself up against the tree trunk I was nearest to, the coldness of its bark seeping into my back. The rustling ceased and after a moment I continued forward. Eventually, I reached a clearing in the forest and my hand was met with another tree trunk, however, the bark of it was smooth and not coarse, like the others. I reached my hand upwards, my fingertips grazing against something fleshy. I gasped at its touch, reeling backwards. The fog continued to roll but it cleared enough to allow me to look up. I cried out louder this time, falling backwards onto the bed of fallen leaves.

I was met with the sight of a forest of a different kind, a forest of stakes, and from them hung the bleeding bodies of my family. My father, my step-grandmother, my brother, even my long-deceased grandfather and mother. Their bodies were contorted in a way that meant they had met death with much pain and suffering. Their mouths hung open and the tips of the stakes burst through them. Then, at the forefront and center, hung my sister. Her body did not hang like the others, instead she had been impaled through her back. Her arms, legs, and head hung limp before her. It was her foot that I had touched. I regained my footing as I stared, mouth agape, at my beloved sister covered in blood. I reached gingerly for her foot again when suddenly it twitched. I screamed at the top of my lungs. I felt such a weight envelop my neck and chest that it began to suffocate me, forcing the air out of my body.

I was going to die. Darkness began to creep in the corners of my eyes and then I heard a voice growling something over and over again. With my last ounce of strength, I threw myself forward, propelling myself into darkness.

I sat up, drenched in sweat, my chest heaving for the air I had lost. My hands thrust out and I clutched a handful of fabric, pulling the curtains aside from the four-poster bed. Seeing Helene asleep on the floor reassured me that I hadn't screamed aloud in my slumber, and as my feet touched the cold floorboards, I was careful to slip out of the room. I crept with speed down the hallway and out onto the overlook, allowing the crisp night air to wash away any remnants of slumber that remained. Moreso, any remnants of that nightmare, as I wished to completely erase it from my memory.

Never before had I had such a violent and hideous nightmare. Not only did it contain such gore and horror, it felt utterly realistic.

As I leaned forward against the wooden railing of the overlook, I murmured a prayer, asking God to wipe those scenes from my mind. The crisp, cold air dried the sweat on my body, chilling my skin, so I reentered my room before I could catch an illness. It was enough that I was losing sleep quite a bit lately, I didn't need an illness as well. But before I laid my head back down on my pillow, I took the small brown book from underneath it and buried it deep within my trunk, back to where it was found, feeling satisfied to leave it there until I had a moment alone and could pitch it into the flames of my fireplace.

VII

IN A DESPERATE ATTEMPT to forget what I had read in that book and saw in my nightmare, I plunged myself into painting the following day, desperate to turn my attention elsewhere so I would no longer be plagued. My body felt better and rested after sleep eventually came, but my mind felt diseased. I longed to speak with a priest, hoping to be absolved of the betrayal of my own mind, but I was concerned about raising suspicion. Especially since we only had four days left before we departed and knowing Helene would begin the preparations tomorrow. Intermittently, I prayed that Prince Vlad would not return and I could flee to Austria. The humiliation I would face there was far better than what lay in wait for me here.

Once again today, I was left alone, fortunately. Helene said I looked better and well-rested. If she was suspicious that things were still amiss, she did not let it on. Instead, she went on her way with endless tasks that she found for herself. I had set aside my painting of the castle for now as it was nearly finished, and moved on to painting the tabernacle inside the chapel of the imperial palace of Innsbruck. After imagining nothing but the images which had haunted my mind the last day and a half, it was calming to paint the chapel I had been to numerous times throughout my life.

My progress was interrupted when Helene rushed in, not bothering to knock first.

"Your Highness," she said breathlessly, pausing to emit a cough which she covered prudently with a handkerchief. "Your Highness," she continued, her voice coming out in a little croak, then getting stronger as she went on. "The prince is here. He is coming up the road now with a party of men. He has kept his promise."

My stomach did a little flip and I could not discern if it was from fear or nervousness—perhaps both—and I stopped my painting immediately, looking at her, my eyes as round as an owl's. "Why are we hearing about it now? Did he not send a courier ahead to alert us of his arrival and no one told me?" A flush began to spread across my body and it felt as though I was coming down with a sudden ailment.

"He did not, Madam, we only know of it now as Ioana heard them coming when she was returning from the town. She rushed here at once to alert us, though I'm certain they were not far behind her as they were on horseback."

"Very well," I replied, resuming my painting and determined to escape into it. It was the only thing keeping me from entirely unraveling.

Helene's eyebrow lifted. "Are you not going to greet His Highness?"

"I do not see why I should, considering he kept us waiting for nearly three weeks and then didn't even have the courtesy to send a courier ahead to notify us of his arrival." What I did not tell her was that I did not want to, that I wished to hide behind my painting.

For a second, I thought I saw a smirk dance on Helene's lips. I had not told her what I had seen, so she must have thought I was playing a courtship game. That was the farthest from the truth. "Very well," she repeated, "I will go ahead and prepare what I can for his arrival. Then, I assume I will return to dress you for dinner with the prince?"

"If it comes to that. But we shall see, won't we? Perhaps it might do him some good to wait a little while." I squatted down as I dabbled a bit of gray paint to mimic the shadow that accompanied the light which used to come through the chapel window early in the morning.

Helene curtsied silently and backed out of the room.

I had to admit my curiosity was growing. After all, I had been waiting in the castle for this man for nearly three weeks, and far longer prior to that to finally meet him. My curiosity had been growing ever since Ambassador Ionescu showed up at my father's court to negotiate for my hand on the prince's behalf. I had no indication of what this man looked like, but if he bore any resemblance to the woodcut I saw of his father—no, I promised myself I would not think of that book any longer. Not until I could cast it into the fire.

There was a commotion downstairs, muffled male voices filled the air rapidly speaking in Romanian, and then Helene's softer feminine tone lifted into the air, halting as she did her best through the foreign language she had learned alongside me. Then things went quiet. I continued on, shading the chapel, crouching forward and moving slowly so as to not disturb my progress. I imagined Helene telling the Voivode that I was unable to come down to greet him at this time but that there was a chance I might be able to meet him for dinner. I strained to hear while I mixed white with black to get the perfectly blended gray I needed.

Just then, there was another commotion. The sound of boots hitting the floorboards in a sweeping crescendo followed by Helene's voice, growing louder with the sound of thundering boots. She was protesting, switching to German in frustration. The sound of the boots grew louder, indicating that they were just outside my door.

And then the door flew open.

I straightened quicker than a bolt of lightning as a man stepped into my bedchamber, his back straight and his presence both imposing and invasive.

Before I could fully comprehend what was happening, I was met with the most startling green eyes I had ever seen. They were mesmerizing, and I was unable to do anything else but stand there with my paintbrush in one hand and my pallet in the other, transfixed by the deep emerald shade of them as he assessed me. My breath trapped in my throat as I suddenly grew self-conscious under his gaze as I remembered my messy, unbound hair and the painting smock over the plain indigo gown I wore beneath it. However, self-consciousness was beneath my station, and I straightened a little bit more as I assessed the owner of those emerald green eyes.

There was no doubt that the prince himself stood before me. He was tall and his arms hung somewhat stiffly at his sides. His chest and shoulders were broad and I could tell, even with the cut of his plain black riding cloak, that he was well-muscled, lean, and fit. What was most striking—accompanying those stunning emerald eyes fringed with long black eyelashes—was a handsome face. The stubble growing in on his cheeks could not disguise his somewhat narrow and sharply angled jaw, his high cheekbones, his long, straight nose, and his eyes which were rather round but angled slightly upwards at the outer corners. He had perfectly arched eyebrows and was crowned with thick, unruly black hair. In the light coming in through the window behind me, I could see reddish chestnut strands mixed in with the jet black strands.

Just then, Ambassador Ionescu stepped forward after standing awkwardly in the doorway. "My Lord, may I present to you Her Imperial Highness, Shoshana Eleanor Marie, House of Habsburg, Countess of Hainaut, and Archduchess of Austria."

"Your Highness," the prince finally said in flawless German, to my great surprise. He threw his cloak back to reveal a black, fur-lined tunic and bowed before me. He had a pleasant, and admittedly very becoming, baritone voice.

I set aside my painting supplies. "Your Highness," I murmured while dipping into a curtsy. "It is nice that you finally have joined us." I could not help the ice in my voice as I straightened and met his eyes levelly.

"It is most regrettable that I was unable to welcome you to Romania after your long journey," he replied coolly, as if he hadn't heard the sharpness of my tone, "but after I received evidence of threats to your well-being, I could not leave them unanswered and felt it most wise to answer them myself, swiftly and without mercy."

Now a chill skittered down my spine. "Threats?"

"Yes. My scouts intercepted a message indicating the Ottoman Turks had dispatched a small troupe of men to kidnap

Your Highness. For a generous ransom from your notable father and to insult me, no doubt."

I felt my cheeks burn with shame and hoped they did not glow red for him to see. I did not often blush, but this time I could not help it. "Well, you have my gratitude for taking the matter seriously and seeing to it that I arrived safely."

I finally noticed Helene's fretful face lingering behind him, the concern in her features only increasing with the talk of my potential kidnapping. I thought for a moment she was going to faint. Ambassador Ionescu lurked in the hallway outside of the door, shifting his weight uneasily from one foot to the other, along with another man I did not originally notice.

"I do take the matter very seriously," the prince continued. His arms loosened and he straightened further. I could not discern anything he might have been thinking as he kept his features inscrutable. "And I thank you for remaining and giving me time to honor the agreement of our betrothal. I hope now that you will feel at ease furnishing the place."

"I intend to as I am not one to back out of my promises." At this time I switched to Romanian. It was still halting, but not as bad as it was when I first arrived. I'd had a lot of time to practice. "Should I purchase furnishings with the intention of you remaining here at Bran Castle, or should I anticipate your return to Târgoviște?"

If he caught my meaning, he did not indicate it, remaining inscrutable. However, the intensity of his stare made me feel almost as if he not only caught my meaning, but read my very mind. I was unsettled by the thought. "I intend to stay as long as I can, however, I will be required to return to Târgoviște eventually. I would appreciate it if you would furnish this house with the comforts of myself and my men in mind." He followed my lead, speaking in Romanian. The language only enhanced the pleasant-sounding tone of his voice.

"Very well, I will do so. As for our wedding? With all of the hindrance already, I should think it imperative that there be no further delay." I found myself surprised at my own words, my sense of duty had taken over the fear I had developed in learning about his father.

Again, his face remained indecipherable. I found it surprising that this man was older than me but somehow appeared both younger and older. Foolish, I know, but there was something about him that I could not pinpoint... It was both intriguing and unsettling. "The wedding will take place at the end of this week. The arrangements have all been made." Again, my stomach did that same odd turn as before. "Now, I will take my leave of you."

With that, he bowed again and was gone before I straightened from my curtsy in reply.

"I do not know what I was expecting, but he is incredibly handsome," Helene said, surprising me as she spoke of men rarely, and never like that.

"Yes, I suppose I am fortunate he is not homely, but there is something about him that makes me uneasy." My eyes fixated on the door, but I was not necessarily looking at it as my thoughts drifted away. He did not look like the image I had seen of his father. I left that thought unsaid, and for that I was truly grateful. He must have shared some of his father's traits, but because his father was no longer alive, I would never know for sure. There was a reservation in his eyes that could be interpreted as hardness, but there was no outward cruelty that stood out to me.

"I am sure that is just nervousness. It was your first time meeting him, after all. Oh, I am so glad your wedding gown will be used after all! I cannot wait to see you in it again."

Helene exuded an excitement that I was not sure I shared. My mind was churning with juxtaposing feelings. I was relieved he was attractive, at least, but he had an impenetrable presence that made me uneasy. Furthermore, I did not like that it seemed like he could read my thoughts, nor how those emerald eyes penetrated mine. Then again, on the other side, I was relieved I would not have to go back to my father in shame and that my future seemed clearer. I wasn't sure that we would come to love each other, but I hoped that we could at least come to a pleasant understanding. I also worried that I would always be uneasy in his presence, knowing about his father as I did.

"Did you hear what I said?" Helene's voice came in sharp, interrupting my interpretations of all the feelings that were swarming me. I blinked back to the present and glanced at her. "I said that I will see to it that we set up a bath for you and get you ready, as I assume you will be dining with the prince tonight."

"On which floor will the Voivode be staying?" I asked.

"I am uncertain, but I will find out. I think we should go with that lovely red gown you have. Red definitely suits you." With that, she whisked away to see to it that Prince Vlad's men were fed and my bath was prepared. Meanwhile, I lingered in front of my painting of the chapel back at my father's home, realizing that it was no longer my home and I may not ever see that chapel again. Suddenly, the shadow I had painted over the tabernacle seemed foreboding and menacing.

VIII

I HAD BATHED AND was dressed in the gown I wore when I first arrived, the gown meant to dazzle the Voivode when we first met. But, of course, he had not been here. Instead, when he first met me, I appeared dowdy in a plain gown and a painting smock with my hair askew. Now, we renewed the vision, gold caul and all, and once the effect was complete, I sat alone in the dining room sipping on the wine Ambassador Ionescu had gifted me. The candles on the wall sconces were new and burned brightly, matching the candelabra on the table.

I was certain I was on time, as Helene confirmed that Prince Vlad had agreed to meet me for dinner—"insisted upon it" had been her words—but he had not yet arrived. Part of me was not shocked as he had already displayed a habit of keeping me waiting, though admittedly, his reasons for keeping me waiting the first time were valid, and I was grateful for them. But what was his excuse now?

I drummed the fingers of my right hand along the surface of the table between sips of my wine, mimicking the movements of an old Austrian folk song I used to play on the harpsichord.

"I understand you are quite talented on the harpsichord. I hope to hear you play some time."

A baritone voice from behind startled me and I stopped immediately, my hand clenching in reflex. My cheeks burned in mortification at being caught off guard, and again, I hoped that they did not show it. I was not fond of the fact that this was the second time it had happened today.

"I do play, and I enjoy it very much. I have been told I am talented, though I am not sure of it myself," I replied, trying to recover from my embarrassment.

Prince Vlad swept through the room just as silently as he had arrived with a small slender man trailing behind him, his steward I deduced, and he assumed his place opposite me. He was clean shaven and his hair was combed. He wore a deep maroon velvet tunic trimmed with black fur at the cuffs and collar, and black trousers capped with leather riding boots. His attire only further emphasized his imposing and impenetrable presence. His emerald eyes fixed on me and for the first time—and completely out of character for me—I found myself hoping he found me just as becoming. I was used to my appearance being scrutinized all my life. It used to bother me as a child, then it morphed into a semblance of detachment coated with jadedness as I never seemed to be an object of approval to the male gaze. As a result, I had stopped caring about how I appeared to men, but now suddenly, and rather foolishly, I cared. Though it shifted when

I could feel the heat on my cheeks again under his gaze, masking my thoughts in case he could actually read them. His gaze was so intense.

"I am no musician," he admitted, "so, talented or not, I will not be able to tell the difference. I am aware of your father's patronage of the arts and the best tutors he hired for his children. If your skill at the harpsichord is anywhere near your skill with the paint brush, I have no doubt you are talented."

His flattery disarmed me. "You are very kind, My Lord. Were you not tutored in any form of art?"

"I was not. The focus of my education was warfare and combat—archery, fencing, horseback riding, history, languages, diplomacy—nothing in the arts. It was seen as unnecessary." He bore no judgment in his tone as it related to his last statement, and remained matter-of-fact. Then again, that seemed to be his general demeanor; he was very difficult to read.

"Perhaps I could tutor you," I said without thinking. As soon as it was out of my mouth I felt awfully foolish. Here I was, guffawing like a child. What was it about this man that disarmed me so?

With this foolish statement, I was finally able to draw a smile to his lips. It tugged at the corner of his mouth when he replied. "I doubt you will find an apt pupil, but I am open to trying."

Fortunately, dinner arrived before I could continue to make myself look even more childish. The servants laid out a number of dishes on the table before us: roast pheasant, dates, figs, grapes, and cheese, all smelling delicious. I didn't realize how hungry I was until my eyes beheld the various platters. Once they were laid out, Ioana, the female servant I

had met shortly after I arrived here, cut into the meat and began to lay items out onto a plate for me. Then, she refilled my
cup and walked away before serving the prince, something
I found rather odd. His manservant reappeared holding a
goblet on a tray, and he placed it before the prince before
disappearing once more.

A conflict picked at me as to whether to mention something or brush it off, lest I sound moronic again. I couldn't
help myself, though, as it was odd that neither servant had
prepared a plate for him. "I have become fond of Romanian
wine myself since my arrival. Ambassador Ionescu was kind
enough to gift me a cask of it."

His eyes glittered for a moment, so brief that it could
have been easily missed. "There is nothing else like it in the
world." Then he took a long swallow of the contents within
his silver goblet. He liked to imbibe, it seemed, to the point
of even refraining from eating. How strange. Perhaps it was
only for this evening. Maybe travel had lessened his appetite.
Or perhaps it was because he was nervous? Though that was
doubtful. He did not strike me as being nervous in any setting. I also reminded myself that I would not be his first wife;
he was familiar with the company of women. This made me
think of our upcoming wedding night. Perhaps it was best
he was familiar with the company of women, for I would
certainly be nervous on that night.

"I hope your journey here was not too long and strenuous."

"A bit long, yes, but not terribly strenuous. It is kind of
you to consider," I said, then bit into the pheasant, all too
uncomfortable with the idea of eating in front of him while
he merely watched and sipped from his goblet. "Are you not
hungry, My Lord?"

"I am not. I found what I had eaten on the journey here was enough to sustain me for the rest of the evening." He sat back in his chair and ran the tip of his finger along the rim of his goblet absentmindedly. This allowed me to notice how long his fingers were and thought what a shame it was that he never learned how to play the harpsichord. With such a long finger span, he would have found it easy to glide across the keys and he could have been very talented.

"I must say you are missing out as this is one of the best dinners I have had in a little while." Again with the foolishness coming out of my mouth. Why was I telling him this? To be fair, it was, having eaten only broth and bread the day before.

He said nothing, but a smirk tugged at the corner of his lips as he lifted the cup to drink from it once more. I took notice of the shape of his lips, then, which ignited a spark of heat in my belly. I quickly lowered my gaze to focus on the contents of my plate before I gave away any indication of my embarrassment.

Little was said for the rest of the duration of dinner, and finally, it was over. We said our goodnights to one another and parted ways, to our respective rooms, the prince taking the floor above mine. Helene had been busy during dinner. Now that we knew we were to be staying, she had unpacked every single one of my trunks. Now my room looked completely occupied, instead of just partially. All of the gowns had been shaken out. The everyday dresses were draped in the wardrobe in my bedchamber, and the ornate gowns for stately occasions and banquets had been squirreled away into a proper storage room. The little brown book waiting to be engulfed in flames had been moved from its trunk, buried between two canvases in my art supplies in fear that Helene might have found it and opened it. It appeared as though she had completely forgotten about its existence, which was for the better. In addition to unpacking my belongings, Helene declared that, since I was to be a married woman, she would be occupying her own room. She would be taking a room nearest mine, though, so as to attend to my needs. Tonight was to be the first night I had ever slept alone.

When night had fallen and the entire castle was seemingly asleep, I sat on my bed in wonder at being completely alone for the first time in my entire life. The flames in the fireplace were low and the windows were shuttered to keep the heat in as the nights were not only getting longer, but colder as well. The spot in which Helene previously slept was bare, replaced with a rug. I sighed and reminded myself of my mission, throwing my feet over the side of the bed and rising to slip from my bedchamber and into the chamber where I was storing my painting supplies. I retrieved the book right where I had left it and moved swiftly back into my bedchamber. Stopping in front of the fireplace, I lowered to my knees, ready to cast the vile book into the flames before they got any lower, but then I stopped short, quivering a little from both chill and something else I could not quite put my finger on. Before I could stop myself, I flipped the pages, avoiding the ones that filled the images I would not name, and opened to the page that showcased the prince's father.

I studied it again. He hardly looked anything like his son, I thought. This man was ugly and cruel-looking whereas my betrothed was not ugly, though it remained to be seen if he was cruel. The only physical similarities I could draw from the portrait were their noses and cheekbones for, based on this portrait, his father also had high cheekbones. The prince had a somewhat thinner lower lip, similar to that of his father, but it was becoming, and not abrasive and bulbous as his father's appeared in the book.

One had to assume that Prince Vlad was aware of the atrocities his father had committed, but did he consider them to be atrocities? Did he have that same streak of cruelty coursing through his veins? Would any children we produced have that same streak as well? My stomach churned at the thought of it.

I was unable to cast the small book into the flames. Something was gnawing at me to keep it. Some unspoken instinct told me to preserve it as a reminder and warning to undo any damage and raise my heirs right, using my father as an example and not my betrothed's.

IX

T WO ROUND EYES PEERED at me, the irises so gray that they appeared silver, and encased with a thick fringe of long, black eyelashes. Above them perched two sharply arched eyebrows and between the eyebrows, the nose sloped straightly downwards until the tip, where it curved slightly upwards, flaring delicately at the nostrils. Below them sat the pair of lips, frowning as the round silver eyes beheld the oval face they were peering at.

Helene was able to mount the gold-framed mirror I had brought with me from Austria now that we were staying. It was a parting gift from my father as I could not bring the large one originally propped up in my former bedchamber. I was peering at my own reflection, frowning at the faint dark circles that had appeared under my eyes. Today was the day of my wedding, a terribly inconvenient time to have dark circles under my eyes. But, a full night's sleep continued to evade me. Every night was filled with thoughts of everything and anything, but more specifically, worries about my wedding and wedding night, as well as the unknown future that lay before me since I could not make out the personality of my betrothed. The Voivode did not give me any indication of what he had planned, and even more troubling, I had not seen him once since the day of his arrival. He mostly stayed in his rooms, keeping to himself, holding meetings with Ambassador Ionescu, dispatching letters, and other business that I was not privy to. So I had no idea what to expect. The ambassador was far too busy now that the Voivode had arrived, so I was unable to ask him. Helene was a whirlwind herself, preparing this and that, cleaning this and that, directing the influx of servants we had acquired to do this and that, and leaving me to write to my father, informing him that the wedding was still on. What I did not divulge to my father was how I felt incredibly excluded as everyone around me was increasingly busy. I did include a letter to my sister, as I wanted to inform her that I received her warning. I anticipated that my letter would be read prior to its dispatch so I was careful in what I wrote.

"Do not worry, Your Highness," Helene said, catching me frowning at my reflection. "You will look beautiful. The silver threading and buttons on your gown will enhance your eyes and all of Romania will see the beautiful gem they plucked from Austria."

"I suppose they will not think of me as the daughter of a Gypsy king here," I remarked, "as a lot of them have dark features. Dark eyes, dark hair..."

"Keep frowning like that and those creases on your forehead will stay. Here, apply this to your face."

"Will this help with the dark circles?" I opened the jar and could smell the animal fat the ointment was made from.

"It will help some, but once it dries, I will apply a little powder to your face to lessen them. Besides, most of those attending will not be focusing on your eyes as they will be too far away to see any dark circles."

"It's not them I am worried about, but my groom. He will be seeing me up close." The ointment was cool on my face but refreshing, and I caught a hint of jasmine.

"You will be so stunning, he won't even notice. Besides, it is almost befuddling how little men notice certain things. You will learn that as you get comfortable in your marriage. Come now, let me help you change your chemise while the ointment dries."

I flung the chemise I was wearing off over my head and stepped into the fresh one Helene held out for me. She allowed me to step back into my dressing gown to combat any chill in the air while she applied a light coat of powder to my face, which did minimize the appearance of the dark circles, though they weren't gone entirely. Once she blended the powder to ensure it wouldn't surface anywhere on my clothes, she helped me into my gown.

It was an incredible gown of a deep red velvet brocade with slashed sleeves and trimmed with silver lace. Silver buttons lined up the bodice until it flared open, revealing a silver insert that squared at the top. Worn over the top would be a long matching cloak that attached at the shoulders, a train which would drag along the floor as I walked down the aisle, edged with black ermine. It would be removed during the wedding banquet, which I assumed would be taking place after the ceremony. I stepped into the gown and Helene laced the back together. It was dazzling, I had to admit.

Once the gown was laced and fitted, Helene draped a lengthy gold chain around my neck, then followed it with a second, slightly shorter one. Then, last to join the other two chains was a black pearl necklace that had once belonged to my mother. I was shocked to see it.

"How did you convince my father to part with them?" I asked, staring at the necklaces incredulously in the mirror.

"I did no such convincing. It was all his idea; he wanted you to have them."

I was awestruck, falling silent and transfixed on how beautiful the black pearls were as Helene brushed my hair and swept it into a gold hairnet. She finished with a gold circlet around my forehead which assisted in keeping the caul in place. Two strands of hair escaped it, framing my face. Helene tried to pin them back but I insisted she leave them, appreciating how they looked. Finally, Helene slipped gold slippers onto my feet and we were finished.

By the time we were done, I barely recognized myself. Maybe I had some potential to be attractive after all.

Helene assisted me down the stairs where Ambassador Ionescu was waiting at the bottom, dressed in his Romanian finery. At the sound of our descent, he turned to face me.

"Your Highness," he nearly gasped, "you are a vision. Forgive me for any imprudence, but you look exquisite."

His gaze remained on me, seemingly spellbound, and while I did believe I looked comely enough, I was certain he was merely being kind. "You are kind, ambassador."

"I mean it, Your Highness. All that behold you are sure to fall in love with you. You are an angel."

"I do not think angels have hair as dark as mine, ambassador, but I appreciate the sentiment nonetheless."

"Perhaps you are just an extraordinary one." He bowed and took my hand, planting a kiss on the back of it.

He escorted me to the carriage that would take us to the church in which the prince and I would be married, the Church of Saint Mary, in the middle of Brașov. The construction of this church was completed nineteen years ago, and we were the first royalty to be wed there. People were lining the streets once again to see me in my wedding finery. The air was crackling with excitement. I was touched to see some of the townspeople dressed in their very best. Helene and Ambassador Ionescu accompanied me in my carriage, and together, Helene and I dipped our hands into the satchel of coins we carried and threw them out into the crowd as we passed. The people cheered as they scrambled to the side of the road to snatch up the coins that clinked onto the cobblestone roads.

"This is marvelous!" Helene cried out, beaming with the giddiness of a child.

Admittedly, my own reservations and fears subsided as I, too, got caught up in the fervor and excitement reverberating all around us. My laughter joined Helene's as we watched the merriment of the townspeople. The cheering followed us all the way to the cathedral and continued as I stepped out of the carriage with Ambassador Ionescu guiding me. If anything, the cheers of the townspeople grew louder as the full effect of my dazzling wedding attire was revealed, befitting a Habsburg archduchess. The merry sounds calmed the racing thoughts I'd had leading up to this day.

I stood, waving at the cheering crowd, as Helene was assisted from the carriage by Ambassador Ionescu. She hurried over to readjust my gown, pulling out the train for all to see. This elicited another swell of cheers from the people and, admittedly, I relished in their positive response. My entire life I had been set aside, doubted, and met with suspicion; it was invigorating to receive such a warm reception of approval. It was also lovely to be in the presence of them, seeing the details of the faces of both the old and young—the men, women, and children of this town. Ambassador Ionescu was kind enough to let me relish in this wonderful reception for several minutes when suddenly, a woman broke out from the crowd, bolting towards me and crying out. With my face suddenly going numb with shock and confusion, all I could do was stand there doe-eyed as she threw herself at my feet, speaking rapidly. Two of my father's knights, who had escorted us to the church, charged towards her as she threw herself down. I thought I heard her say, "may God protect your soul" as she pressed something small and hard into the palm of my hand, tears streaming down her cheeks, but it was difficult to discern all the things she said with the roar of the crowd behind her. I could only stand and stare as the guards removed her forcefully, dragging her away somewhere unseen. I looked down at my palm and saw a small wood-carved crucifix embedded in it.

Taking this as his cue to remove me from the situation lest someone else have similar or even worse ideas, Ambassador Ionescu took his place at my side to escort me into the church. He was standing in the place of my father to give me away to my groom. Trying to shake myself from the unsettling scene, I made sure to tuck the crucifix in my opposite sleeve so that he did not feel it there.

The sight of the church itself was breathtaking—a titan towering over all of the surrounding houses, taverns, and businesses in the town square. It was made of brick, with a single bell tower that stood imposingly, its spire piercing the blue of the sky. Behind it was the long stretching body of the church. It was crowned with a peaked roof that fell in step behind the bell tower, and surrounding the roof were smaller, shorter spires which dipped down into buttresses that housed figures of various stone-carved saints.

We approached the entrance and were met with another small group of my father's guards that had traveled with us, dressed in their best and draped in the emblem of my father's empire. The ambassador, Helene, and I were surrounded by them, two rows of two in front of us and three rows of two behind us. Then two guards bearing a dragon on their shields and tunics opened the door to let us in. Together, we entered the church with this great display of the two houses joining together. Helene kept my train lifted as we walked. The doors closed behind us and the sound of the crowd cheering was drowned out in the solemnity of this great church. The distant sound of a harpsichord filled the air, replacing the cries of the people.

The interior of the church was just as exquisite as the exterior, stretching on like a great hall in a great palace, arches springing from one to the other like the ripples from a pebble dropped into a pond. Tall, brick pillars met the arches that bloomed over them in the high ceiling. The sun was beaming in through the great windows that extended nearly to the ceiling and the light emphasized the brilliance of the architecture. The floor was capped with a sea of pews that stretched almost as far as the eye could see, and they were filled with finely dressed nobles, their wives, and families who all turned to face me as we entered. I hardly noticed their curious stares as I took in the awe-inspiring view of the beauty around me.

Together, the ambassador, whose arm I leaned on, Helene, who continued to carry my train, and my father's guards around me, we moved forward down the boundless aisle with all eyes upon us. The distant harpsichord continued to shimmer in the air. Just then, the cheerfulness I had once felt, having caught it from the people as they greeted me, grew into nervousness. The aisle seemed to go on forever. A thought in the back corners of my mind crept in, nagging at me, reminding me what I had seen in that little brown book. The intensity of my heartbeat thundered in my ears, drowning out the glitter of the harpsichord. Very subtly, I tried to scan the faces of the crowd to see if I would be met with the sight of my betrothed's father glaring back at me, then I chided myself, reminding myself that the book had said he was dead. All for the better.

I did my best to fix my attention on the final destination ahead of me and that was a beautiful mural of Christ Himself at the end of the aisle, His arms outstretched comfortingly. *Lord*, I thought to myself, thinking of the wood-carved crucifix in my sleeve, *take me into Your keeping. Let this marriage be blessed by Your mercy.*

Surrounding this mural was the altar itself and standing before it, in the middle, was the priest, and beside him was the imposing figure of the man I was here to marry. I saw a couple of other men standing beside him, one whose dark brown eyes were fixed intensely on me, but they paled in comparison to the Voivode's upright stature and wedding finery. It wasn't until I was closer that I could make out the details of his attire. Despite being slightly outdated, he wore it rather splendidly and it suited him well, almost like a second skin. He was dressed rather simply and his silhouette was straight, emphasizing his impressive posture, and he wore a deep black knee-length sleeveless robe. Under the robe, he wore a dark blue velvet doublet with black fur edging the cuffs. Black trousers were once again topped with his knee-length black leather riding boots, which had been polished for the occasion. At his hip hung his sword, exposed by his grand black fur cloak he wore, fastened with a large gold brooch at the center bearing the same curled dragon that emblazoned the tunics of his knights. Finally, his head of unruly hair was donned in a round black fur cap that matched the cloak.

His emerald-green eyes bore into me seemingly without blinking. I wondered if he thought of his first wife as he gazed at me and suddenly I felt self-conscious that perhaps I paled in comparison to her, picturing her to look like one of the flaxen-haired beauties at my father's court.

As we approached the altar, the two rows of knights ahead of me made quite a show of clearing the way to allow the ambassador to lead me the rest of the way to the altar alone. Ambassador Ionescu saw me to the top of the short steps, and Prince Vlad moved towards us as Ambassador Ionescu extended my hand, offering it to the Voivode. He took it in his, leading me to the final remaining steps of the altar so that we stood before the priest. I could not focus on the priest, however, instead focusing on the touch of the Voivode's hand, which was not at all warm but not cold, either. It was odd. I glanced up at his face, unable to determine what was in his mind, as usual. His mouth was set in a firm line and his eyes betrayed no emotion. I did notice, however, he appeared a bit pale.

The wedding mass had begun and the Voivode and I knelt before the priest as he blessed our union. The ceremony went a little over an hour before our rings were exchanged and we could consider ourselves wed. The harpsichord sounded again and Prince Vlad extended his arm to me and I took it. I noticed Helene weeping gently at Ambassador Ionescu's side as she dabbed a handkerchief to the corner of her eye. Ambassador Ionescu was beaming widely, his pride no secret to anyone who looked at him. I was forced to tear my attention away from the others as Prince Vlad began to move forward and for the first time as man and wife, we walked down the aisle together, accompanied by the polite clapping of the nobles who witnessed our union.

His knights mingled with my father's and together they escorted us out of the church and to the waiting carriage. Yet again, I marveled at the cool touch of Prince Vlad's hand as he helped me up, Helene sweeping my train inside so it did not get caught in the door, and then he placed himself next to me.

"It is done," he said as he adjusted himself to get more comfortable, catching me a bit off guard. I was taken aback by such a statement, his first words to his new wife, though it seemed to be stated more to himself than to me.

The carriage lurched and we made the short journey back to Bran Castle to have our wedding banquet. We were coated in uncomfortable silence during the journey and I tried to fill it with something to say, but no words would come to me. It felt as though my tongue was coated with lead. This was the first time I had been alone with a man who wasn't my father or my brother, and I wasn't sure how to speak with men. Perhaps he expected me to say something or was having second thoughts. I could not be sure as he gave no indication of how he was feeling in how he carried himself. Fortunately, the journey was a short one.

The grounds at the bottom of the castle had been converted into a temporary little village. Tents and pavilions had been erected as the next several days would contain wedding celebrations. The air was cool as winter was coming, but bonfires would be lit and warmed ale and mulled wine would be served to keep the guests warm. There would be games, banquets, festivities, archery contests, and dancing. This opportunity to show off Prince Vlad's new wife, the daughter of the Holy Roman Emperor, could not be passed up, and nobles from all of Romania would be traveling to attend, even if they had not been able to make the wedding. Only a select few guests would be joining us immediately after, however, for a light supper within the walls of Bran.

I was whisked away upstairs to remove the train of my gown and to descend back downstairs to greet the guests in the dining hall, which had been rearranged to accommodate more guests. I was impressed with Helene. She had clearly outdone herself by organizing all of it.

Prince Vlad and I were seated in the middle of the long table and nobles pushed their way in to meet me. They would exchange a few words with me, congratulating me on my nuptials and sometimes commenting on the fine quality of my gown. It would only be a matter of time before the noblewomen began to emulate my gowns, but for now they were beside themselves with the sight of it, kind words mixed in with hidden streaks of envy. All of the faces began to blur and I could not remember who it was I had met or spoken to. The occasional brief glances I was able to get of Prince Vlad told me that he was also overcome, particularly by the men trying to get in a word or two with him, no doubt to whisper requests in his ear or rub shoulders with him in order to get favors down the road. Men had done it all the time with my father. They sometimes would clap the back of the Voivode, laughing uproariously at some of his remarks as if he was the most clever man to walk the earth. Though he might have been, I did not know, for despite being now married to him, I barely knew my husband.

The meal came and went. Admittedly, more wine passed my lips than I would have preferred but it was to quell how overwhelming the room was. Helene was nowhere to be found as she was conducting the banquet, making sure the servants never slacked on filling cups or refilling dishes. There was so much going on, and it was overwhelming to my senses, leading me to encounter everything in a trancelike state. I almost felt as though I was watching everything from afar instead of experiencing it firsthand. Even during the banquet, the prince and I exchanged no words seeing as there was an endless parade of men and women seeking our attention. People were speaking in Romanian so rapidly, and some with accents so heavy, it was difficult at times to keep up. It was rare when I heard the familiar German being spoken, but even still, it was laden with such a thick dialect that it could be little comfort to me.

After dinner, the prince took my hand and together, we led the guests out onto the grounds to continue the festivities. The sun was setting and the bonfires had been lit, and servants pressed cups of mulled wine into our hands as we passed them. We settled into the largest pavilion where two high-backed chairs had been placed on top of a short platform. Prince Vlad escorted me to one and I sat as he took the chair immediately beside me. People continued to make their tributes to us, though not as frequently as they had during the banquet. This time, some of them bore little gifts and trinkets which were taken back up to the castle by servants lest they were to go missing. A slew of male guests continued to take the time to plant kisses on the back of my hand. There was also more to occupy their attention as there was a band of men playing music, one wielding a drum, one a lute, and finally, one with a flute. Tumblers and jugglers occupied the grounds, entertaining the guests, and there was a jester making his rounds as well, making the ladies blush with lewd comments and guffawing with the men.

Admittedly, this spectacle was enough to rival the numerous festivals my father had held back in Austria. I had to give Prince Vlad laudation. I had been thinking this to myself as the guests paying tribute to us thinned out, allowing themselves to be entertained by the happenings surrounding us.

"What do you think?" Prince Vlad asked, finally addressing me directly. "Is this a celebration to rival that of one held by your father?"

I blinked at him, owl-eyed. It was almost as though he had read my mind. "Why... yes it is... I was just thinking the very same thing. How peculiar."

His paleness had disappeared and he seemed more vibrant than he had this morning. His gloved hand reached for mine and he squeezed it gently. "Excellent," he replied, looking back out to the crowd. "An emperor's daughter should have a wedding celebration to rival his own."

He let go of my hand, patted it, and then stood to make his way to mingle into the crowd. It was then that I recalled the delicate nature of his position. These men who were trying to flatter us—and whom Prince Vlad was trying to flatter in return—would determine our position as rulers of Romania based on their voting system. It was a brilliant strategy by Prince Vlad, though, to marry the Holy Roman Emperor's daughter. It would force these nobles to risk facing my father's ire by removing us from the Romanian throne. Prince Vlad's position was quite safe, though not guaranteed, so he still needed to make his rounds to keep the boyars happy.

The music stopped and the crowd was ushered aside by a handful of servants to create a clearing. Then, a man carrying a fiddle joined the band of musicians and he began to lead them in a new musical piece. I recognized it at once—the *basse danse*, a popular dance within the courts of Burgundy, where my mother was from. Customarily, it was a dance for the monarchs to lead with, inviting the rest of the gentry to participate once they had the chance to strut their finery. But after a few bars of the music, Prince Vlad had not joined me on the dais as I had expected him to. Instead, Ambassador Ionescu approached, his eyes meeting mine. There was a glint of mischief in them and he bowed before extending his hand to me. I curtsied back to him and put my hand in his, then he led me off of the dais to the clearing. In unison, we knelt briefly before gliding across the clearing in the dance's basic two-step glides, alternating between stepping, clasping hands, and turning.

"Does the prince not dance?" I asked the ambassador as he continued to lead me around the clearing in the slow-paced dance.

"It is not his forte," he replied.

"He did indicate on the night of our first meeting that he didn't have much talent for music. I take it that includes rhythm as well."

"His Highness has other talents, some of which you will see for yourself soon enough."

What those talents were, I couldn't help but wonder. I refrained from telling him that I was beginning to get the impression the prince was avoiding me, seeing as we hadn't shared more than a few words.

Though, just then, as Ambassador Ionescu and I continued to move wordlessly across the clearing, I caught Prince Vlad watching me fixedly. A smile then moved across his mouth and it was the first time I had seen him smile fully. In the light of the bonfires and torches, I could see he had a brilliant display of white and rather straight teeth, and the corners of his eyes met his smile in a rather surprisingly charming and endearing way. Perhaps it was the wine, but at the sight of it, I felt my heart skip a beat and my stomach felt like butterflies were fluttering within it.

It had to have been the wine.

As the *basse danse* ended, my gaze was unable to peel itself away from Prince Vlad until I was interrupted by an older man asking me to join him for the next dance. As I turned my attention back to the prince, I saw he had gone, rejoining some of the men who appeared to be gambling with a pair of dice at one of the tents nearby. I agreed to my new partner's request and was engaged in the next one, which accompanied simple steps and the occasional clapping. Then, after that dance, I was caught up in another, the Italian *ballo*, with a new partner who shyly asked me if I would join him, then another and another, and I had no shortage of dance partners for the rest of the evening, though my husband was not one of them. In fact, I didn't see him again for the rest of the evening's festivities.

I stopped to catch my breath when Ambassador Ionescu appeared before me for another turn with me. "May I inquire as to be your partner for the next one?"

"I did not know you to be such a dancer, ambassador, but I would be glad to."

"Why, I love dancing! I could never get enough of it in my youth, but now I do not have the dexterity I used to. Now, I must preserve what dexterity I have left to impress my new princess."

Princess. I had forgotten that was to be added to my series of titles: Princess of Romania. "I am sure you could outdance any of these gentlemen."

He beamed at the compliment, taking my hand to lead me into the next dance, a large group number this time.

"What do you think of your new husband?" he asked quietly as we joined hands and moved in a small circle with some of the other guests.

"A bit of a mystery," I replied. "I was told very little about him before coming here and now he is here and I still don't know very much about him. I have married an absolute stranger." We stopped, extended our right foot and clapped, then the ambassador took my hands and we promenaded around in a wide circle to the rhythm.

"You will get to know him in time," the ambassador continued.

"Everything about him seems to be such a secret," I pressed.

"Your Highness, you should know by now that there are no secrets in a palace. You would do best to remember that, especially now." We repeated the same step as before, but this time extending our left foot, then promenading around again. "You have been the talk of the entire evening, yourself."

I was shocked to hear that I had been subject to whispers and murmurs, though I don't know why I had been so naive to think that I would be spared. Although, I was also so used to being overlooked that I did not think I was worth talking about. I thought my secrets were safe under the shroud of being generally ignored.

"I suppose you are right," I replied thoughtfully, saying no more on the subject. My eyes scanned the crowd of guests, suddenly very aware that I would be the subject of everyone's whispers tonight.

X

I T WAS WELL INTO the evening when Helene finally reappeared. She looked worn and exhausted yet determined
to carry out the task at hand.

"Your Highness," she said, waving away the servant who
appeared with yet another goblet. My head was swirling
with dancing and mulled wine and it felt like I was on a
cloud. But then I sobered up quickly at the realization as to
why she was summoning me. She escorted me to the castle along with a guard. Behind me, I could hear the guests'
laughter as they continued to enjoy tonight's festivities. I
had hoped that perhaps I could hide among them and shirk
the duty I had to perform tonight, except, alas, that was not
to be the case. But then I recalled the prince smiling at me as I
danced, watching me intently as I glided across the clearing,
and my cheeks grew warm. I had never had mulled wine before tonight and perhaps it should have remained that way.

Helene and I went up to my chamber where she freed me from my voluminous gown. She assisted me into a clean floor-length chemise and my satin dressing gown, then she freed my hair from its bonds and brushed it out so it tumbled over my shoulders.

"Remember everything I told you," she said as she brushed out my hair. I glanced behind me in the mirror and could see her face bore the utmost seriousness. "It may hurt at first, and it is wanton to enjoy it. He, of course, may enjoy it and is allowed to take as much time as he needs, but your task is to let it happen. Then, when he is done, he may stay the night with you or he may not, it is his choice."

"I have not forgotten."

"Good." With that, she finished and placed a kiss on top of my head. "I am very proud of you and I have no doubt your father is too. Your mother would have been incredibly proud of you, that is for certain."

Our eyes met in the mirror and she smiled. Then, she patted me on the shoulders, further emphasizing that she was done. She spun on her heel to add another log into the fireplace so that it would last the majority of the evening.

"You will be just fine," she said in a brief moment of encouragement, and she winked at me before whisking out of the door and leaving me absolutely alone.

The house was absolutely quiet; not a single sound echoed through the castle. Everyone remained at the celebration and every servant was needed to ensure the guests were attended to. It was some time that I lingered in my room, trying not to let my nerves get the best of me. Then, I heard footsteps outside of my door. Someone was approaching very quietly, the floorboards creaking, giving them away. I set the book I was reading aside by the fireplace and turned towards the door, expecting my husband to come through. He did not however, and the footsteps subsided.

I sat for a moment and waited, thinking perhaps he was nervous. It remained silent for another few moments, then the footsteps continued, pacing in front of my door. I took a deep breath and released it, then rose to my feet. Perhaps he did not want to intrude. Perhaps he wanted an invitation. I reached for the door, still hearing the footsteps.

Then, I pulled it open only to find the corridor empty.

I jerked back with the shock of finding no one there and quickly closed the door, utterly shaken. I swore I had heard footsteps. I was sober enough that the effects of the wine weren't as strong. I returned to my place by the fire as it was the spot furthest away from the door and poured myself a goblet of wine from the amphora Helene had prepared. Then, the footsteps started up yet again, growing with intensity this time and the door opened. I gasped rather loudly. The Voivode had entered.

He stopped and eyed me curiously. "My apologies, I did not mean to disturb you."

I quickly composed myself. "No, My Lord, you are not... not disturbing me. In fact, I have been e-e... expecting you."

It was so frustrating that his gaze seemed all-knowing. "I should have knocked," he offered.

I smiled weakly. "It is all right. Here, would you like some wine? It is... lighter than what they are serving outside. Not as dense." Before he could answer, I began to pour some into the unused goblet and held it out for him to take. It was comforting to fill the air with anything other than what he had come here to do. I worried that maybe now I would find out that he inherited his father's cruelty.

"Thank you," he said, lifting it as a toast to me and then taking a sip.

An awkward silence filled the air for what felt like an eternity.

"Why don't we take a moment to sit by the fire?" he offered further. "I would appreciate some rare moments of quiet."

Nodding wordlessly, I resumed my seat by the fire as he reached for the poker and shifted the logs within, provoking the fire to glow brighter. Then, he took the cushioned chair opposite me, taking another sip of his wine.

"Are you comfortable, My Lord?" My back was rigid in my chair, my hands folded in my lap. I could not get myself to relax. Meanwhile, he relaxed in his chair, leaning back in it completely at ease. Any trace of his pale visage was entirely gone, and instead he appeared more vital and strong—glowing almost.

"Quite, thank you. You have done well with this room and I look forward to seeing what you do with the rest of the estate. Fortunately, Brașov is a trading town so you should meet no difficulty in getting what you need or like to have. Imported goods make their way through here all the time, and I am certain that any merchant would grant the Princess of Romania priority."

"It seems as though everyone wants priority for themselves," I replied, grateful for the conversation. "I don't remember the names of anyone I have met tonight—it is all a blur."

"A lot of their names aren't worth remembering, despite what they would like to believe." There was a glint of mischief in his eyes and I couldn't help but laugh. Perhaps he *was* terribly clever.

"Don't ever let them hear you say that," I quipped back as I laughed.

"Well," he said with a small shrug, "if they weren't so utterly uninteresting and boring, it wouldn't be an issue, would it?"

I laughed again. "And what is it that you would find interesting in a person, My Lord?"

A rare smile tugged at his lips again, not a full one this time but enough to let on he was amused. I wondered if he quite enjoyed making me laugh. "A person that had an original thought in their head as a start. Not sidling up to me or my wife in hopes to gain favors as another."

My wife. I noted how foreign it felt to be referred to that way, despite having been born and bred to be a wife and mother. "It's the crux of our position, I'm afraid. What else?"

"What else?" he echoed. "Well, I think another thing would be honesty. But I suppose that falls in line with what I mentioned before, as there is nothing honest about befriending someone merely to get what they desire. Especially someone in power who just arrived in a foreign country, with little to no friends."

"I hope there *are* honest and kind people here." My voice was entrenched with subtle coldness in reply to his observations.

His smile faded away and we slipped into awkward silence again for some time, something I was growing to dislike very much. Why could I not feel entirely at ease around this man? Then, I remembered, and prevented my thoughts from straying to the little brown book lest it show on my face.

Prince Vlad shifted to his feet. Then he held out his hand to me and it seemed as though any warmness that had been blossoming between us melted away. After all, this is what he came here to do, the final act of making our marriage valid and sealing the contract. I took his hand and allowed him to lead me to the bed. Dutifully, I laid down on my back and turned my head away from him in a gesture I thought to be considerate. The mattress shifted as it bore his weight, then I felt his cool hands graze the hem of my nightgown then the rush of cool air as he lifted the hem gently. He lowered himself over me slowly, careful not to crush me with the entirety of his weight, and then all of a sudden I felt an immense stinging pressure between my legs. I gasped and winced despite my determination to not make any sort of sound as I had been instructed. I could not help it.

He lingered there for a moment, perhaps to see if I would protest, but I knew my duty and did not. Then he began to pump into me. I bit my lip to keep from wincing again, keeping my head turned towards the wall. This went on for less than a minute before he pulled away, and as I turned my head, he was already gone and the door was closing slowly behind him.

XI

THE SKY HAD GRAYED the next day, despite starting off with some sunshine. Sunshine would have been nice as the wedding celebrations continued, and there was to be a day of outdoor games which included a fencing contest, a horse-riding race, and an archery contest. As the bride and new Princess of Romania, I held the esteemed position of granting prizes to the winners of each. So, I was stuffed into another costly gown, in a French style this time, with a matching French hood, one I had received from my sister. The gray day coincided with my mood as I continued to play last night's event over in my head. I had been distracted all morning while Helene dressed me. The prince's change in demeanor had been my fault, but not because of what I had said, more so what I had implied. I had hoped to discuss this with him before the games began but I had not seen him, and it was again my assumption that he was avoiding me. And now I sat here in this pavilion on a raised dais with the chair beside me empty.

I was resolved to no longer allow myself to think of the last event from the evening prior. It was a path I did not want to go down as I feared being crippled with shame and embarrassment now that I knew firsthand what my duty as a wife entailed. It was better to leave it well alone so as to endure it more easily. Fortunately, Helene said not a single word about it; she didn't ask about it nor make a comment. She simply stripped the bedding off of the mattress without a word of that or my bad mood.

"What a cloudy day we are having," said a voice next to me, "and it's such a shame on a day like today."

I turned and saw a man standing near the dais looking up at me with a wide smile. Now what? Though he looked familiar and I sensed I had seen him some time in the last twenty-four hours.

"Indeed it is a shame." I had hoped my curt reply would discourage him from speaking to me any further but, alas, it did not.

"I imagine the sun is hiding today in shame knowing its rays cannot surpass your illuminating beauty."

His blatant attempt at flirtation made me go rigid at once. Who was this brazen man? He was tall, nearly meeting me at eye level even though I sat on a platform. His wide grin was what caught my eye at once, followed by his sandy brown hair and deep, russet eyes. He wore a tabard bearing my husband's dragon over his clothes and that's when I recalled that he had stood beside my husband at the altar yesterday as we were married. I did not remember specifically speaking to him though.

"You are not from here," I said, noticing his dialect was out of place here in Romania.

"A very acute observation from a well-traveled lady," he replied with a chuckle. "No, as it just so happens, I am not." Then very easily, he switched into a language I had not heard in some time. "I hail from France."

"You are a long way from there," I responded, falling easily into the native language of my mother. "What is your name?"

"Is it ever my honor to give the lady my name! My name is Simon Gagnon."

"And how did you end up so far from home, Simon?"

"I was kidnapped by the Ottoman Turks as a child and sold into slavery. I was on a passenger ship on its way to the Italian Peninsula when they seized the ship, took all of us captive, and there I was until the Voivode's father released me, taking ownership of me as his ward. I had the pleasure to grow up with His Highness." He told his tale so casually that it almost didn't sound like the tragedy it so clearly was. I was surprised he had divulged this information to me so early in our acquaintance. I was also taken aback by a display of kindness shown by the prince's father, per Simon's account, which was contrary to the atrocities he had committed according to that little brown book I kept in my possession.

"I am sincerely sorry to hear of what happened to you."

"You are kind, Your Highness, but I can hardly carry any remorse or melancholy to what happened to me in the past, because it has allowed me the pleasure to lay eyes on the most beautiful woman I have ever seen." His brown eyes shone with unbridled lust as he took my hand and planted a lingering kiss on the back of it. Never in all my life had a man paid that sort of attention to me. The courtiers of my father's court stayed away from me, choosing instead to give their attentions to the fairer ladies. So, I had seen that lusty look before, but never had such a look been cast in my direction until now. I did not know how to respond to Simon's attention at that moment, instead my eyes only rounded dumbfoundedly in reply.

"Closing in on my bride already, Simon?" Another voice sounded beside us. "It hasn't even been twenty-four hours, you knave." Prince Vlad stepped onto the dais, taking his seat beside me.

"You mistake me, My Lord," Simon replied, immediately pulling his lips away from the kiss that had gone on just a little too long. Romanian sounded odd coming from his lips now that I was certain he was French. "I had merely come to introduce myself as I didn't have the chance last night. Especially as her Highness was in no short supply of dance partners throughout the evening."

"Are you participating in the contests this afternoon, old man?" Prince Vlad asked, changing the subject.

"As it so happens, I will be. I have entered the riding and archery contests."

"Good, then I will see you on the field for the archery competition and remind you how it is done."

"We will see about that," Simon laughed. "See you on the field, old man." Then, he sauntered off with an air of cockiness.

"An interesting character," I ventured when he was out of earshot.

"Yes, he has always been that way, his cockiness getting him into trouble all the time. I have had to beat that cockiness out of him from time to time, though it clearly never worked." Just then, he reached into his doublet and pulled out a piece of parchment. "Here."

I took it from him and unfolded it only to be met with strange looking characters written on it. "What is this?"

"'Austrian party is traveling southeast through Hungary into Romania. Approximately one hundred guards accompany her. Task is recommended to be augmented at nightfall three weeks hence,'" he translated and I realized it was Turkish written on the parchment. Blotted on the parchment were brown stains which I had first thought to be ink, but then it dawned on me that it was blood.

Folding it quickly, I handed it back to him, feeling my stomach churn at the sight of it. "I realize I was rather coarse in my remark to you last night. For that, I am sorry."

He turned to look at me for the first time since joining me on the dais, his emerald eyes assessing my sincerity for a moment, and then he replied, "I understand. It is forgiven." He took the parchment from me and tucked it back into his doublet.

It was then that our attention was taken over by a steward calling out for the beginning of the horse race. Eight men had signed up, and would travel the grounds in three laps. The first to finish would be the winner. Simon's haughty stature stood out among the men as he shot a grin in my direction, holding his hand to his heart. I turned away to display disinterest so as to not provoke any jealousy from my husband, but his face fell into its usual inscrutable position and I could not tell if he had even noticed.

To my dismay, Simon ended up being the winner of the horse race. He was quick to come and claim his prize. He knelt before me as I passed him the small satchel of silver and then pinned a ribbon above his heart. Afterward, he

kissed his own fingertips and planted them onto the ribbon,
a gesture I guessed was supposed to represent his desire to
kiss me. What a brazen, doltish man. Then, he thanked me by
planting another long lingering kiss on the back of my hand.
He turned and began to wave at the audience that cheered
for him.

"Insufferable scoundrel," Prince Vlad snorted next to me,
showing no signs of being actually annoyed at his companion's antics but amused. "Insufferable" was a perfect word
for it.

Next was the fencing competition, something I enjoyed
much more than the horse races as I wasn't particularly fond
of horses. To my delight, some of the men from my travel
entourage had signed up, and they each wore tabards with
my father's emblem. I was incredibly touched by the display, especially seeing as they would be departing from me
and returning to Austria after my wedding festivities were
concluded. Each of them did wonderfully, though one knight
shone particularly bright. He had a crop of blonde hair and a
dashing smile, reminding me so much of my brother. Every
opponent of his paled in comparison and as he made it
through several rounds, parrying this way and that with
such ease that it was more of a dance than a sword fight.
It was clear that he would be the victor. His final opponent,
however, was also very talented—a dark, burly man from the
Voivode's entourage with striking, onyx-colored eyes and
thick, menacing brows shrouding them. Now it was a competition between Austria and Romania.

Declared as the two finalists of the competition, they each
approached one side of the clearing. The Voivode's champion was covered in sweat and ferocity; my champion remained at ease, sweat hardly dotting his forehead, definite-

ly catching the eyes of some of the younger women in the crowd who nearly swooned at him.

He stepped forward and raised his blade, turning in my direction. "To my lady and to my emperor!" he cried. His challenger merely grunted in reply. It was the very image of David and Goliath come to life as he thrust his blade toward my champion, who then pivoted and clashed his blade against the other's in reply. While Prince Vlad's challenger had strength and size as his advantages, mine had swiftness and grace as he danced around him, blocking every offense his challenger offered. The Voivode's champion was soon growing breathless, trying to keep up with mine; he seemingly did not have the stamina for a long battle, but was better in bursts. Realizing this, my champion switched tactics and went on the offensive, thrusting his saber with such speed and dexterity that his opponent could barely block them, not doing so until the last split second. Finally, with all of his might, my champion performed one long lunge and the blade sliced the skin of his opponent's arm, drawing blood and therefore declaring him the winner.

My champion raised his arms over his head as if to welcome the applause and occasional cheers, then he came over to me to collect his prize. His brilliant smile made my heart wince as he reminded me of my brother so much, especially up close. He bowed deeply, murmuring "My Lady, it is my greatest honor to compete in your name. I dedicate this victory to you."

Unable to contain the smile from my lips, I pressed the satchel of silver into his palm. "I accept your dedication as I am very pleased with your victory." I then pinned the ribbon to his chest and said, "Take this ribbon back to our home and remember me fondly when you see it." He took my hand

and kissed it lightly, taking the amount of time that was appropriate and not lingering like that scoundrel, Simon. He bowed and stepped away from the dais to be congratulated by his companions who were gathered nearby.

At last was the archery competition, but there was to be a moment before it began as targets made of hay had to be set up in place. During this brief intermission, people temporarily dispersed, and by this time, Helene had joined me, sitting on a stool in the pavilion. Prince Vlad had left to participate in this contest. We talked softly of the fencing, commenting on how nice it was to have an Austrian win. It was pleasant to sit with Helene, for I had not seen her much in the last several days.

When the targets were set, the crowd began to hush and resume their places in anticipation for the last contest of the day, with another banquet and more dancing to follow. The contestants lined up—this contest had the most participants by far. There were not enough targets to accommodate all the men—a total of twenty five with only eight targets. They would have to take turns shooting in waves. If they did not have a bow and quiver, they were lent a set, but most of them had come prepared. The first wave of men took their places about fifty paces from their targets. Nearly in synchrony, they placed their arrows on their bows, cocked the strings, and let the arrows fly. Anyone who got their arrow closest to the red center painted on the target was allowed to stay for the next round. Anyone who missed the target, or those furthest away from the red center, were disqualified. Simon surfaced during the second wave of men and his arrow nearly pierced the center, securing his place in the contest. As they moved aside to let the third wave of men come through to try their aim, he found me and blew a kiss in my direction.

"My goodness. Brazen, isn't he?" Helene crowed, taking no care to hide her dismay.

"Trust me, I am well aware. He hasn't left me alone all day. He is a companion of the Voivode," I told her, pretending as though I hadn't seen his latest antics.

"It's a wonder that the prince hasn't put him in his place, openly flirting with his wife like that."

The third wave of men came and went and the Voivode did not appear, but then he came through as the last one to go. The crowd roared at his appearance as he took his place opposite one of the center targets. He carried a beautiful bow that was stained a deep umber color with rings of gold hand-painted in a regal design, curving elegantly with its limbs sloping down lazily. It was truly an incredible display of craftsmanship. I was eager to see what he could do with that exquisite bow he carried.

Even surrounded by a crowd of people, the Voivode stood out with his formidable figure as he lined himself up with the target before reaching into the leather quiver on his back and drawing out an arrow. He eyed the target one more time before attaching the arrow to the string in a fluid movement that seemed as easy to him as breathing. He drew the drawstring towards his face and in the blink of an eye, the arrow went soaring so quickly to the target that I nearly missed it. He struck so close to the center, it was only a gold coin's width away. The crowd went wild. I could see why; it was difficult not to be impressed with his skill. Perhaps this was the talent that Ambassador Ionescu was referring to only the night before.

Those who had been disqualified departed and there was another round of shooting, going in the same order as before. This continued on until there were five left, then the final two contestants—Simon and Prince Vlad. Both possessed impressive skill with the bow and it was hard to anticipate who was going to be the victor, though I hoped it was the prince, as I did not want to have to pin another ribbon on Simon and be met with another round of his drivel. However, I would have been shocked if it was not to be Prince Vlad, for I had never seen anyone shoot a bow and arrow so quickly. Each round he went through, he went faster and faster, his arrow rarely straying from dead-center. His arms and shoulders rippled with ease every time he held the bow upwards, just before he made the shot.

Simon and Prince Vlad exchanged some words before assuming their positions for the final round. Simon's easy smile met whatever it was that the prince said to him, and they shared a hearty laugh. Then, Simon took his place to shoot first. He took a deep breath, measuring the target before lifting the bow and pulling back the drawstring. He hovered there for a moment before finally releasing the string and the arrow went soaring, thudding loudly into the target as he was the only archer now. From where I was sitting, it appeared as though it was dead center. He threw a grin at the prince and his mouth moved as he spoke, but I certainly could not hear what he said from where I was, nor did I see if the prince replied as his back was facing me.

The Voivode took his place, taking the target next to Simon's so that a judge could measure the two final arrows if necessary. This was sure to be a close call. He lifted his shoulders up and stretched them back, making me think of a predator preparing to pounce on its prey, then he pulled an arrow from the quiver, raised the bow, and shot it all in one smooth, swift motion. The arrow went flying so quickly into the center of the target, it was a blur. The crowd was dead silent as the judge went over to the two targets, evaluating them both as it *was* a close one. I definitely couldn't tell who the victor was from where I sat. The judge took several moments to assess before announcing that it was His Highness, the Voivode, who won the archery competition.

The crowd burst out in a flood of uproarious cheering, and Prince Vlad leaned over, clapping his companion on the shoulder in a display of camaraderie. Then, as the crowd continued to roar, he made his way over to me on the dais and I took this as my cue to rise to my feet. He stopped before me, and I made no attempt to hide my relief on my face as I pinned the ribbon to his doublet right over his heart. Then, in one fluid motion, he hopped up onto the dais, swept me into his arms, leaned me back, and before I could comprehend what was happening, he pressed his lips to mine. Just as if one thought the crowd couldn't get any louder, they erupted into a deafening roar at his display.

Prince Vlad's grip on me was so tight, all I could do was let it happen, careful not to lose my balance as I leaned on his arms for support, entirely at his mercy. I had never been kissed before. His lips were cool on mine. Before I could comprehend the sensation further, he lifted me and placed me back on my feet, and I steadied myself. He wrapped his arm around me, lifting his hand to wave to the crowd and leaving me unsure if this was only another display for the crowd, or a statement of possession.

XII

I T WAS CLEAR THAT the prince wouldn't be coming to my bedchamber again tonight. As a matter of fact, I did not know where he was, as I had seen him very little throughout the evening. It wasn't clear if he was avoiding me or simply had retired early. Last night's conversation had led me to believe that the prince cherished his moments of quiet, so perhaps that was what he was seeking. It was all right, though, for I was rather tired myself, eager to lay down enveloped in silence. It had been another evening of banqueting, with guests trying to rub elbows with royalty, and dancing. My dance partner queue was in no short supply once again, with some familiar faces, some new, though Simon was sure to make his way in, even stealing a dance from another. During which, he was sure to regale me with the tale of the horse race from his view on the saddle—especially the harrowing moments just before he won. Instead of being impressed, I found myself rather ill at ease, so uneasy with horses as I was. It didn't help any that Simon was clearly adding embellishments to make himself seem more impressive than he actually was.

"Is there anything you cannot do?" I had asked him after our second set, noticing that he was a great dancer as well as rider.

"I excel at everything, Your Highness," he replied without a trace of sarcasm. "*Everything.*" My eyebrow shot up at his emphasis of the word "everything" but I did not ask him to clarify. "Perhaps you would oblige me in the *basse danse* as well? Another moment to hold your delicate hand in mine would be absolute bliss."

"Absolutely not."

He laughed at my indignation. "Well, there was no harm in asking. An arrow shot has a chance of landing somewhere, and you miss all of the shots you do not take."

"Do you have a wife, Simon?" His grin faltered at my inquiry. Ah, there it was. Finally, there was something that would weaken that insufferable smirk.

"I do," he replied carefully.

"Is she here tonight?" I couldn't help myself, I had to continue to needle him. "If so, where is she? I would like to meet her."

"She is there," he indicated with a toss of his dark sand-colored locks.

My eyes followed the direction he indicated. A petite Romanian noblewoman stood nearby, a peninsula branching out from the rest of the group of women laughing amongst themselves. She appeared terribly ill at ease, poor thing, shifting her weight from one foot to the other and her dark doe eyes darting back and forth. She was definitely not the image I had of a wife for Simon. She must have been wealthy, as there was no way this was a lovelorn marriage. Her gown, at least, indicated that she carried some wealth.

"Simon," I crowed, "I insist that you introduce her to me at this *very* moment. You failed to mention all day that you have a wife, what a silly oversight! She must have been so proud of your athleticism today. How delightful it was that you brought her a satchel of silver home."

I stopped dead in my tracks despite the song still going and the other dancers still pirouetting around us and began to make my way over to her, unable to help myself after suffering with him all day long. Simon shuffled behind me rather sheepishly as I approached the mousy and nervous woman. Her plain features rounded in surprise as she recognized who it was that approached her. I felt as though I towered over her, though I was not terribly tall myself.

"Your Highness," said Simon, introducing us. "This is my wife, Ana-Maria. Ana-Maria, I do believe that it goes without saying that this is her Royal Highness, Princess Shoshana, Archduchess of Austria."

"I am delighted," I said, my smile genuine. "Out of all of the women I have met yesterday and today, your name is by far the prettiest I have come across, especially as it bears the same name as our Blessed Virgin. How do you do?"

Ana-Maria curtsied deeply before me. Yes, she was wealthy, her curtsy was flawless. "I do well, Your Highness. I am pleased to be meeting you."

"She is beautiful, Simon," I said. Although she was not, she was very plain and physically uninteresting, with the exception of her nose which hooked at the bridge, but it was clear that she hungered for a bit of kindness and it was the least I could do as I was embarrassing her husband at her expense. Not to mention, it must have been unbearable to watch him gawk and flirt with another woman all day long. Not that she could do anything about it. She could protest at her husband all she wanted behind closed doors, but that's not to say it would work, as he would be at liberty to flirt with any woman he wanted, bed any woman he wanted. Such was a woman's curse, and she and I were united in it, entangled in this world of men.

She glowed at my compliment, revealing to me that she did not receive them often. He did not confirm or deny her beauty, merely replied, "I am very fortunate with such a wife."

"Have you been enjoying yourself?" I asked, ignoring him entirely.

"I have been very much, Your Highness." Her voice was soft, almost like a whisper, but not quite. "It has been some time since we have had such an occasion here in Brașov, though we have never had one so splendid."

"Good, I am glad you are enjoying yourself. Be sure you get your hands on some of the mulled wine when you have the chance. I have been unable to stay away from it myself." I winked at her conspiratorially. "Simon, would you be so kind as to fetch your wife some mulled wine? I could not bear to tear myself away from her until she has tried at least one sip of it."

"Of course, Your Highness." He stepped away, unable to say no to me. He might have been a man, but I was still his superior.

I continued my conversation with Ana-Maria. She was rather young, somewhere around my age, perhaps slightly older, though her demeanor made her seem rather young. "Do you like dancing?"

"I do very much so, Your Highness."

"Is that so? I do not recall seeing you out there with the other dancers either last night or tonight."

"I don't think I am very good. Nor has anyone asked me to dance with them."

"Oh, I doubt that you're not very good. Besides, all that matters is that you enjoy it. Your husband hasn't asked you to dance?"

She shook her head. "Not once."

Said husband returned with two goblets of mulled wine. I took one from him, passing it to Ana-Maria and leaving him to hold the other one he was proffering to me.

"Thank you, Your Highness," Ana-Maria said primly and took the goblet from me. Her delicate little lips that resembled a tiny newborn sparrow's beak pressed onto the edge of the cup and she took a sip. "It is just as divine as Your Highness said it was."

"It is divine, isn't it? It is definitely a favorite of mine, especially on such a cold evening. Now, Simon, once she is done with her mulled wine, take your wife for a dance or two. The poor thing tells me she hasn't been out there once. Who better to escort her than her husband? Ana-Maria, find me for tomorrow's festivities and accompany me throughout the day, I would enjoy your company. Good evening."

"Good evening, Your Highness."

Turning on my heel to retire for the evening, I left them alone together, feeling awfully haughty and unable to help it. I sensed Simon staring at me as I left him holding the goblet that was intended for me. I knew that he longed to catch up with me.

I grinned again recalling that moment as I now sat by the roaring fire of my bedroom, waiting for Prince Vlad to return.

My eyes fell upon the crucifix that sat on the table. It was the same one given to me by the woman who had fallen at my feet as I entered the church on my wedding day. I shivered despite the heat of the fire beside me. By now, I assumed he would not be coming. Perhaps it was for the best.

The next day was just more banqueting and mingling, though the crowd of guests had dwindled as many went home, getting weary with the cold, which was growing unrelenting. Those who remained draped themselves in fur, a common occurrence in Romania and not necessarily a clothing item that distinguished rich from poor.

The archery targets had been left up and young men gathered near them, having unofficial archery contests of their own, or sword fighting. The women who lingered watched them, hoping to catch their eyes and flirt. Though it was out of season, a maypole had also been set up and girls danced around it, hoping that their dancing might catch the eye of a courtier. It was obvious that marriage was on everyone's minds, and there were many who were hoping to ensnare someone themselves. Helene had lamented that she had come across several couples caught in romantic embraces as she breezed through the grounds, still overseeing everything.

"These young people," she growled, her cough returning stronger than before. "So careless and brazen. I will be interested to see all the summer babies that suddenly pop up."

"Helene, you had better be careful, you are working yourself to death!" I cried, huddling under the warmth of the fur draped over me. "That cough sounds like it has only gotten worse."

Helene and I were clustered in the pavilion, joined by Ana-Maria, who had seemingly become my talisman against Simon's unwanted attention. He had not bothered me once today. Though he was stalking the grounds, participating in seemingly all of the competitions the men were creating for themselves, not missing out on an opportunity to flex in front of the women. We were content to watch the events unfold before us on the grounds, particularly watching the people as they were quite fun to study.

"It's merely the cold," Helene replied, dismissing my concern. "I will be fine in a few days. Look at that young man over there! He is practically salivating on that girl's gown. What a hound!"

"Helene," I said between laughter, "he's not doing anything obscene! He's merely talking to her. You know it's a sign of age when older people begin to complain about the young, and you're not even old! However, at the moment, you sound positively ancient."

Ana-Maria remained silent but suppressed her giggles with the back of her hand. She sought me out fairly quickly that morning, at my behest last night, and it was clear she was uneasy at first, but since then she had begun to warm up. I was surprised, at first, to learn that she knew German, but then realized with Saxon occupants in Romania, it was not unheard of for Romanians to know both languages. She had also confirmed this.

"Propriety is timeless," Helene said. "There's nothing wrong with wanting to conserve propriety."

"They aren't harming anyone," I insisted. "You're getting yourself worked up over nothing." I turned my attention to Ana-Maria. "Do you have a house in Brașov, then Ana-Maria?"

"We do. We have a home here and then one in Târgoviște, which is our primary residence and much roomier."

"Which do you prefer, Brașov or Târgoviște? I have not been to Târgoviște yet. Brașov has been my only experience with a Romanian town so far."

"I definitely prefer Brașov. It is quieter and more quaint. Târgoviște is busier, filled with more people... more crowded."

"If it is filled with more people, then that probably means it's dirtier," said Helene, wrinkling her nose as she imagined the smell that came with it. "Such was the case with Paris when I was there a long time ago."

That night, there was more dancing and mulled wine. There was something more fun about this evening's revelries than the last two. The wine was flowing and the laughter was more uproarious. Games of dice and cards were going on in the pavilions once again, music filled the night sky, dancing resumed, and a small group of men challenged each other to a wrestling competition while bets were being held on the side. What's more, the men dressed down to the bare minimum as they wrestled, challenging one another on who could stomach the frigid air longer.

The moment Ana-Maria left my side to join the dancing, something she finally gained the confidence to do, Simon appeared at my side. "Will you be among the spectators watching the wrestling, Your Highness? I am participating and know your presence would assure my victory."

"I intend to excuse myself from that event," I said. "Ana-Maria is a lovely creature. I fail to see why you hadn't introduced me to her right away as I am in great need of friends."

He appeared scandalized. "Am I not considered among your friends, Your Highness? First you are withdrawing from spectating the wrestling, and now you don't consider me among your friends? You wound me, Your Highness."

"And what about your poor wife while you pant after another?" Irritably, I grabbed the goblet off of a tray that was passing me, taking a large gulp. I'd had several tonight and was feeling a bit bold.

"What about her? Surely you know that we did not marry for love, something you should know all about by now."

"And what is it you mean by that?" I nearly spluttered my wine at his audacity. He knew he had crossed a line, and at least had the decency to look it. "My marriage is of no concern of yours. The audacity you have to make commentary on it already, it being only three days old. I doubt you would speak so frankly to the Voivode."

"Forgive me, Your Highness, you are right. I have crossed a line, but any man who looks at you would be seething with envy directed at the prince, or any man fortunate enough to receive your hand in marriage."

"Simon, that is quite enough." A voice growled behind me and I whirled around on my heel to see Prince Vlad standing there. He hardly raised his voice though it made me uneasy to see what it would be like if he did. "You have been playing the damned fool these last three days and I have tolerated it this entire time, but now you not only insult my wife, but you insult me as well. It has gone on long enough."

Without a word, Simon swept into a deep bow and excused himself from our presence.

The air between us was tense and I was reluctant to speak. Admittedly, I was a bit afraid of the prince, for I had not seen this side of him before. I did not think this was the worst of it. Should fury envelop him, I was certain it would be most frightening.

"My apologies," he then said, breaking the silence between us. "I display too much tolerance when it comes to him; it has gotten to his head. He should not speak to you that way and for that, I am sorry."

"It is not you that should be apologizing. He is the one offending."

"I see him as a brother, so I often let him get away with it, though things have changed significantly and he needs to remember that."

I nodded, understanding. "Where have you been today? I have not seen you once until now."

"Something came up. Don't worry, nothing for you to worry about, no further kidnapping plots or anything of that nature. Just something small I had to take care of, business remaining in Târgoviște. The responsibilities don't stop, even when the Voivode's own wedding is being celebrated."

"They do not," I agreed. "It was often that many events in my life were interrupted due to my father's vast responsibilities. There never seemed to be a short supply of messages, letters, news, and so on."

"And he has an entire empire to oversee, I can only imagine how difficult that must be." His arms folded across his chest though he seemed to relax a little more.

"Yes, but he doesn't have to deal with the constant threat of the Ottoman Empire knocking on his door." I sipped on my wine, then turned to him again. He was gazing at me curiously. "What is it?"

"Nothing, I was just thinking. You are right, the Ottomans have been plaguing us for decades now. Hopefully, they will begin to ease off now that the Holy Roman Empire sits at our back door. We shall see. Though there's no more need for this kind of talk for tonight. It is much more pleasant out here tonight, isn't it? Less people, quieter, more at ease."

"I had been thinking the same exact thing earlier. Come, let us join them. I see Ambassador Ionescu at the gambling tables—he's been there all night."

"Then he must have a purse spilling with coins. Let's go see if I can win some of that off of him, eh?" He threw me a mischievous smirk and I found myself caught up in it, willing to do anything he asked at that moment.

I never thought I would gamble, but then there I was at that table with both the prince and ambassador, among others, for hours, wine flowing past my lips. I slipped into a reverie, my head swimming in the most delightful way. We were playing cards, until Prince Vlad kept winning hand after hand, nearly emptying Ambassador Ionescu's fat purse. Then, when it was nearly empty, he insisted that they switch to dice. Unable to keep my focus anymore, I excused myself and slipped away from the table. My eyes were glazed over and it was hard to see straight. I wasn't even sure if I could walk in a straight line anymore.

Most of the music had subsided, but there remained a lone musician—the fiddle player. He saw me walking past, intending on finding Helene to escort me back to the castle, and I was held in his gaze. He lifted his bow and held his instrument to his chin, playing one long drawn out note, then dipping into a few rapid ones. I stopped and was transfixed, unable to tear my eyes away from his nimble fingers as the fiddle seemingly called out to me in its low, rich tones. Then, one of the other musicians came forward and began to join in on his drum, keeping the beat to the tune of the fiddle, which was speeding up. Unable to contain myself and emboldened by the wine, I began to sway. My hips began to curl and turn to the music when a second fiddler joined and began to play notes which complimented the other, turning it into almost a duel of fiddles.

Between the two fiddles and the beat of the drum, I became enslaved, unable to control myself as I danced to the music, swaying my arms and rolling my hips. Any propriety and decorum melted away from me and I was no longer an archduchess, born and bred of the court, but a slave girl in a harem. The wine had made me bold. Inviting me to succumb to it as I twirled and moved, my pace quickening alongside the beat of the drum and the melody of the fiddles. People had since stopped what they were doing and watched me, gathering and murmuring to themselves, though I barely noticed. To me, there was only me and the haunting melodies of the strings. In the corner of my eye, I saw Simon staring at me, openmouthed but approvingly. Then, I saw Ambassador Ionescu standing, frozen beside the prince. I could not make out the prince's features, with my head swimming and the corners of my eyes brimming with blurriness.

But then there was one face that stood starkly out to me—sharp and defined compared to the blur of all the others. I stopped immediately and my heart began to pound in my chest.

It was him. I saw him. Glaring back at me. Hate emitting from his almond-shaped eyes. His long hair curled past his shoulders, his cheeks ruddy and reddened, his thick black brows furrowed.

Our eyes met.

Darkness crept at the corner of my eyes, tugging at me. I could no longer see.

I was falling.

XIII

MY HEAD LOLLED AS I floated back to consciousness.

Panic-stricken voices echoed in my ears. Someone was carrying me. My stomach churned.

The eyes. *His* eyes.

How was it possible?

I succumbed to the darkness once more.

XIV

I T WAS MY THROBBING head that first told me I was still alive. It pounded furiously, then almost as if on cue my stomach churned into knots. I groaned.

"Your Highness," a small voice said nearby. Ana-Maria. "Are you all right?"

"No," I croaked. "I have never felt so wretched in my life."

"At least you are awake now."

"What time is it?"

"Well into the afternoon. You have been asleep a long time."

"Please draw the curtains, Ana-Maria. The sunlight is blinding."

I heard scraping as she did so and the room became comfortably dark. "Is there anything else I can do for Your Highness?"

"Ale?"

"Here." She helped me sit up and pressed a tankard to my lips. It was heavily watered down.

"Thank you. What happened?"

She resumed sitting on the stool that sat near my bed. "You were... er, *dancing* when suddenly you stopped with such a look of horror transfixed on your face, and then you fell to the ground. Everyone was afraid you were having a fit of some kind. Then, my husband rushed to your side immediately, picking you up off the ground until the prince came over. He handed you over to him and the prince carried you to your bed. We summoned a doctor and he said it was merely the effects of the wine and perhaps exhaustion, that you would be right by the next day."

Simon, that scoundrel, no doubt leaping on the opportunity to get me into his arms. "I don't feel right. I don't know that I will ever feel right ever again."

"Well, it was past midnight by this point, so he probably meant tomorrow. Let me get a cool wet cloth for your head."

"You are too kind, Ana-Maria," I told her as she returned from fetching the cloth and laying it on my forehead. It was nice.

"It is you that are kind, Your Highness. It is rare when someone takes notice of me." She lowered her eyes and I felt sorry for her, feeling remorseful that I had initially used her to embarrass Simon.

"When you're in my position, you take more notice of people who don't throw themselves at your feet at every opportunity. That is a rarity."

Just then, the door burst open, startling both of us, and Helene came rushing in. She reached for the curtains and ripped them open, making me wince at the bright light. Ana-Maria quickly rose to her feet, curtsied, and left, undeniably wanting to avoid the storm that had just come barreling in.

"Now that you're alive," Helene said forcefully. She stood before me with her hands on her hips. "What is it you thought you were doing last night? Dancing around, making a display of yourself like a whore in a harem?! You are the eldest child and daughter of the Holy Roman Emperor! Your mother would be turning in her grave if she had seen your *display* last night." I scoffed and raised my hand to protest but she denied me the ability to do so. "No, there is no excuse. You have rested plenty, now it is time to get up and act your part, meet your responsibilities instead of acting like a tavern maid. Go on! Get up!"

Helene must have known my head was pounding and sought to punish me by forcefully using the brush on my hair. It was a wonder I wasn't bald by the time she finished brushing it out and braiding it, then stuffing it into a long fabric coil that was crisscrossed with ribbons and a silk hair net topping it, held in place by a thin band around my head. I did not dare complain about the hairstyle she chose for today, knowing full well she had chosen it to punish me, because she was right. I had made a shameful display of myself, getting inebriated, gambling, and dancing in a way not befitting my station. And now, I would have to face everyone as further punishment.

It was definitely a penance, because the moment I entered the dining room, well after everyone else had, all grew quiet and I could hear their whispering. They watched me take my place next to the prince, whose face remained inscrutable as always. There was no telling if he was angry or not. Though, presumably he was and it seemed as though everyone was watching for any sign of his anger. When he did not let them have it, they began to tentatively resume their conversations and the talking gradually grew louder.

"How is your head?" The prince asked after a few moments, finally acknowledging me.

"Horrendous," I answered, deciding on the truth.

His eyes still did not meet mine, but instead, he reached forward and pushed his goblet over to me with his fingertips. "This will help."

"What is it?"

"Wine, of course." My stomach lurched at the thought of letting more wine into it. "It is the only thing that will help. Trust me." That's when he finally turned and there was a smirk in his eyes.

Convinced, I took his wine and he snapped for his manservant to come forward, carrying another goblet with what appeared to be a thicker wine than the one he had just given me. "I take it you have had many bawdy nights that led to a pounding headache the following morning?"

"Absolutely," he replied. "Especially when I was younger. They were nights not entirely unlike last night, except I was in your position. People may talk and whisper, but no matter what you do, they always will. I would not worry about it."

Taking another sip, I thought for a moment before saying, "Thank you. I understand you carried me to my bed after... my episode. You have my gratitude."

"Make no further mention of it."

The food was then served and the guests ate merrily. There would be more games and revelry for the last night and I was dreading going. I was weary and ready for things to slow down. But I knew as hostess, I would have to put on an exhibition of grace and gratitude when deep down I knew people were whispering and gossiping about me, especially after my *display,* as Helene had called it, the evening before.

"Despite emptying Ambassador Ionescu of all of his money last night," the prince continued, "I will be glad to see everyone go. Four days of celebration is enough—the people have had their fill, enough is enough."

"I quite agree, My Lord. Though, fortunately, this will be a celebration for them to remember for the rest of their lives."

"That it certainly will. It was a spectacle showing that we are caught up with the rest of the Western world and not a primitive society as the West believes."

"I have no recollection of anyone thinking such a thing when I was in Austria, but there was an air of mystery surrounding Romania. People didn't know much—what your customs are, what it looks like here, and so on."

"And what is it, do you think? You come to us with fresh eyes."

"That this place is still shrouded in mystery. There's a sense of wildness to it, but there's also an unmistakable air of integrity that lives here too." What I did not include was that ever since coming here, I had been completely unsettled and met with some of the strangest circumstances I had ever experienced. For example, last night. Did I really see... *him?* Or was that a trick of the wine? Then, the other night, I had heard footsteps outside of my door only to find that no one was there. This place was haunted and played with people's minds.

"Hmm," was all he said, sipping from his goblet.

"Your Highness," surfaced a familiar accent. Simon bowed deeply before us. "After your fall last night, I had to come and inquire for myself the state of your well-being. I hope you are feeling better today."

"Much better, thank you." The wine was beginning to help, just as the Voivode said it would, and my head was pounding less fiercely. "I understand that you were among the first to rush to my aid. Please accept my deepest gratitude."

"It was my pleasure," he replied, beaming but not winking like I knew he wanted to, certainly not so close to my husband's scrutinizing eye. He inhaled to say more, but was interrupted with Prince Vlad's interference.

"Simon, it looks as though everyone is finished dining. Why don't you lead everyone out onto the grounds for the last of our events?" he said with a wave of his hand.

"As you wish, My Lord." His eyes twinkled knowingly as they met my gaze one last time and then he turned to do his prince's bidding.

The air was cold and snowflakes fell down languidly from the sky, melting the moment they touched the ground. I stayed on my chair in the pavilion for the majority of the time, watching everyone else make merry. I was utterly aware anytime anyone's eyes fell upon me. Moreover, I eagerly scanned the crowd looking for the face I saw last night to determine whether it was real or not. I was still not certain, but at the time, his face seemed as real as my hand before me.

I swore it was Vlad the Impaler whom I had seen.

But now, as my eyes scanned the faces of each person, I could not be as certain. I almost willed him to reappear so I could prove to myself that I was not going mad.

Just as the sun was setting, I got to the point where I could no longer be outside and stood to excuse myself. Helene and Ana-Maria escorted me back up to the castle where I had Ana-Maria brush out my hair this time, as my scalp was still recovering from Helene's earlier fury. Not only that, but Ana-Maria's gentle hands were a nice change of pace, and my thoughts trailed off to what a whirlwind these last four days had been, starting with my grand wedding all the way until now. I had met so many faces, ate so many new dishes, and tried so many new things after being suspended in time for nearly three weeks of waiting. Now, I wondered what it was going to be like tomorrow, when the servants took down the pavilions and swept away all traces of the guests who had been occupying the grounds for nearly four days straight. I was sure the innkeepers in town were going to be counting their coins with glee, as many guests from out of town had occupied their rooms. I also wondered if the prince was going to return to Târgoviște, and if he was, whether I was to go with him.

Then, another memory stood out, preserved in time, pushing its way to the front of my thoughts. My eyes darted to the wooden crucifix that sat on the table beside my bed. The look on that woman's face when she fell to my feet, speaking so rapidly, and the tears streaming down her face. I never did find out what happened to her. What was it that she had known? It would have been easy to dismiss her as perhaps a former lover of my husband's who was upset with his marriage, but had that been the case, there is no way she would have gifted me a crucifix. More like a dagger to the side. "May God protect your soul," she had said.

Protect my soul from what?

Then I remembered.

The devil himself seemed to be walking the earth, for I had seen him myself.

XV

FOR A WHILE, AFTER I swore I had seen Vlad the Impaler among the wedding guests, I was constantly looking over my shoulder with paranoia chewing away at me, certain that I would see him again. I would jump easily when someone entered a room when I did not hear them approaching. I could barely bring myself to eat for several days afterward due to that same paranoia twisting itself in my stomach. Though, after a while, I began to ease as the strange occurrences I had come across upon my arrival seemingly ceased, and eventually I dismissed them as manifestations of my anxiety that developed from moving to a strange country and marrying a man I knew nothing of. Daily mass was helpful to calm my nerves, going to the services at the Church of St. Mary each day and elevating my worries to the Lord.

Then, once my paranoia began to ease, I allowed myself to be further distracted with picking out furniture, wall hangings, and other assortments to furnish Bran Castle for the next several weeks. Helene and I first began by hiring more staff. A slew of applicants came flooding in from the town in droves, hoping to gain the employment of their new princess. We needed more staff in the kitchen, for one thing, and then we needed staff to maintain the grounds, more specifically. The stablemaster needed a few assistants on top of it all, so Helene and I spent our mornings interviewing candidates, then in the afternoons, we shopped for furnishings, placing orders to have the house done by Christmas.

I had seen very little of Prince Vlad during this time. He kept to himself in his quarters, holding meetings, responding to correspondence, receiving audiences, and other things I wasn't privy to. Besides, I was so busy, I didn't have the time to worry about what he was doing. Every night, typically, I would fall asleep immediately upon laying my head down on my pillow. He had not made any attempt to come to my bed since our wedding night, and for now I was perfectly content with it. Though I knew the time would come where we would need to fret about an heir... though we probably should have been worrying about one right away...

It seemed as though Christmas was not far away as winter had made itself comfortable around us, covering us in a blanket of white snow mere days after the last day of our celebrations. As a result, we had to hurry to get more rugs and tapestries to cover the walls to help keep us warm. Now, with the extra hands to help, fires could also be lit and maintained in every room bearing a fireplace, and baths could be warmer.

Ambassador Ionescu had long since returned home after our wedding, rejoining his own family. He had no wife, for she had passed away a few years ago, but he had several children and grandchildren with whom he was spending time, taking some time to reside with each. After having spent months in Austria, he was definitely owed this chance to reconvene with his family before Prince Vlad might have sent him off on another mission. Though, admittedly, I did miss his jovial presence and often forgot at first that he was no longer residing with us, at least for now.

Ana-Maria would often come by, offering input for some of the items Helene and I looked over with the merchants, carpenters, and so on. I think she rather enjoyed it and was becoming more confident than the woman I had initially met. Her husband sometimes escorted her and other times did not. He was behaving himself, mostly, though he definitely made a comment about my dancing on the first day I saw him since that night. When he escorted his wife to the castle, he would deposit her into my company, then disappear to join Prince Vlad, wherever he was in the house, and then he would come to collect her once it was time for them to return home. On the rare moments I inquired as to the state of their marriage, Ana-Maria said very little other than he was kind to her, but never anything else. She did reveal at one time that they had been married a year already, though there was no sign that an heir of their own was going to be coming any time soon. She let on that he never came to her bed, something I could relate to, but instead of being content, she was mournful about it. It then became apparent that she loved her handsome and dashing husband, but her love for him was left unrequited, as Simon had confirmed to me himself.

Naturally, I compared her situation to mine, unable to help myself. Ana-Maria had married for love, at least on her part, whereas I did not. She longed for her husband's presence, whereas I did not. She desired a child and a family, whereas I wasn't sure that I did. To build a family was expected of me, but I had never taken the time to consider if it was something I actually wanted. Our husbands also could not have been more contrasting. While both equally handsome in their own ways, they could not have been more different, as their personalities were near opposites. Simon was loud, abrasive, and quick to speak what was on his mind while Prince Vlad was quiet, more reserved, and never revealed what was on his mind, not even in his eyes. If I had a choice, which would I have preferred? I could not say.

By the end of these few weeks, I had received letters of congratulations on my nuptials from my family, and I allowed myself a reprieve for once to let myself read them after dinner. I saw the familiar long, winding penmanship of my father's, congratulating me and anticipating the return of his soldiers. His letter was overall brief, to my disappointment, and I found myself missing that evening we had shared by the fireplace in his quarters the night before I left. Then there was the perfect and elegant handwriting of my sister, also congratulating me. Her letter went on to describe the excitement back at home with the preparations of her own marriage to the Spanish Prince. She was to be traveling to the Netherlands after Christmas, waiting there and continuing preparations. She was to leave for Spain late next year. She also informed me that Father had finalized the date for our brother Philip's wedding to Juana, Princess of Spain, in the new year. It was to be held in October. She made no mention of the vile brown book she left wrapped in my linens, probably because she was aware that royal letters were often intercepted and read by spies and other nosy miscreants.

Next, there was a letter from my step-grandmother in her small, prim penmanship, expressing that her pride knew no bounds. Finally, a letter from Philip containing his spidery scrawl, short and brief in his congratulations.

I was somewhat jealous that my siblings were going to be able to live so close to one another as their betrotheds were children of the King and Queen of Spain, an ironclad alliance between them and my father, while I was all the way on the complete opposite side of Europe, practically at the very edge of the world it seemed. Allowing myself only a small time to wallow in this, I let Helene—who had since forgiven me for my transgressions—dress me for bed, and I spent the rest of the evening writing back to them.

It wasn't until I woke up with my face embedded on a pile of parchment that I realized I had dozed off. I was about to prepare a letter to my brother congratulating him on the date of his wedding when I laid my head down for what was going to be only a moment. I was awoken by the sound of shuffling and scraping outside my window near the writing desk at which I sat.

Confused, I sat up, peeling my face away from the parchment to see the fire had died down and the room was nearly black. I lit a single candle and readjusted the beautifully embroidered wool shawl around my shoulders—one among the many gifts I had received after my wedding. I hadn't heard the shuffling and scraping again, but there was some sort of commotion, as if someone was ascending the stairs to the floor above me very slowly.

I opened the door gradually to see what was going on. Not that I could see anything; the whole area was shadowy with the exception of my single candle. Slowly, I moved towards the direction of the sound, but it had since stopped. I went up the stairs by the lone light of my candle, careful not to trip on anything. Everything was very still and quiet, nothing seemed amiss, so I turned to make my way back downstairs to put myself to bed when I heard a muffled moan.

Glancing over my shoulder, I lingered for a moment, then I turned back, my curiosity getting the best of me. I went towards the moan, which had come from down the corridor on the floor containing the prince's quarters. I felt the sides of my face prickle as I went down the corridor, as my body warned me that perhaps I should not be there. However, my curiosity had grown and I could not will myself to turn back. My candle managed to cast a wide net of light down the corridor and it fell on a shadow huddled against the corner, where the walls adjoined. A sigh escaped from the shadow and my eyes widened as the shadow began to take shape. The minimal light began to form the narrow face of Ioana, thrown back in a look of ecstasy, eyes closed. Her long, pale neck was exposed, her auburn hair was askew. Her body was obscured by the shadow, but the light created an outline for me to see a little better.

The prickling that had started on the edges of my face spread down my neck to my chest and the hairs on the back of my neck began to rise as a familiar crop of obsidian hair brushed along the edge of her jaw, cheekbone, and neck. Long pale fingers draped along her arm.

Deciding I wanted to see no more, I turned, making my way down the corridor the same way I came. From the corner of my eye, I could see the face of the second shadow beginning to turn towards me only to succumb to the darkness once more as I hurried away. He would see me and the light of the candle moving swiftly down the hallway, there was no doubt of that, but I did not care.

My cheeks burned despite willing them to stop. A lowly servant? Truly? Storming down the corridor, tears flooded my eyes, blurring the house around me into obscurity. I had been prepared for this possibility, but I was not prepared for the torrent of hurt that it would cause, and that caught me off guard.

I cried out as something suddenly clamped on my wrist. "Shh, shhh, Your Highness, it's only me." I blinked away my tears to see Helene there, her long hair braided and thrown over her shoulder. "What are you doing out here? You'll freeze to death. Come, come."

She took me back to my room, sitting me on my bed, then going over to tend to the fire. After several attempts, it was ablaze and she came over to me, concern drenching her features. She pushed my hair back away from my eyes. "What is it? What is the matter?"

"I heard a noise and I went to investigate it... only to be met—with—he... a lowly servant, Helene!" My hurt quickly turned to anger. "His insults know no bounds!"

Helene gathered me into her arms, placing my head onto her shoulder. She shushed me gently. "I know, *mein liebling.* I know, cherub." It had been so long since she had called me "cherub", something she used to call me as a child. "As much as we try to steel ourselves against certain things in life, we never truly can steel ourselves from hurt. No matter how much we try."

"I've had enough of his insults, Helene, I can hardly bear it." I was fortunate the tears hadn't spilled from my eyes, instead drying and turning into indignation. "I hope he goes to Târgoviște and he stays there and rots. I wish to God I never had to lay eyes on him, and I hope I never have to again."

Instead of chastising me, Helene let me ramble on, spewing my frustrations. Neither did she remind me that she had warned me this could happen, leaving the unfair rules that women had to stomach unspoken. What she personally felt she also left unspoken, but her eyes told me that I would get used to it.

XVI

ANA-MARIA AND I WERE sitting in my private drawing room, playing a hand of cards. While we sat, Helene drifted in, unnaturally quiet.

"You usually make your presence known when you enter a room, Helene," I said to her, putting my final hand down to beat Ana-Maria this round. I had beaten her so much I was starting to feel bad and was considering perhaps letting her win once or twice. "What are you keeping so secret?"

I had excused myself from any further work on furnishing the castle, allowing myself a free afternoon. In any case, it was nearly done, and there wasn't much left to do but wait for the carpenters to finish their work and the merchants to deliver the items I had ordered. I had a stack of receipts that I would have to take to the prince in order to pay the funds, but I had decided I would wait to take them lest I attempt to claw out his eyes. Now that he was my husband, he had absorbed the dowry provided by my father, and while I was given an allowance, it was not enough to cover the expenses accrued.

She turned around and there was an odd look on her face that ranged from playful to expecting to be cuffed on the side of the head. "There has been a delivery for you, Madam."

"Not already, surely? We have another week at least."

"No, Madam, this isn't something you ordered." Her eyes flickered and I got the impression she was trying to tell me something that she didn't want Ana-Maria to know. "A *gift*."

I caught her meaning immediately. If he thought I could be bought with gifts, he was sorely mistaken. "Oh, I see. Well, where is it?"

"I asked that they bring it into the solar. It should be there now."

"Let's go see what it is, shall we?" With that, I made my way to the room I had designated as a solar, a room where I would receive guests and entertain them. The three of us made our way there and I was met with a beautiful German harpsichord, its angular case something I recognized at once upon entering the room. It was decorated rather simply but its wood was bright. Along the edges were painted little gold floral decals, a nice touch that added quaint elegance. A small matching stool had come with it, a lovely lace cushion on top of it.

This man had an irksome habit of disarming me, even as I wanted to bear nothing but disdain for any gift he might give me. But I found I could not hold that disdain, for it was a beautiful instrument. I flipped the lid back carefully and ran my fingers along the wooden keys, grazing their texture at first and then pressing down to hear the first few notes of an old Austrian folk song. I grinned at the sound. The instrument was perfectly in tune, and even after a long hiatus, I still could play after being forced to leave my old harpsichord back in Austria. I lowered the lid that covered the keys and lifted the lid of the case. Resting on top of the strings inside was a portfolio of pages. I opened it and inside was a small collection of sheet music containing Romanian folk songs. On top of them was a letter.

It read, "*I still hope to hear you play, if you would oblige me. Hopefully tonight after sunset.*"

I handed the portfolio to Helene with the letter inside and sat on the bench before the harpsichord and began to play. She knowingly opened the portfolio while Ana-Maria fluttered over to me, peering over my shoulder to watch my hands glide across the keyboard. But by then I was already in a reverie, succumbing to it quickly as it had been so long since I had played.

"Well," Helene said, finishing the short letter containing the scrawling words, "this room has yet to be finished, but shall I see what I can do, Your Highness?"

I finished my piece with a glittering crescendo, then stopped abruptly, meeting a dramatic conclusion. "Please. I will be here just after sunset as he requests."

I was there early as I could hardly wait to get back to the harpsichord. I had almost forgotten how its tones soothed me, allowing me to slip into a dream-like state while my hands traversed across its keys. Now I had my own once more, and even if I was torn away from this charming castle I was growing to love, I could take it with me and no one could object. It was like I was being embraced by an old friend as the notes I played fell around me. They were crisp, underlined with a subtle undercurrent of the vibrations created to make the sound.

As I remained bent over the keyboard while I continued to play, my focus was suddenly interrupted when I felt what seemed to be a hand caressing softly along my jaw, down my neck, and along my collarbone. It elicited a gasp, then a hiss from my mouth as I leapt away from the harpsichord, so startled by the sensation. My immediate reaction was one of outrage, angry that someone would put their hand on me so flagrantly. My breath rattled in my chest as my eyes traveled the room, searching for the owner of that hand, ready to berate them, but my outrage withered away.

No one was there.

I lingered, frozen in my place, confused as to what I had just experienced. The sensation felt so real. When I was certain that no one was there, I sat back tentatively on my seat in front of the harpsichord, playing slowly at first, then crescendoing with more confidence, dismissing what had happened as a figment of my imagination.

The door creaked open behind me though my focus remained on the music emitting from the instrument. The flames from the fireplace cast a tall shadow over me as the prince watched me play. I did not let thoughts of last night interrupt this musical reverie I was in, banning any further thoughts of shadows from my mind. There was only the music, an old French piece I had learned in honor of my mother. My father used to love it when I played it once and a great while, always asking me to play it one more time once it was finished. It was a joyous melody with lots of trills and intricate triplets, but the tempo was quick and it required a skilled player to meet its speed on time. Because of this, it had taken me some time to learn. I went away at it for a few more minutes, finishing the song, then ending with a flourish of trills, one succeeding another until they trailed off.

"I see you are making good use of it," said Prince Vlad behind me. He gave no acknowledgement of what I had seen last night and instead presented as though it never happened. Or perhaps he did not know that I had seen. "You are excellent. I admit, when I first heard some of the notes, I found it a rather piercing noise, but now hearing what you can do with it, I have changed my mind. Perhaps you should sell these instead of the man I purchased it from."

"Your words are kind," I said with cool courtesy. "It was also kind of you to have this delivered. I had missed playing terribly."

Helene had left behind a small spread of bread and cheese with butter, as well as a decanter of wine. She made do with what she could with the nearly empty room. The harpsichord had been moved further in, near the windows for the natural light, then she borrowed some of the chairs from my private sitting room along with a small table.

"You seem to be a natural," he told me, pouring me a glass of wine and handing it to me. Then, he took a seat at one of the chairs opposite me.

"I started learning to play practically when I learned to walk. Not literally, but not much longer after," I said, taking it from him. "I may be a natural at the harpsichord but you are a natural when it comes to archery. Where did you learn to shoot like that?"

"Well," he began, leaning forward, clasping his hands together and resting his elbows on his knees. "Same as you, almost, but with the bow instead of the harpsichord. I was learning to shoot not long after I was expelled from the nursery."

"Expelled?"

"Not literally, but it was deemed a waste that I should spend more time there as a child than necessary."

"By your father?" It came out before I could stop it; I blurted it entirely without thinking. How utterly stupid.

"Yes," he said, rather cautiously I thought. "A military man himself, he felt that his sons should not be wasted, idling themselves with trifling things, and instead needed to be out in the field as quickly as possible." *Sons*. Did the prince have a brother? Multiple? I did not know this. But then again, I knew very little about him. "So out into the field I went by the time I was five or so, learning to ride a horse, shoot a bow, and wield a sword. I always felt my skills were better with a bow than with a sword."

"And yet you did not participate in the horse races that were held. Why?"

"I couldn't decimate Simon at every competition, could I?" That mischief returned.

I was nearly taken aback at how easily we slipped into conversation after not seeing each other much in a few weeks, and *especially* after what I had come across last night. "No, you could not, as that would have been a massive blow to that inflated pride of his." He laughed and, surprisingly, I was delighted at the sound of his laughter, hearing it for the first time. It was a hearty laugh that resonated in his chest, and it was hard not to smile at the sound of it. It was infectious. "I have never touched a bow before. I wonder how easy it would be to learn…"

The same easy conversation went on for some time and I finally learned some things about him. He had traveled extensively as a child, coursing all through Romania to the various castles and fortresses. On several occasions he had traveled so far as Hungary where he lived for a time in Buda, as his mother was a relative of the Hungarian king at that time. In addition to speaking German flawlessly, he spoke Hungarian effortlessly. He wasn't terribly close with his uncle, from whom he had inherited the throne, but he was the only surviving and suitable heir—his suitability having been determined by the boyars who still held sway. Noticeably, he never once mentioned his father again as we talked. In our easy and effortless conversation, I found myself wanting to believe that he hadn't inherited his cruelty, but I still couldn't be sure as there were many sides to one's personality.

"...then my sister is to be married to the Spanish Prince shortly after," I concluded, telling him about my own siblings. He shared with me that he had two brothers, one was deceased and one was missing, having disappeared long before his uncle's reign.

"And you miss them." He stated it so matter-of-factly, it was more a statement than a question. That sense of feeling disarmed around him began to resurface.

"I do, in a way," I said, cautiously. "I did not grow up much with my sister, and we were only beginning to get close after she returned from France. My brother has always been the favorite, so while we enjoyed each other's company, he was often whisked away by his studies or the girls in the court. They always fancied him and he always charmed them, no matter how old he was..." I trailed off, wondering if I would ever see him again—or Margaret for that matter.

"Would you oblige me in playing another piece?" asked Prince Vlad, his voice pulling me out of my contemplation. Our eyes met and, not for the first time, I still wondered if he could read my thoughts despite such a thing not being possible.

"Gladly," I replied, grateful not to dance around the awkwardness that seeped in and out as I was occasionally reminded throughout our discussions of what I had seen last night. Deciding I still did not trust him no matter how easy our conversations had been this evening, I drew a piece of music from the portfolio he had gifted me along with the harpsichord and settled on a Romanian song. I had never seen it before, naturally, but glancing at it, it seemed fun to play with its triplets and glides.

"Truly incredible," he said from behind me again as I finished. I had not realized he was standing directly behind me to watch me play. "Had I not known better, I would have thought you had learned that piece prior to tonight."

"It's not difficult, anyone could do it."

"I very much doubt that."

"I assure you, watch. The left hand manages the beat while the right takes on the melody." I leaned back to give him a better view of the keyboard while I illustrated my point. "See? Even you could do it. You have an incredible handspan, that you could definitely play well if you learned. Try it. Take your left hand like this and allow the fingers to arch over these keys here." He leaned forward to humor me and tried imitating my left hand over the keys as I instructed. "Not quite—like this." I took his hand and adjusted the placement of his fingers. "There you are. Now, keep pressing down on this beat every so often, like this." I held my hand over his, pressing lightly to instruct him when he should hit the chord. "There, do you sense that? Keep doing that and while you do..." I played a few notes of the melody with my right hand, still holding my left over his.

Suddenly, I became aware of the proximity of his body to mine as he leaned over me, his chest nearly grazing my back. I could feel the softness of his breath on my neck. His hand under mine felt cool to the touch. At my realization, I turned and our eyes met, holding one another's gaze. In his emerald eyes, I saw a glimpse of something I hadn't seen before, something that slipped unchecked. Then, his eyes steeled themselves once more and it was gone.

"It's getting rather late," I said, my voice unintentionally soft.

"I suppose it is," he replied, his voice low. He stepped away slowly, but this did not break the heat that seemed to be surfacing on my skin.

"Good night, My Lord," I said, having made my way to the door.

"Good night."

XVII

1496

CHRISTMAS CAME AND WENT, though fortunately, the castle was furnished just in time. Our celebrations were kept quite at a minimum considering how elaborate our wedding celebrations were not long before. The festivities consisted of a small banquet, of which a handful of boyars, including the mayor of Brașov, and their wives attended. The feast, however, was not kept to a minimum. We had boar's head, suckling pig, as well as many other savory dishes. Then, after it was over, there was dancing, and once the boyars had left we had a gift exchange amongst those who resided within the castle. I had organized small gifts of sweets and trinkets to be given to our servants, so once the banquet hall was cleaned, the servants lined up and the Voivode and I personally gave each of their gifts to them. Along with the servants, we gave gifts to those most near and dear to us. On the other hand, I was the recipient of some lovely gifts as well. However, Simon, that impertinent fool, gifted me a fiddle with a note that said, *"since you dance so beautifully to the sounds of this instrument, you should learn to play it too,"* reminding me of that night that still made my cheeks burn with shame.

While all of the gifts I received were exceptional, the one that stood out the most was the gift from the Voivode. He gifted me a bow with a quiver full of arrows, something I had not been expecting. He explained that because I taught him to appreciate the harpsichord, he thought it only fair to return the favor, which made me recall that night. My cheeks always grew warm at the memory of him so close to me while he sat at the harpsichord. It was a beautiful bow, smaller than the standard size and curved dramatically. The wood was stained a beautiful reddish color; it was quite elegant. It was a shame I would have to wait until spring to use it as this winter was particularly relentless, forcing us to remain indoors to keep away from the bitter cold.

After the holidays, things grew quiet, but it was a pleasant time. I no longer was plagued by the strange happenings I had experienced when I first arrived, and by now, I found it to be almost laughable that my imagination had conjured up such silly things. I occupied my time by painting the beautiful winter scenery, learning to play the fiddle Simon had gifted me with the help of a tutor—thinking it would be a shame to let any instrument go to waste—and reading. I had also taken up patronage for the Church of Saint Mary's, where I was married, donating funds so that they could assist the poor. In addition to my patronage of Saint Mary's, I sent funds to the new school that had been completed, the one which the Voivode's uncle had started during his reign.

Then, before we knew it, the new year had come and gone and soon spring was nearing.

I wouldn't say I knew my husband much better than when I first arrived, but I did somewhat. He remained incredibly busy during these first several months of his reign as Voivode, so I saw him very little. From what I did hear, I learned that he had made trade concessions for the merchants, lowering the export tax and lowering the amount it cost to dock at entry ports. This led me to suspect he wanted to encourage Romanian exports so the world would know that this little country was keeping up with the times in the production of goods and textiles and, in turn, the rest of the world would take an interest in what Romania had to offer, spending the coin to procure some of those goods.

In addition, he renewed the military class—something that had somewhat fallen apart with the reign of his uncle—feeling it was important for Romania to have a robust military, especially as I caught word that he was planning to no longer pay the Ottomans their annual tribute—something his uncle resumed doing after he assumed the throne. Two thousand ducats were paid annually to prevent the Ottomans from attacking, a mighty and steep cost, hence needing a robust military for such a bold measure. If he did take this measure, it was clear my husband had confidence in his alliance with the Holy Roman Emperor, though time would only tell if this gamble would work.

Additionally, my husband was determined to lower the crime rate, which had risen in the last decade or so. He increased the fines and penalties for petty crimes, and any man that could not pay was required to join the military. Women would be forced into indentured servitude, at least until their fine was paid off, depending on the severity of the crime.

I was impressed with the velocity at which the Voivode worked. Time would only tell if these measures would work and were beneficial, particularly the lowering of the various taxes. Military expenses were steep. Were the checks and balances of lowering taxes while increasing criminal fines enough for the country to not only reach financial stability, but allow it to grow as well? I could not be sure, but it was clear that the Voivode was considering this. Some of this I had heard straight from him (on the rare occasions I did see him), other tidbits of information I had heard from Ambassador Ionescu, who came to call upon occasion.

Such was the occasion on this particular day. The ambassador came by to talk with me after having had an appointment with the Voivode earlier in the afternoon. Helene and I lingered in our quarters—she sewed while I painted a scene of the blossoms that were beginning to bud on the trees surrounding us, when there was a soft knock at the door. One of the servants appeared behind the door after Helene opened it and she announced the arrival of the ambassador. I bid her to have him wait for I would meet him downstairs to take a walk as I needed a reprieve from my work anyhow.

"Our Voivode has another assignment for me," the ambassador announced as we walked together on the grounds, his arm extended and mine draped loosely around it. Helene walked with us a step behind. "It requires a bit of traveling again."

"Traveling? Surely not as long of a distance as Austria? I speak in nothing but kindness when I say that you are reaching an age where you should be comfortable on a chair surrounded by your grandchildren."

"No, no, fortunately that is not the case as I do not think I could make such an extensive trip in this lifetime again.

Those days are behind me if these past several months have taught me anything."

"So then where are you going if the Voivode won't finally grant your retirement? Perhaps I could persuade him to send someone else," I said, though knowing it was unlikely I had any ability to persuade the Voivode of anything.

"There is no need, Your Highness, despite how kind your offer is. His Lordship promised me that after this assignment, I will be eligible to retire if I so wish, he just feels that there is no one else to be trusted with the mission he has given me."

Helene made a soft little noise behind me, and I glanced over my shoulder to see if she was all right. Her face did not betray anything was amiss. "Is this assignment such a dire secret that you cannot tell me what it is?"

"Not at all. His Highness did not indicate that I was bound to secrecy. I am to be sent as an envoy to the Turks to inform them that Romania will no longer be paying the annual tribute, as well as deliver notice of some other sanctions—especially the end of *devşirme*."

"*Devşirme*?" I replied, chewing on this foreign word for the first time.

"In addition to the annual tribute, we Romanians have been forced to provide the Ottomans with a collection of our good Christian boys who are converted to Islam, circumcised, and then serve in the Ottoman army as *janissaries*. Something we will not be allowing any longer."

Helene and I mirrored each other, sharing a look of shock. I had never heard of such a grotesque thing. It took me a moment to regain my ability to speak as I processed the horrific practice. "More often than not, I have heard what a serious threat the Ottoman Empire is to us. Is the Voivode serious about the measures he wishes to take? With sanctions on top of it? Is that wise? Yes, this horrific practice should end, but perhaps the tribute in gold should not."

"He is quite serious, Your Highness, though his measures are not too unfamiliar in recent history. His own father did the same during his tenures."

It took every ounce of my will to refrain from jolting at this mention of the Voivode's father, especially as this was the first time the ambassador had mentioned him to me. I had grown comfortable and had since expelled that awful book from my mind, but hearing the mention of him made it all come flooding back. Although, I took this as my chance. "I have heard very little about the Voivode's father. What was he like?"

Ambassador Ionescu thought for a minute and I wondered if maybe he realized he had made a mistake in mentioning him. I could not be certain. "I was but a young man when he reigned, but he was a fearsome warrior, completely unafraid of the Turks unlike his half-brother. He was the only person willing to stand up to them, it seemed." Was he choosing his words carefully, I wondered. "Other than the battles between his army and that of the Ottomans, Romania was the safest it had ever been in recent memory. Crime was at an all-time low, to the point where Vlad Dracula left a gold cup near the town's fountain. Anyone could drink out of it, but no one dared take it lest they faced the consequences."

Dracula. That was the first I had heard this name. "And what *were* the consequences?"

There was a beat before the ambassador answered. "Execution," he said.

"I see... It would seem that his son is more merciful in that he requires military service instead of death sentences for petty crimes such as thievery." I could not keep the ice from entering my voice. "'*Dracula*'. What does that name mean?"

"'Son of the Dragon.' His father was named Vlad Dracul so therefore he was named after him."

I recalled my father mentioning this my last night in Austria. "Is that why the Voivode's emblem bears a dragon?"

"That's it exactly—it's an image carried on through the generations." Ambassador Ionescu released a smile brimming with pride. "Fitting for their bravery, something also carried through the generations of the Drăculeşti clan."

His usual contagious smile found its way over to me and I couldn't help but meet it with my own. "You are granting me so much of my husband's family history for the first time since I have known you, where was all of this knowledge before?"

"You never asked," he said with a wink. "Besides, facing the Turks, one can't help but feel a swell of pride for God and country—they have been our enemies for so long. I am honored to be serving His Lordship this way."

A churning in my stomach had begun. "When do you leave?"

"Beginning of next week."

"That's hardly any time at all to prepare," Helene said unexpectedly. She caught up to us and was now walking on the ambassador's other side.

"Not much," he admitted, "but it is enough time to pack what I need. I only have to ride just over the border and cross the Danube River. The Voivode has arranged a meeting with the sultan's envoy, although they think that they are receiving the annual tribute. It will be such a delight to see their faces when they realize that is not the purpose of our meeting at all. I expect to be back in a couple of months at the very latest, depending on how any potential negotiations that arise go based on the sanctions the Voivode is imposing. He has given me permission to negotiate on behalf of Romania should the terms meet our overall expectations."

It did not seem as though he was talking to me any longer. "Perhaps it will be sooner than that," Helene replied, hope coating her voice.

"Hopefully," I chimed in. "Please remain safe as this seems to be an utterly dangerous assignment." Then, I lifted my hand to my forehead. "My goodness, am I feeling a bit light-headed. Please do excuse me, I may lay my head down for a moment so that this passes."

Helene perked up. "Let me escort you, I will walk you back."

I smiled. "That is not necessary, Helene, I will be fine on my own. I am sure it will pass. Besides, it's such a lovely day, one of our first warm ones. There is no need for you to miss out on it because of me. Continue to walk with our good ambassador. I will be fine. Good day to you, ambassador."

Before Helene could insist any further, I spun on my heel and moved quickly back to the castle, quicker than anyone who had lightheadedness probably would move, but I wasn't exactly telling the truth, was I?

"Grinning to see me, eh? I knew you would come around."

My grin faded away at a moment's notice. "Good afternoon, Simon," I said as I allowed him to scoop my hand up to kiss the back of it. "I was going to inquire as to what brings you here but I have since learned better and would rather not know."

Simon chuckled heartily. "I am on my way to the stables. The Voivode and I are going out for a ride. It would be such a waste to spend this beautiful day indoors, no? Though, this beautiful day can't compare to your radiant beauty."

"Enough with that minstrel nonsense and carry on your way, you knave," Prince Vlad said, coming down the steps from the castle.

"I cannot help that I have a way with words that you do not possess, my dear friend," Simon chuckled. "I was born a silver-tongued devil."

"A 'devil' all right," Prince Vlad retorted without malice. "See to it that our horses are saddled. Off you go."

Simon swept into a dramatic bow before me, and then he sauntered off to do his master's bidding.

"You can take the Frenchman out of France, but you can't take the French out of a Frenchman," Prince Vlad told me somewhat apologetically, the smirk dancing around his lips in typical fashion.

"And what is that supposed to mean?" I teased him with mock indignance. "I happen to be French as well, on my mother's side."

"Good God, I am surrounded by them," he replied, casting his glance heavenward. "Lord take pity on me."

"You should be thanking Him," I replied, laughing.

"You are not going in, are you?" he asked, changing the subject. "Come and join Simon and me for a ride."

I blanched at the suggestion. "I'm afraid I can't, I am working on a painting, you see, and it's almost finished. I only stepped away for a little while—"

His facial features rearranged suddenly and his eyes bore into mine compellingly. "Nothing will happen to you, I promise. I will make sure of it."

I nearly winced at his words as he seemed to see through my attempts to mask my fear of horses. "So you have heard of my mother's fate then?"

"How could I have not? All of Europe stopped at the news of it. Your mother was well-renowned."

"Then you know of my fear of riding on horseback too?"

"It is not... unknown to me."

I marveled at how he still disarmed me, could read me as easily as words on a written page.

"I won't let anything happen to you," he reassured me again, those emerald eyes becoming malleable, letting me see something in them that I had only seen briefly a moment before. Something I wasn't sure I could discern.

"Come on then, old man," Simon called over, holding the reins of two horses and leading them over from the stable.

"What say you?" Prince Vlad asked. "You can ride with me. Or you could ride with Simon, if you really wanted." With that we broke out into another round of laughter.

My heart was beating mercilessly in my chest. I truly hated the idea of riding on the back of the horse, the very thing that stole my mother from me. Yet, there was something about the way Prince Vlad asked me, almost as if he was imploring me...

"Very well," I replied reluctantly, hoping I wouldn't regret it later.

Then, within moments, I was on the back of the saddle I had given the Voivode for Christmas and he was seated on it behind me. Once again, I was reminded of that night in the solar with the harpsichord as he was again so close to me that I could feel his breath in my hair. Though, this time, even though I sat with my legs draped over one side, I was cradled between his legs, practically on his lap. I almost would have been scandalized at this position had I not been so utterly terrified with what I was about to do.

"Hold onto the pommel here, and if you can't, the horse's mane will do. I will keep you steady with my arms as I hold the reins," the Voivode told me, though I was barely listening. My heart was pounding in my ears. I worried I wouldn't even be able to grasp the pommel as my palms were beginning to sweat.

"Her Highness looks a little worse for wear," Simon observed, having mounted his horse already.

"Her Highness will be just fine," Prince Vlad assured. "She will overcome anything she sets her mind to."

"That is true, she's married *you* after all, an incredibly brave thing to do."

Ignoring him, the Voivode clicked his tongue and the black stallion started to move, and I emitted a little gasp. My knuckles went white as I gripped the pommel. This beast was so large, it carried both of us with ease. I just hoped that it could not sense my fear. The prince was kind and said nothing, merely craning his head slightly over me to see the way ahead, keeping the horse at a slow walk.

"See? It's not so bad, is it?" he asked after several minutes of keeping this pace.

"I suppose not," I said, unclenching my teeth finally and easing a little, though I still remained mistrusting. Simon was calling over to us, running his gray stallion in circles around us, but I paid little attention to him. I was just praying I wouldn't fall off.

"I'm going to have him go a little faster, but you are going to have to release the tension in your body and allow it to move with the horse. Follow his rhythm, otherwise it may

hurt after a while. Do you understand?" Prince Vlad instructed, his voice very close to my ear.

"Yes. I will try," I replied, wiping the moisture from my
palms onto my skirt.

He clicked his tongue again and the horse began to trot.
I very quickly realized that, despite being told so, I had not
released the tension in my body like he suggested as the
pommel went very uncomfortably into my seat as I lurched
forward.

"I would have thought that the Voivode would have
shown you what a good rider he is by now," Simon bellowed
over to us, laughing at his double entendre.

"Maybe it's time I put him in his place," the prince said.

"It *is* time," I replied instantly, "for I am getting quite
weary of his commentary."

"Then, it might be better to swing your leg over the other
side." He released one of his hands off the reins so I could take
it for balance as I moved my skirts over and swung my leg
over the side of the horse. Propriety be damned. While I was
eager to get off this beast, I was more eager to have Simon
put in his place as he was getting on my last nerve.

Once I was better balanced on the saddle—much better
now that I sat astride—the prince wrapped his arm around
my waist, then he clicked his tongue again and the horse took
off. Simon, who was ahead of us, realized what was occurring and scrambled to get his horse to move faster, but we
were gaining on him too quickly. The wind whipped through
my face and hair and, admittedly, it was exhilarating even
though strands of my hair tore from my braid. All of my
fear was washed away by the wind as laughter escaped my
throat, also being carried away by the wind. We blazed past
Simon but kept going past him and then past Helene and

Ambassador Ionescu, whose faces were drenched in shock as we thundered by. We stretched by the edge of the town, following the wall that encased it and beyond, passing a field of bleating sheep that scrambled away as we rushed headlong into a thicket of trees. Before we made it through, the Voivode slowed the stallion to a cantor. When we got into the thick part of the forest, the horse slowed to a trot and then to a steady walk until we reached a stream, where we stopped.

The sun blared through the trees as there were no leaves yet for shade, but the sun was gentle and not too overbearing, just bright. The branches had little buds on them, and if the weather stayed like this, it wouldn't be long before leaves emerged. The stream wasn't terribly wide, but its loud trickling filled the air, abundant with water because of the snow that had since completely melted.

"Do you think we have our victory?" The prince asked, assisting me from the horse. I was suddenly very aware of his hands on my waist.

"I would say so. Hopefully that will teach him to clamp that awful mouth of his," I said.

"Probably not, but it will be good to remind him of this from time to time." He went to the saddle and extracted a waterskin from it. As he went over to the stream to fill it, I patted my stray strands of hair, which had escaped from their bondage. After taking several swigs from the waterskin himself, he handed it over to me and I drank from it, finding it rather refreshing. My mouth had gone dry from laughing in the wind.

"Well, that wasn't so bad, was it?" he asked. He went over to the horse, grabbed the reins, and led the horse to drink from the stream.

"I enjoyed it more than I thought I would," I admitted. "During my youth, they attempted to teach me to ride a horse in my lessons, but I would make such a fuss that, after a while, they just abandoned any further attempts to instruct me. You see, after my mother..." I faltered, unsure of why I suddenly felt compelled to confess my fears to him. I had never spoken of this to anyone.

"I understand. It is difficult to overcome one's fears, though I am glad you came around. We will have to get you set up with your own mare and saddle."

"We could try, though I do not think I have inherited my mother's passion for horses. Furthermore, I will never be as good a rider as you," I told him, passing the waterskin back. His fingers grazed mine as he took it from me, gooseflesh immediately rippling across my skin. Our eyes met and a moment of silence fell between us until the sound of thundering hooves grew and Simon's flushed face came charging in on the back of his stallion.

"That stallion of yours is a bat straight from hell," he said, heaving himself from his saddle. "The two of you came out of nowhere."

The Voivode's eyes lingered on me a moment before turning to Simon and tossing the waterskin over to him, which he drank from greedily. "Serves you right after spewing all of that nonsense."

XVIII

"H OW LONG HAVE YOU been keeping this from me?" I asked Helene, unable to contain my mirth. "You sneaky, saucy vixen!"

"Hush now," she chided me, a blush I would have never expected blooming on her cheeks. She looked the most beautiful I had ever seen. "It has been months, though. Nearly a year."

"Months? Nearly a year! You *are* a vixen, Helene! All this time, you and the ambassador, courting one another right under my nose."

It was well after dinner and she was assisting me for bed. I had spent the rest of the afternoon with Simon and the Voivode, riding back with them at a much more casual pace. I joined them for dinner, where I noticed the prince ate nothing while Simon ate ravenously, seemingly enough for the both of them. One would think he had never eaten before in his life. Then I said goodnight to have a bath. Now, Helene was combing out my hair as we talked quietly into the night.

"Both of us had a duty that we needed to fulfill," she explained. "Making sure that you were married and settled was our primary concern, everything else came after."

"Though I would have never expected him to be one you would find to be attractive, I admit."

"There are other forms of attraction. Physical beauty isn't everything. Besides, I am too old to be so frivolous about something so quickly to fade as beauty. When you get to my age, everything changes."

I reached behind me and took her hand in mine, meeting her eyes in the mirror. "I am happy for you, Helene. I really am. He's a wonderful man and you deserve this." She lowered her eyes again girlishly and smiled. "I brought the matter you asked me about to the Voivode this evening during dinner. I asked if there was someone else he would be willing to send. Now, before you protest, no, I did *not* say anything about the two of you. I just said what I thought and that was that Ambassador Ionescu deserves to retire now instead of later."

"And what did he say?"

"The same as what the ambassador told us earlier—that there is no one else he trusts for this assignment, and that once he returns, Ambassador Ionescu will be gifted with a generous commission. I am sorry, Helene, but I am sure he will be back soon. Then he can return and ask for your hand and we can have a large, beautiful wedding for the two of you."

"I just hope he returns safely."

"He will. I am certain he will."

I was not sure what had awoken me.

I jerked in my sleep and lay there for a while, hoping sleep would overtake me again, but it did not, so I stepped out for some fresh air. The floorboards were chilled under my feet, cooling after the sun went down, so I threw my shawl around my shoulders and padded out of my bedroom, down the hall, and onto the balcony. Yes, it had definitely cooled since this afternoon, but it was still a pleasant evening. The three-quarter moon hung in the sky, casting a gentle glaze of ivory onto everything below, allowing me to see the familiar courtyard silhouettes such as the well and the retaining wall. The courtyard had unofficially become an extra space of storage for crates as the occupants of this castle had doubled since I first arrived, between the newly hired servants and extra guards. We would be remaining at Bran for the rest of summer and into the fall, leaving for Târgoviște before the winter. I couldn't say I was overly fond of the idea of leaving this castle, but it was definitely a summer home and not one in which a prince needed to hold court and proper audiences.

Leaning forward to gaze down at the courtyard below, my daydreams of what Târgoviște looked like were interrupted when I heard the sound of wings flapping. Not a rapid flapping, but the wings of what could have been a large bird, like an eagle or an owl, wings with a wide span. It stopped suddenly and the night was silent again for a moment or two. Then, whatever it was landed on the roof with a soft thud, though it sounded almost too heavy to be an eagle, even. I jolted, startled by the sound of it.

Not wasting a moment, I raced back inside to the floor where the Voivode resided. Any thoughts of what I had stumbled upon the last time I wandered to his floor I pushed away, determined as I was to awaken and alert him with what I had heard. When I turned into the corridor and approached his bedchamber, I saw that there was a light in his room. He was awake already.

Had he heard what I had heard? The sound came from the direction of his quarters after all. Still, I should make sure he was aware. It would be unseemly for me to alert the guards in nothing but my shift. I came to the door and raised my hand to knock when I heard voices.

I could distinguish the Voivode immediately. He was talking to someone, but the voice that responded wasn't one I would have anticipated. Thinking back to the time I had discovered him with Ioana, I would expect her to be keeping him company at such a late hour, or perhaps some other woman. But the sound of the male's voice made me hesitate as it had such a quality to it that I found disturbing. It had a similar timbre to the Voivode, was also a baritone voice, but it was harsh and laced with a knife's edge—not at all pleasant like the prince's. I couldn't quite make out what he was saying, but he was speaking rapidly while remaining hushed. Then it stopped and I swore they could hear the breath shuddering from my chest, so I clamped my hand over my mouth.

Then that same harsh voice said, "We are not alone."

Before I knew it, the door had swung open and I could only stand there like a fool, wide-eyed, as the Voivode's frame filled the doorway. His eyes bore sternly into mine and I had a passing thought noting how feral he looked. His hair was wild and unkempt in a halo around his face, which was pulled into a taut expression. His clothes were in a state of disarray and his jaw clenched tightly. I'm not sure what I was more frightened of anymore at that moment, the thing I heard on the roof or him.

I expected him to yell at me, but he did not. Instead, he asked me in a very firm tone, "What is it?"

My throat tightened as I struggled to find words. "I-I... I thought I... heard something on the r-roof. An... intruder perhaps."

A small exhalation escaped from his mouth and he released his jaw before stepping out into the corridor with me and closing the door behind him. He guided me away from the door and placed his hand on my shoulder, albeit not roughly but with purpose, and led me down the hallway. The darkness was seemingly not a hindrance to him, and we stepped onto the balcony. We stood in silence as he listened for anything amiss. When he was satisfied there was nothing, he led me back inside, assuring me that there was nothing. As he escorted me back down to my quarters, he told me that he would summon guards to remain posted outside of my door, just in case.

"There are all sorts of wild birds that live out here, eagles, owls, ravens—they like to prey on the mice that sometimes skitter along the roof here, I'm sure. It is not uncommon," he told me as we approached the door to my bedchamber. "I am certain it was nothing more than that." I was taken aback by his agitation and abruptness, for it was the first time I had encountered it from him. Yes, he had a reservation about his person more often than not, and there were times when we had gotten along, but there had never been anything such as this. It was rather unexpected.

When we got to my door, he stopped and released my shoulder. His eyes averted for a moment as he seemed he wanted to say something else. Then he settled on "goodnight." I said nothing in reply, but merely took that as my cue to slip back into my bedchamber in confused silence, feeling as though I had been sent to my room like a child being punished for telling lies.

I stood at the bottom of the steps of the castle beside the Voivode, my arm draped over his in a show of unity I did not particularly feel. I had said very little to him, leaving it as only a cold greeting and nothing else. It was the first time I had seen him since that night, and we were bidding Ambassador Ionescu farewell before he left for his assignment across the border. He certainly was more polished than he had been the other evening, displaying himself to be rather imperial instead of a heathen. Helene stood dutifully behind me, but I knew she had said her goodbyes in a far more intimate and private setting over the last couple of days. I had given her leave so that she could spend some time with the ambassador. I was surrounded by lovelorn women, between Helene and Ana-Maria, who had announced only the day before that she was expecting a child. Spring was certainly in the air. I was ecstatic for her as she had longed for a child from her unloving husband, though I certainly did not inquire as to how she had finally got her husband into her bed. All that mattered was that she would have the child she wanted, and one could almost tell by just looking at her as she was positively glowing, despite being still early in her pregnancy.

Ambassador Ionescu had taken the final inventory of his supplies and was now prepared to ride off with a small party. He approached the prince and me to bid his final farewell. Bowing deeply, he said, "I will keep you apprised of everything, My Lord, leaving no detail out, whether it be large or small. Farewell, My Lord, farewell My Princess. Keep me in your prayers that I come back successful."

"You haven't let me down yet, Avram, I expect nothing short of your success. I almost envy your ability to see the reaction directly from the Turks themselves when you tell them that we will no longer be beholden to them." He clapped him jovially on the arm, undoubtedly envisioning the scene himself.

"Again, I will leave out no detail, especially that moment," Ambassador Ionescu replied, laughing as if he shared the vision of his prince. "It's been a long time coming."

"Yes, thirteen years of appeasing them is far too long. It is definitely high time that we tell them that enough is enough. I will be interested to hear what their negotiations are on the sanctions we are imposing."

"We will find out, My Lord. I promise to not be lenient and keep Romania's best interests at heart." Then he turned to me. "I will miss our visits, Your Highness, your presence is always most enlightening. I look forward to when we may resume them."

"You will be sorely missed, ambassador. I have grown so used to your company that it will be strange to not have you so near, but it is only temporary at least. Come back to us as you are, won't you? I expect to share another small barrel of that fine wine with you upon your return—or perhaps a large one and a game of dice or two with it. "

"You have my word, Your Highness." He bowed deeply again before me, taking my hand and placing a kiss upon the back of it, a kiss I knew that wasn't necessarily meant for me.

Just before he mounted his horse and sped off with his travel party, he glanced at Helene and their eyes locked one last time.

XIX

I T WAS SOME TIME before the Voivode finally got correspondence from Ambassador Ionescu. He reached the border
safely with his party and was prepared to make contact with
the sultan's envoy within the next few days from the date of
his letter. During that time, Helene became quite subdued,
far quieter than I believe I had ever seen her. It was a bit of a
challenge to distract her, especially at first, for her thoughts
were far away from us, but eventually, she relented. I knew
she worried. The Ottoman Empire, their way of life, and
their temperament wasn't familiar to us Austrian women.
At one time they seemed to be a distant monster, a faraway
phantom. But now they were before us, and we could no
longer turn away as they were playing a dangerous game,
one that had been going on long before our arrival. Fortunately, a letter addressed to me but clearly meant for Helene

was included in his correspondence to the prince, which had cheered her immensely.

In the meantime, I served as an envoy of sorts for the prince as well. Spring was in full bloom now, and with the warm weather came the invitations for various events, such as a banquet held at the mayor's house, which I ended up attending alone in the prince's stead.

At the banquet, we were presented with a play—a rather crude satire that had surfaced in Germany and had somehow managed to find its way here. Shortly after the mayor's banquet, the other boyars felt compelled to try and one-up each other with banquets presenting similar plays. It was also around this time I noticed the boyars' wives had begun imitating some of the fashions I had brought with me. At first, there were whispers about me attending these events alone, or sometimes with Ana-Maria, but after a while they ceased. I was never given any reason why the prince did not attend, but I wasn't unhappy with the arrangement. During these banquets, I began to develop some standing of my own, making acquaintances and breaking the monotony of the winter. None of my new acquaintances could take the place of Ana-Maria who, other than Helene, had become my closest confidante. She helped me keep track of who was who among the nobility, as she herself was well-known among them. She was also useful in telling me who to be wary of, as well as filling me in on what was spoken of when it came to the Voivode and me, especially since no one would be direct and honest with me themselves. Our lack of an heir was a common topic, it would so seem, particularly for the mayor's wife who seemed to find amusement in it when, to my face, she was nothing but kind and eager to please me.

One particularly warm evening, Ana-Maria informed me that the topic had come up again while we attended yet another round of festivities at the mayor's house, this time in honor of my birthday, which had been earlier in the week. We were escorting Ana-Maria home in our carriage at a rather late hour.

"What has she said now?" I asked, genuinely interested.

"She suspects that the Voivode finds you repulsive," Ana-Maria replied reluctantly.

I burst out laughing, unable to contain myself. "Perhaps he does!"

"Do you really feel that way?" she asked, putting her hand on her own belly absentmindedly, though she still didn't show obvious signs of carrying a child. "You never speak of the matter."

No, it was true, I rarely did, especially since I could hardly make sense of the dynamics of my relationship with the Voivode myself. One would think he would be eager to have an heir, but all signs pointed elsewhere. "I am not certain," I replied, settling for the truth. "The Voivode and I are cordial, but then there are these moments that seem to drive a barrier between us. We have not... *known* each other since our wedding night. So maybe she is right. Perhaps he does find me repulsive."

"I am uncertain how any man could find you repulsive," she said, casting her eyes downward. "You have to be the most beautiful woman that I have ever seen, to the point where you do not even seem real. At least, that's what I first thought when I saw you. Others have said... similar things."

"What sort of things?"

She kept her eyes downcast, something she still did upon occasion despite becoming more confident since I had first met her. "Well," she continued, "as you may have learned, the Romanians are a superstitious people, especially the peasants, and since your arrival, many stories have traveled amongst the nobility." She giggled nervously. "Most of them are ridiculous, really, hardly worth even telling you."

My curiosity was piqued. "Go on, Ana-Maria. You have become one of my most trusted friends—my only friend, really, since I have been here. You must tell me now."

She giggled nervously again before looking up at me between her eyelashes. Then, she saw the seriousness written on my face. A shadow shuddered across her features. It was a beat or two before she finally spoke and she did not giggle nervously this time. "There are... rumors, Your Highness." She took a deep breath. "Some say you made a deal with *Muma Pădurii* deep in the forest on your way to the castle, asking her for ethereal beauty so that the Voivode would find you beautiful upon your arrival. In exchange, you would give her your firstborn child, which is why you are not expecting a child yet—to prevent you from having to meet your end of the bargain."

"*Muma Pădurii?*" I repeated.

"The mad old woman that lives in the forest. A witch who brews potions and casts spells. It is also said that she enslaves children, which is why she demanded your first born in exchange for beauty."

I almost laughed out loud, but the seriousness in Ana-Maria's eyes stopped me, though I still couldn't help but smile in amusement. "Is that all they say?"

"No," she replied. "Some say that you are actually one of the *iele* that strayed from her sisters and you have bewitched the Voivode, holding great power over him." I raised my eyebrow in question at the unfamiliar word. "Oh, I am sorry. The *iele* are fairies that live in groups of three or seven, and they not only can cast magic but have great seductive powers over men. This rumor ran rampant shortly after your wedding festivities, after that one night where you... danced... as the *iele* often dance during the night." Her eyes lowered again.

"And do you think I am one? A fairy?" I couldn't help but wonder as I did have the misfortune of holding some sway over her husband, despite my best attempts not to. Perhaps she thought I had cast a spell on him too.

She sighed, embarrassment beginning to surface. "I did. Early on. My husband was... *is*... so enamored with you, I thought perhaps you were *iele*. But since I have gotten to know you, I know you are not."

"Never once have you struck me as superstitious, Ana-Maria, I am quite surprised," I said.

"Superstitions run strong in Romanian blood, Your Highness, and I am Romanian through and through," she replied.

"Well, surely people must know I am not one of these fairies, especially as the mayor's wife helpfully draws attention to the fact that I have yet to beget a child by my husband. I truly could not have bewitched him if he won't even come to me at night." I suddenly remembered the woman on my wedding day, the one that fell weeping to my feet and pressed the wooden crucifix to my palm. Then, I swiftly recalled the flapping I heard on the rooftop. "Do they say similar things about my husband?"

"I don't know that I should say, it seems like an act of treason."

"I will protect you from any such charges." My heart was rattling in my rib cage. Suddenly, this conversation didn't seem so amusing. "I need to know, Ana-Maria." Perhaps desperation seeped through my voice, because Ana-Maria's eyes flickered up to meet mine, fear welling up in them. I steadied myself and quietly released the breath I was holding. "Please." I had hoped the adjustment to my tone would be less startling as I took her hands in mine and squeezed them coaxingly.

She peered at me suspiciously for a moment. The carriage halted in front of her home and we sat in stillness. "It has been noticed that your husband has some strange routines, which has led to some talk."

"Such as?" I didn't mean to dominate her natural timid demeanor, but I had to know.

"He is rarely seen, if ever, eating in front of others. He keeps strange hours, he mostly keeps to himself, or those closest to him. His presence itself unsettles many people, making them nervous. What's more is that there have been whispers of sightings of his father, who died almost twenty years ago. People say his father rises from the grave to feed on the blood of the living—a *strigoi*. Therefore, making his son, the Voivode, a *moroi*."

"What is a *moroi*?" I asked, my voice reduced to a whisper.

"A *moroi* is the offspring of a *strigoi*, a being that wanders the earth feeding off the life source energy of the living."

"You are cruel," I snarled as an uncontrollable heat spread across my body, starting with my cheeks. "You and everyone else that spread these ugly rumors are cruel. There is no such thing, these are all just terrible stories and falsehoods spread to tarnish my name and my family."

Ana-Maria recoiled but did not take her gaze off of me. "You have seen something. What have you seen?" she asked, her voice low, her eyes knowing.

"Get out!" I cried in an outburst. "Get out! Now! Take your ghoulish stories and get out of my sight."

Ana-Maria scrambled out of the carriage silently, regarding me suspiciously. Her gaze was laced with fear. I
was not prone to outbursts such as this, but I had heard
enough—fantastical stories of fictional beings walking the
earth and feeding off the living—it was too much and made
me swiftly defensive, paranoid, and frightened. I felt as
though I had plummeted into a den of wolves and there was
no escape as they whispered about me, used me for their own
benefit, and laughed behind my back. Even though I had bid
Ana-Maria to tell me, I felt as though she was one of them in
that moment, a wolf in sheep's clothing.

I tapped on the roof of the carriage, bidding the driver
to carry on, and we lurched forward. I didn't even care if
Ana-Maria stood there, watching with her mouth agape as
the carriage sped off, coating her in dust. I was just eager
to get back to Helene, where I felt safe in her presence—her
solid, maternal presence that would see the utter nonsense
in these ghoulish stories.

Ana-Maria knew, though. She knew better, as she had
asked me what I had seen.

I saw him that night. The night I had danced like a cour-
tesan, a harlot, like one of the *iele*. He was there, glaring back
at me, his face among the crowd; a face that should have
been old, but instead was youthful. My rage wasn't, in truth,
rage, but fear in the guise of rage. It was far easier to rage
at Ana-Maria than be frightened at what she offered—the
reality that what I saw wasn't merely a manifestation of my
anxieties. The reality that I had truly seen him, risen from the
grave—the reality that ultimately went against God Himself.

"I will escort her from here," Helene said, dismissing the guards who always escorted me to every place from which I came and went. It was late, but she had waited up for me loyally, as she always did. The house was quiet; the servants had long since gone to bed, and only the guards, scattered at their various posts throughout the grounds and first floor, were awake. Helene led me from the foyer up to our quarters, holding a candelabra which softly illuminated the familiar cream-colored walls and dark-colored wood floors around us.

"Was there anything noteworthy about tonight's banquet at the mayor's house?" she asked me.

"No," I told her, deciding to keep the truth from her for now as I was exhausted. "I am quite weary of banquets and social gatherings, Helene. If there are any that come forward, please reject them right away. I need a rest." I would tell her the truth in the morning, about the silly rumors swirling about the prince and me. We would have a good laugh about these ridiculous stories over breakfast, and I would use the light of day to banish any shadows that had come with them.

"I will do so, Your Highness," she replied. "I think time away from them will be good for your health. Not to mention, such indulgent eating will only expand one's waistline—"

"Helene! What is that?" I interrupted. Something on the floor down the corridor near my bedchamber made me stop dead in my tracks, clutching at Helene's sleeve.

She saw it almost immediately, too. The wall sconces flickered dimly making it difficult to make out exactly what it was. It looked like a heap of laundry on the floor.

Helene and I approached slowly with the intention of getting a better look with the light of her candelabra. A pale hand extended out, feminine fingers with short nails curled around the palm, and we followed the sleeve to see the form of Ioana lying there, her face turned away. Her hair had come loose from her braids and lay partially sprawled out on the floor around her, covering most of her face.

"Ioana?" Helene called softly. "Here, hold onto this for a moment and lower the light so I can see. I hope she is not ill." She passed me the candelabra and knelt to help Ioana up as I crouched down to give her better light. It was then that I noticed Helene was kneeling in something, but at the same moment, Ioana's head lolled back as Helene attempted to lift her onto her lap.

Her neck became exposed and, by the light of the candelabra, revealed a hideous gash across her throat, the open flaps of skin arranged in what looked like a macabre, sardonic grin.

Helene was kneeling in a pool of Ioana's blood.

XX

THE FULL MOON HUNG high in the sky. Its beams came flooding in through the windows, bathing me in bright light as I sat on the windowsill of my room staring up at it, dumbfounded. I was lost to the moment as I tried to comprehend what had happened. In the distance, I thought I heard the faint howl of a wolf crying out for its pack, but it sounded so far away, it could have been merely the howling of the wind. The sound pulled me from my state of shock that had carried me far away from the chamber I was in, far away from myself.

At the realization of what we had stumbled across, Helene screeched a bloodcurdling scream and I lurched back, nearly dropping the candelabra. We remained frozen in utter terror until we were surrounded by the sounds of boots trudging up the steps. The guards swarmed in at nearly a moment's notice and one would have thought they were coming to arrest us, but no, we only had the misfortune of discovering the horror.

"What is it?" Prince Vlad appeared among the guards surrounding us, coming to my side to assess what had happened. With gentle hands, he removed the candelabra from my grip and leaned in towards Helene. With one arm, he assisted her to her feet. Then, after taking in the scene, he barked orders at the guards. To my ears, though, he sounded far away as my mind receded elsewhere, my eyes fixed on the gore in front of me. He guided Helene into my arms as the guards shuffled to do his bidding, waking up the servants to assist Helene and me as well as scouring the castle to make sure the perpetrator didn't escape. Prince Vlad turned his attention back to the slain Ioana and it was then I saw that it wasn't only her throat that had been slashed, but also from her abdomen to her chest, which seemed deflated. It was difficult to fully make out the extent of the carnage, but I did not wish to see. Instead, my mind snapped back. I guided Helene, who was shaking uncontrollably and covered in Ioana's blood, away.

From that moment on, the rest of the evening was a blur entrenched in chaos. Servants came with a bath for Helene, who I had helped out of her bloodstained clothes all while still in my own finery from the evening's banquet. I did not mind, though. After all the times she had done the same for me, it was the least I could do. The house thundered and clashed with the sounds of guards rushing through the halls, servants hurrying about, and voices calling out to one another. Helene and I remained in my chamber after it had been cleared and a fire had been stoked in the fireplace. We said very little as Helene, who was washed and clean by now, undressed me, her hands tremoring all the while. I insisted that she stop, but she was persistent. I believe it calmed her somewhat to have a task to do. Once she was done, she took a seat by the fire, staring into it while I remained by the window, bathed in the light of the full moon. Below, the guards' torches flickered as they surrounded the grounds, searching for Ioana's murderer.

Both of us jumped at the sound of the gentle rap at the door. Before I could answer, Prince Vlad had appeared in the doorway, and I noticed his sword tied at his hip though he wasn't fully dressed, appearing only in a loose linen shirt, trousers, and boots.

"I am sorry to have frightened you," he said, closing the door behind him. "So far, we have not found who committed this atrocity—they may have escaped. The maidservant's body has been removed and will be returned to her family for burial. Then, there will be an inquiry for the incident. I will send for the mayor first thing in the morning and confer with him, and we will have a third-party official come to investigate. Once the murderer is apprehended and charges are brought forth, we will issue adequate justice. In the meantime, twice the amount of guards will remain posted on every floor until he is caught."

I eyed him harshly from where I sat, looking for any signs that he mourned her. As usual, though, his demeanor remained inscrutable. Reading his thoughts was impossible, making me wonder if perhaps it was *him* who had done it. Perhaps in a jealous rage after finding out she had taken on another lover? Bloodlust ran in his family after all.

"What serves as 'adequate justice' for such a gruesome murder? Impalement?" I challenged him impetuously, snapping out of my trance of shock, confusion, and horror.

His eyebrow shot up at this remark. *Finally,* I had gotten a reaction out of him, penetrating that infuriating enigmatic expression of his that he almost always wore. It was also the first time I had alluded to his father while speaking with him. "It is apparent that you have been spending quite a bit of time with the boyars," he replied, "maybe a bit *too* much time. Execution may be warranted, however, it depends on the nature of the investigation. Time will tell."

"Depending on if it was a member of the upper class that killed her, you mean?" I shot back. I met his eyes levelly, my heart pounding furiously in my chest. Helene remained seated near the fireplace resembling a skittish animal as she trembled, despite being very close to the heat of the fire.

"Yes," he replied unflinchingly. "Nothing has been taken from the castle that we can discern so far. All of the servants will be questioned during the inquisition."

"Had there been an adequate number of guards, this would not have happened to begin with. You have always been incredibly negligent about having an adequate number posted. Instead, they meander the grounds playing cards and carousing when they should be guarding every corner of this castle. My father was never so negligent. In the imperial palace, there were guards—"

"This is *not* the imperial palace," Prince Vlad interjected impatiently.

"That's *quite* clear, isn't it?" I shot back coldly.

"Your Highness," he continued, "I am not the enemy here—"

"That remains to be seen." Our eyes met and the blood rushed through my veins in heated anger. The scene from the night I saw Ioana in his arms kindled freshly in my memory.

We stood like this for what seemed an eternity, each waiting for the other to break the tension by submitting.

"I will keep you apprised of the investigation," he finally said in a dangerously quiet voice, moving towards the door and seeing himself out. The sounds of his boots fell away as he moved down the corridor.

"You believe it was him?" Helene asked from behind me, her voice tugging me away from my thoughts and bringing me back to the room. It was the first time she had spoken since we had found Ioana.

I sighed, releasing the tension that had gathered in my chest. "I don't know. Possibly. I caught them together that one night near his chambers, she was in his arms and the scene was... well..." I sighed once more. "Don't you remember?"

"Yes. What benefit would he have in killing her though?" Her ability to return to her logical self was a bit surprising, catching me completely off guard.

"She took on another lover and he killed her in a jealous rage, perhaps?"

Helene shook her head slowly, wearily. "No. I do not believe so. This place may be wild compared to that of Austria, but the prince is not above the law, not here. You know how precarious his throne is. His uncle was the longest voivode in recent history after the crown being thrown from one voivode to another. His own father reigned for barely six years."

"How do you know this?"

"Avram told me. No, the prince may take on lovers and they may bear his children but he is not so careless to kill one in a jealous rage. The prince has yet to display such volatility." Her voice was coated with weariness. No, perhaps not.

Helene was right. Something told me that the boyars would not tolerate another blood-hungry voivode after experiencing such a long tenure of peace.

"Come, you are exhausted," I said, reaching for her and helping her onto her feet. She allowed me to do so and I escorted her to my bed, our roles reversed as I tucked the bedcovers around her. Neither of us felt compelled to sleep alone, though I wasn't sure I would be sleeping at all. Guards were posted outside of my door, so I knew I would be safe, but settling into bed beside Helene, I did not feel safe. I laid awake feeling poorly for what I had said to the Voivode, feeling as though I had been unnecessarily cruel. I was so certain that he was guilty in Ioana's death, but even in these moments of tragedy, Helene's logic remained steadfast, and I came to terms that she was most likely right.

If it was not him, though, then who?

Helene succumbed to sleep rather swiftly, eager to escape the night's events, I'm sure, whereas I could not. I laid in this frustrating state of wakefulness for at least an hour—perhaps more—time ebbing away from me. Very slowly, to avoid disturbing her, I pulled back the bedcovers and flung my feet over the side of the bed. I threw my shawl over my shoulders, shivering despite its immediate warmth, and stepped out of the room.

"Your Highness," I heard a voice softly beside me. One of the two guards posted at my door faced me. "The Voivode requested that you remain inside your room for your safety," he continued, "and that you most certainly do not go anywhere unescorted."

"Is the Voivode still awake?" I asked.

"I do not know, Your Highness."

"Will you escort me to his chamber?"

He thought for a moment, but then he could not refuse me, seeing no reason as to why I should be kept away from my husband. "Very well, Your Highness."

"Just one of you. I need the other to remain and make sure my handmaid is protected," I told them.

The one who spoke escorted me through the hallways up to the floor above us. The silence that curled around us was eerie considering what had happened only hours before. Torches remained lit throughout the halls as the darkness was now unsafe. The murderer could still be lurking within, though it would be entirely stupid to remain in the house with everyone on high alert.

I could see light coming from under the door of the Voivode's chamber. He was still awake. No guards posted outside of his own door. The guard rapped on it for me and his voice called from within.

"Enter."

The guard opened the door and stepped aside, allowing me to cross the threshold. This was the first time I had stepped into the Voivode's chamber. The first thing I noticed was heavy maroon drapes covering the windows, keeping the room dim with the exception of the candles that remained lit. Otherwise, the room was decorated minimally. There was a Turkish rug covering the wooden floor. I wondered if he had plundered the rug in his conquests with the Turks. On the left side of the room was his four-poster bed with maroon coverings that matched the windows, which remained undisturbed. I saw him draped over a large desk on the opposite side of the room. The desk was scattered with papers, and currently he was bent over the desk writing a letter.

Upon my entry, he glanced up from his writing. "Good evening."

The guard closed the door behind me, leaving me in the Voivode's safekeeping. There was no turning back, though I began to feel maybe I should not have come. This setting was too intimate, making me feel uneasy. Wearing only my nightgown and slippers with a shawl draped around me, I might as well have been standing before him naked, a thought that made my cheeks burn.

"Good evening," I replied, forcing those thoughts away and clasping the shawl tighter around me.

"Please, take a seat," he said, indicating to the chairs that sat opposite his desk on the other side of the room, near the door. "I need to finish this correspondence and I will be with you shortly."

I did so and waited in uncomfortable silence, the only sound filling the air being the scratching of his quill.

"I am composing a letter to the mayor," he said, finally, when he concluded, "bidding him to make time for a meeting with me tomorrow morning so we may discuss this evening's events. This will be dispatched shortly after dawn. It will be best to begin the work on this matter sooner rather than later. What is it I can do for you?"

"I came to offer my apologies," I said, pushing through my pride that was blended with nervousness. "I was unnecessarily cruel to you earlier and it was unacceptable."

Prince Vlad leaned back in his plain wooden chair and regarded me for a moment. A long moment. "I have long since come to terms that this is how it is going to be between us, this strange fencing that we seem to do. I do not expect you to particularly like me, nor do I require it. What I do ask is that you trust me and at least maintain a basic level of respect.

Is that something you can do so that we can maintain some semblance of a tolerable marriage?"

I was flooded with an unexpected sense of injury. "Do you find our marriage intolerable, My Lord?" I asked, then wondered why I had. Wasn't I content with the distance between us? Isn't that what I had wanted? But on the other hand, I didn't think it was intolerable—that I was intolerable.

He stared at me again in thought. "No, I do not. I think it has potential. Especially when we have such pleasant times as we did horse riding or even that night in the solar. But then we fall into moments as we did again tonight. These moments where your mistrust in me takes hold and you combat me. What is it that makes you distrust me so?"

I bit my lip lest I say something I would later regret. Did I dare tell him about the book my sister had placed in my belongings? Did I tell him that I knew what a monster his father was and that I worried he was exactly the same? Should I be so bold as to mention the rumors being spread about him?

Fortunately, I did not have to. He spared me from having to do so. I must have taken too long to answer because he said, "Very well, you do not have to answer. Mistrust me if you feel you must. All I ask is that we at least stop with these games. Perhaps that is how it is done in the courts of Austria, some strange display of courtly etiquette and flirtation, but I do not care to have that here. I have neither the time nor the patience." He reached for the letter he had written to the mayor and began to seal it with his wax seal.

"Why is it that you don't visit my bedchamber?" I blurted before I could stop myself. It was only a matter of time before I said something I would regret. This was the worst thing I could have said—it was as if my mind had completely shut off and I ceased thinking entirely, overcome by all the whispering I had caught wind of over the last several months. How utterly foolish.

He stopped what he was doing and stared at me once more. My cheeks burned with embarrassment. "People are beginning to talk," I continued in an attempt to recover, "questioning why there is no heir. Even my own family is beginning to question it in the correspondence I receive from them."

"Is that what this is about?" he asked, his eyebrow raising in what I assumed to be vexation.

I didn't know how to recover from this exceedingly embarrassing moment. Instead, my throat tightened and I gaped stupidly, like a mouse in the pantry caught unawares.

He sighed and ran his hand across his forehead, rubbing it. It was the first time I had seen such an open display of exasperation from him. "You *have* been spending too much time with the boyars," he muttered, though it was clearly to himself and not actually to me. "It is a fair thing to be curious about, especially coming from the family that you do. In fact, your father has written to me about it himself, lecturing me about the lack of an heir, so I am not altogether shocked that this has come up. It was really only a matter of time."

He paused again, gathering his thoughts. "As I explained to your father, things are different here. Heirs do not need to be produced from a marriage, any blood relative can be a direct heir whether it be a child of a mistress, a nephew, a cousin. There is no urgency here as there is in the West. My uncle was not my grandfather's legitimate child, he was born from his mistress and before that, my grandfather was an illegitimate son. That being said, it is best that an heir be a legitimate child of the voivode, it is the strongest claim. Any child of ours *would* have the strongest claim with the

Holy Roman Emperor's blood in his veins. On the other hand, contrary to popular belief, I am not a deviant. I do not enjoy the act of forcing myself on any woman, even if she is my wife."

Silence filled the air once more. I was a bit stunned by what I was hearing. Never before had I heard of a man unwilling to go to any means to conceive an heir, whether his wife wanted to perform the marriage act or not. It was unheard of. Even the most unhappy of marriages produced heirs, my grandparents being an example of that, their strained union having produced several.

"I understand the hypocrisy of what I am saying," he continued, "considering I came to you on our wedding night, but that was only out of necessity. I could not have your father actively seeking an annulment, especially considering he has more influence with the Pope than I."

"Is it not a necessity to conceive an heir?"

"Yes, but again, it doesn't necessarily have to be the product of a marriage," he indicated again. "Bastards do just as well here."

He was not returning the cruelty I had displayed earlier, he was very matter-of-fact in his demeanor, but I still felt wounded by his words. The only purpose I served for him was a tie to the Holy Roman Emperor. That was it. He didn't even need me to produce an heir. I had no other purpose. The comprehension of it took the form of a weight crushing my chest, making my breathing turn into a great effort.

"Your Highness," he continued, his tone softening, "it is clear you do not wish to have me in your bed. I do not say that to cajole my way in, to manipulate you into doing something you do not want to, I merely point out the truth. So, out of respect for your person and to honor your wishes, I stay away. Does that answer your question?"

"It does."

"Good. I'm afraid the boyars' wives are just going to have to continue to talk. I am certain you have the fortitude to withstand it as I strongly assume that gossip ran just as rampant at the imperial court of Austria as it does here. Therefore, it is something you are used to. Now, is there anything else I can help you with? I have much to do yet."

"Not at this time."

"Very well. Can we conclude this meeting with an understanding that from here on, we respect each other and grant each other a bit more trust? I will not ask anything else of you."

I could see in his eyes that he was being earnest. I also could not help but notice how vibrant he appeared this evening. His skin had lost some of his usual pallor, a bit flush with health and vitality. His eyes were alert and keen and his hair shone in the light of the candles, even the reddish undertones that normally couldn't be seen unless it was bright out.

"I am willing," I replied finally.

"Excellent. Now, dawn is nearly upon us and you will need to get some sleep." He knocked loudly on his desk a couple of times and the guard who escorted me appeared once again, this time to take me back to my chambers.

XXI

"A<small>ND THAT IS ALL</small> I can tell you for I know nothing else,"
I said, concluding my retelling of what Helene and
I stumbled upon that night to the bushy-browed investigator that the Voivode and mayor hired to investigate Ioana's
murder.

He arrived several days after the murder happened to
speak to Helene and me individually. I met with him in the
solar after I was notified of his arrival and recounted all that
I knew. He listened intently while a scribe who accompanied
him wrote everything I said. Other than the guard who now
escorted me at all times until the murderer was found, there
was no one else in the room since it was deemed best that
there be no one present to potentially sway my telling of
what I had witnessed. Helene was also assigned a guard, and
she would be next to share her version of the story.

"I imagine this has been a devastating experience for you, Your Highness," the investigator said. His mustache was so thick, it was a wonder it did not muffle his words.

"It has not been ideal," I confirmed, not going into detail at how unsettling the castle had been and how I had slept very little since.

"Well, you have given me everything I need, Your Highness. If you would be so kind as to have one of your servants fetch your handmaid, I will get her account next."

I summoned a servant lingering outside of the room and bid that he fetch Helene. I waited until she appeared. Poor thing looked drawn and exhausted. I wished that I could bid Ambassador Ionescu to return as his presence would be a great comfort to her, but he was concluding his negotiations with the Ottomans, which I had heard was an overall success, and he anticipated returning by the end of the month. This was some news that had cheered Helene up a little, but like me, she was eager to get this matter over with. We couldn't rest until the murderer was caught as the air was frigid with fear that the murderer would strike again.

I exited the solar with my guard behind me and was going to make my way back to my chambers when Simon rushed past me. He noticed at the last second that he was in my presence so he halted and dipped into a low bow.

"Your Most Eminent Grace," he said in the silky tone he seemingly reserved just for me.

"Good afternoon, Simon," I replied, gesturing to him to straighten. "It is a nice afternoon at that. Would you care to walk with me?"

"It would be my utmost honor, Your Highness," he replied, all but winking at me.

"Unfortunately for you, we will not be alone. The Voivode has ordered that a guard be with me at all times." I wasn't sure if he caught my initial sarcasm.

"As he should have. Any harm to your person would be devastating. A dreadful business this all is." There was an odd note in his voice that I could not discern.

"Terribly devastating, and I look forward to it being over. These last several days have been difficult." We were met with the sun beaming brightly in the sky over us and all of the trees full and lush with leaves. The blossoms still remained and they greeted us with their pink and purple petals. Everything was so beautiful, it was hard to believe that a murder had occurred here only so recently.

"I have only just heard of what happened," Simon continued as we began to walk across the grounds, my armed guard following a few paces behind us. "The Voivode told me in his study, summoning me to inform me of the situation. However, I knew something was amiss when I arrived as it seemed as if I was suddenly at a prison. The guards were quick to confiscate any weapon I had on my person. Never before have the walls of Bran been so suffocating."

"It does seem to be a prison now," I agreed. "I am not free to leave as I please anymore, and I am constantly followed, as you can see. Not to mention that danger seems to be lurking in every corner now."

"They will find him, Your Highness," Simon said in a tone I had never heard from him before, a tone that was gentle and almost sad. He also slipped into speaking French instead of Romanian, something he rarely, if ever, did. "The Voivode is nothing if not determined."

"I am sure they will," I replied, feeling comfort in my mother's native tongue. "It seems that his capture has become the Voivode's main priority. Anyway, discussing this is not why I have asked you to join me this afternoon."

He halted in his tracks and with a sigh, he lifted his hand to his heart. "Can it be?" he cried. "Can it be that you have come to your senses and wish to declare your elusive love for me?"

"That couldn't be the case, Simon, as you are entirely unlovable," I retorted.

"You wound me, Madame, but I gladly accept any and all of your blows, for even they keep my heart beating as they are from you, the very content of my heart."

"Please, Simon, I need you to be serious with me, just for a moment. Then you can resume your foolery."

He straightened and continued to walk beside me. "As you wish, Your Highness. Now, what is it you wish to ask me?"

"You have known the prince for a long time, isn't that correct? Since you were boys, if I am remembering correctly?"

"You are correct, Your Highness."

"I understand you are his only confidante, the one man he trusts entirely."

"You are correct again, Your Highness."

"So then, please tell me, are there any children of his that I should be aware of? Any potential heirs?"

Simon became uncharacteristically quiet, lowering his gaze to the verdant grass beneath our feet. I was under the impression that he felt himself trapped between a rock and a hard place, between his best companion and his best companion's wife—a place no man ever wanted to be.

"Come now, Simon," I chided him, "I can hardly ever get you to stop talking, and now, the moment I need you to, you refrain from saying a word."

He waited another beat before sighing. "My wife tells me that your childlessness has become a frequent topic at all the banquets the two of you have been attending," he said. I was glad to hear that Simon and Ana-Maria actually spoke to one another, despite the subject matter on which they spoke of. I had always been of the impression that they never spent more than two minutes together—apart from their union that produced a child, I assume. "She has also told me that the two of you had a bit of a falling-out as well."

"Has she told you why?"

"No, she did not reveal that part of the conversation to me."

"It was because I felt she was cruel for telling me the things people have been saying about the Voivode and me. Now, looking back on it, I was the one who was harsh, as it was me who implored her to tell me. However, with everything going on, I have not had the chance to summon her and make amends for my behavior. I do not wish to be left in the dark, as I so often feel that I am, that I am still a stranger to this place, which is why I ask you if the Voivode has any children I should be aware of. Any information you do have will go no further than this."

Simon's russet-colored eyes met mine. "Your eyes are so gray and bright that they almost appear to be like molten silver. I have never seen eyes like that before."

"Please answer the question, Simon. I assure you, I am not setting you up to be ensnared."

"But you already have ensnared me, My Lady." He smirked. "I must say, I think I could get very used to you begging me. If I were to answer your question, what is it that Your Highness would do with such information?" His lips fluttered into a brief smirk, tantalizing me.

While it was meant to be a jest, I found it a formidable question. There was truly not much I could do with the information, really. Had the Voivode sired any children, I would be utterly helpless to do anything about it, especially if he recognized them as his heirs. I blanched, unable to answer his question.

"The Voivode hasn't fathered any children. On this, I swear." His smirk ebbed away and his eyes met mine again, searching for something I could not discern.

"Not even with his first wife?" I ventured further.

Simon's gaze strayed from mine and resumed staring at the grass again. "No, their union did not produce any heirs."

I released the breath I was holding onto. "What happened to her?"

"She died."

"How?"

"She died in childbirth. Neither she nor the son she bore survived."

The next day, I received notice that Ana-Maria had requested an audience with me as soon as possible. Admittedly, I wondered if this was due to Simon's interference after I told him I wished to make amends. Nevertheless, I granted it and agreed to meet with her. She came to me in the afternoon where I had a light lunch prepared in the dining room. The weather had turned, and we were being pelted with heavy rain that bore down on us continuously with unforgiving dark cerulean clouds looming over us.

Ana-Maria's arrival was announced, and she curtsied to me the moment she entered the dining room. I gestured for her to sit.

"I am glad you are here, Ana-Maria," I began right away, eager to make amends. "I am sorry for what transpired between us. I was harsh, especially since you were only doing what I had asked of you."

"Your words are kind, Your Highness, and I too regret my participation in causing you distress, but that is not why I am here," she replied with haste. Her eyes darted nervously in the direction of my guard, who sat nearby on the opposite side of the room. In my desire to rectify our friendship, I did not notice how anguished she looked. Her olive complexion was pale today and her brows were furrowed. Tears were gathering in her eyes.

"Is everything well?" I asked, worried that perhaps she was having complications with the child she carried.

Her eyes darted towards my guard again and she began to speak in a hushed tone. "The child is fine, I am physically fine, but I am distressed. The Voivode has sent Simon away unexpectedly, with little to no notice and indefinitely."

"When?"

"He was informed of this decision yesterday."

"Yesterday?" I had seen Simon the day before and he did not make mention of it. "What was the Voivode's reason for sending him away? And where is he sending him?"

"I don't know—I don't know anything. Simon wouldn't say, only that he was going and he wasn't sure when he was to return. He didn't say where. It isn't unlike Simon to disappear for a few days here and there, but he always returns. This time it does not sound like he is going to, and if he does, it won't be for a long time." Her tears spilled over and she began to openly weep. "I am worried he won't be here in time for the birth of our child. I waited so long for this babe and what if he isn't here for its arrival? What am I to do?"

It was clear to me then that she saw the babe she was carrying as the adhesive of their union, an indication that Simon did have feelings for her, and that its arrival would be the conduit of their familial happiness. Simon did indicate that their marriage was not out of love on his part, but perhaps that had changed, perhaps the arrival of his child had stirred something within him.

"Is he on a diplomatic mission on behalf of the Voivode?" I asked, thinking of Ambassador Ionescu.

"I do not know," she repeated through her tears. "Again, he didn't say, but to me, it seems as though it's an exile."

"An exile? For what? What has Simon done?"

She was sobbing so hard that her words were obstructed by little gasps. "I-I b-b-believe h-he offended h-his M-Majesty s-somehow... B-but I'm n-not sure h-how." I shushed her gently, encouraging her to breathe through her sobbing. I did not tell her that I had an idea as to how Simon might have offended Prince Vlad. I assumed that a man could only tolerate another man declaring his affections for his wife for so long before it became offensive and tedious. Maybe it was for the best.

When her sobs eased, Ana-Maria asked, "Would you be willing to speak with the Voivode on my behalf? Will you try to get him to agree to allow Simon to return in time for the birth of our child?"

I did not think that was an unfair request, so I assured her I would speak to the Voivode on her behalf and see if I could convince him to agree to it. I was not confident in my ability to persuade him of anything, but for the sake of my friend,

I would try. Besides, I owed her a favor after my harshness towards her, especially since she had been so forgiving to look past it immediately.

After her departure, I sent a note to Prince Vlad's manservant to deliver, requesting an audience. It was eventually granted, and the Voivode agreed to meet with me later in the evening. I was playing a somber piece on the harpsichord when he entered.

"Good evening," I said, not taking my eyes away from the keys. This would be the first time I had spoken to him directly since that night in his bedchamber.

"Good evening." He took a seat on the cushioned bench nearest me.

"I hope you are well," I said, in an attempt to meet my end of the agreement we had made that night; the one of respect. Trust was something I still had to work towards, admittedly.

"I am quite well, thank you."

I concluded my piece and sat back on the harpsichord bench so I could see the Voivode better.

"That was a new one," he told me, referring to the piece I had just played. "It's rather somber."

"It is a French song, one I learned a long time ago and haven't played for some time. It is an ode to *Tristan and Isolde*."

"I cannot say that is something I am familiar with."

"It's a story from the West about two lovers—a knight who falls in love with the princess destined to marry his uncle. Eventually she returns the knight's love but is unable to break her marriage contract, so they steal away to be lovers. It used to be very popular, but I suppose it hasn't made its way here as the story originates from England. A bard from my mother's court had come at the request of my step-grandmother, and he composed this song in honor of my parents' marriage, which is how I eventually came by it."

"A bit of a somber piece for a wedding—one would think it would be more suitable for a funerary march."

"It is quite the somber story."

"As pleasant as you play it, I can't imagine this song is why you have summoned me this evening."

"No, I did have a purpose as there is something I would like to discuss with you. Ana-Maria tells me Simon has been sent away. What for?"

His eyes became steely at the question. I sensed his rigidness rather than saw it as he sat perfectly still. "It is a private matter."

"Very well," I replied, knowing full well that he would not say anything further. "I am sure you are aware that Ana-Maria is with child. She asks that Simon be allowed to return in time for the birth. She is still early yet, the child shouldn't be here for another seven months or so, perhaps six at the earliest, should all go well. I would implore you to allow him to return by then on her behalf."

His eyebrow cocked. "It is a bit mystifying that you would request for his return as I would think, out of anyone, you would be thrilled with his absence."

While he was not wrong, I felt I owed a favor to Ana-Maria. "It is for Ana-Maria. She has proven herself a worthy friend—it is the least I can do for her. It is important to her that her husband return for the birth of their child."

He contemplated for a moment before finally agreeing to it. "You may inform Ana-Maria that her request is granted. It makes sense that he at least be present for the birth of his child. I will be sure to issue correspondence informing him that he is to return by then. Once the child is born, however, I will review the matter once more."

"I am sure Ana-Maria will be delighted," I said. "May I tell her where her husband is? She is distraught that she doesn't even know where he is at this time nor where to send correspondence."

"I am not at liberty to say at this time, per his request. Is there anything else you wish to speak to me about?"

"No, that is all."

"Very well. Good evening, then." He rose to his feet and was gone. Perhaps I shouldn't have followed up with that question, it seemed as though perhaps I had pushed my luck.

I glanced over at my guard who sat twisting his dagger in his hands, and met his glance. "Good evening, indeed."

XXII

THE INVESTIGATION INTO IOANA'S murder continued for another couple of weeks when we finally received word
of some news. Her family had long since buried her in a
quiet ceremony in which the Voivode paid for as a courtesy
since she had perished while in our service. We had grown
somewhat more at ease within the castle, as it was assumed
that her murderer had long since fled and so we had nothing
to fear, but the Voivode kept the guards posted, and I was
still required to have one with me at all times. However,
we finally received the news we had been longing for. The
perpetrator had been captured at long last, and we could
finally release our bated breath. Helene and I could finally get
a decent night's sleep, not having to worry about stumbling
into something horrific hiding in the shadows. Not only that,
but Helene could return to her own bedchamber at night, as

we still shared my bed. She had been too unsettled to sleep in her room alone all this time.

It turns out that the murderer was a known thief, a former servant of ours, and he had broken into the castle with the intention of making off with some riches. He confessed that Ioana had tried to stop him and he murdered her. With his confession, he was sentenced to be executed, death by hanging.

I refrained from attending the execution, but the Voivode did attend. This was the first death warrant he had signed off on since becoming voivode, and he felt compelled to see it to the end. Especially because it occurred within our own house, which no doubt had led to numerous whispers and gossip. It was clever of the Voivode to get the mayor involved immediately as well as an outside investigator. The Lord knows we didn't need any implications that we had somehow been complacent in her murder. Internally, I was grateful that the criminal was to be executed by hanging and *not* by impalement. A scaffold was quickly erected in the town square, and from my understanding, the execution drew a large crowd. It was the largest crowd since our wedding and it went soundlessly and without difficulty, which was a relief, and the end to a very challenging chapter. As a result, I was no longer required to have a guard trail my every move, but the increased number of those posted remained so that one could be quickly and easily summoned if necessary.

Ana-Maria had been elated to learn that the Voivode had agreed for Simon to return for the birth of her child. She was content with that and did not ask me to press for his location any further. Nor did she express any disappointment that she would still not know why he was sent away by the

Voivode. It seemed that she did not want to press her fortune by asking more of him.

I was sitting in my study going through correspondence I had received. So far, it was the usual—letters from my family, specifically—but then there was a letter bearing no seal, just a lump of pressed wax. I unsealed it and a little note fell from within. No wonder I did not recognize this seal, it had been opened and resealed to include this little note. I decided on reading the larger letter before turning my attention to the note inside, seeing as that one contained the remnants of what appeared to be a royal seal. The letter read:

Greetings most esteemed Archduchess of Austria, daughter of the Holy Roman Emperor, Princess Consort of Romania, Countess of Hainaut and dearest cousin,

May I offer my extensive congratulations on your recent nuptials, thus adding to your already lengthy list of titles. I am writing to you not only to share my well wishes but to propose a meeting between me and your esteemed self as well as your husband. It has been too long since I have paid heed to my friends in the east and with your somewhat recent marriage, I cannot think of a better event on which to kindle warm relations between ourselves and our nations. Hungary and Romania have long since been intertwined in their histories and with both facing the ongoing Ottoman threat, it would be in our best interest to make a display of our friendly intentions with one another.

I hope that you would consider a meeting of some sort, doing me the honor of moving past the former transgressions I have had with your father. I can assure you that I bear you no ill will for his doings, just as I bear your husband no ill will for the actions of his uncle, who had allowed the armies of Bayezid through his borders to attack my armies as I claimed my Hungarian throne. While modern politics is not lost on me, we are also not beholden to the

actions of the generations before us. Therefore, again, I reiterate
my desire to stage a reception with both you and your husband,
and while customarily the voivodes of Romania have come to
Hungary to pay homage, I am willing to forgo that as a display of
my good intentions. So, whether it be upon my invitation or yours,
I leave that up to you.

I look forward to receiving your response.

Yours truly,

Wladislas, King of Hungary, Bohemia, Dalmatia, Croatia,
Slavonia, Rama, Serbia, Galicia, Lodomeria, Cumania and Bul-
garia, Prince of Silesia and Luxembourg, Margrave of Moravia
and Upper and Lower Lusatia

A letter from King Wladislas, how intriguing. His letter
brought back memories from nearly six years ago now, when
my father entered the conflict to gain the throne of Hungary based on a treaty that was established by my grandfather before him. The matter was settled in the year fourteen hundred and ninety-one with the Peace of Pressburg
Treaty, in which my father agreed to withdraw his troops
on the agreement that Wladislas would renounce his Austrian territories. This treaty was also the finale to the military
conflict between his predecessor and my grandfather, which
had lasted a good portion of my lifetime. These were the
"transgressions" and events he referred to in his letter.

I also found it intriguing that he referred to me as his
"cousin". Yes, we were related, but so distantly that a stan-
dard-sized parchment wouldn't suffice; a much larger one
would be needed just to fit both of our names on the same
family tree. His mother was a very distant cousin of my father's, therefore making us very far-removed cousins. Fascinating that he had thought to reach out to me directly
instead of Prince Vlad, but perhaps it was due to our dis-

tant relations. This was a letter I would have to bring to the Voivode to get his thoughts on the matter. I was not certain of his relationship with the King of Hungary—if he had any—and this was a significant decision that required his input. Especially considering I was not entirely aware of the history between Hungary and Romania and where they stood currently.

I turned my attention to the small note that fell out of the Hungarian king's letter, annoyed that it had been tampered with to accommodate this one, but it was not uncommon for letters to be opened and read numerous times before reaching the hands of the intended recipient. No letter was ever safe. Too bad my father's ingenious postal service had not reached here, thus minimizing the time letters were spent in others' hands due to time efficiency. Perhaps that was something I needed to discuss with the Voivode—extending Father's system here in the East, especially considering I often got his correspondence far beyond the date it was originally written.

The parchment was far less elegant than that of the Hungarian King's note, it was far more coarse, and the penmanship was clearly written in haste as it was homely and filled with spelling errors.

My beautiful princess,

I am writing to you through the help of a friend who had learned to read and write as I did not. I hope that you will do me the kindness to read my final thoughts and words as I am sentenced to die. I saw you on your wedding day and was struck by your beauty. I hope you are full of grace as well as beauty, like our Virgin Lady. I confess to you that I did not kill your maidservant, I am innocent.

I doubt you would remember me but I served in your household, and yes, I was sent away and jailed after stealing some silver, but I swear to you, murder is not among my sins, it was just simple to pin it on me through torture. Trust me when I say that after being tortured, anyone will confess to anything. I know my time here is done, so I do not expect you to intercede on my behalf but I write to you so that you know the truth. Someone must *know the truth. And you, you were always so kind to me.*

Trust no one in your household, except the good lady that came with you. Your life may depend on it. Grace and mercy unto you, Your Highness.

A chill ran down my spine. Then, it was followed by a strange prickling sensation that started on the corners of my face and raced down to my hands. There was no signature on the letter but it was quite obvious from whom the note came. All of those feelings of fearing the shadows lest a murderer spring out from within came flooding back in a torrent.

After mulling over its contents for a minute or so, I stood and went to my bedchamber, where I paced nervously. My mouth grew dry and my throat felt constricted. I did not know what to make of the letter as my palms grew clammy. I wiped them on my skirt as I paced. It was as though the walls were closing in on me. This was a letter that I most definitely would not be bringing to the Voivode, and I needed time to know what to do with the information it contained. I settled on burying it at the bottom of my linen chest where the little brown book was also housed. I would return to it later when the eeriness it had brought with it subsided. Until then, I returned to my study and summoned Helene.

"Helene," I began after she entered. "Did we recently terminate the employment of a servant here due to theft?"

"We have, Your Highness, last month. In fact, he was the man who murdered Ioana, the prisoner the Voivode had executed earlier this week."

"I am aware of the murderer's identity. Why wasn't I notified of his termination?"

"I didn't wish to try Your Highness over such a trivial matter."

"I appreciate all of your work, Helene. You have filled the shoes of my mother, overseeing all aspects of my life for as long as I can remember, but from now on, I wish to be apprised of every matter when it comes to the household. Nothing is to be kept from me, no matter how trivial, do you understand?"

"Yes, Your Highness."

"Where is the Voivode this afternoon?"

"He is currently in his study, madam."

Determined to set aside that matter for now, despite anxiety pooling in the pits of my stomach, I rose and went up to the Voivode's study, taking my letter from the Hungarian King. He permitted me to enter after I knocked on the door. I had been to his study various times before to drop off receipts of purchases I had made over the last several months, especially when I was furnishing the castle. It was definitely less bare than his bedchamber, and the walls were covered with various maps and shelves, some of which contained books, others displaying various daggers he had collected over the years. One was, as I understood, Hungarian, fittingly enough. The other was Turkish, its curved blade and garish hilt drowning in jewels and giving away its identity. Finally, there was one with a golden inlaid hilt that I believe had belonged to his father or grandfather, but I was not certain. My only clue that it belonged to a male member of his family was that it bore the dragon insignia that was carried through the generations of his family, so I assumed it was a family heirloom. The desk in his study was far larger than the one in his bedchamber and it took up the majority of the room, scattered with even more papers than the other one. There seemed to be no end to the flurry of petitions, inquiries, and proposals that had landed on its surface.

At my entry, he leaned back in his elegantly carved wooden chair—this one cushioned—and regarded me. Swallowing any remaining anxiety that had welled up in my throat, being nervous that he was one of the enemies that the mysterious note thrust upon me alluded to, I lifted the letter in my hand to illustrate my purpose in interrupting him this afternoon. "I received a letter from the Hungarian King," I told him, approaching the desk and handing it to him. "I thought it may interest you."

He took it from me and read it silently to himself. Then, he scoffed. "He makes reference to your growing titles but then proceeds to add his numerous ones in his signature, flaunting them in your face—one of which rightfully belongs to your family. More than one, in all probability."

I couldn't help but smirk, my heart still fluttering nervously despite my attempts to stifle it. "I noticed that too. I also found it interesting that he addressed it directly to me instead of writing to you."

"It is not by accident, I am certain," he replied, returning the letter to me. "Perhaps he thought he would get further by contacting you, due to your familial relations. Or, perhaps he thinks you are young and foolish and that he will find it easier to compel you than me. Regardless, he isn't wrong that a meeting would benefit both countries to establish a relationship."

"Didn't you spend some of your childhood there? You are far more familiar with Hungary than I am, so it would have made sense to write directly to you rather than me."

"Yes, it would have, but it seems as though he couldn't surpass an opportunity to add insult to injury to a member of the Habsburg family seeing as the conflict between you happened much more recently."

"I cannot say I am particularly eager to meet him. Would we travel to Hungary then?"

"No, absolutely not. That is another thing he includes in his letter, a reminder of the power Hungarian kings held over voivodes in the past, something he clearly wants me to remember. But given your status and the recent fraught relations with your family, he would not presume you would come to him. We would extend the invitation for him and his queen to come here."

"My Lord, there is no way we could accommodate an imperial entourage here at Bran. We simply do not have the capacity."

He leaned back in his chair and thought for a moment, his elbow resting on the surface of his desk and his fingers absentmindedly curling as he did so. "No, that is true, but we could accommodate him and his party in Târgoviște. You may write to him to extend an invitation to join us there this autumn. This also means that we will have to cut short our stay here at Bran to prepare for his arrival. We will prepare to leave by mid-summer."

"Well, I suppose it is then time to freshen up my Hungarian," I said, relenting at the order in which we would have to leave Bran earlier than scheduled. "I have not touched it since I was a child, I'm sure it's worse than my Romanian."

"It will undoubtedly return quickly to you. There is one more thing I would like to mention before you leave." He stood and extracted a paper from his desk, handing it to me. I perused the contents of the document and saw it was a law that he had signed, raising the tax on imported goods from foreign merchants.

"This is all very well and makes sense," I said. "I should think this would offset the lowered export taxes and port fees you established earlier this year."

"It most assuredly has, surpassing both of those and turning a profit into the treasury," he said. This time a smirk tugged at the corner of his mouth. "All thanks to you. I signed this not long after our wedding and it has certainly paid off, as we have had a flood of Florentine and Milanese merchants cross our borders, providing the noblewomen with textiles and materials so that they may order gowns that resemble yours."

I could not help but meet his smirk with a smile of my own, growing warm at this praise from him. "I have noticed that the women have been emulating my gowns over time. Perhaps it isn't the worst that I spend time among the boyars as long as it continues to fill the treasury."

"Perhaps not," he agreed, taking the document back from me. "Still, remain cautious in their company. While I have installed some of the boyars of my choosing, one can never be too careful."

Still warmed by his praise, my mind flooded with many things at once—some of which were the things Ana-Maria told me the boyars said about him, not regarding our lack of heir but the superstitions, and I wondered if he knew about them too. At that moment, I recognized that I had heard so many things about the Voivode from everyone but him. He had told me very little about himself.

I recalled the note I now had tucked away in my linen chest. Was he one not to be trusted in my household, as the author of that note had alluded to? Was he capable of harming me? He had the blood of Vlad the Impaler in his veins after all. Were there others? If so, who were the others?

All of these questions chilled my spine, making me feel as if something unknown was closing in around me, a phantom enemy that I could neither see nor touch. Like a specter that had been haunting me since the moment I set foot in Romania, a ghost that I had been suspecting but dismissed as a folly of my own head. Perhaps there was truth in the Romanian folklore that Ana-Maria had told me about, or maybe I had an enemy out there that I wasn't aware of.

All I knew now was that I needed to get out of here.

I may have been in danger. At the very least, something was amiss here, but it was clear that I was not getting out of Romania anytime soon due to my marriage. My father would help—Prince Vlad had said it himself, my father had more influence with the Pope than he did. My father could petition on my behalf for an annulment, but he would not offer me refuge without due cause. The Church would also require evidence to grant an annulment, so I had to find out for myself if there was cause or not. The easiest cause for dissolving a marriage through the Church was lack of consummation of said marriage, but that option was out of the question—Prince Vlad had made sure of it. Perhaps with my accrual of sufficient evidence, I could persuade my father that my marriage was not in my best interest, and not in the best interests of his empire, that it was perhaps even dangerous. Then, he could take my case to the Pope and an annulment would be granted. Whether that evidence would be enough, though, I was not sure. I wasn't sure if seeing the face of my husband's dead father would prove anything but my insanity. But perhaps my security, or lack thereof, was grounds enough, or at least a start. After all, a murder had recently occurred in the corridors of this castle—clearly I was not safe. I would have to find something.

Then I could go home and be free.

I had to get out of the shadows and into the light, I had to find out what was going on around me, I had to figure out where to begin to build my case before presenting it to my father.

That was when an idea came to me.

As my desperation closed in around me, determination accompanied it. I bit my lip in an effort to suppress any reluctance that was welling up.

"It is another beautiful day," I pressed onward, getting swept up in my sudden swelling determination, "and you have yet to show me how to use the bow you gifted me on Christmas. Maybe we could take advantage of this afternoon so that I could learn."

I would have to wait to reread the note until tonight. I would mull over where to begin, then, but at least this was a start.

Prince Vlad said nothing at first and I wondered if maybe he was taken aback by my offer. I arranged my features to show willingness to disguise my innermost thoughts as I waited for his reply.

"It's true that I promised to show you how and I have yet to do so. Give me an hour to conclude these items I have been working on, then I will escort you out to the grounds."

"You will be pulling the string back in your dominant hand, so grip the bow in your weaker one, and hold your arm out, slightly bending at the elbow," Prince Vlad instructed me. I took the bow in my left hand and ran my right forefinger along the string.

Yes, it was a warm lovely day, but the sun warming my back began to subside as thick clouds made their way through, obscuring the sun's rays. My attention was pulled away from his instruction as I began to notice the weather turning.

"It will be all right, we will have time for you to shoot at least one arrow should rain come," he assured me, though I hadn't said anything about the turning weather. "Now wrap your left forefinger around the bow as this will balance the arrow to straighten your shot. Line up to the target with your left foot in front of the other, and keep your back straight, twisting your body to keep it aligned with the bow."

He stood behind me, wrapping his arms around me to straighten my hold on the bow and rearranging my posture. His hand covered mine on the bow, and frustratingly, my heart leapt in my breast at his touch. We hadn't been so close to each other since that day I rode on his horse with him. His hips grazed mine as he imitated my posture behind me. He lifted the bow and adjusted it to my eye level.

"Do you see how this helps you keep the bow steady?" he asked softly in my ear.

"Yes," I said a little more breathlessly than I intended. My stomach began to twist in little knots as I tried to maintain focus on his instruction.

"Now, pull the string back, keeping your inner elbow here parallel to the ground. The bow must always remain straight, and you must keep your hand away from your face. Keep the bow pointed at the target and pull the string back as far back as you can to keep it taut. Do not release, however. Dry firing isn't good for the bow. Bring the string slowly back into position instead. Excellent, let's try that again with the arrow."

He guided me on how to place the arrow on the string and we resumed the position with him remaining behind me, his hand still over mine on the bow and his other under finding my right elbow as I pulled the string back with the arrow attached this time. "Point the tip of the arrow so that it lines up with where you want it to land. When you are ready, follow your instinct, and release it, breathing all the while."

It was surprising how steady I was able to keep the string taut even though Prince Vlad was helping me steady the bow. A gust of wind picked up as the ominous gray clouds tinted with blue continued to roll through, entirely blocking out the sun. In the distance, a roll of thunder growled softly.

"It is all right," the Voivode reassured me again. "Stay focused, release it when you are ready." I took a deep breath and on the exhale, I released the arrow, which went soaring, landing in the grass beneath the straw target.

"Well done," he said, releasing me. "Now try again. I will step away this time." He handed me another arrow from the quiver and I placed it exactly as he had shown me. As I released it, I began to feel the pecking of raindrops beginning to drip from the sky and onto my gown. They started off sporadically before picking up in intensity. I glanced over and saw that I had missed the target once again. Then, the rain went from mere pecking to a sudden downfall, and there we were trapped in the middle of it.

The prince moved over to the targets, grabbed the arrows, and he guided me towards the nearest shelter, which was the stables. We rushed under the protective roof, but by this time we were already drenched. We stood without words watching the rain beat relentlessly onto the land below it.

"Once it lets up a little, I will escort you back to the castle." He took the bow from me and slung it over his shoulder along with the quiver.

"It looks like it may be a minute before it does," I said, assessing the damage done to my gown. I was inspecting my sleeve when, in the corner of my eye, I caught him peering at me. "What is it?"

"I was just thinking how very becoming you look covered in rainwater."

I halted my inspection at the realization of what he had just said. It was the first time he had ever complimented my appearance and I wasn't sure how to respond. Out of all the times I had appeared before him in my finest attire, he had complimented me the moment I was certain I resembled a drowned rat.

As I stumbled with my reply, I also noticed how handsome he looked covered in rainwater. The wetness in his hair emphasized the waves framing his face, and his light summer tunic, which was drenched, was pressed against him like a second skin, drawing attention to the lean muscled shapes of his arms and torso. My eyes fell on his lips, which were slightly parted, and the memory of him kissing me during the wedding festivities all that time ago came flooding back to me. There was a small voice in the corners of my mind that told me in that moment that I should like for him to do it again.

"It looks like the rain is letting up a bit," he said quietly. "Come, I'll take you back to the castle before it starts falling heavily again."

XXIII

H ELENE CLUCKED AT THE sight of my gown when I came in from the rain, but she seemed confident that it wasn't completely destroyed. The rain went on the rest of the afternoon and into the evening, accompanied by some thunder and lightning early on. It was still raining as I retreated to the library after dinner, and I was able to start combing through the books that had been collected since I had already written my response to the Hungarian King. Each of the walls were covered with shelves containing books I had brought with me, some purchased after my arrival and some the prince had brought with him. Many had been gifts sent to me as either in welcome or as wedding gifts. The shelves were not completely full, but already there was a sizable collection that had accrued.

It had darkened early, so I was alone in the library with nothing but the illumination from the wall sconces and the gentle beating of the rain on the windows to keep me company. Holding a candelabra in one hand, I combed through the books for anything that might provide me with some insight about the Voivode, Romania's history, folklore, and even, regrettably, about his father. Anything and everything could perhaps be useful for presenting a case to my father to have my marriage annulled.

I crouched in front of the bookcase to peruse the titles on the bottom shelf. The candelabra was in one hand and the other grazed the spines of leather-bound books. Then the sound of footsteps echoed in my ears. Turning, I expected a servant to be bowing behind me, here to let me know that my presence was required somewhere else. But, no one was there. Believing I had been mistaken, I turned my attention back to the spines of the books when the back of my neck began to prickle and I began to feel as though I was being watched.

I turned again. "Is someone there?"

I was met with an eerie silence, so I straightened and moved to the corridor, looking out but finding no one there, only the guard posted, but I doubted he would want to snoop on me. Not long after, the feeling of being watched subsided, and I went back to my search still feeling rather uneasy but determined in my quest.

Luck, so far, was not on my side—everything we possessed were books of romance, poetry, theological texts, and military practices in warfare. I combed through the pages of some of these to see if there was absolutely anything they could provide, particularly the theological and military texts. Any history or other clue might help, but they yielded nothing. After a couple of hours, I set the candelabra down on the table and sat frustrated on the cushioned bench in the middle of the room. So far, there was nothing to help me gain information. I remained where I was, thinking about what I would do next.

I would ask Ana-Maria if she had a library I could peruse. That's where I would start first. Then, my next route would be to contact the monasteries nearby to see if they had any helpful texts. Unfortunately, that would have to wait until the next day at least.

My thoughts were interrupted when I heard a faint flapping noise, a sound I definitely had heard before. Holding very still, I waited to see if I could hear it again, but there was nothing. I stood and went towards the window, looking out into the night. Only the quarter moon hung in the sky, so there was not much light for me to see out into the shadows. I took the candelabra and stepped out into the corridor, listening for the sound again. But there was nothing, only the guard, shifting his weight from one foot to the other in the light of the wall sconces.

I left him standing alone as I went downstairs. I wandered through the two lower floors of the castle, trying to determine if I could hear that sound once more, but again I was met with nothing. Only the occasional acknowledgments from the posted guards or the servants who were tidying up before going to bed. No one else gave the impression that they had heard such a thing, so perhaps it had been the wind. Since my courage was wearing off, I went back upstairs to my floor, knocking on Helene's door for her to come and ready me for bed. She did so, and when she retired to her own room again I threw my cape around my shoulders and stepped out onto the balcony. I probably shouldn't have gone out without shoes because rainwater had seeped onto the wooden floor, making it slick. I stared out into the darkness that enveloped the courtyard, unable to see below, and listened intently for any flapping, but it was silent with the exception of the lazy patter of the rain and the occasional sound of the wind rushing through.

I unbound my hair and let the wind run through it as my thoughts drifted to this afternoon, weary from this evening's fruitless research. Why had I longed for the prince to kiss me at that moment? Was it just sheer lust? I had never had lustful tendencies before, and it had unsettled me, but yet, at the same time, it was oddly thrilling. Then all the thoughts of mistrust and everything else strange between us came streaming back, blending together with the rare but pleasant moments with him, leaving me in a state of confusion.

What was it about this man?

That was a question I still could not seem to answer for myself.

My ears abruptly surged with the sound of rushing air, followed by the flapping noise that I had heard for the third time, but this time it was so loud that it could hardly be from a bird, no matter how large. Surely there wasn't a bird alive whose wingspan made such a noise—it would have to be enormous. Because the sky was coated in deep shadows, I was unable to see where the noise was coming from, but it sounded as though it was coming from right above me. I raced downstairs, determined to try to catch a glimpse of it if I could.

"Your Highness?" A male voice questioned from behind me as I raced past the guards. "Your Highness?" My feet thundered down each staircase with the guards pursuing behind me until I made it to the front door. The guards posted there stared stupidly at me as I barked at them to open it at once. To my irritation, they refused, remarking on the rain, saying it wasn't safe for me to go out there. I turned to travel across the courtyard, then moved blindly through the kitchen and out the side door, through the entrance that the servants used.

Rain doused my hair and cape as I continued running across the sleek grass, my face turned up towards the sky, willing my eyes to find the source of the flapping noise. I could find nothing. I wasn't even sure if I was following in the direction it had been traveling. I had become disoriented in the shadows that enveloped me, and there was no doubt that whatever it was, it had long since gone.

"Your Highness?" came a male voice behind me as I stood under the canopy of the trees. I turned and saw one of the guards standing there, bearing a torch and looking at me curiously as the rain continued to pelt us. My chest heaved for air as it had been some time since I had run like that. "Your Highness," he repeated again, coming towards me. Behind him were a few more guards, all eyeing me reproachfully as if I were a cornered wild animal that might strike at any moment. "Come in from the rain, Your Highness, otherwise you'll catch your death of cold." He came to me, extending his arm. I took it and allowed him to lead me away.

I bolted upright from my trancelike state. I was shaken from this state of being not quite awake but not asleep either by the sensation of my skin crawling. My room was dimly lit with the single thick votive candle I had lit before falling asleep. The nights were warm enough now where I did not have to draw the curtains of my four-poster bed, so they remained open. I could have sworn I was being watched. I remained still, expecting to hear someone else's breath among my own. There was nothing, but the sensation did not go away.

"Who are you?" I whispered. "I know you're there."

Silence was the only thing that responded to me.

I remained like that for another moment or two, waiting for some sort of sound, some sort of movement, but there was nothing. Once I was satisfied I was alone, I sighed and lay back down.

The rain continued into the following day as a lazy drizzle with gray clouds still looming over us, so I waited in the carriage while the guard grasped the iron handle on the door and knocked loudly. The door opened and a maidservant appeared, her eyes rounding as she recognized who had been knocking on the door unannounced. They exchanged words for a moment until the guard returned to me, taking my hand and helping me out of the carriage.

"Your Highness," the maidservant said while she swept into a curtsy as I approached the open door.

"Is the mistress of the house in?" I asked her.

"She is. Please come in out of the rain."

She led me through the foyer and into a pleasant solar where a fire was roaring, keeping the room at a warm temperature. "My mistress tends to be cold now that she is expecting," the maidservant explained as she assisted me in removing my cloak. "Please have a seat. I will announce your arrival to my mistress."

I sat down on one of the arm chairs near the fire and examined the brightly-colored Romanian tapestries hanging on the wall. This was the first time I had entered Simon and Ana-Maria's home in Brașov, and it was a lovely two-story home. The foyer had been rather plain, but this room was coated with bright tapestries exploding with flowers in all sorts of vibrant colors. On the floor was a Romanian rug busy with all sorts of flamboyant patterns resembling flowers and vines. On the far side, opposite the fireplace with the deep mahogany mantle, was a brightly-colored chest coated with red, white, blue, and gold and atop it was a pewter pitcher with matching goblets. An overall visually busy room, but it very much captured Ana-Maria's Romanian heritage.

"Your Highness," came her soft voice as she entered. "What a pleasure it is to have you come by!"

She came to me and I greeted her with an embrace, then she sat across from me, occupying the other armchair.

"I am sorry to arrive without notice," I told her.

"It is no trouble at all, Your Highness. I welcome the company. As you can tell, it is quite quiet here without Simon."

"Have you heard a word from him since his departure?"

"No, not a word."

"Well, hopefully wherever he is, he will find a moment to write to at least let you know that he is all right." My guard had been taken away to dry off and get a tankard of ale, so Ana-Maria and I were quite alone. I leaned in towards her and said, "Ana-Maria, I need to ask you more about those things you were telling me about—those things that you had said the people were discussing."

"The *iele*?"

"No, not them, the other things. The ones that feed off of the living."

"The *strigoi*." She began to look uneasy and reproachful, seeming to think I was going to have another outburst like the last time we discussed such things. I was careful not to move too suddenly or talk too loudly so as to indicate that I was not planning to have another outburst again. I kept a smile fixed on my lips to further emphasize my desire for peace.

"Yes, that. You said that the people have told tales that the Voivode's father was one." She now leaned in closer to me. My smile had long since faltered. "That night, you asked me what I had seen. Do you remember?"

Her voice was merely a murmur. "Yes, I remember."

We leaned in even closer to one another. "I have seen him too," I whispered. "That night, after my wedding, the night I... danced. I saw his face among the crowd, staring back at me. It was his face that caused me to fall. I was so frightened, I fainted." Ana-Maria's mouth fell agape as I revealed to her one of my deepest secrets. "I had seen his face before in a book my sister hid in my belongings before I left Austria. A pamphlet, really, telling the tale about Vlad Dracula. And that is why I have come here today. I need to know more."

She stared dumbfounded at me, little stuttering sounds coming out of her agape mouth. "Are you certain?"

"I believe I am," I said. "I haven't told anyone about this before, but ever since I stepped foot in this country, I have been plagued with strange occurrences—noises, voices, presences, footsteps, the feeling of being watched. They subsided for a little while and I thought it was all a trick of my imagination, a result of my distress from having left my home, my family, of having my whole life upended... but they have since picked up again. Then I received this." I procured the note that I found tucked in the Hungarian King's letter and handed it to Ana-Maria. I paused while she read it. When she finished, I continued. "So now you see? I must know more. There have been too many occurrences now for me to ignore that there's something amiss in my house. Or worse—that I may be in danger."

"I believe you," Ana-Maria said quietly. "Come with me." She stood and led me through her house to a room on the first floor. She knocked quietly on the door, and at the bidding of the occupant, she went in, beckoning me to follow her.

"*Bunica*," she said softly to the old woman sitting by the window in this small bedroom. She was a wrinkled old woman with the whitest hair I had ever seen. I did not know that I had seen a person so old before. Ana-Maria knelt in front of her and clasped her withered, gnarled hands. "*Bunica*," she continued, "the princess is here to see us."

The old woman turned to me and as elderly and decrepit as she appeared, her eyes were as sharp as broken glass as she peered at me. "Come, come closer to me so that I may see you better." Her voice was as dry as sand warming in the sun. I did as she asked, not expecting this woman to rise and curtsy as I was not sure she was even capable of doing so. Ana-Maria moved aside so that her grandmother could appraise me.

"What is it that brings you to me?" the grandmother inquired.

I imitated Ana-Maria and knelt in front of her, a posture that seemed utterly foreign to me. I had never knelt before anyone other than my father.

"She will be able to tell you about the impaler lord," Ana-Maria explained to me. "She was there."

"The impaler lord, you say?" the old woman questioned. "Yes, I remember him. I remember him quite well. It was through his generosity that my husband and I were able to rise in status, loyal to him as we were. You have married his son."

"That's right, I have," I said to her, "and I need you to tell me all that you remember about his father, Vlad Dracula."

"He was brave," she continued. "The bravest man I had ever heard of. He was one of the last crusaders, always in an endless fight with the Ottomans who terrorized us and practically used us as their slaves." She paused to release a barking cough. "We were safe under his reign. No one dared cross him in both fear and reverence to the great lord. He fought until he could fight no more. He was kidnapped and taken prisoner in Hungary, where he remained as the pet of the Hungarian King while his brother sat undeservingly on the throne. There, his son, the Voivode, was born. Finally, he was released. Sent to fight the Turks on the behalf of the Hungarians. He became voivode again for only a month. He was ambushed, betrayed, and assassinated. His headless body was said to have been found by monks, who took it to be buried. His head was supposedly taken to Constantinople where it was impaled on a stake for all to see. That is a lie, I say. The brave lord was not killed. He got away." She began to bark in a coughing fit once again. "He got away."

I stepped back to allow Ana-Maria to tend to her ailing grandmother. The woman's racking coughs continued, rattling her whole body. "He will rise again," she croaked between coughs, "he will rise again to liberate Romania."

"You now understand that my family owes everything to Vlad Dracula," Ana-Maria told me after we had left her grandmother to rest, retreating to the room we had been in before. This time a servant brought us some claret which Ana-Maria and I sipped on together. "As cruel as his methods could be, he was very generous as well. He carried the hearts of the Romanian people."

"It does not make sense, though, from what I have encountered. I was informed that he committed atrocities—great evil to innocent people."

"Where did you hear these things? Vlad Dracula made many enemies, you know. After he died, they spread many evil things about him. That does not necessarily mean they are true."

I withheld telling her more of the details from the little brown book my sister had slipped into my personal effects before I arrived here. I got the sense that perhaps she felt similar towards him as her grandmother did and it would be useless to continue to debate her on the subject. "What else can you tell me, Ana-Maria? How is it that the dead can walk among the living?"

"I cannot say for sure. But the legends say that one *strigoi* can turn someone into one with a blood exchange. The *strigoi* feeds on their blood and they feed on his. Another legend says that a witch can curse someone to become a *strigoi*. Two *strigoi* can mate, and their offspring will be born one as well. Then, finally, it is also said that if a spirit is troubled enough, they can rise from their grave having been transformed into one."

"How does one keep a *strigoi* away?"

"I am not completely certain, but I have heard that a crucifix or a talisman from a witch can keep them away. I have also heard that garlic can. Oh, and holy water."

"On my wedding day," I told her, "a woman managed to escape the crowd. She fell at my feet, and pressed a crucifix into my hand. Did she perhaps have some sort of knowledge about this? About Dracula returning as a *strigoi*?"

"It's possible. There are many who wish for his return, people like my grandmother, but there are also many that fear his return."

"Do you happen to have any literature related to any of this in your library?"

"I am not certain, but if we do, I doubt it would be in our library here, but in our library at Târgoviște. Our book collection here is very small. Although, I do not think there will be a chance you will find anything written on these things, as they tend to be passed down from mouth to mouth through generations. Regardless, you are welcome to my library, both this one and the one in my Târgoviște manor."

"As it turns out, we will be going to Târgoviște earlier than originally scheduled because the Hungarian King is going to be paying us a visit some time this autumn. Therefore, depending on the dates he confirms, we will be leaving for the capital in mid-summer. I hope you will travel there with me, for I need someone to watch over me in a brand new city."

"You know I will. I should be well enough to travel, only just beginning to show, really." Ana-Maria's lips fluttered into a reassuring smile, which began to falter just as quickly as it appeared. "In the meantime, stay out of the shadows, for one never truly knows what lurks within. I will pray for you, Your Highness."

XXIV

I LEFT ANA-MARIA'S HOUSE with a small stack of books and an understanding as to why Prince Vlad was cautious to step foot in Hungary, despite having grown up there. His father had been imprisoned by the Hungarians for what sounded like a vast amount of time. I had also understood there was quite a conflict when it came to public opinion of Vlad Dracula. He was either quite loved or quite hated, depending on who you asked.

After a short duration, the carriage halted again in front of the Church of Saint Mary's. The town was quiet due to the rain, but that did not stop the occasional passersby from stopping and staring at me as I entered the church escorted by my guard. I never tired of the beauty of the church and the smell of incense that overcame me every time I visited. I was about to slip into a pew for a moment of prayer when I heard a familiar voice greet me.

"Your Imperial Highness." Father Căianu was descending the steps of the balcony, his round face lit with delight. We had become friends through my patronage of the church, starting when he had paid me a personal visit a few months back to inform me of the progress my donations had allowed. I had taken to his warm personality right away, feeling him to be a great comfort to me.

"Greetings, Father," I replied, holding out my hand for him to take. "I am glad to find you still here, I was worried perhaps you had already gone home."

"I try to be here as often as I can," he told me, his podgy cheeks holding up his smile. As we were the same height, his sable eyes met mine directly. "What brings you here on this rainy day? Are you here for prayer? Or confession perhaps?"

"I was hoping to speak with you on a private matter. However, confession after our discussion would be appreciated too, if you have the time."

"For you, I always have the time. Come and sit, then we will go to the confessional afterwards." He ushered me into one of the back pews and we sat beside one another. "Now, what did you wish to speak to me about?" He had a high voice for a man but it was pleasant and soothing, not at all irksome.

"First and foremost, I had hoped you would be willing to assist me in retrieving some texts and documentation relating to the history of Romania."

"Our history is so vast, is there any period of time in particular?"

"Yes, as a matter of fact, I am looking for history pertaining to the reigns of the last few voivodes before my husband. I was hoping that on top of the general history, I could find documentation about the country's laws and information about the Voivode's father, Vlad Dracula." I wanted to further ask him about any documentation regarding the Church's stance on plausible reasons for annulment too, but I could not just yet. I could not give myself away just now. "Lastly, I would love anything on Romanian culture and folklore as well."

Father Căianu all but winced at the mention of the word. "I see. Well, I am sure texts containing such information exist. Give me time to collect some material for you, would that be all right? A couple of weeks at most, as I will have to make some inquiries to some colleagues. I will bring to you anything that I discover. However, we may have little fortune finding texts about folklore as those things tend to be passed down in the form of oral tradition through the generations."

"Whatever you can find would be perfect. I know of your love for books and history so it felt natural to come to you, as I was certain you would know where to collect books containing specific topics. Thank you."

"Naturally, I am more than delighted to help you. Besides, I get the chance to scour for more books. Anytime there is a chance to do so, you can always count on me." His face fell grave for a moment. "I must urge caution about the pursuit of certain topics, however, such as folklore. It can lead you down a dark path, spiritually, if you are not careful."

"You have my word that I will remain cautious, Father."

His warm demeanor returned and he took my hand gently, clasping it in both of his in a show of friendship. "Was there anything else I could help you with, Your Highness?"

I looked away to the crucifix that hung at the front of the church, by the chapel. The grimace on poor Christ's face as He hung in agony gave me second thoughts. "No, that would be all, thank you. But there is one more thing." I procured a small bag of coins from my sleeve. "I trust that this would be enough to maintain the utmost secrecy, keeping my request between the two of us."

"Your Highness," Father Căianu gasped at the sight of my bribe. "You always have my confidentiality. Such measures aren't necessary." His eyebrows knitted together for a moment. "But, donations to the church are always welcome."

"Good, then I donate this to the church. Now, I would like to confess if you still have the time."

I traced the map with my finger, trying to summon the locations in my memory that I needed to illustrate my point. "My memory fails me at this time, but I know the first postal route created was from Mechelen to Innsbruck." I indicated where each was on the map of Austria, which had been posted on the wall beside the map of Romania. "The overall structure of this system is to allow the couriers to change horses in order to hasten the speed of sending correspondence or any other information that needs to be spread. They are required to ride at about a league and a half per hour, covering around thirty-seven leagues per day.

"Romania is not the same size as the Holy Roman Empire, so that alone would reduce the costs required for this project, seeing as we would not need nearly a fraction of the number of postal stations. We can impose a monopoly on it as well, making it available to anyone, and further filling the treasury. Most importantly, it would provide security to any and all of our correspondence due to its speed, which would prevent things from falling into the wrong hands—something that I think individuals would definitely be willing to pay money for. However, we would need to hire a postmaster general to oversee the implementation of the project as well as its long-term maintenance."

"An impressive system," Prince Vlad said, leaning up against the edge of his desk in his study, arms folded across his chest.

"I cannot take credit for it, as it was my grandfather's innovation, which my father expanded upon. I know Father only intended for its use within the Empire, but seeing as we are on allied terms with him, it would serve all our interests to set up something similar here. After all, he is extending it further west than Austria. Why not have it in the east as well? With King Wladislas' arrival in the autumn, we can discuss working alongside him on this so he might establish something similar in Hungary as well."

"That is all very well, but what about the security of the postal stations themselves? We also could not advertise the couriers as being employed within the postal service. With the Ottomans constantly crossing our borders, they would undoubtedly seek to raid the postal stations first, potentially causing harm to the couriers, if not outright killing them. It would not serve well to have this information fall into the wrong hands, as you said yourself."

I had not thought of that. Security was becoming a concern once again after we had received word from Ambassador Ionescu. The Ottomans were turning back on the negotiations which they had established, being stubborn about the loss of their annual tribute to which they had grown so accustomed. Much to our disappointment, his return would be delayed. The Voivode had informed him of our intention to travel to Târgoviște early, and so he was to return to us there.

Then the idea struck me. "As far as the security for the courier, I can't speak to that. I haven't thought that far, but for the post stations themselves, they do not have to be advertised as post stations. They can be made to resemble ordinary houses, especially further down south, near the border."

"It *is* an impressive system," Prince Vlad further emphasized, "but it is security that concerns me. Speed is not enough to assure that security, especially if the Ottomans were to catch on. I will have to think about that before making a final decision. Hopefully an idea will come to me about tightening the security of the couriers and the post stations. Not that it is exceptional now, but I would hate for the Turks to learn of these station locations only to set fire to them and so on."

"I understand the problem they pose," I replied. "If there is something I can think of too, I will let you know, though you know better than me as to what they are capable of." I tried to quell the sinking feeling of defeat that was beginning to pool in my belly. If the Voivode did not agree to this system, I was not sure how my petition for an annulment would be delivered safely, swiftly, and secretly to my father's hands once I was ready to provide it to him. I had to be certain the Voivode would not find out my plans.

While we were finishing our discussion, as if on cue, there was a knock on the door. "Enter," the Voivode called out. A servant entered, bowing as soon as the door was opened.

"Your Highness," he said, turning to me with another bow, "Father Căianu has arrived, requesting an audience."

The good father had impeccable timing, for it had been a couple of weeks since I made my request to him. "Escort him to the library, I will meet with him shortly." The servant bowed once again, leaving to do my bidding.

"A visit from the priest," Prince Vlad commented. "Hopefully nothing dire."

"Nothing of the sort," I replied. "I had sent him on an excursion to collect some books for me to borrow. The shelves in our library still have yet to be filled and there was nothing that interested me since I had read everything at least once, with the exception of the books on military tactics in there. Those don't interest me in the very least."

"They don't?" he asked with a hint of mischief. "I am certain you would make an excellent tactician."

"Somehow I doubt that," I replied, amused. "As you saw, I could hardly shoot a bow and arrow."

"It will take time," he said. "Go on then, meet with the priest. Let me know if there is anything interesting in his collection."

Father Căianu was waiting for me in the library, with various volumes already spread out. As always, he was smiling when I entered. He showed me each volume individually, describing them with excitement each time, as if he had made a great discovery. While his excitement was catching, I just hoped they contained what I needed.

"How long may I borrow them? We leave for Târgoviște in a fortnight and will remain there until next summer, perhaps indefinitely, and I would hate to keep the owners waiting for their return."

"'Borrow'? Why, these are gifts, Your Highness, to expand your collection. We cannot have our dear princess ignorant of Romania's rich history and culture!"

"You are too kind, Father. I did not mean for you to go through all of this trouble, but it is a great help to me. Please, the least I can do for all of your trouble is to invite you to join me for lunch this afternoon, which should be served shortly if it is on schedule."

"I would be delighted to accept your invitation, Your Highness."

Father Căianu had long since left. I was pouring through the books and scrolls left behind in the library until late into the night. It took some time before I finally found any mention on the Voivode's father. What I did find confirmed everything that I had heard from Ambassador Ionescu and Ana-Maria's grandmother, and what I had read in that little pamphlet squirreled away by my sister.

The only new information presented to me was that Vlad Dracula had been in the custody of the Turks, imprisoned as a child as the result of being caught alongside his father. His father had offered both of his sons, Dracula and his brother Radu, up as hostages as a measure of good faith of his loyalty to the sultan. He ended up betraying the sultan, and his sons were forced to remain as the Turks' prisoners. After his father was killed, only Dracula was released to serve as voivode under the thumb of the sultan, though this did not end up the case, as Dracula rebelled almost immediately upon taking his throne.

Both Ana-Maria and Father Căianu had also been correct—I could find nothing on Romanian folklore. Once my eyes could no longer focus on the words on the page, I forced myself to retreat to my bedchamber where Helene had fallen asleep on the chair near the fireplace waiting for me to return. I told her she did not need to wait, but she had insisted.

"Helene," I said to her gently, so as not to frighten her. "Helene."

I shook her gently to wake her. Her head lolled, and she groaned, struggling to awaken. Then her head flopped to one side, and in the light of the dying flames I noticed two small, round wounds on her neck, side by side and separated by a small space between. They were not large, but were reddened and swollen. "Helene? Are you all right?" She looked rather pale, and my heart began to race as I shook her with more urgency.

"Your Highness?" she mumbled, finally opening her eyes.

"What is that on your neck?"

She stumbled onto her feet, swaying a bit and going over to the mirror. "I am sure it is nothing," she told me with a yawn. "A spider that bit me while I slept, perhaps."

"I have never seen a spider bite get that red or swollen," I replied skeptically. "Do you feel well? You look pale."

"Other than a bit weary, I feel just fine. Something a good night's sleep will take care of—I'll be perfectly normal in the morning. Let us get you dressed for bed."

XXV

THE NEXT DAY, HELENE was rather groggy, seeming far away and inattentive. When I asked her about it, all she said was that she was merely disappointed at Ambassador Ionescu's delayed return. The wounds on her neck did lessen overnight and by morning they were much less angry, as the swelling had gone down. She insisted they did not hurt, that she barely felt them, and only knew they were there because I had pointed them out. Despite her dismissiveness, the wounds made me uneasy, but I could not force her to attend to them if she did not wish to.

She and I had begun the process of packing for our journey to Târgoviște. It would only be a day and a half journey, but I wished to take many of my things with me, such as my painting supplies, clothes, instruments, and other items I had brought with me from Austria. Yes, I was even taking the harpsichord that the Voivode had gifted me. It was strange to be packing up again so soon. I wasn't keen on undertaking yet another journey, but again, at least it was a much shorter one. Besides, I could tell the Voivode was eager to return. Bran had not allowed him the space he needed for conferences and hearing petitions.

Before my linens chest was swept through, I went to it, to take the little brown book and note from out of their hiding place. I had tucked the note inside of the book, and kept the book near the bottom of the chest. However, when I went in search of them, they were gone.

Heat rushed to my cheeks as panic coursed through me. Had Helene removed the book? If she had, she would have asked me about it, I know she would have as she tended to be very direct with me. No one else was allowed to access my linens—or even my bedchamber, for that matter—other than her. She was adamant that she be the only one to tidy my room, change my bed linens, and handle my gowns.

I did not know what to do.

A thought swept through my panic and I went to the library, shocked to see the Voivode there, flicking through one of the books Father Căianu had gifted me.

Hearing my hurried arrival, he turned to look at me. "I see you are reading up on Romania's history and laws," he commented. His facial features shifted at the sight of mine. "Is everything all right? You look flushed."

I could not read his expression. Was he being contemptuous? Was he taunting me? After all, he had the ability to comb through any chest, wardrobe, or chamber that he wanted. Did he know anything? I could not tell any of it. I could barely hear him over my heart pounding in my ears. "Helene and I are packing, and I thought I left something behind that I wanted to take with me to Târgoviște," I said weakly. "I can see that I was mistaken."

"What was it? Perhaps I can keep an eye out for it."

"A-a letter from my sister," I stammered. "It is no matter." I turned on my heel and left, hurrying away as quickly as possible, as I was certain he could read my thoughts and that he knew what I had been hiding all this time. I thought I was being careful, but clearly, I wasn't.

For our remaining time at Bran, my paranoia grew. I felt that I was being watched, so I refrained from drawing any attention to myself by continuing my research. Fortunately, I hadn't begun to write my letter to my father regarding my desire for an annulment just yet. I felt it was safest to wait until I had all the information. A letter could be easily found, just as the letter from the executed thief and little brown book had been.

Instead, in order to detract any attention away from what I had been planning, I wrote letters to scholars and artists from all over Europe, inviting them to join our court in Târgoviște where I would serve as their patroness. I anticipated rejection as scholars, musicians, and artists would most likely rather try their hand in the more opportunistic courts of Florence, Venice, Castile, and so on, but I was determined to apply my father's practices of a well-rounded, scholarly, and artistic court of my own for as long as I had to remain in this country. All of Europe trembled with this growing renaissance, and I was not going to be left behind.

The day finally came for us to depart. I never did end up finding the letter and little brown book, much to my anxiety-ridden discomfort. The wagons were packed and the guards were ready to escort us. A small group had been sent ahead to make sure that our journey was clear and safe of bandits or Ottomans. Helene and Ana-Maria were tucked away into the carriage and I was the last to be assisted inside. As I stepped up, I recalled the tediously long journey from Austria to Romania, filling me with dread as it now seemed as if hardly any time had passed since then, although it had nearly been a year since I had departed.

The Voivode was eager as he mounted his horse, looking robust as he exchanged words with some of the men of our entourage—boyars and their families who would be following us to Târgoviște. They threw jests at one another, reminding me of the camaraderie the Voivode had with some of these men. It was odd that Simon was not among them, and I wondered if Prince Vlad missed his closest companion. I sat beside Ana-Maria and adjusted my skirts before glancing at my two ladies. Ana-Maria's gowns had been let out a little as she was finally starting to show. She seemed content and had made little to no mention of Simon since, though I assumed she did miss him. Or perhaps she did not, perhaps she was content with not seeing her husband lust after another woman.

The carriage lurched forward and off we went to the Princely Court of Târgoviște. We kept the carriage windows unsealed to let the warm air in. Helene and Ana-Maria talked quietly amongst themselves while I stared out into the scenery, trying to commit some of it to memory so that I could paint it later.

"Perhaps we should have tied your harpsichord upright so that you could entertain us all throughout the duration of the journey," Prince Vlad said, pulling his stallion up beside us. He was somewhat pale, but that did not detract from his vigor.

I couldn't help but laugh at the idea. "Could you imagine? The princess consort is also a traveling troubadour."

"You could charge a fee," he offered with a grin.

"No one could afford it," I said, still laughing. "You would also have to tie me to the bench so that I don't tip off should the wagon hit a bump in the road." We shared another laugh.

When my laughter died away, we fell silent for a moment. Then he said, "I am sorry for embarrassing you in the library."

"You did not, My Lord."

"Admittedly, I was curious to see what you were spending all of your time on. I was passing by and happened to see the books lying there. I did not realize you were interested in Romania's history, but I suppose I didn't prepare you prior to your arrival here. I should have taken that measure long before you came by sending some items along once our betrothal agreement was sealed."

He said nothing about the little brown book or the note tucked inside of it, nor was I going to bring light to it. I shuddered to think what had happened to it. I had not moved past my anxiety over its whereabouts. "It is no matter. The end of the whole betrothal process was a bit of a whirlwind affair anyhow, there wouldn't have been time for them to get there before I left."

"That is true—once your father was finally open to negotiating, it was a rather rushed affair. On the other hand, I have given further thought on your proposal to extend the postal service here. Once we get to Târgoviște, I would like to get to work on setting up a couple of postal stations between there and Brașov. Anything further south than Târgoviște is too great a risk, but I don't see why we couldn't go along the north of the country."

"Marvelous!" I said, unable to contain my smile. My suspicions that he knew anything about my plans, the little brown book, and the letter from the executed thief began to subside, at least for the moment. Otherwise, why would he agree to approve my postal system?

"I was wondering if you would serve as an advisor on the project. After all, you would be the most familiar with your father's practices. It would make sense for it to be you."

"I absolutely would." My cheeks grew warm at the compliment, and I was slightly taken aback by it. I had not anticipated him asking me to serve his country as anything other than a conduit for an alliance with my father.

"Excellent. Once the ambassador returns, I would like to offer him the postmaster general role, if he is willing. If he is not entirely ready to commit fully to retirement, that is."

In the corner of my eye, I could see Helene whispering something in Ana-Maria's ear. I couldn't hear what she said, but when a grin spread across Ana-Maria's lips, it was clear what they were whispering about. Heat bloomed on my cheeks and I hoped that the Voivode could not see me flush as he coaxed his stallion into a cantor to lead the way. I paid them no further mind as I contained a grin from spreading across my lips. Part of my plan to return home was coming into fruition, and it was thrilling. The faster my request for an annulment made it to Father, the faster I would be able to return home.

"Have you discovered anything further?" Ana-Maria whispered to me. Night had fallen and a camp had been set up for us to rest. We would resume our travels in the morning. The three of us shared a tent—Helene, Ana-Maria, and me. Helene was fast asleep, leaving Ana-Maria and me to whisper.

"Not much," I told her. "I got a little nervous continuing my research, worried about getting caught and questioned."

"I understand. I imagine it is hard to do anything when eyes are on you nearly all the time."

"That note I showed you—someone took it. I could not find it, and was still unable to locate it when we departed."

"Perhaps Helene disposed of it?"

"I had considered that, but she would have questioned me about it. It seems someone else was rifling through my room."

"And the Voivode made no mention of it?"

"He hasn't. I cannot tell if he knows about it or not. It is always difficult to tell what he is thinking. Generally he tells me very little."

"Well, I thought of something I had forgotten to tell you. The *strigoi* tend to prefer the nighttime, growing stronger after the sun sets. They can walk under the sun, but they grow weaker, and their powers are diminished."

"What powers are those, Ana-Maria?"

"It is said that they can turn invisible or turn into mist. They can also shapeshift into creatures of the night—wolves, owls, bats. It is said that they possess strength stronger than any living man."

"While I appreciate this additional information, Ana-Maria, perhaps it could have waited until later, and not when we are completely exposed with a tent as our only shelter in the dark forest in the middle of the night."

✣✣✣

Târgoviște was unlike anything I had encountered yet in Romania. It was louder than Brașov and far more busy—a different pace entirely.

As we traveled through the sprawling and disheveled streets, merchants swarmed the marketplace, weaving through the large square. Yes, Brașov was a merchant town as well, but Târgoviște appeared to mostly be just one large marketplace. It was also clear we had entered the heart of Romania, for the Saxon influences in the architecture that we saw in Brașov had faded. Houses here were more plain—basic, wooden structures without the half-timbered look that was more common in Brașov. Mixed among the plain houses were two-story Byzantine-style homes with their orange, slightly-slanted roofs peering down on the wooden houses below them.

I assumed these belonged to the boyars because they tended to have walls erected around them. Everything seemed far more dusty, too, as there were more dirt roads. It was flatter compared to Brașov, which had been cradled in the mountains, whereas Târgoviște was surrounded by openness. Seeing as it was the Voivode's capital, it was more crowded as well.

The one thing that was a welcome sight to me was that the city sat on the bank of the Ialomița River, which explained the thick humidity enveloping us. As we passed through the town in our carriage, Ana-Maria told me that there were also lakes nearby where fishermen harvested trout.

"My welcome here has been far less warm than when I arrived in Brașov," I remarked as we passed. I noticed how the people cheered loudly for the Voivode, who was at the front of the entourage, and grew quiet as my carriage passed them. They seem to regard me more suspiciously.

"You are a foreigner and a Catholic," Ana-Maria explained, trying to comfort me. "Roman Catholicism is seen as more foreign here, therefore they mistrust it."

"But the Voivode is Catholic."

"Yes, but he is still one of them. His family's conversion to Catholicism was more out of necessity and the people understand that—to them, his heart and soul is still Orthodox. He still provides patronages to the Orthodox monasteries and supports them just as much, if not more, than Catholic ones. Give them time, Your Highness. Romanians can be a distrusting people, especially out here."

"Aren't there Saxons out here as well?" Helene asked.

"Yes, though not as many. Not as many as there used to be."

I could tell I was going to miss the quaint charm of Brașov, and was already longing to go back. But, at least for now, I had to be at peace with the situation.

Our entourage dwindled as the boyars who traveled with us broke off and went to their separate homes. In the northeast part of the city, we finally made it to the castle. It was a fortress, really, surrounded by two thick walls separated by a space for at least two men to walk side by side. Brick and river stone had been used to construct both the walls surrounding the complex as well as the castle itself. We came through the primary entrance—a gate embedded in the thick walls. I wasn't sure what I was expecting, but the castle itself was not terribly impressive. It was rather modest in size and rectangular in shape. From the outside, it appeared to have one, maybe two floors. But the Voivode had been right, as far as I could tell, it did probably hold more room for another royal entourage than Bran Castle. We passed a small and simple chapel as we went through the main gate, and straight ahead, to the north, was a tall tower with a square base that molded into a round pillar forcing its way into the sky. There were other battlements that thrust upwards, but none that could compete with this one. To the west, I noticed a semblance of a garden, but it hadn't been maintained, something that would have to change. We then came to a halt at the entrance.

"I look forward to getting to know the layout of yet another new castle," Helene said dryly. Her neck had long since healed up, giving her no further trouble, and she had resumed her normal no-nonsense self.

"I will do my best to help you. I have only been here once before, but between us, we can work through it," Ana-Maria said optimistically.

Servants came flooding out, both those whom we had brought with us, having left some behind to maintain Bran while we were away, and from out of the castle. I was assisted out first and then Helene and Ana-Maria followed. Helene, with Ana-Maria's help, began to bark orders at the servants, leaving me to feel lost and useless.

"Perhaps we should get out of the way while they get us settled," Prince Vlad suggested, coming up behind me. In that moment, the breeze swept up, taking his hair with it and mussing it, making him look rather roguish. "Care to join me for a walk?"

I gawked at him for a moment, unsure of how to reply. I wanted to stay away from him lest he were to discover something written on my face that I was trying to leave Romania once and for all. But as another gust of breeze swept up, ruffling his hair again... perhaps a brief walk wouldn't hurt. "I wouldn't mind that after having sat in that carriage for so long," I said. "Besides, it will be good to get to know the grounds."

We walked slowly side by side away from the bustle of the servants moving furniture, taking the horses, and so on, walking towards the enormous tower to the north.

"That is Chindia Tower, built about thirty years ago or so," he explained as we came up to it.

"It's impressive," I admitted. And it was. "May we go up?"

Prince Vlad led the way as we climbed an extensive winding staircase that seemed to go on for ages until we got to the top. He guided me out, taking my hand as I carefully avoided tripping over my skirts. Despite myself, I felt my cheeks warm at the cool touch of his hand. I inched towards the edge and looked out, overtaken by the view. The entire city and beyond was visible, the rolling landscapes stretching to the horizon as far as the eye could see. It was breathtaking. From there, I had a better view of the grounds and could see servants leading the horses into the stables. Then outside of the walls, in the east, I could see a small house, which Prince Vlad indicated were the servants' quarters. Twilight was upon us, and thin clouds streaked across the indigo sky. The sun was hanging low, radiating with a pink glow, casting everything in that same hue of pink.

"It's beautiful," I exhaled, the breeze sweeping up more strongly and carrying my breath with it. "I'll have to capture this in a painting, especially while it's warm enough to be up here."

"Any paintings of yours would be a welcome addition to the walls of the castle, as it's in sore need of revisions," Prince Vlad said. "I hadn't lived here long after I was anointed prince, but my uncle occupied it this last decade and his taste is quite outdated. You will see what I mean when we go inside."

As he spoke, I became aware of the proximity—or lack thereof—between us as he stood behind me, also looking out. "Well, perhaps I could work on refurnishing over the next couple of weeks," I said, my voice low and more breathless than I intended.

"Whatever you need to make it feel like home," he replied softly.

I was skeptical it would ever feel like home, but I was willing to try—at least until I was able to leave after the approval of my annulment.

"This is incredible," I said, my eyes surveying the high, brick ceilings that curved out in classic Roman arches.

"It's too decadent," Helene grumbled. "Practically barbaric."

As beautiful as it was, I was inclined to agree with Helene. It didn't seem right to utilize this large bathing space located beneath the castle, as it seemed excessive and immodest. Though, I was in desperate need of a bath, and the servants had gone through the trouble of preparing it for my use.

"It's inspired by the bathing methods that the Turks use," Ana-Maria explained.

"All the more so," Helene said, standing firm. "I thought the Romanians and Ottomans hated one another. Why would they, then, adopt their customs?"

"It's not always that simple, Helene," I told her. "The Romanians and Ottomans have been intertwined for some time, it's natural for there to be some overlap."

As I said, the ceiling was high and rounded, cascading down into curved arches that held the ceiling up. At the center of the room was a sizable octagonal pool of shallow water, probably thigh high at most, and on the sides of the pool were stone benches to rest upon. Torches kept the space illuminated along with elegant floor candelabras. It was getting warm as we stood there assessing it; beads of moisture began to surface on my skin.

"Besides, we might as well since it has been prepared. It's either this or go to bed filthy." Helene grunted at my decision but said nothing as she peeled off my gown and allowed me to step into the pool wearing my bathing shift. The water was pleasant, a perfect temperature as I stepped into it. Helene released a gasp and startled. I glanced up to see Ana-Maria removing all of her clothes, entirely, and wrapping a towel around herself before wading into the pool.

"This is how it is done," she replied meekly under Helene's scrutinizing gaze.

To draw away any further ire directed at Ana-Maria, I peeled my own bathing gown off and followed suit, wrapping a towel around myself as well. Helene cast her eyes heavenward, lips moving silently, murmuring a prayer, then she moved to me, using one of the bowls to pour water over my hair to wash it.

As Helene's fingertips worked on my scalp, I leaned back and closed my eyes. Perhaps the move from Bran wasn't the worst thing as it did not have this feature. Despite the bath scandalizing Helene, I thought I could get used to this quite easily. I wasn't in love with the rest of the castle, admittedly. It seemed cold, as the walls were all made of that same brick and river stone, and the windows were not as big, not casting enough natural light, so torches had to be lit at all times.

The layout was pretty basic, with square chambers laid out perpendicularly, long halls connecting them. The ground floor contained the armory, guards' quarters, bedchambers for guests, and then the main hall. The main hall wasn't terribly impressive, large enough to accommodate about one hundred people in it at a time, perhaps one hundred and twenty. Still, that was larger than our banquet hall at Bran.

The second floor, then, was smaller as the roof narrowed at that point. It allowed room for really only the Voivode and I to have separate chambers, his lying to the southwest and mine east of his. I had my bedchamber, of course, but then I was able to have a solar and a study. The Voivode had a study and bedchamber as well, then another room that contained his own personal armory. There was a library lodged between our quarters, connecting the two to one another. As soon as I was able, I would be in there, combing the shelves for materials I may need to continue the work on my petition to my father.

The area we were in now, the bath, was one part of the extensive underground area. The kitchens were down here, and the ovens were connected to the bathing room in order to heat the room and the pool—rather ingenious in my opinion. Wine and other necessities were also stored down here, as well as prisoner cells. However, the walls were so thick down here that one hardly had to worry about hearing the sounds of the prisoners, if there were any. I did not care to find out. The cellar area was quite extensive and overall very impressive, as each chamber down here was quite roomy.

The castle's furnishings weren't extraordinary, but they were suitable enough, at least for now. Carpets and runners were laid onto the cold stone floors, and tapestries and drapes hung on the walls to keep any chill out during the winter months. Torches lined the walls between the tapestries and drapes, far enough to prevent any unfortunate accidents. There was not much I would have to purchase at this time, for we had plenty of chairs, benches, chests, and so on. The only thing the castle really could have used was some artwork to bring some vibrancy to its drabness.

XXVI

THE NEXT MORNING I was awoken and dressed expediently, as I was expected to join the Voivode in the audience chamber as we welcomed the boyars and officially opened court now that he had returned to Târgoviște with his wife. We were to host a banquet this afternoon, so I dressed in a Milanese gown of cloth-of-gold. The bodice was somewhat low-cut so I paired it with ropes of pearls of varying length, as I always had preferred pearls. The cut of the waist was at my natural waist level, emphasizing its slimness. My hair was wrapped in a coil of matching gold thread with my gold silk netted cap resting on my head. Pearl earrings dangled from my ears to match the ropes of pearls. This dress was one of my most costly, and admittedly, I felt more like an ornament in it than a woman. But that was the intended effect in its design, I was certain—for a royal woman was more of a bauble to be gawked at than a flesh and blood woman to be loved and appreciated.

Helene and Ana-Maria, also dressed in their best, accompanied me down to the first floor, where the Voivode was waiting with a handful of his men. We were to go into the main hall together, hand in hand for ceremonial purposes, to signify that our court was officially opened. The Voivode's eyes fell on me coolly as he assessed my attire. I noticed he was dressed impeccably in a navy knee-length tunic with silver buttons running down the center, cinched with a black leather belt. The belt buckle bore the dragon insignia of his forefathers. Over his tunic he wore a black coat of lighter material meant for the warm season, cuffed tightly at his wrists. He wore his typical black trousers covered with his black leather riding boots. Overall, it was a handsome effect, with the exception of the hat he wore. It was a formfitting cap with a thick brim, which matched the color of his tunic. At the center was the insignia of the dragon once again, but smaller. His cap was similar to the one I had seen his father wear in that little brown book, and it sent a shiver down my spine. All that it lacked were the feathers sprouting from the brooch at the center. However, those caps remained very much in fashion among the boyars.

"I look forward to what happens after their wives catch sight of that gown you are wearing," he told me.

I smiled at him. "That's exactly why I wore it."

He met my smile and lifted his arm to me. I laid mine on top of his and we faced the doors, indicating to the guards that we were ready to enter. The wooden doors opened and the boyars and their families rose as we appeared. All the faces blended together as we passed them making our way towards the dais at the other side of the room. Except one face sprung out at me. I had to contain my gasp of surprise as Ambassador Ionescu beamed brilliantly at me as we passed, extending his goblet in our direction in a silent toast. I did not know that he had returned—he must have come late the night before. I wondered if Helene knew before walking into the great hall. She must have, surely.

We took our seats at the table on the dais and everyone resumed theirs afterwards. Several courses were brought to us—plates containing trout, suckling pig, cheeses, figs, and stews in bowls made of bread. There was a roar of sound as the nobles talked and laughed amongst one another, almost drowning out the musicians who played in the corner. During all of this, I watched the Voivode out of the corner of my eye. He was eating the items laid out for us.

He and I talked quietly amongst ourselves, hesitantly at first, as we were the only two seated at the dais. He pointed out specific people that I hadn't met before and gave me a little information about them, who they were, where they came from, and so on.

When dinner was done, the tables were pushed aside and the benches pushed up against the wall. The musicians began to play louder and dancing commenced. Those who did not wish to dance remained on the benches against the walls, sipping their wine.

It was then that Ambassador Ionescu reappeared, his cheeks bright red from his wine. "Your Highness," he said, addressing me and holding up his goblet, "it's our favorite!"

I laughed, suppressing the urge to throw myself at him for an embrace. "Indeed it is!" I cried, holding my goblet up to him as a toast. We clinked goblets and threw some wine back, laughing. I had forgotten what a delight his presence was. "When did you return?"

"Late last night," he replied. "Those damned Turks finally relented after further negotiations, and I was finally free to return."

"It sounds like you gave them hell," the Voivode interjected, a smirk tugging at the corner of his lips.

"You gave them hell, My Lord, I only did as you asked. They are not pleased at the increased tax rates that have been imposed on their merchants, I will tell you that much. They are not overly fond of not being able to fish near our borders, either, without the large fees they have to pay in order to do so."

"Well, we are no longer their stewards," the Voivode replied coolly, "and it's only fitting that we impose these actions on them—especially when it comes to no longer giving up our boys to serve in their armies."

"I was certain that Bayezid would put up more of a fight than he did."

"It would appear he is a bit distracted with tensions rising between his empire and Poland," Prince Vlad explained. "I received correspondence from King John Albert, asking for assistance should military conflict arise between them again. Their truce has long since expired and I wouldn't be in the least bit surprised if John Albert is preparing for another raid. Bayezid is too occupied to worry about us at the moment."

"I would think having lost his annual tribute from Romania would be enough to warrant a response on his part," I said. "Two thousand ducats a year would only help add to his war chest. War is an expensive business." I knew that all too well from my father, who always seemed to run into financial issues despite being such an impressive ruler.

"That is true," Prince Vlad conceded. "But how many fronts can he fight without entirely exhausting his war chest? He is not only skirmishing with Poland on and off, but Venice too. Right now, Poland serves as the greater threat than we do. Bayezid is certainly not his father, he can only handle so much. This is why it was the perfect time to impose these sanctions on him, while he is in this weakened state. He may turn his attention back to us, but he won't anytime soon. Not with rising tensions between Venice and Poland. "

"Do you think you will honor the Polish King's request, My Lord?" Ambassador Ionescu asked.

"I am not sure," the Voivode answered honestly. "To aid him would be to potentially send Romanian men to their deaths, and I am not willing to risk their lives for a war that is not our own. It would depend on the surety of Poland being victorious. Besides, when the Ottomans do turn their attention back to us, we will need to be ready."

My own attention was pulled away from the Voivode as an odd quietness filled the great hall. The music halted and the voices dipped into whispers, before subsiding entirely. Then I heard a familiar sound—a long drawn out note, dipping into a few rapid ones. I turned and saw that the fiddle player had taken everyone's attention at the center of the great hall. He played a few more low, rich notes, and the crowd of people began to laugh, recalling all too well the last time we had heard this tune.

"Now that's just cruel," Ambassador Ionescu said hotly beside me.

Eyes of the boyars and their wives began to fall on me, and whispering resumed among the occasional bursts of giggling. There was one woman in particular who caught my attention, a redhead I had never seen before, but she was undoubtedly the wife of a nobleman. Which nobleman, I did not know. Something about her demeanor made me think she was behind this, particularly as her hard gaze fell upon me, her lips tight in triumph.

Unexpectedly, the Voivode raised his arm to silence the audacious fiddle player, who wasn't really that good anyway, but I stopped him. "Do not trouble yourself, My Lord," I said, grazing my fingertips along his forearm. "It's not the musician's fault, I am sure he was put up to it. Let them have their amusement at my expense." Ana-Maria's words came flooding back to me. *You are a foreigner...*

Before Prince Vlad could say anything further, I stepped off the dais and made my way to the fiddle player. "Are you going to give us a dance, your Royal Highness?" a male voice called out imprudently. Everyone else whispered while they watched me curiously, snickering uproariously once more at the remark. The redhead's eyes glittered and narrowed, reminding me of a venomous serpent.

The fiddle player halted at my presence and I could tell he was completely unaware of the significance of the piece he was playing, for innocence rounded his eyes. I reached my hands out to him. "May I?"

He lowered his bow and fiddle and handed it sheepishly over to me, slinking away in a low bow afterwards. The silence that fell in the great hall was eerie as I placed the fiddle under my chin and adjusted my posture to support it properly. I lifted the bow and ran it against the strings only to discover it was slightly out of tune. After getting it back in tune within a brief moment or two, I ran the bow again across the strings, sweeping into a high rich note. I swept the bow across to play a few more notes, dipping into lower tones and volleying between them with a dramatic decrescendo until soaring into a crescendo, which then led me to play a triplet of swift notes, my fingers darting quickly across the neck. I continued to speed through a jaunty tune that showcased the dexterity and swiftness of my fingers moving across the neck, going faster and faster, playing far faster than what the actual tempo of the song was. Then, I halted, putting a far more dramatic ending in place. I lifted the bow and fiddle while the room erupted in applause for the musician to take back, which he did, again sheepishly.

Feeling quite haughty, I returned to my place at the dais.

"It appears the princess consort *is* a troubadour," the Voivode commented upon my return, referring to the jest made during our journey here about tying my harpsichord upright on the wagon. I could not tell if he was amused or annoyed—my display was rather common and not one of royalty—but to be truthful, I did not care. It felt too good to take charge of a situation meant to humiliate me, turning it on its head. If anything, it seemed to be successful. They talked excitedly amongst themselves and the music resumed. The redhead disappeared.

"You certainly put them in their place," Ambassador Ionescu observed. "Well done, Your Highness."

"Thank you, Ambassador," I replied, still feeling rather haughty. We picked up another conversation in which the ambassador was telling me about his travels to the border, Helene having joined him at his side. Their arms grazed one another's as they stood side by side, a seemingly innocent gesture to anyone else, but I knew better, knowing that after all this time apart, they longed to be alone. As the ambassador spoke, from the corners of my eyes, I could sense the Voivode's eyes upon me. Not wanting to interrupt the ambassador speaking, I did not meet his gaze, but it was hard to ignore the feeling as my scalp tingled with sensation—a sensation that traveled from my scalp, down my neck, and ending at the center of my waist.

The rest of the evening went by rather uneventfully for the most part, until something captured my attention, making my skin rise in gooseflesh. I was asked to dance by several boyars, most of whom complimented me on my musical skills or boasted of their various accomplishments.

It was during one of these dances that I happened to glance out into the crowd and see *him*.

At first glance, I blinked, wondering if it was a trick of the light, but when he remained there, standing partially obscured by the stone column, I knew it was no trick. I had only a small amount of wine with dinner, so my sight was not tampered with by drink this time. I glanced in the Voivode's direction, wondering if he also saw, but his attention was taken by a group of men who I understood to be his new military captains. My eyes searched the hall to see if there was anyone else, particularly Ana-Maria, but no one appeared to be paying attention. My eyes fell upon him once more.

Our eyes met.

My dancing partner was babbling at me, but I paid no notice to what he was saying, though I kept my steps uninterrupted so as to not draw attention to myself that anything was amiss.

Our gazes held one another and I assessed his long straight nose, the cold cruel moss-colored eyes, the thick brows and mustache, and the long, wavy ebony-colored hair. His eyes held a strange mix of amusement, callousness, and interest. A passing thought of mine wondered what he thought as his eyes beheld me. My heart thumped in my chest, fear rattled in my ribcage, but I would not avert my gaze. The dance ended and I moved away from my partner, who continued to babble incoherent nonsense that I cared little about, and I made my way towards the column.

The impaler prince, shadowed in his cloak, turned on his heel and exited the great hall into the corridor. The doors of the great hall had been left open all night, so he exited without notice. As I passed, some of the women tried to get my attention, complimenting my gown or my hair, but I excused myself from their attentions. I made it out into the hall and saw his cloak wrap around as he turned the corner, moving quite swiftly. I bit my lip and carried on, but now my skin rose in goose pimples again, accompanying my thundering heartbeat.

This was foolish. I wasn't entirely sure what I was walking into. Was I walking straight ahead into danger? Was it too late to turn back now? What was I even doing?

I turned the corner and saw him thunder down the corridor before turning another corner. I increased my pace and turned the corner behind him only to find that he had entirely vanished. I released the held breath burning in my lungs, my chest famished for more air, and waited for my heart to slow. After taking a couple of deep breaths to steady myself, I turned on my heel only to be met with a face in mine, causing me to reel backward and cry out.

XXVII

B EFORE I KNEW IT, I was being propelled back even further,
my cry stifled from the force. My back crashed roughly
into the stone wall, my head jolting back as well, but it was
my back that took the brunt of the impact. I had been turned
slightly to my side so that one of my arms was smashed up
against the wall and the other pinned at my side. Despite my
desperate attempts to get away, I was immobilized by a great
weight.

"Shh, shh," said a voice in my ear. "As much I like hearing
you cry out, this is not the context I would have hoped for."

It was a voice I had not heard in some time, speaking
French softly. "Simon?" I asked, though my mouth was covered by his hand, my voice muffled.

"Indeed, it is." With our faces nearly touching, his eyes
bore into mine, looking black in the dimly lit corridor. His
hair had grown longer and his face was bordered with a

reddish beard. He was rather unkempt, a rather shocking sight as he had always been particular about his looks. Now he looked like a feral madman. Not to mention the odor of stale sweat that he carried with him. "If you promise not to cry out, I will remove my hand. Do you agree?" I nodded vigorously, and he removed his hand. "You are an absolute vision in gold. A golden idol I would gladly worship." His beard parted to reveal a wolfish grin.

"What are you doing here?" I hissed. He removed his hand but did not remove his person, which still had me pinned against the wall. I was well aware of his body pressed against mine, and the fear I had felt earlier was returning but was taking a different shape. My skin began to prickle at the back of my neck.

"I came here to see you, if only to catch a glimpse."

"That's foolish, Simon, and you know it. You have been exiled, you shouldn't be here." The feeling of being a rabbit caught in a wolf's jaws began to grow as I remained pinned between him and the wall as his eyes ravenously searched my face.

"How I have longed to have you in my arms, especially these lonely nights over the last several weeks," he said softly, leaning in closer to my neck as I turned my head away, trying to squirm my way out. "Your face haunts me during the darkest hours of the night. I can't get you out of my mind."

"Simon, that's enough!"

He breathed deeply, inhaling my scent. "I have often wondered how you smell. Just as lovely as I imagined." His lips grazed along my flesh.

I managed to get my hand that was pinned at my side free, and I lifted it to slap him across the face. But just as my palm was going to strike, he caught my wrist, holding it up over my head and pinning it against the wall. His face lowered to my breast as he continued to inhale.

"This is indecent! Think of your wife, pregnant with *your* child!" My fear was heightening, my heart rattling in my chest.

"Yes, she may be carrying my child, but it was you I was thinking of the night the child was conceived."

"Simon, what is the matter with you!"

"I'm a man madly in love and wild with desire." To further illustrate what he meant, his other hand started reaching for my skirts while pressing his hips closer to me. "Surely you must know by now how I worship you, how I love you." His hand successfully entered the folds of my skirts and his fingers caressed my knee towards my outer thigh. I struggled to pull it away from his grasp, but it was futile. I was not strong enough to free myself from him.

"You know I am married, just as you are! We cannot do this! I *will not* do this."

His gaze returned to mine and it was hard, cruel, and black. "Married to a man you know *nothing* about. You do not know him like I do, and you would not like it if you did. He cannot pleasure you like I can—he does not love you like I do." Just then, he lowered his hand, pressing his thumb along my lower lip before slipping it into my mouth entirely. I tore my head away, unable to stifle my gag.

Suddenly, there was a clatter and his hand pulled away from my thigh, dropping my skirts. He cocked his head, listening, reminding me of a dog perking its ears. Voices could be heard in the distance, then giggling. They grew louder. In an instant, Simon pulled away from me and disappeared into the shadows. Immediately, I readjusted my skirts, trying to shake off the disgust crawling up my skin. Upon the onset of more giggling, I turned to see who my liberators were. A guard and a maidservant carrying a tray of emptied goblets turned the corner. At once, they saw me, and the maidservant gasped. Guiltily, they pulled apart as the guard's arm had been slung around her waist, and they each dipped into a bow and curtsy.

Straightening, I said to the maidservant, "You may return to the kitchens." She bobbed again awkwardly still carrying the tray. I turned to the guard. "And you may escort me back to the banquet." I hoped I had been able to regain my composure and not let on to what had just happened to me.

I was able to slip back into the banquet unnoticed. Or almost unnoticed, for when I returned, I felt the sensation of someone's eyes on me. Glancing over, I saw that Prince Vlad was staring at me. Our eyes met and his emerald green eyes were as hard as steel. I did my best to fix my features to be as unreadable as his, but deep inside, I was trembling, wanting nothing more than to flee to the baths to scrub away the shame and disgust that was crawling all over my skin.

XXVIII

ANA-MARIA AND HELENE ESCORTED me to the grand hall the
next day, which had been converted back to its original form as the throne room. The Voivode and some of his
courtiers were already there as I took my place on the throne
beside the prince. He requested that I be at his side as he had
an audience with some of his subjects. They would present
problems, conflicts, requests, and so on, before him for a
couple of hours. This was something not unfamiliar to me,
as I had sat in on audiences before in my father's court. I
settled into my new throne immediately, feeling as though
I had stepped into a gown that fit perfectly and needed no
tailoring.

On my side sat a tangle of women who were to serve as my
ladies-in-waiting. Helene would manage them and would
still be my right-hand woman, but she insisted I needed a
retinue as any other royal woman had, much to my chagrin.

I had a small retinue back in Austria, but since my departure, I had since grown used to having some independence—less busyness in my life—and I enjoyed it. But Helene was right. I needed to have the retinue to reward the men who had since been promoted to various ranks in the Voivode's military, as these ladies were their wives. Having them serve me was a high compliment in their ranks and role within the Voivode's kingdom, therefore I had to relinquish my newfound freedom and relent. I was further dismayed when I glanced at them in passing and saw the redhead among them, her eyes fixed unabashedly on me. I trusted Helene would watch all of them like a hawk, especially the redhead. With his courtiers and my ladies, and with us sitting on our thrones side-by-side, we made the portrait of a proper royal court.

All that was needed now was an heir.

The audience went by quickly as we heard the petitions of the people, which consisted of a property line squabble, an artisan being shorted by his client, a farmer who had lost some of his flock of sheep, and so on. It was fascinating that no matter where you went, people always had the same troubles. Even so, I couldn't help but listen with interest, and it made the time pass rather swiftly. It also served as a distraction to the disgust that had accompanied me all morning after what happened the night before. It further gave me an excuse to avoid meeting the Voivode's gaze, as I was worried that perhaps the stale sweat odor had lingered on my person and he would know that I had been in the arms of another man—even though it was against my will. In the event that Simon's abominable behavior did come to light, it would be Simon's word versus mine, and I was not sure I would be believed. I was a foreigner after all, *not* to be trusted.

When the petitions were over, Prince Vlad left with his retinue which included Ambassador Ionescu. They were to discuss the elements of his return. I retired with my ladies, greatly relieved to further avoid the Voivode.

"When will you and the ambassador be married?" Ana-Maria asked Helene quietly, the three of us huddled together in the solar while the other ladies amused themselves with sewing or playing cards. Ana-Maria leaned back in her chair, looking pale and fanning herself with a fan. I kept my eyes averted from hers in shame after what her husband had attempted the night before. Still, I had noticed that since we arrived she was looking pale and increasingly uncomfortable. She insisted it was nothing—only a combination of the heat and her pregnancy giving her a bit of trouble. Her gowns had been let out in the belly even more so than before, though it mostly appeared as if she had eaten far too much.

"Hopefully soon, with yours and the Voivode's permission," Helene replied, turning to me.

I had to prevent myself from startling as her attention turned to me, being so caught up in my discomfort and disgust in remembering the feeling of Simon's hands on me. "Of course you have my permission—in fact, I insist on it!" I attempted to recover from only half paying attention, not taking my eyes off of the book I had plucked from the library that served as a cover with which to hide my face from them. I had been worried the disgust was as plain on my face as were the words on each page of the book I held.

"Avram has a private audience with the Voivode after their meeting with the other advisors to discuss the matter. Hopefully, he will look upon it favorably."

"I can't imagine he would not," Ana-Maria offered merrily, totally ignorant of her husband's transgressions. "Be-

sides, Her Highness can always intercede on your behalf."
She smiled at me, recalling, no doubt, how I convinced the
Voivode to allow her husband to return from exile to attend
the birth of their child.

I met her smile with a weak one of my own, my stomach
churning. Naturally, I hadn't told her what had happened,
as I wasn't sure I had the courage to do so, especially when
she had been so pale as of late. I would hate to cause her any
distress that could potentially harm her or the baby. Besides,
I still had not quite moved past the disgust lingering on my
skin.

"I can't imagine he would not either," I agreed. From the
corner of my eye, I noticed Ana-Maria wince. I lowered my
book. "Is everything all right?"

"Yes, Your Highness. My mother tells me that aches and
pains can be normal while with child." She winced again as
if to illustrate her mother's point. And I, who knew nothing
about childbirth, could say nothing to refute it, but I did
know how lucky she was to still have her mother's counsel.
I was eager to tell her, however, about who else I had seen
last night, but I couldn't until we were alone. And now the
odds of us being entirely alone were slim with all these new
additions.

"Your mother struggled with aches and pains while carrying you," Helene told me. "She was such an active thing
that it was difficult to get her to slow down and rest." Normally, I craved anecdotes about my mother, but this afternoon I was too distracted to focus on that. I kept playing last
night's events over and over again in my head, eager to tell
Ana-Maria about some of it. Instead, I was surrounded by the
tittering of women speaking rapidly about the new gowns

and shoes they were going to order and who looked the most handsome last night.

"I thought the Voivode looked particularly handsome," said the redhead softly but still loud enough for me to hear. Lacramioara was her name. Her husband, who served mine almost as diligently as Simon—though, one could say he had practically replaced Simon by now—had been promoted to a general.

I wondered why I could not particularly recall seeing her face among those at my wedding, but so many new faces had been thrust at me that night. Perhaps there was a chance we had met already. Though, after having seen her last night, I felt like I would have remembered her, as her red hair was so striking. I paid no attention to her remark, instead making a show of scouring the book in my hands as she played cards with the other ladies. I could feel furtive glances being tossed my way, however. She was beating Ihrini and Bianca—whose husbands had been promoted to captain and lieutenant, respectively—by quite a bit. Elisabeta and Sofia sat at the fireplace, sewing.

I understood quickly that Lacramioara was the leader amongst them and they all looked to her for direction, second only to me. I did not trust her, but again, I was obligated to welcome her and the others with open arms into my retinue, when I truly just preferred the company of Helene and Ana-Maria.

"I thought all the men last night looked particularly handsome," Sofia offered, trying to draw the attention away from Lacramioara's brazen taunt.

"Clearly we have to watch that one," Helene said to me, switching to French, the language these ladies were least likely to understand. German merchants came through Ro-

mania all the time, so there was a chance they could understand that language. Helene spoke French well enough, but it
was halting and thick with our native accent. Having learned
so young, I was able to discard any trace of my native accent.

"It would appear we do," I agreed. "I was told she paid the
fiddler last night to play that song."

"Well, the jest of hers backfired, didn't it? Your lessons
have gone a long way. But who else knows what she may
be planning? She's clearly competing with you." Helene
scowled at her sewing as she spoke. Ana-Maria did not understand us, but I believe she got the impression of what it
was we spoke about—or rather, *who* we spoke about.

I forced myself not to glance her way, to take in her thick,
bright copper-colored hair, her oval face which came to a
delicate point at the chin, and her azure eyes. Lacramioara
was beautiful, very beautiful, and she knew it, for she wore
gowns that were cut just a bit too low, meant to show off her
ample bosom, and wore her hair in styles that were not quite
overtly suggestive but just enough to tantalize. Her beauty
made me feel small, dark, and insignificant next to her, and
it was irksome that it drew out my insecurities once more.
The other ladies paled in comparison to her, especially poor
Ana-Maria who was so plain, yet the dearest to me out of all
of them.

"She may compete all she likes," I replied. "It will get her
nowhere."

"Except perhaps in the Voivode's bed," Helene replied, her
eyes rising from her sewing to meet my gaze, reminding me
that any child that Prince Vlad sired would be considered his
heir.

"There is nothing I can do about that, as you have made so plain numerous times," I snapped back at her. "You have told me time and time again, he may take mistresses."

I knew their ears perked up to try and figure out what we were talking about, but it was obvious they could not understand. Helene evaded continuing the conversation, falling silent and returning to her sewing. I wished that Ana-Maria and I spoke a language that only we could understand, for I wanted to tell her to find a time to meet with me alone.

The time finally came, well into the evening. I had excused Helene, who had received the good news that the Voivode granted his blessing for her to marry the ambassador. She went off so that they could celebrate amongst themselves. I doubted they'd had much time together since his return, so they had earned this time alone. I also excused the other ladies for the evening, and then it was just Ana-Maria and me in my bedchamber, sharing a plate of cheese and bread before bed.

"That is because she was not at your wedding," Ana-Maria said, answering my inquiry as to why I had never seen Lacramioara before. "*She* was hoping to become Prince Vlad's wife, and many thought she would. But then the Voivode turned his attention to finding a foreign royal bride and was she ever furious. Then, coincidentally, she fell ill just before your wedding and was supposedly bedridden for an entire week straight. Whether she was truly ill or it was a fake sickness to prevent her having to attend the wedding, no one truly knows.

"I do not know if there was actually anything between her and the Voivode, but Lacramioara threw herself before him any chance she could get. She even married one of his closest men only to get closer to him, rumors say, shortly after your own wedding. Then, when the rumors started swirling that you were one of the *iele*, that only irked her further. She can't stand when any other woman's beauty is spoken of; she gets wildly jealous."

"Yes, Helene isn't particularly fond of her," I replied, savoring the bread and cheese I had just taken a bite out of. "She's intent on keeping a close eye on her."

"She is wise to," Ana-Maria said, "and if she is keeping a close eye, then I will too. The trick she played on you last night was particularly cruel. It seemed the full moon was bringing the worst out in everyone last night." Ana-Maria leaned back in her chair, her hands absentmindedly on her belly. She was still pale and seemed exhausted. Suddenly, I felt guilty for keeping her from her home and her bed.

"Are you certain you are all right?"

"Yes, like my mother said, pregnancy is different for everyone, though part of me wonders..." she trailed off and stared straight ahead. Then she scoffed and smiled. "It is no matter. Regardless of how uncomfortable I am, I am happy."

"Well, as long as you are up for it, there is something I have been wanting to tell you all day, but I could not get a moment alone with you."

She turned to me, extending her legs out before her. "Go on."

"I saw him again last night."

She suddenly became alert and sat up. "The impaler prince! Where?"

"He was here at the banquet last night. I saw him as I danced, standing by the column nearest the door. He was watching me. I know he was there, my mind was not altered with drink this time. He was standing there as clearly as you are sitting before me."

"And then what?" Her dark eyes nearly glowing.

"I pursued him."

"You what!"

"Pursued him. I followed him down the corridor and around the corner. But when I turned the corner, he was gone. He had simply vanished."

"I don't know if that was very wise, Your Highness. You didn't know what his intentions were, he could very well be trying to harm you."

"Well, I had to find out, didn't I? Who else could I tell that I have seen him? Everyone else would think I have gone positively mad, especially as it seemed that no one else saw him last night. But it seems your grandmother was right, that he would rise again. For twice I have seen him now, though I am not sure why."

"To save Romania."

"Is that not my husband's task?"

Ana-Maria said nothing, instead she lowered her gaze. I lifted my brow at her silence but chose not to pursue what she was thinking. "Perhaps he does see me as a threat then, as do the townspeople here. Perhaps he *does* mean to harm me. If that's the case then what am I to do?"

Ana-Maria tugged at the braid that bound her mousy brown hair as she thought for a moment. "Garlic," she then announced. "*Strigoi* are repelled by garlic. I think it would be wise to have some at your bedside and windowsill. Then, perhaps on your person, if you are able."

"Would that not raise questions?"

"It may, but the alternative would be much worse. You said that woman on your wedding day who fell at your feet pressed a crucifix in your hand, right? Well, keep that at your bedside at all times, as well as your rosary. They are repelled at the sight of anything holy."

"I keep my rosary on me nearly all the time anyway, perhaps that is why he fled from me last night. Do we know for certain that the impaler prince is a *strigoi*? Perhaps he wasn't assassinated after all, perhaps he did get away."

"No, but regardless, it wouldn't hurt to have these things near you in the event that he is. One cannot be too careful."

XXIX

"WHAT DO YOU THINK of these designs for the new coin I am issuing?" the Voivode asked as I sat in his study. We had our audience after breaking our fast this morning, then we had a meeting regarding plans for our postal system that I wanted to implement in Romania. The ambassador enthusiastically agreed to serve as postmaster general, feeling he was not entirely ready for a life in which he had nothing but free time. This would still challenge his mind, he insisted.

It was a relief to hear, as it meant I could proceed with my plans. I now had two accounts that I could present to my father with certainty that my person was in danger—one being my attempted kidnapping by the Ottomans on my journey here, and the other being Simon's molestation attempts. The other things I had experienced since coming here, the seemingly supernatural things, would take a little convincing, still, but I would continue my research for something tangible.

Prince Vlad held out a sheet of parchment to me, and I took it hesitantly. His demeanor was pleasant, giving no indication of knowing what happened the other night with Simon, or even any awareness that Simon had returned. When I took the parchment from him, my fingers grazed his accidentally. They were cool to the touch, unlike my cheeks, which burned instantly at this unintentional intimacy on my part. I raised the parchment to my face, hoping it would disguise any blush, and I saw there were images drawn of enlarged coins, one side bearing the Habsburg eagles and the other side displaying the Drăculești dragon.

I swallowed my embarrassment and instead chose to fixate on how flattered I was that he had asked for my opinion. But I did have a question. "Will the people not think that this insinuates that Romania is now an extension of the Holy Roman Empire?" Despite my attempts, I could not ignore the fluttering in my belly as I recalled his cool touch and I forced myself to focus.

"Perhaps, but that is not necessarily what I had in mind for its design. My intentions are to show that Romania has the support of the Holy Roman Empire should the Ottomans try to invade. It is a symbol of our union, commemorating nearly a year of our marriage."

"We are still some months away from it being a year."

"This is true, but we are closer to a year than not at this point. The people need to be reminded of the Drăculești-Habsburg alliance and what better way to embody it than with a coin? Besides, by the time the designs are finalized and the coin is minted and circulating we will be just about a year since our union."

He was right, considering coins were being passed around all the time and it was a perfect way to signal his newfound, powerful alliance. "When will it be minted?"

"As soon as possible. I was hoping to get your approval on it first." There was a knock at the door signaling Prince Vlad's next meeting and my departure.

His eyes bore into mine, and I got the faintest trace of enthusiasm emitting from him, though I couldn't be sure. Since when did he need my approval? Perhaps he thought of me as a stand-in for my father and whether *he* would approve. "Its design is suitable and it definitely has my approval." I handed the parchment back to him, careful not to graze his hand again.

"Excellent! Then I will request that they begin on them right away." He flashed a smile and I was reminded how incredibly white his teeth were. "You may enter." He bowed to me, and I curtsied to him as his next appointment came shuffling in.

I exited the Voivode's study quickly, determined to rid myself of this feeling in my belly, and saw Helene was still where I had left her, but not Ana-Maria. "Where is Ana-Maria?" I asked.

"I took the liberty of dismissing her," Helene explained, rising to her feet. "She did not look well and I assumed you wouldn't mind."

"No, I do not mind. I hope she is all right."

"She will be fine, Your Highness," she insisted. "She said it herself yesterday—aches and pains are normal with any pregnancy."

Still, something gnawed at me. Perhaps Ana-Maria wasn't entirely all right. "And where are the other ladies?"

Helene cast her eyes heavenward before answering. "They are playing in the baths."

"From whom did they receive permission to enter the royal baths?"

"Lacramioara, it would seem, even though I insisted that they weren't to enter without permission."

"And they did not take your word seriously?"

"It would appear not."

I sighed, my irritation rising. "Very well. Summon them at once to my study, as I wish to speak with them. If they do not come they will be dismissed from my service immediately. I do not care whose wives they are."

Helene curtsied in reply and went to do my bidding. I whisked away to my study, and when I entered, the hairs on the back of my neck began to rise. I stopped for a moment to listen for any movement while my eyes scanned the room.

"Are you there?" I said in a whisper. I was answered only with the sun pouring in through the narrow windows. Cautiously, I moved to sit at my desk though the feeling of being watched did not go away. I took it upon myself to light the candelabra on my desk for a little more light so that I could read the stack of letters waiting for me. It was not long before I was interrupted by a knock at my door. It allowed for a welcome distraction from the feeling of not being alone.

"You may come in."

My ladies shuffled in through the door, their wet hair bound in braids, with Sofia leading them in. Lacramioara was the last to enter. Helene was ushering them in wordlessly, and when they were all lined up before my desk, they curtsied in near synchronization.

Then Bianca blurted out, "Please do not be cross with us, Your Highness! We were only curious, especially since we heard of the marvels that Radu the Handsome built, and we had to see for ourselves!" I realized then that Bianca couldn't have been more than fifteen and the youngest of the lot.

"Radu the Handsome?" I repeated.

"The Voivode's uncle, *Your Highness*," Lacramioara answered, and even though she masked it well, I could sense her smugness at bearing knowledge of something I did not. "He was voivode before his father's brief third reign in the year fourteen hundred and seventy-seven. He was known to be incredibly handsome and indulge in the *most* decadent things."

"Yet another bastard?" I asked, regretting it immediately when her smugness now displayed itself openly with a grin.

"On the contrary, Your Highness, he was legitimate."

"I see." My jaw clenched uncontrollably and I had to force myself to loosen it before continuing. "Regardless, you are not to enter the royal baths without my permission. You are to consider Helene's word second only to my own. Is that understood?"

"Yes, Your Highness," they murmured. Lacramioara's mouth was set in a firm line and her jaw was tight. She clearly did not like being reprimanded like a child.

"Very well. You are dismissed for the day." Helene opened the door for them, and they each filed out wordlessly.

When they were gone, I pressed my fingers to my temples and rubbed. "Is it supposed to be this tedious?"

"I am afraid so, Your Highness."

"I miss our quiet days back at Bran already." Then I remembered that there was a chance we weren't alone. "Helene, I just remembered something I needed to ask you. Could you fetch some garlic from the kitchen and bring it to my bedchamber?"

"Garlic, Your Highness?" Helene asked me incredulously.

"Yes. I know it sounds silly, but it's some ridiculous superstition that Ana-Maria is insisting on. She claims it wards away evil, and with her condition I really don't feel I should be rejecting her insistence. She seems extra on edge lately." I hated how easily the lies slid off my tongue but I had no choice. How was I to explain it all otherwise?

Helene's eyebrow flickered up. "Why now? Why not before?"

"I am not sure. I'm guessing she's having all sorts of revelations now that she is with child. Perhaps she thinks she's an easier target now compared to before."

"I should think a rosary would ward off evil well enough."

"I agree, but I see no harm in indulging her if it makes her happy. At least until the pregnancy is over."

Helene eyed me as if I had lost my mind. "All right, if you say so. But don't be upset and come to me to complain that you smell of garlic."

The bulbs of garlic dutifully waited for me in my chamber, and I did as Ana-Maria instructed by placing them along my windows and keeping a bulb on the table beside my bed, right next to the crucifix. When they were all placed, I sat on my bed and stared at them for a moment before falling into a fit of laughter. How ridiculous this was. What could a bulb of garlic do? But then again, Ana-Maria had insisted, and she knew more about these matters than I did. Oddly though, they gave me some strange sort of comfort. The feelings I had of being watched began to ebb away.

My bedchamber here was far larger than at Bran, with an enormous four-poster bed complete with red velvet curtains and spiraling bedposts. It was not nearly as warm and cozy, though, because of the stone floors and walls. The dense tapestries stifled any airflow making it stuffy; it was more of a tomb than a bedchamber.

There was a soft knock at the door, so I pulled back my bed covers. Since Helene had already gone to bed, I went to it, opening the door to find the Voivode on the other side. My eyes rounded in surprise at his appearance.

"My Lord," I murmured, stepping into a curtsy. It had been a long while since we spent an *evening* alone together, and even longer since he had visited my bedchamber. In fact, the last time was our wedding night, nearly a year ago as the Voivode had pointed out earlier in the day. It made me suspicious at once.

"Good evening," he said, sweeping into my room after accepting my invitation. His eyes instantly fell onto the garlic bulbs littering my bedchamber. "What are these for?" He reached for one near my window and his fingertips grazed the edge of one of the bulbs.

"It was Ana-Maria's suggestion," I said, repeating what I told Helene earlier. "It seems that her pregnancy is making her overly superstitious, for she senses evil all around her. I felt it better to oblige her in her condition."

"That was probably wise," he replied, amusement coating his tone. "It is inadvisable to refuse a woman carrying a child of anything."

At once I couldn't help but wonder if he spoke from experience, thinking of his first wife carrying his child as Simon had told me. "It does seem as though the Romanians tend to be rather superstitious. I am afraid I don't have any refreshments to offer as I did not expect your arrival this evening," I explained. I caught myself wringing my hands and forced myself to stop, worried about why he had come.

"That is all right, I did not come for refreshments," he replied, smirking at the garlic bulbs one more time before turning his face in my direction. He was not dressed for bed, nor was he dressed in daytime attire. As I had seen before, he was in a white linen shirt with his black trousers and riding boots. Heat rose to my cheeks and I made a point to not look over to the wide bed behind me as he continued. "I heard what occurred today between you and your ladies."

"Oh, I see. My, word reaches you fast."

"I make it a point to always know what is going on in my kingdom, but I am not here to reprimand you, only to extend my support. While I appreciate you honoring the wives of my most trusted men, do not feel obligated to keep them if they continue to be insubordinate."

"I shall keep that in mind, My Lord." My heart was pounding in my ears as I waited for him to come to me, insisting that we get into bed. But then I recalled the night at Bran, the night of Ioana's murder, when he said he did not take pleasure in forcing himself upon women. Had he changed his mind? Had being back at court jogged his sense of duty? Was he here to insist upon it?

"I also sent word to the Hungarian King of our arrival in Târgoviște. So, now we await a specific date from him as to his intended arrival, but in the meantime I would like us to prepare. Would you charge Helene with overseeing the preparations?"

"I will, My Lord. I am sure she would be honored."

Just then, in the distance, I heard the flapping sound I had heard over the past several months. It took everything I had not to excuse myself and dart from the chamber in pursuit, lest I draw the Voivode's attention. He gave no indication that he heard it as well.

"Excellent. I have no doubt we can trust her to make adequate preparations." Silence fell around us, and I got the faint indication that there was something else he wanted to say. I kept from biting my lip. I fully anticipated that he would demand his marital rights. Then he broke the silence, saying, "Well that was the only matter of business I had to attend to. I saw the lights of your chamber under the door and just thought I would relay these to you. Good evening."

"Good evening, My Lord." He swept into a bow and was gone before I could complete my curtsy.

I longed to follow him, to see if he was going to bed or if he would stay up a while yet. I was suddenly ill at ease with being alone. I wanted to pursue the flapping I had heard too, but there were so many guards posted in the dark corridors of the castle that I was hesitant. I did not want to draw attention to myself, not just yet. The garlic bulbs raised enough suspicion. It would be damaging to my efforts to draw any further notice. For now, I had to content myself with waiting.

S UMMER WAS CONCLUDING AND autumn was approaching, bringing the one-year anniversary of my arrival to Romania rapidly—only a month and a half away. It was odd to think I had been away from Austria for over a year now; so much had happened since then. While I never lost sight of my intentions to convince my father to have my marriage annulled and return home, the remaining summer months had been busy, so my research had to be done in the brief moments I had to myself.

The Voivode's coin had been minted and was circulating, Helene and I were very busy scheduling banquets and events for the Hungarian King's arrival now that we had a set date agreed upon, and our first postal route had been created between Târgoviște and Brașov, which was a huge step in my progress toward returning home. But most importantly, Helene and Ambassador Ionescu were married. The Voivode and I were the only witnesses to their charming wedding in the royal chapel on the evening they were married. With preparations for King Wladislas' impending arrival, Helene could not, unfortunately, get time away to be with her new husband. That would have to wait until after the king's departure. I wondered how her nuptials would fit into my plans as I began outlining my letter to my father. Perhaps it would allow Helene to retire from my service so she could live happily with her new husband. While I would miss her so, she deserved every happiness, having set aside her own my entire life to care for me.

King Wladislas would be staying with us for a dreaded month of constantly entertaining him and keeping him happy. I wasn't sure how I would survive it, especially considering it would further delay my plans. He would be with us for the remaining warm weather, so there would still be plenty of time for some outdoor entertainment at the very least. Some of the troubadours and scholars whom I had invited from throughout Europe began to arrive, which was timely as I could utilize their skills in keeping the Hungarian king entertained. There was one in particular I was struck by—a small man from Florence who was the first to answer my summons and demonstrated great talent. I desired to get to know him better, but it would have to wait.

Despite keeping busy, I remained ever vigilant for the impaler prince lurking in the halls, though I did not see him again. I wondered if perhaps Ana-Maria's trick was working. Simon had not made another appearance, either, though his child was certainly making its appearance; Ana-Maria's belly grew quite round. Her disposition had not improved, however, and she seemed exhausted all the time. When she was not exhausted, she was in pain. She excused herself from my presence often. Selfishly, I felt I needed her to keep me sane while in the tiresome company of my other ladies, especially Lacramioara, as not only did she continue wearing her low-cut gowns and making allusions to my husband's handsomeness, but she was particularly attentive to him when in his presence. He humored her, responding to her jests and remarks but nothing more that I saw. She was always sure to send an innocent smile my way in these instances.

I always pretended I didn't notice.

The others seemed scandalized by her behavior but did not question it lest they provoke her ire. I had come to learn that the other ladies were cautious and perhaps even afraid of her. I noticed this particularly on days of leisure, when we walked the gardens or had picnics by the lake. Though there was nothing obvious to reprimand her for, there were subtle things—backhanded compliments or moments when she would come over and one of the other women would get up immediately to relinquish the spot to her. While she may have been clever enough to mask her rudeness to myself and the others—making it difficult for me to reprimand her for it, as she could easily deny it all—she wasn't clever enough to hide her true intentions from me. I saw right through her. I found her to be tedious and merely waited for a slip that would allow me to excommunicate her from my retinue.

The Voivode and I saw very little of one another since the night he came to my bedchamber. When we did, it was during our audiences, which happened twice a week, or during updates from the ambassador about the progress on our postal system. Occasionally, we would exchange words after exiting the audience chamber together, but that was about it.

On the day of King Wladislas' announced arrival, when messengers had been sent ahead to notify us that the king's party was only an hour away, Helene quickly pulled me to my chamber to stuff me into a grand gown—the one I had been married in. Ana-Maria watched from a chair as Helene dressed me, insisting she was well enough for the occasion.

Then, when I had met Helene's approval, the two of them escorted me out to the corridor where the rest of my ladies waited, following behind us as we descended the stairs and into the great hall. Prince Vlad and his courtiers waited there, Prince Vlad dressed in a thigh-length maroon tunic festooned with black brocade and a light cloak over it, pinned together with his dragon insignia broach. He wore the same hat from the night of our arrival banquet, his hair curling out from underneath it.

It was not long before the arrival of King Wladislas was announced, and he came barreling into the great hall with his rotund wife, Queen Beatrice, at his arm. She was his predecessor's wife, originally. When he died, the Hungarian nobility insisted that Wladislas marry her, and I had heard their marriage wasn't a particularly happy one. But then again, I was not one to talk; my marriage also fell into the usual mold of unloving marriages amongst royalty. Though, admittedly, mine was fine enough with the friendship my husband and I had developed—even if it was primarily founded upon business-related matters. I was content with that.

King Wladislas, who was three years older than my father, had a very broad face shrouded in a heavy beard flecked with gray. He wore his brown hair streaked with gray long, though it only emphasized the length of his forehead. He was rather short compared to my father and Prince Vlad, and rather petite, which did his wife no favors. Though she smiled widely, it was very becoming in contrast to King Wladislas' tight, thin-lipped attempt at a smile. His dark eyes darted between us as if he expected one of us to strike. His wife's sky-blue eyes settled on me warmly. I could see the cunning in her gaze and knew at once there was more to Queen Beatrice than what she presented.

Introductions were made, and as gracious hosts, we personally showed them to their quarters where they would rest and clean up before the banquet being held in their honor that evening. In the meantime, I would change from that gown into another—a lighter dress that was easier to dance in. King Wladislas and Queen Beatrice sat on the royal dais with us during dinner with their courtiers and ladies mingling with our own.

"Romania is beautiful," Queen Beatrice, who sat on my left, told me, her second chin wobbling as she did so. "I had underestimated its beauty."

"As did I when I first arrived," I told her in my heavily accented Hungarian. She was originally from Naples, but all of her time in Hungary erased any trace of it, whereas it was clear Hungarian was foreign to me.

"I have been told you are quite a painter. That you have painted numerous landscapes of Romania since you have been here." Her voice, like her smile, was sweet with a honey-eyed tone.

"I have. I will be sure to give one to you before you return home so that you remember us and your time here always. I know just the one—one of the first ones I painted when I was in Brașov, one of the great forests surrounding the town."

"It is wonderful that we can come together, our nations forming an alliance despite our challenges in the past. I am delighted to be here." She threw me one of her charming smiles, one that made me feel as if there was a great secret only the two of us knew, before taking a drink of her claret.

From what I could tell, Prince Vlad and King Wladislas were getting on just fine as they talked amongst themselves. Despite the endearing letter he had sent me initially, the Hungarian King avoided me entirely. I wondered if he had planned to avoid me the entire month that he was going to be here.

"Do not fret about my husband," Queen Beatrice told me, catching onto my furtive glance sent his way. "He is intimidated by you. Not only are you a great beauty, but there are a lot of damaged feelings he still bears from the actions of your grandfather and father."

"Is that not why he is here? His letter indicated he was more than willing to look past those things."

"He is willing, just give him time. He is a bit nervous but also very agreeable. He will come around. I am sure you heard of the scandal earlier this year, when our treasurer embezzled an extensive amount of funds. Well, he has been a bit more nervous than usual since then. Not to mention, our common enemy is still acting up in Croatia, continuing to raid in spite of the truce made last year."

"The Ottomans?"

"Precisely."

"They are troublesome and seem to never go away, always remaining a continuous problem. They are no better than the plague."

"They are a plague in themselves. But we will pay no mind to that for now. Let's leave that kind of talk to the men. Tell me more about yourself."

I was growing to like Queen Beatrice quickly. She and I spent a good deal of time during the banquet talking, even past when the dancing had long since begun. Our conversation was interrupted, though, when there was a small tap on my shoulder.

"Your Highness," said a voice at my side. "Cousin. I would be honored if you would accompany me in a dance."

I extended my hand to King Wladislas, and allowed him to escort me to the dance floor as the next dance was about to begin.

"You must forgive me," said the king, "for giving you the cold shoulder this evening. Your husband and I have much to discuss during our stay here, as you can imagine." He had an interesting speech pattern, one that was drawn out with every word chewed on and chosen carefully.

"Yes, I understand the Ottomans are giving you grief. Though, I was under the impression that your visit was also meant to put aside all of your differences with my family. Was I under the incorrect impression?"

"Not in the least bit, cousin. I have nothing but good will towards you. Please forgive me."

The king was a clumsy dancer. He knew the steps, but there was no feeling in them, only the motions. Regardless, I praised his ability as a courtesy.

"Your Highness," said a feminine voice at our side. Simultaneously, we both turned to see Lacramioara standing there, holding a bow and fiddle in her hands.

"Your Highnesses," she said again, batting her eyelashes and instantly catching the king's attention. "Her Highness' skill with the fiddle is unmatched, and I think it would be a great honor for you to hear it for yourself." Ah, here she was again trying to embarrass me, especially since her last attempt had failed.

"I had heard you were quite the musician," the king replied to me, but was unable to take his eyes off of her. His gaze traced along the length of her swan-like neck. "I would be delighted."

She lowered her head demurely as she held the instrument out to me. Seething, I took the instrument from her. I didn't have a choice. Rejecting King Wladislas' insistence could be seen as an insult on my part. Lacramioara escorted the king back to the dais where Queen Beatrice and the Voivode were, whispering in his ear all the while. Before he resumed his seat, they shared a laugh and he kissed the back of her elegant hand. Queen Beatrice's light sapphire-colored eyes darted away at that moment, and she sipped on her claret to hide her overturned lips.

The crowd parted, clearing the floor, and all eyes were on me. I lifted the fiddle to my chin and drew the bow across one string, eliciting a drawn-out note. I opted for a mournful tune, a piece I typically played on the harpsichord but had been able to transcribe to the fiddle. It was a song that transported me every time I played it, carrying me from where I was to a plane not of this world. It was no different this time, and by the time I had gotten to the end I had forgotten I was standing in the center of the dance floor with every single set of eyes in the room peering at me. Everything was still, and everyone seemed to be holding their breath during the last few notes, but when I concluded, applause thundered through the great hall.

Yet again, another humiliation attempt by Lacramioara became a moment of triumph for me.

The Hungarian King was openly weeping, swept up by the piece I had just played while everyone applauded.

"That was the most beautiful thing I have ever heard," he told me as I resumed my place on the dais. His hand found its way over mine.

"My wife is incredibly talented," the Voivode explained to the Hungarian king. "Every instrument she tries she excels at. She even tried to teach me once, but alas, I am more suited to a bow and arrow than I am a harpsichord."

"I hope to hear more," the Hungarian King said, pulling his hand away like he had touched something hot; as if just remembering my husband was there.

"You have a very brazen lady-in-waiting," Queen Beatrice told me some time later. "What is that about?"

"It is a long story, but yes, brazen she is."

Queen Beatrice was just as cunning as I had originally thought. "Jealous, is she?"

"That's what others have observed."

"It's what I observe too. Let me guess: she tried to seduce your husband, hopeful for an eventual marriage, but he chose you instead?"

I laughed. Queen Beatrice was a bundle of surprises, and her frankness was incredibly amusing. "You are absolutely accurate, from what I have been told."

She joined me in my laughter. "You mustn't let your mind go to waste, my dear. Once you do, it is all over. Always listen to your instinct. But, heed my advice when I say that you must put an end to that little strumpet's behavior quickly, as it will cause you nothing but trouble."

The night went on for a long time, but I did not mind this time, for I was very taken with Queen Beatrice's company. Guests dwindled away, even the Hungarian King himself opting to go to bed—at least that's what he told us. We remained, things getting rowdier when Ambassador Ionescu came over, convincing us to join him in a game of dice. One game of dice led to several, and Queen Beatrice proved a ruthless player, nearly draining us dry until Prince Vlad came back around, taking the winnings for himself. The game went on well past midnight until there was no more wine to be had and we had no choice but to retire for the evening. Between sheer exhaustion and excessive wine drinking, sleep overcame me in hardly any time at all.

"It will be no time before the Ottomans turn their attention back to you, realizing what a mistake it was to allow your ambassador to leave after they relented to your wishes. To no longer receive their annual tribute? That will come back to haunt you, mark my words." King Wladislas' eyes were wide as he spoke more hurriedly than usual.

It was a beautiful breezy and sunny day as we floated on a barge across the lake outside of the city. It was Queen Beatrice, King Wladislas, Prince Vlad, and myself accompanied by a handful of guards and attendants as we drifted across the water's clear blue surface.

"If that is the case, then we will be ready," Prince Vlad replied lightly, not a trace of worry coating his voice. "In fact, I anticipate it won't be long before Bayezid sends envoys to renegotiate. I am counting on it."

"If we are going to draw up an alliance of our own, I would appreciate it if you would not inflame the anger of the Ottomans. I do not want to lose precious Hungarian lives due to another sovereign's provocations."

"They do not need to be provoked to attack. They are hungry for land and power, no provocations are needed. You should know that yourself already. You have been nothing but agreeable, yet they still attack your border. I will not supply their war chest only for it to be used against me and all of Christendom later on."

"The Voivode makes a valid point," Queen Beatrice chimed in. "An alliance is absolutely necessary. We need to muster all the power we can to prevent them from taking any more than they already have."

King Wladislas scowled, conceding that she was right. "Very well. We will have our men draw up our terms and meet on them next week. From there, we will collude and negotiate on our terms, drawing up an official alliance. Does that sound agreeable to you?"

"I find it satisfactory," said Prince Vlad. "Though I think we should review the other's terms prior to meeting in order to prepare."

"Very well, if that is what you think."

I now understood why the Hungarians called King Wladislas "King Very Well". As Queen Beatrice said, he was very agreeable, and it didn't take much to persuade him, something his enemies took advantage of, no doubt.

"How is your father?" he asked, turning to me. His cheeks were becoming ruddy from sitting directly under the sun instead of under the shade like the rest of us.

"Last I heard, he is doing quite well. My brother Philip is due to marry Juana of Castile in less than two months, marking a long-awaited alliance finally coming to fruition. Then, not long after that, my sister Margaret is due to travel to Spain for her own wedding to the prince, strengthening that same alliance." I took this as my cue to discuss the items I wanted to discuss with the Hungarian King, something I had been nearly dying with eagerness to do since he arrived.

"That reminds me, there was a matter I was hoping to discuss with you, cousin."

I explained to him my plans for the postal service I was hoping to expand into Hungary with his cooperation, giving him the same explanation I had given Prince Vlad initially. He was receptive and rather enamored with the idea, especially considering our new potential alliance. When we docked, he was eager to meet with Ambassador Ionescu to discuss the idea further. At my earliest opportunity, I would write to my father to get his cooperation as well, thrilled at the prospect of our letters reaching one another sooner than they did—he would be able to receive my petition sooner once I was ready to complete it.

The lazy day of floating on the lake turned into another banquet that evening, just as extravagant as the last, although we did not stay up as late.

"He's a rather odd sort, isn't he?" Prince Vlad asked me as he escorted me to my wing of the castle.

"He is. He certainly lives up to his nickname, it hardly takes any effort to convince him of anything."

"Yes, a dangerous quality in a ruler. Hopefully it does not come back to haunt him."

"Do you really anticipate the Ottomans to send envoys to our court so soon?"

"I do. They will soon realize what a loss our annual tribute is, especially as they keep stirring conflict among so many kingdoms. But I also stand by what I said, that we will be ready." His fingers absentmindedly grazed along the back of my arm before settling on my elbow as he escorted me. "On another note, he was quite pleased with your idea. Well done."

My attention was taken by his touch, sending a wave of flush across my chest. "Thank you, My Lord."

We arrived at my bedchamber, where Helene was waiting inside to dress me for bed. We stopped and silence fell around us. His eyes met mine and lingered for a moment or two.

"Good evening, My Lord," I said softly, breaking the silence and interrupting the flush on my chest from traveling anywhere else.

He took my hand and placed a brief kiss atop it. "Good evening." He lingered as I reached for the door and disappeared behind it.

The weeks flew by filled with picnics, banquets, dancing, plays, riding, and archery contests. The troubadours and scholars I hired to enlighten my court were paying off to the point that King Wladislas remarked that there was no doubt I was my father's daughter, having taken a page from his book by creating a court focused on greater learning. His predecessor, King Matthias, had been concerned about making Hungary a center for art, literature, and culture whereas King Wladislas did not seem as terribly concerned. He did appreciate my efforts, regardless, and insisted that I entertain him with the harpsichord at every available opportunity. Queen Beatrice was more practical, and while she kindly sat during these moments it was clear her interests lay elsewhere. It almost seemed as though their places should be switched; that she be the leading sovereign, since she seemed to have more interest in stately matters, and so on, whereas King

Wladislas had an almost childlike quality in that he was easily entertained.

By now, I was exhausted, and grateful that all attention was occupied by the drafts of the alliance terms between Hungary and Romania. Prince Vlad and his men were reviewing the draft proposed by King Wladislas and vice versa. It gave me a much needed reprieve, but Ambassador Ionescu and I found time in between treaty negotiations to begin our work with the king on our postal service, by discussing locations and laying down the foundations to draw the two countries together. The revisions and renegotiations took another week before a final draft was accepted, dwindling down their stay to only one more week.

The terms were fairly standard. The primary function was that each country would answer calls for help from the other in the event of an Ottoman invasion, supplying men, weapons, cannons, horses, and other supplies to aid one another in the fighting. The negotiations primarily considered how many men and how many horses, supplies, and so on. King Wladislas pushed heavily that Romania provide more men, something Prince Vlad was hesitant towards, while Prince Vlad pushed for more cannons, pistols, and gunpowder.

There was one stipulation, though, which caused a bit more of a standstill, and that was language in the document that stated that, in the event that Hungary should take on arms with the Holy Roman Empire, Romania would not come to their assistance. While King Wladislas was less than enthused with that stipulation, it must have made sense seeing as Romania's treaty with the Holy Roman Empire was a stipulation of my marriage contract. It was the sole reason for my being in Romania to begin with. Prince Vlad understood the importance of that clause, too, for he had included it himself and without my insistence.

King Wladislas eventually came around after nursing his injured feelings, and the contract was signed and sealed. The occasion called for yet another grand banquet to celebrate our new alliance, not to mention celebrating the last night the Hungarian King and Queen would be staying with us. I had thought I would never grow tired of banquets, music, and dancing, but needless to say that by this point, I had, especially as I was eager to get back to my personal plans. The only point of interest for this banquet was a group of tumblers who also juggled swords, spit fire, and performed an incredible sword dance. Naturally, their spectacle was set up outside on this warm October evening, and they kept us entertained for a good portion of the night. Their spectacle had just concluded and we clapped politely while some of our guests threw them coins. The Hungarian King was particularly in awe of their display, choosing to stand as he applauded them.

"Warm nights like this are numbered," Helene said, bringing me a goblet of wine and still brimming like a young newly-wed.

"They are," I replied, looking out at the guests as they resumed dancing and drinking. Men surrounded my husband and King Wladislas, congratulating them on the new alliance. "Can you believe we have been here a year now?"

"In some ways, I can't. Time goes by faster and faster as you get older, so in some ways it doesn't seem like a year, but then there are other days where it seems longer."

"Next month, the Voivode and I will have been married for a year." Instead of being swept up in the merrymaking, I felt contemplative, especially as I watched Lacramioara weave her way through the crowd and heading straight toward the Voivode. She was latched onto the arm of her husband, but her eyes were possessed by Prince Vlad, her mouth dancing all the while. There were moments when she would toss her hair aside to reveal the length of her neck, or lower her eyes demurely when spoken to. Then there were times when her fingers would float up to her mouth, her fingertips grazing along her lush lips, drawing attention to their fullness. When she laughed, her bosom seemed particularly vivacious, just barely not spilling out entirely over her low-cut bodice. She was quite adept at the art of flirting, something I had never learned, though I had seen it enough in the court of my father to understand that's what was occurring. Prince Vlad's attention was fixed on her, but whether out of politeness or something more, I was not certain.

"You have a lot to show for," said a voice coming up on my other side. "Do not let them reduce you into being only the source of an heir—prove to them that you have other things to offer." Queen Beatrice seemed to have read my mind with her eyes directed knowingly on the brazen Lacramioara. "Though, it seems you have done a marvelous job already. My husband was quite taken with your plans to expand your father's postal service, and the Voivode has gifted us some of the coins minted with your family's crest on it. At this rate, your court could rival those of the West."

"I hope so," I admitted. "But despite my efforts, it seems all I am reduced to is my ability to conceive an heir. Or lack thereof."

"I am childless as well," she reminded me, "but that hasn't stopped me. I know the king did not want to wed me, he had someone else in mind, but I proved to the nobles that I would be a valuable asset. They agreed, and I have done nothing but prove my worth ever since. Those are the types of women that stand out in history. Women like her are common and all too abundant. Do not let yourself be so easily dissuaded by the gossip and ridicule. Rise above it. You are a Habsburg, after all. You are young, and I suspect great things are in store for you yet."

I smiled. It wasn't common that people spoke to me like that. "I shall miss you," I told her, meaning it wholehearted-ly. Queen Beatrice had been a delightful companion with her no-nonsense and practical ways. She was witty, clever, edu-cated, with an unabashed sense of humor. I was fortunate to have her in the next kingdom over.

"And I will miss you," she told me. "I insist that you come visit me in Hungary, hopefully some time next year. In the meantime, never hesitate to write to me, for I already con-sider you to be a very great friend."

The next morning, after our farewells, my very great friend and her husband swept up their retinue with one of my paintings stored among their things. I was sorry to see them on their way, for I was going to miss Queen Beatrice. It wasn't long before they were gone, taking the rest of October's warm air with them and leaving behind cold frigid winds that seemed to settle into one's very veins.

XXXI

T HE WIND HOWLED OUTSIDE of the castle relentlessly. Despite my attempts to stay warm, all the furs I possessed could not shake the coldness that gnawed on my bones. Autumn did not seem to linger at all and winter swept right in, pushing it out of the way and making itself smugly comfortable. November had settled in, and we were encroaching upon the first anniversary of my marriage. After the extravagance of the Hungarian King's stay, the Voivode and I agreed that celebrations would be kept to a minimum, honoring the occasion with a simple banquet which included his most loyal boyars and their wives.

The Voivode and I sat side by side on the dais watching as a handful of our guests took time to toast us and our union—even Lacramioara. As she did so, she diligently displayed the large ruby ring she had received as a token from the Hungarian King, a trinket she was quite proud of since his departure. After the toasts, the servants swarmed the great hall, laying down platters of suckling pig, geese stuffed with sage, pears, garlic, and other spices, bread bowls of stew, followed by Santa Lucia buns, sugar plums, and posset.

The Voivode indulged very little in the evening's feast, and I wondered perhaps if he was feeling ill. I contemplated asking him, not wishing to draw attention to something he would have preferred to keep to himself. But then my curiosity got the best of me. "What ails you, My Lord?" I asked him quietly.

"I have no appetite," he answered honestly.

"Any reason in particular?"

"No reason in particular. It is peculiar, all of these platters look divine, but yet, I do not feel compelled to try even a bite."

"Hopefully you are not coming down with something," I said, earnestly. We had made great strides in setting up our postal system, which had already begun operating within Romania, and we anticipated our system throughout Hungary would begin its operations in the spring. But beyond our discussions and progress of our postal system, I still saw the Voivode very little, and it was becoming difficult to engage in conversation with him, as I was unsure what to talk about with him. Despite it being our one-year anniversary celebration, we seemed to be friendly acquaintances at most. "It is the season for illness."

"I appreciate your concern, but I am sure it is nothing and I will be fine." He offered me a courteous grin and drank from the goblet he was holding.

His manservant came sidling in, then, but instead of leaning into the Voivode's ear, he whispered into mine.

"There is a messenger here for you, Your Highness," Casimir told me. "He comes from Lady Ana-Maria's manor, requesting your presence at your earliest convenience."

My brow furrowed and my stomach did a little flip, not caring for the sound of that. "Tell him to wait for me. He may escort me to his mistress' home right away. Then order a carriage, I am ready to depart as soon as it's ready."

He bowed and slithered away.

"That does not signal anything good," I said to Prince Vlad, whose furrowed brow mirrored mine.

"I can't lie and say it does," he agreed.

"I hope it isn't a problem with the child, but I'm not sure what else it could be. Please excuse me, My Lord, I must attend to her right away."

"I expect nothing less. If there is anything she needs, everything we have will be at her disposal."

I did not even bother to change out of my finery. Prince Vlad's manservant came back for me, escorting me to the carriage. It carried me across town to Ana-Maria's home, the first time I had been to it since arriving in Târgoviște. Everything was such a blur as I arrived with maidservants and grooms everywhere, their faces etched with worry. One escorted me to the second floor to Ana-Maria's bedchamber. There was a midwife and her two assistants and also a brunette woman I did not know, though I assumed it to be Ana-Maria's mother.

They all curtsied at my arrival and the dark-haired woman stepped forward. "She is not well, Your Highness" she said softly to me. "Some complications with the babe. They are not optimistic."

I turned to the bed and saw Ana-Maria. Ghastly pale, she lay in the center of her bed, slick with sweat, her hair matted and pressed against her face and neck. Her breath was shallow. I could see the swift rise and fall of her chest above the mound of her belly. Her arms fell limply at her sides on the surface of the bed.

"She has been asking for you, Your Highness," said her mother solemnly in my ear. "I am grateful you have come." She moved over to her daughter, kneeling at her side and placing her lips to her forehead. "Her Highness has come, my darling girl, she is here to see you just as you asked."

At the sound of her mother's voice, Ana-Maria stirred, her eyes fluttering open as if it were a great task. "Your Highness?" she said meekly.

Breaking protocol at the sound of her weakened voice, I went to her bedside immediately and took her hand, kneeling beside her. "I am here, Ana-Maria, my dearest friend."

Following the sound of my voice, she turned her head and smiled. "I am so happy you are here."

"I came as quickly as I could," I told her, a lump gathering in my throat at seeing my dearest friend in such a wretched state.

"I am sorry to have missed your wedding anniversary celebration," she began to say before I interrupted her.

"Shh, shh, do not even start to say such a ridiculous thing," I told her, squeezing her hand gently. "You needed to stay here and rest so that you can get better. Once you are well, we can laugh once again at that gaggle of women I call my 'ladies-in-waiting' and remark upon how low cut Lacramoiara's gown is once again. I expect nothing less."

"They are not optimistic. No one will say anything, but I can tell that they do not expect me to... make it."

"They are utterly foolish, of course you will be fine. There are complications with pregnancies all the time, and plenty of women come around to complain of it later on. You will be no different."

She then smiled again. "Even still, I am happy. Even if I don't live, I am still happy, and I wouldn't have given up this babe for anything. I love him more than anything. He has made me undeniably happy, even in the worst of my pains. He is quiet. Quiet for the first time in months, but I know it is a boy. I just know he is, but he is quiet. If something is to happen to me, Your Highness, you must promise that you will watch over him."

"Of course I promise. Should that happen. But that isn't going to happen. He will have his mother with him, that is not going to change. No one could take the place of his mother."

Her breathing was labored and her eyes fluttered closed again. "You have done so much for me already, Your Highness, but I wonder... wonder if there is one more thing I could ask of you. One more thing."

My eyes were filling with tears. "Anything you want, my dear friend. My entire person is at your disposal."

"I wonder if you would be so kind as to intercede on my behalf one more time to ask the Voivode if he may allow my husband to come to me. I would like to see him again."

"Anything you wish. I will send a messenger right away." Ana-Maria's mother nodded and she went to one of the attendants, murmuring in her ear to do my bidding. They returned with a quill and parchment on which I wrote a brief message to the Voivode to be dispatched right away. It wasn't long before I received a reply from him. In reading his reply, I was touched by his kindness and mercy in granting Ana-Maria's request, offering to handle Simon's summons himself. I only prayed that Simon would show his wife at least one kindness in answering her request.

I remained at her bedside for nearly three days, unable to detach myself from her. My love for Ana-Maria was great, and I could not abandon her, not until she showed signs of getting well. When I had informed the Voivode that I would be staying at my dearest friend's bedside until her husband arrived, he kindly replied by sending Helene along with a change of clothing, insisting that I take all the time I needed. An adjoining room was set up for me, and I sat with her as often as I could as she fluctuated between consciousness and unconsciousness, taking shifts with her mother so that we could switch off getting some rest.

Occasionally, when Ana-Maria would come to consciousness, we would talk, finding little moments here and there to laugh even, but more often she was asleep. I watched the midwives with intense scrutiny as they worked, insisting they do everything they could to help her. They assured me that they were doing their best as they mixed herbs, feeding them to her and applying warm, dampened cloths to her forehead. None of them could tell me what the matter was.

It was my turn to sit at her bedside, and I was praying the rosary when she began to stir. It was late in the evening, and the others were trying to get some rest while they could. I had offered to sit with her in the late evening hours, giving me the privacy I needed to pray over my rosary. She had become slick with fresh sweat, but she was the most alert I had seen her since I arrived.

"You are still here, Your Highness," she said, granting me a smile.

"Of course I am Ana-Maria, how could I leave you?"

"The Voivode..." she began.

"He knows I am here and he sends you his best wishes. He has honored your request and Simon should be here any day now. He insists that anything else you wish will be granted."

"The Voivode is kind... you are kind. I wonder if you would fetch something for me, Your Highness? I am hesitant to ask, for it is improper to make requests of my sovereign, but I have something for you. Meant for your eyes only."

"What is it? I will fetch it for you, propriety be damned."

She lifted her hand, pointing to a dresser behind me. "In the drawer there, under my linens. It is there."

Rising to my feet and putting my rosary into my pocket, I went to the drawer. I opened it and reached inside feeling something hard underneath her linens. I withdrew it. "A wooden stake?"

"Yes. I have been meaning to give it to you for some time now... but I have been unable. It is made from a hawthorn tree."

"What is it for?"

"Should you... be attacked by a *strigoi*, you must plunge that into their heart. It is one of the only means to destroy them—only a hawthorn tree will work. You must protect yourself, Your Highness." It was not long, no longer than my forearm, but its point was sharp. "Remember everything I have told you about *strigoi*. Protect yourself." Then she winced and groaned. I thrust the stake back into the drawer and rushed to her side.

She cried out again, her body convulsing. "Someone, please, help!" I cried out in panic, taking her hand and squeezing it all the while feeling so utterly useless. "Ana-Maria, it will be all right. Help is coming... you are strong—you can make it through this."

Sweat dripped along her forehead, and her eyes flew open. They bore into mine wildly. "I can no longer feel him moving! Please don't let anything happen to my baby!" Her eyes were so wild, I no longer recognized her. I wasn't even sure if she truly saw me.

With a rush of strength, her hand gripped mine, crushing it. "Please, someone come! Immediately!" I cried out again.

Ana-Maria screeched, her back arching as the midwives came rushing in. One threw back the covers while the other grabbed her ankles. Her mother came in as another midwife thrust apart Ana-Maria's knees, reaching her hand between her legs.

"She is ejecting the babe," the midwife announced as the other two midwives tried to steady her.

"No, no-no-no-no, no!" Ana-Maria cried, still crushing my hand in hers. Her eyes were still wild and wider than what should've been humanly possible. "It is too early! He is not ready!" Her whole face contorted and she let out a wail. Her mother went to her other side, brushing her hair back from her forehead and murmuring little encouragements in her ear.

I could only stand there stupidly, holding Ana-Maria's hand in mine, willing her to find the strength to survive, and praying fervently. Then she began to scream, crying out for Simon, her back arching as the midwives tried to work swiftly. There was a rush of liquid followed by blood streaming from between her legs.

"We must staunch the bleeding," cried out the midwife between Ana-Maria's legs. The others scrambled to fetch linens, packing them between Ana-Maria's legs where the main midwife directed. It was absolute carnage, a sight I certainly wasn't prepared for. Silently, I begged Simon to come, to please consider his wife for once as she was becoming more and more pale, every scream seemingly draining her of vitality.

"You must push!" the midwife urged her.

"No! I can't! I can't lose my baby!" Ana-Maria cried, struggling against them holding her down. Her legs bobbed and clenched as she reflexively tried to close them as if doing so would prevent the babe from leaving her body, but the midwives began to hold her down by her ankles again.

"You must, darling," her mother coaxed her. "There will be other children. You have to let this one go."

"I can't!" Ana-Maria cried out, tears pouring from her eyes, and her face contorted with a mixture of grief and pain. "I won't!"

But it seemed as if she had no choice because the midwife began to push down on her belly, guiding the child from her womb, ignoring Ana-Maria's wailing protestations. Then, when its head began to surface the midwife continued guiding it out.

It did not scream.

Instead, it came out blue.

I could not see anything clearly at first, but I watched as the midwife worked hurriedly, swaddling the baby in a blanket. As she did so, I could see the child was a boy, as Ana-Maria had known, but I also saw something else. A gasp rose in my throat. I was only able to stop it so as not to cause Ana-Maria any more distress.

The child was horribly deformed. There was no nose where a nose should have been, and his head was flattened on one side where the skull should have formed. He was also incredibly small. At the sight of it and all of the chaos I had not noticed that Ana-Maria had gone quiet. But then I noticed her hand lay limp in mine. Screams bellowed through the room once more, but they were not Ana-Maria's.

They were her mother's.

Ana-Maria had gone whiter than the sheets beneath her. Her eyes had glazed over, staring at the ceiling above us.

I fell to my knees, squeezing her hand. "No, Ana-Maria, don't leave me. You cannot go anywhere. I order you. You must remain at my side, do you understand me? I order you!" I could not stop the tears from falling in my attempts to coax her back to life. But it was futile.

I may have had power as a reigning monarch, but I had nothing over the will of God.

What happened next was a blur. There was nothing but the painstaking grief that welled up in my chest, crushing my breastbone. This did not feel real. It was as though I had fallen into a dream—a horrible nightmare—an event that was happening to someone else and not to me. That I was only a spectator to this immense grief crushing me under its weight. I drifted far away. Even Ana-Maria's mother's wailing grew distant. Hands gripped at my shoulders, pulling me away, but I refused to let go of Ana-Maria's hand, hoping that maybe with this physical connection she could siphon some of my life into her body. Then she would rise up and smile at me once more. That everything would be all right—that this would be like a scene from a play, and everything would go back to the way it was once the play was over. I was no longer there in the room as the force trying to pull me away finally succeeded.

There was so much blood.

The last thing I saw before I was taken from the room was the midwife carrying a small bundle and placing it on Ana-Maria's breast.

"I am terribly sorry for your loss," the Voivode said, kneeling at my side and taking my hand in his.

I nodded. Grief had stolen my ability to speak. It lingered, a great weight on my chest. I was in my bedchamber, seated by the fire. I could not move, could not speak, could not think. I was still far away. I could only marvel at the weight of despair that consumed me.

"She is to take all the time she needs," the Voivode said to someone. Helene, I think. She was the most likely. "She is to have no visitors, excuse all of her ladies, send them home. She is not to be pestered by anyone or anything until she is ready."

As of that moment, I did not think I was ever going to be ready to face the world ever again.

I could not focus on what the priest was saying. I had become withdrawn, receding into myself these last few days, rising only to attend Ana-Maria's funeral. It was the least I could do for my beloved friend. We stood in the churchyard after the service where the priest bestowed his final blessings on the casket containing both mother and child. Many had come to pay their respects, but not the one whom I had prayed would come. It filled me with such fury that I could rip his eyes out if he dared to show his face.

When the service was over, I asked if we could accompany Ana-Maria's mother and father back to their home.

The Voivode, in his kindness, obliged my request, offering to come with me. I felt obligated to accompany her grieving parents as one last favor to Ana-Maria who had become my dearest friend and confidant. I did not know what I was going to do without her now that she was gone. There was no one else I could trust.

Alone, I went to her bedchamber which had been cleaned up since I had last been there. I stood melting in my own tears, and it almost seemed like she would turn the corner and appear in the doorway, dropping into a curtsy before asking me what I was doing there. But alas, she did not. She never would again. I prayed that God Himself welcomed her into His arms. If there was anyone that deserved it, it was she.

My eyes fell on the dresser opposite her bed, and I remembered the thing she had given me before succumbing to eternal slumber. I opened the drawer, and it was still there. I took it and folded it within my skirts.

Prince Vlad had waited kindly with her parents as I said my final farewells, standing as I reappeared looking much like a ghost myself. We bid them farewell, her mother desperately clasping my hand with both of hers and pressing a kiss onto the back of it before we departed. As we crossed the threshold and stepped out the front door, a figure appeared before us.

"Your Highnesses," the figure said, dropping into a bow.

That fury returned in an instant, flooding me. "*Now* you have the decency to come?" I asked coldly. "Or is it merely that you've come to collect your dead wife's estate? Your wife, who *died* giving birth to *your* child!"

At least Simon had the decency to look ashamed. He also had the decency to clean himself up since the last time I saw him. "I tried to get here as soon as I could. Once I received your summons, I departed immediately." He looked to Prince Vlad helplessly. "It is the truth."

"Do you even feel a *morsel* of grief at her passing?" I demanded. "Are you even capable of it after everything you have done to that poor woman?" He lowered his eyes, fiddling with the cap he held in his hands. He looked so pitiful and vile that I had to suppress the urge to spit in his face, especially as my memory flashed with images of him molesting me in the corridors of the castle. Thank God Ana-Maria had not taken knowledge of that to her deathbed.

"Come," Prince Vlad said softly to me, urging me into the carriage, wrapping his arms around me to lead me away, as my fingers unconsciously flexed into hooks I so desperately wanted to use to claw Simon's eyes out.

"You are a miserable wretch and I never want to lay eyes on you ever again!" I called out to him as Prince Vlad ushered me away. "You disgust me!"

I cursed him then and there, meaning what I said. I hoped to never lay eyes on him ever again, as the hawthorn stake pressed against my side within the folds of my skirt when I entered the carriage.

XXXII

1497

I WORE MY GRIEF like a shroud. I was unable to shake it off as the days melted into each other, and before I knew it, it was Christmas and then the new year.

Grief had not presented itself this way even when my mother passed away—I was too young to really understand. Since then, I had not experienced another loss of a loved one. The first weeks after Ana-Maria's death were nearly unbearable and I felt as though I was but a specter going through the motions of life, longing for what had been before I felt such pain. I no longer pursued my quest to discover anything I could about Dracula, nor to persuade my father to allow me to return to Austria. Being entrenched in my grief, I found I did not care.

Eventually, when there was a shift in the tides of grief, I found a small spark of life which allowed me to resume some of my normal duties. I also allowed my court to distract me. Scholars whom I had hired tried to debate philosophy with me, and musicians tried to coax me into playing the harpsichord for them, but even still, I never felt entirely present. My ladies had long since given up, no longer persuading me into a game of cards or encouraging me to show them how to paint. Even Lacramioara lost interest in trying to instigate me, turning her pernicious attentions elsewhere. So far gone was I that I did not even care if she ended up in my husband's bed.

At night, when I was alone, I was haunted by Ana-Maria's violent death and her deformed child, waking up from plaguing nightmares in cold sweats. There were times when I swore I could hear her wailing in the shadows of night, her cries echoing in the corridors, but when I woke they were gone. There were even times I thought I heard the wailing of a baby—cries that Ana-Maria's child was robbed of in life. It had all been a stark awakening about the reality of childbearing, about the dangers women faced with a task that was not only expected of us, but required. I grew grateful in my grief that the Voivode left me alone and did not try to get me with child now that I knew of the reality of it.

The Voivode had been kind during this time. He gave me the isolation I needed as I traversed through grief, and when I was eventually ready to return to our audiences, he welcomed me back warmly, never expecting me to do more than I felt capable of. I had missed the audiences, and wondered why I hadn't returned to them earlier. They proved to be a welcome distraction, offering a moment to forget the grief that plagued me like a specter.

Grief was an odd thing. At first, it feels like you are crumbling apart, dying, turning to ash only to come to terms with it, piece by piece. A companion that you can never shake off, but one with which you reach a mutual agreement. A companion that never goes away, but one that will leave you alone from time to time until he reminds you of his presence, and you crumble once more only to get back up and do it all over again.

The winter had been difficult. We suffered through furious winter storms, burying us in blankets of snow for what seemed an eternity, but then finally the sun began to linger, then grow stronger, and the snow began to melt away, allowing spring to push its way in. I permitted myself to be swept up in it as winter was a suitable season for grief and spring was not, especially when the buds on the trees were beginning to burst open. A chill remained in the air, but it was tolerable—nothing like the frigid winds whipping through us through the majority of the winter.

I was privy to some news regarding the rest of my family during this time. My brother was settling well in his inherited lands, his new wife of several months utterly devoted and madly in love with him. Philip was also trying to placate King Charles of France, something that apparently frustrated our father who had bad blood with the French king, and my brother pushed back against Father in yet another squabble between them. In my brother's defense, it seemed as though our father had bad blood with nearly everyone. On the other hand, my sister Margaret encountered some misfortune yet again as it related to her marriage to the Spanish Prince. A horrendous storm had struck the ship taking her to Spain, a storm that was certain to overturn the ship and kill everyone aboard. But, Margaret's fortune had turned, and she made it safely to Spain to marry the prince after taking a detour in England, awaiting the storm to pass before continuing her journey. She wrote to me shortly after her wedding and from her telling, the marriage seemed to be a promising one. With that, Father's plans for all three of his children were complete. We were spread all over Europe with our own respective kingdoms to serve his interests for the empire. Both of my siblings seemed very content with their nuptials, and while I remained coated with grief, I found myself spiteful and envious of them, taking this letter and throwing it into the fireplace.

One spring afternoon, I was sitting in the solar with my ladies, indulging myself on the harpsichord, at long-last feeling inspiration returning to me. My musicians had composed many pieces since their arrival, and I was playing one of them when a servant entered the chamber.

"Yes?" I said, not taking my eyes from the sheet music as my fingers fluttered across the keys. Helene sat near me sewing, her eagle eyes watching the servant.

"I was wondering if you would like to join me for a ride today for some fresh air. After this long harsh winter, it might do us some good to escape these walls for a little while."

My skin prickled at the back of my neck with the realization of my mistake. I turned to see the Voivode standing there, an amused smirk pulling at his lips. My ladies were aware of his arrival and they had already risen to their feet, dipping into deep curtsies. Lacramioara's curtsy was low enough so that not only could the Voivode get a good look at her wares spilling over her bodice, but so could all of us present.

My eyes rounded at the suggestion. While I had ridden with him once before, we hadn't since then. Even when the Hungarian King was here, I withdrew from any invitation to go riding, still afraid of horses. The Voivode had offered to teach me, but that offer had long since fallen through.

"I recall I offered you some time ago to teach you how to ride," he said, as if reading my thoughts. "It seems that I am horrible at keeping my promises, but the offer still stands if you are willing."

Side-eyeing my ladies, they remained dipped, but I could see they were brimming with eagerness to be outside after the long harsh winter that forced us indoors for many months. Not to mention, there was no chance I could let on that I was unsettled by horses, for there was no shadow of a doubt that Lacramioara would exploit that fact. As far as I knew, she wasn't currently aware of my disdain for them. "Very well, My Lord."

He extended his hand to me, and I allowed him to guide me through the castle, my ladies tittering behind us. "I have something for you," he said softly, only for me to hear. "A birthday present."

"My birthday is not for another week," I reminded him.

"An early present, based on another promise I made but did not keep, so I hope you will forgive me one day for that."

"One day, I might," I said, surprised at my sudden desire to tease him. It was a glimmer of my former self, before I was overcome with grief. "We shall see."

He made a show of a frown, but then continued. "I thought you could use some cheering up. I hope you like it. If not, you can be honest with me, my feelings won't be injured." We entered the courtyard, and a smoky gray mare stood there with a lovely black mane and tail, all saddled and ready to go. "There she is."

"My, is she beautiful!" Lacramioara cooed, obviously annoyed at the shared murmurs between the Voivode and me.

She brushed past me, heading for the horse as if the Voivode had gifted it to her. She reached for the bridle and began to stroke the mare's snout, making it quite clear that she had a way with horses. As she stroked the horse she threw a glare at me, making her jealousy quite evident, her ruby ring glinting in the sunlight.

I did not know what to say. Instead, I bit my lip as I tried to come up with a response, not wanting to appear ungrateful. Again, Prince Vlad seemed to read my mind. "It is all right, she is well tempered and very docile, something I felt was a perfect fit. She won't hurt you. Why don't you come over and introduce yourself?"

He guided me over, his hand hovering over the curve of my lower back, his other hand taking hold of the bridle.

"She is beautiful," Lacramioara cooed again, her eyes eager to get Prince Vlad's. But he hardly paid her any notice. "How fortunate you are, Your Highness, to be presented with such a beautiful beast."

"You are very kind," I told the Voivode, finally managing a response.

"Would you like to ride her?" he asked me, quiet enough to prevent Lacramioara from hearing as she ran her hand across the back of the horse. "I can show you how."

It was no use, though, because she heard anyway. "I think we should all ride and make a day of it. How lovely would that be? It is a perfect day for it." Her eyes flickered at me once again. "And perhaps when the Voivode is unable to, I could take his place in teaching you how to ride." The clever "strumpet," as Queen Beatrice called her, had already picked up on my inexperience with horses.

"Well, I don't think I could deny my ladies a day outside," I replied to Prince Vlad. "It appears I am outnumbered anyhow and don't have a choice."

"You always have a choice, don't let anyone persuade you otherwise. No matter how... flagrant they may be." His eyes darted in Lacramioara's direction and I couldn't help but feel a moment of triumph. I hoped the Voivode also saw through her ways.

So then it was set. Prince Vlad's courtiers joined us, and soon we became a whole riding party. The courtiers and ladies set off ahead on their horses, eager to compete with one another, while Prince Vlad lingered behind with me. He showed me how to mount the saddle, taking the reins and urging the mare forward while his manservant followed with his horse behind.

"Are you certain you want to do this?" I asked him, feeling stupid atop the saddle sitting sideways as he took the reins, walking alongside my horse. "Wouldn't you rather charge ahead with the others? I don't mind, I can withdraw back to the solar and busy myself with my music. I would hate to hold anyone back."

"It is no matter," he assured me. "Besides, I promised you I would set you up with your own horse and saddle. Naturally, I would have to teach you as well."

"I am surprised you remembered. That was about a year ago already." My thighs clenched as I sat sitting on the saddle as if doing so would keep me on the horse more securely. My nervousness was ever-present.

His eyebrow cocked. "A year ago? Are you certain?"

"Absolutely certain, My Lord. It was last spring."

He scoffed to himself and the mare responded by snuffling his hair in the most endearing way. Maybe this horse wasn't so bad. "It's funny how quickly time moves when you're not paying attention." The mare snorted in reply. "Do you think you want to take the reins?"

Biting my lip, I answered, "If I must."

"We can keep going as we are. I don't mind. I used to do this for my younger brother when we were boys."

"No, no, I suppose now is as good as ever. Besides, I don't need to give Lacramioara any further cause for ridicule." Then I perked up, having nearly forgotten that the Voivode had brothers, something he had told me some time ago. One was deceased and the other was missing. "Was it your younger brother who passed away?"

"Yes. He passed away about eleven years ago, now."

Having a newfound understanding of the full scope of grief, I could empathize with him. "Where is your other brother? Have you had any word of his whereabouts at all?"

"I am not sure where my older brother is," he said with a shrug. "He could be dead, or he could be starting a rebellion against me. Who is to say?"

I nearly shivered at the prospect of yet another enemy out there wanting to do us harm. Just then, before we had reached the gate to exit the castle compound, a manservant came running towards us.

"My Lord!" he cried out, struggling to catch his breath. "Your Highnesses!" Prince Vlad stopped my mare and turned. "Envoys have arrived! Turkish envoys! They request an immediate audience with you, My Lord!"

My heart nearly stopped in my chest. Turkish envoys? That could only mean one thing—Prince Vlad's prediction had come true. They were returning for their annual tribute. They must have been feeling the loss heavily already. He turned to look at me and our eyes met knowingly.

"The princess and I will be there to grant them an audience shortly," Prince Vlad told the servant. "In the meantime, see that they are fed and rested. They will be summoned when we are ready."

My heart thundered in my ears as Prince Vlad and I sat on our thrones in the great hall. After the servant departed, Prince Vlad and I returned to the castle while his manservant summoned the others so that we could all change to appear as a fearsome and regal court not to be trifled with. I opted for a deep violet gown made of silk trimmed with lace—it had been quite costly when I commissioned it to be made. The glare Lacramioara gave me when she saw it made me think she was going to burst right then and there, and I knew I had made the right choice in selecting it. I just hoped that I did not ruin it by having my nervousness turn to sweat. I glanced at Prince Vlad from the corner of my eye, but he appeared calm and collected by this sudden turn of events and not at all ruffled.

The grand wooden doors opened and three men came striding in, their faces fixed in grim lines. All three had some varying degree of facial hair, from a long beard to a dark curling mustache. Their attire was striking and exotic—great long pleated robes that nearly grazed the floor, and on their heads they wore caps that folded over clinging close to their scalps. The exception was the man in the middle, the oldest of the three. He wore a lengthy garish feather in the center of his cap. His face was the hardest, with its long crooked nose and thick bushy eyebrows above his cold, black, deep-set eyes. His complexion was also the darkest of the three, a tan olive color indicating that he spent much time out in the sun.

"Your Highnesses," he began in flawless Romanian, bowing, those onyx eyes falling first on the Voivode and then me. A shiver ran down my spine, but still, I straightened in my throne and arranged my features to look as hard as his own, determined to disguise my nervousness. This was the first time I had come face-to-face with our mysterious enemies.

"Welcome to my court, ambassadors," Prince Vlad said pleasantly. "To what do I owe the great pleasure of your arrival?"

"I should think our arrival is no great surprise to Your Highness," the envoy continued. His voice reminded me of that of a snake, hissing and low.

"Don't tell me you wish to circle back on our previous negotiations?" Prince Vlad asked, his tone traced with a slight hint of mockery. It was so subtle, however, that I was not certain if anyone else picked up on it but me.

"The previous arrangements all remain suitable to our accommodating sultan but one. It is the matter of the annual tribute, which was paid loyally and on time by your successor."

"Then you are correct," Prince Vlad said, "your arrival is no great surprise to me. The only thing that does come as a surprise is how long it took for your sultan to reverse course on our agreement. The sultan must have comprehended what a great loss it was to him after all. Tell me, are all of his attempted coups proving to be too costly?"

"A 'coup' would insinuate that the sultan is engaging in unlawful actions to wrestle power from a government reigning over the sultan himself, Your Highness. The good sultan *is* the government," the ambassador said.

"It is nefarious to attempt to seize European lands, lands that do not belong to the 'good' sultan."

"By whose authority do you make such an observation?"

"By God's authority," the Voivode said.

"We do not follow *your* god's authority, therefore it is not unlawful. We are not bound by any laws but our own."

"I kindly remind you to refrain from debasing this court with your sacrilegious outbursts, good ambassador," growled Ambassador Ionescu, coming forward at the Voivode's other side. "Remember on whose soil you stand."

"God's authority is the only authority I am concerned about, not your 'good' sultan's," Prince Vlad continued. "And as His anointed prince, I serve His interests and His interests only, not your 'good' sultan's. Therefore, this being His realm, I stand firm on my decision. I will not debase my good people to fund your sultan's attempts to seize lands from European sovereigns—*Christian* lands."

The envoy's eyebrow cocked. "Are you certain this is wise, Your Highness? Consider your country's history with our great empire. Your nation stands as the doorway to the rest of Europe. Time and time again we have burst through that door. We will not hesitate to do so again."

"Yes, I have not forgotten our history and past aggressions, but I have now what historically we did not have before. Strong, beneficial alliances should the Ottomans arrive on my doorstep once again." With that, Prince Vlad reached over and took my hand in his, holding it firmly to further illustrate his point.

The envoy's eyes flickered to me once more. "Ah yes, your coveted Habsburg bride. You sit there confident this alliance will prove fruitful to you, but are you certain it is one you can count on? Romania's alliances have fallen short before, especially with Hungary, and if my sources are correct, you have created yet another alliance with Hungary. Who is to say that this Hungarian King won't fall short as did his successor with your father? Who is to say that Maximilian won't fall in step with them as well? He makes a great show of wanting to take up arms against us, but he always falls flat."

"Who is to say that Bayezid won't fall short should I agree to reestablish the old agreement of an annual tribute? How long will it be before he asks for more beyond the original tribute amount? How long will it be before he demands our Romanian sons be enslaved once more? How long will it be before he turns his attention back to Romania to try to conquer us once again? No, I would rather cast my lot in with the West. You may tell your sultan that I stand firm and will not relent to his demands."

"My sultan is just and may overlook your impudence for now, but mark my words, you *will* live to regret this, Prince Vlad Drăculești of Romania," said the envoy, his black eyes darkening even more. With that, he bowed reluctantly then spun on his heels and left with the other two following behind him.

After the doors thundered to a close behind them, Prince Vlad said, "Ionescu, Princess, let us convene in my study. We have much to discuss and prepare for."

"If you would wait just a moment," Prince Vlad said to me as our discussion had concluded and we were all dispersing.

It was late into the night by the time our discussion ended, and as exhausted as I was, I lingered until the last man had left before turning back to him. "What is it, My Lord?"

"Would you assist me by writing to your father, apprising him of what happened today? Notify him that I anticipate a conflict will arise between ourselves and the Ottomans, and that we call on him for assistance."

I didn't think it would be so soon that he would call on the alliance established with our marriage. "Do you think my father will answer you?" I asked earnestly, the Turkish envoy's words echoing in my mind.

"I do," Prince Vlad insisted, rising from his chair to pace back and forth along his desk, which was scattered with maps and papers. "It was one of the terms of our alliance."

"And if he doesn't?"

He stopped and his eyes fell on me. "Then, we shall have to count on King Wladislas. I will be writing to him a letter to be dispatched tomorrow."

"And if *he* doesn't answer?"

"Then we are on our own," he told me, confirming my worst fears.

"Well," I said, biting my lip. "In the very least, I could try to appeal to my brother, Philip, and my sister, Margaret. With Margaret married to the Spanish heir, they are certain to have their own reinforcements. The Spanish King and Queen have always been such advocates for the security of Christianity in Europe."

"There is no harm in trying," Prince Vlad agreed. "The queen may not be able to resist the chance to humiliate the Muslims once again, as she did in Granada five years ago." As he resumed his pacing, I studied him. The rest of us had been exhausted as the night went on, but he seemed alert and very much alive. The way he paced reminded me of a caged predator, buying its time before pouncing upon its prey. He stopped again, noticing me staring at him as I got caught up in my own thoughts. "What is it?"

I blinked. "It is nothing, My Lord," I said sheepishly, lowering my gaze. I felt stupid for being caught staring at him.

"Forgive me, you must be quite tired. Allow me to escort you to your room." He started towards me.

"It is all right, I can go myself. You seem rather restless, and I know you have much to do yet. I will leave you to it."

"Let me escort you to the door at least," he said, his long stride continuing my way. He reached for the door and held it open for me. I moved toward the threshold and then stopped, turning to him. The memory from last year of our time together in the stables while it rained flashed before my eyes as my gaze fell on his lips. Then there was the time after our wedding when he kissed me theatrically in front of our guests. The urge to lean forward, to kiss him again came bubbling up. I wanted to remember what that was like.

He was looking at me, expecting me to say something. "Good evening, My Lord," I said, shaking myself out of my reverie. I was clearly exhausted and needed to go to bed.

"Good evening," he replied softly. I could sense him watching me as I left him behind in his study, after which I am sure he wrote promptly to King Wladislas. His letter would be dispatched right away, making use of the postal system which was now up and running in Hungary as originally scheduled.

My ladies were not waiting outside of the Voivode's study, having not waited to be dismissed before departing. Helene would be waiting loyally in my bedchamber to undress me, but otherwise the castle was quite silent as I walked down the dimly-lit corridor. I turned the corner to see a huddled mass pushed up against the wall. It was moving, shifting in the shadows, reminding me of the moment in Bran Castle when I found Prince Vlad in a clandestine position with Ioana. My breath caught in my throat when I saw a shapely leg emerge from a fold of skirts, wrapping it around the waist of another in the shadows. I had just left Prince Vlad in his study where he lingered, so I knew this wasn't him. I questioned if it even *had* been him the last time. Regardless of who, it was definitely the passionate embrace of a man and woman I had stumbled upon.

In the soft glow of the torch a few paces away from them, the face of Lacramioara fell into focus as her head fell to one side, her eyes closed and lips curled in ecstasy. Her lover had pushed her up against the wall, his face to her elegant neck. Tired and not in the mood to deal with this, I made up my mind to turn on my heel and go the other way. Just as I was about to do so, her lover turned to face me.

I gasped, stumbling back.

The impaler prince glared at me, fangs protruding from his lips and dripping with crimson blood that glittered in the torch light, the shadows making it resemble ink more than blood. Visible on Lacramioara's neck were two large puncture marks, seeping with the very same blood dripping from the impaler prince's mouth.

I ran as swiftly as I could. Behind me there was a growl that turned to laughter. The sound chased me through the corridor until I reached my room. I threw open the door and stumbled inside, slamming it behind me. Wildly, I took in the sight of the garlic still sitting at my windows and bedside, a practice I had continued, changing the bulbs out every few days. Everyone thought it was a silly practice that I continued to honor Ana-Maria, and I let them think that. In reality it was for exactly what I had seen this very evening. My eyes darted to my bed where I kept her wooden stake under it. I went to it and thrust my hand under, feeling it still there.

"Your Highness? My goodness, what is the matter?" Helene said, coming to me from the other side of the room with my nightgown thrown over her arm. "You look as though you have seen a ghost!"

I did not tell her that I had, only that it wasn't a ghost that I saw, but a *strigoi*.

XXXIII

SLEEP NO LONGER CAME easily to me the next couple of nights. I kept the hawthorn stake folded in my skirts every time I left my bedchamber, and a bulb of garlic in a satchel hanging at my waist. A crucifix also now hung on my neck in addition to my rosary that I always carried, and I refused to go anywhere alone. I expected to see him every time I walked into a room or turned a corner, his heinous, blood-stained fangs haunting my every thought.

Lacramioara did not seem to remember what had happened that night. However, she was pale and subdued, the most I had ever seen her, and her low-cut gowns had been replaced with high-necked ones. Looking at her, I recalled how Helene had two puncture wounds on her neck at one point and it made my stomach churn as I now knew what they had truly been.

Every moment I was not pulled into an audience or con-
ference with the Voivode and his men, I spent in the chapel
praying my rosary. I knew it irritated my ladies, who longed
to be out in the warm sunny weather, but I did not care. I
prayed rapidly for deliverance from this evil, for my soul and
my husband's, for Ana-Maria, and even Simon. We seemed
to be cursed, and now that Ana-Maria was no longer with
us, I was alone in facing this evil. I had no one else to turn to
but God Himself. Between my prayers, I meditated on how
to solve this problem. Between the oncoming wrath of the
Ottomans and now this, it was far more than I could ever
manage myself, and so I also prayed for a resolution, for the
resolve to unravel this situation.

After dinner, I excused myself early, dismissing my ladies
beforehand. Helene brushed out my hair and spoke quietly,
but my thoughts were far away. Despite it having been a few
days since the Ottoman envoys left and the reappearance of
the impaler prince, I was restless and ill at ease. I worried
that perhaps Prince Vlad had made a mistake angering the
Ottomans, but I also had no choice but to trust him for now.
Not only was he the reigning voivode, but he had been deal-
ing with the Ottomans long before I came, so he had more
experience. He was confident that his alliances were secure,
but alliances were broken all the time. Who could say about
King Wladislas with how easily persuaded he was? But the
realization came to me that perhaps I must allow Prince Vlad
to handle that matter while I handled the other, so wishing
I had Ana-Maria's guidance.

I knew now was the time to write to my father to tell
him I needed to be rescued from this place, that I wasn't
safe here. I had to compile all of the evidence I had accrued.
Surely, I would have enough now to emphasize my need

for an annulment—between the murder within Bran Castle, Simon's assault on my person, the threats of the Ottomans, and my lack of heir. I yearned for that long-lost letter from the executed thief—it would have strengthened my petition to my father, but I would have to do without it. I had no choice. With the postal service, hopefully my petition would all reach him without prying eyes invading it. Though I didn't have enough yet to prove the supernatural events happening around me, I hoped that everything else would be enough. At the very least, I had to try. What other choice did I have? I couldn't spend another minute in this castle. Waiting for my father's response would be more than agonizing in itself.

Helene patted my shoulders, announcing she was finished, and I stood to have her assist me out of my dress. As she did so, a maidservant came in handing me some concoction steeped with herbs that Helene had requested after remarking that I appeared as though I might be coming down with something. I sipped it as Helene shuffled me out of my skirts and took them away to put them in storage. When she had left me alone, I went to the window, looking out into the courtyard. I could not shake this feeling of unsettledness.

Soon it was replaced as a strange feeling started to sweep over me. My skin seemed to prickle, then, and the sensation began to spread across my body, making my body become heavy and burdensome. The room began to spin around me and my feet became wobbly. I could hardly stand, and fell to my knees, buckling under my own weight. My eyes opened and closed as my head spun. The sound of my bedchamber door opening reverberated through my skull, which was followed by the sound of boots approaching. My vision blurred as whoever it was stood before me, and I thought I heard a low growl, perhaps someone chuckling.

A sound I had heard before.

My body was betraying me, and I could no longer keep my eyes open as my head began to droop. The last thing I remembered was the coolness of the stone floor as I laid my face down upon it.

XXXIV

T HERE WAS A RINGING sound followed by a shooting pain. Even though my eyes were closed, it was blinding. It was my head that ached so horrendously. My eyes fluttered open, and I was met only with the glowing flame of a single candle. I lay on my side, which was the third thing I noticed after coming to, following my throbbing head and the candle. I lifted my hand to rub my forehead but noticed I could not. I tried to focus my gaze on them, but the room was still spinning. My hands were bound by rope at the wrists.

"Good evening, Your Highness," a voice hissed through the shadows. I jerked at the sound of it, trying to sit up. My eyes followed the sound of the voice, and I saw a figure enter the room I was in. The figure held a lantern, which revealed him to be none other than the envoy who had spoken to my husband in our great hall. And it wasn't a room I was in, but a tent. "We have not been properly introduced. Allow me to do so. My name is Cihangir Ali Bey, a most esteemed ambassador of the great sultan, Bayezid the Second." His lips curled in a grin. As he spoke, a servant began to light more candles to illuminate the area around us better.

"Where am I?" I demanded, trying to sound imposing despite my hoarse voice and compromising position.

"You are hours upon hours from Târgoviște at this point, just outside of the Romanian-Ottoman border in our encampment," he answered. "It will only be a few days before we cross the border, and from there... well, that depends."

"Depends on what?"

"Depends on what it is the sultan wishes to do with you. He may either ransom you to your insolent husband, or better yet, ransom you to your great father. Or perhaps even both, an outcome that would reap the most benefits. On the other hand, he may just decide to keep you as a concubine for his vast harem—a Habsburg Princess in his harem would be quite the prize. I cannot say what he will decide. In the meantime, you must be famished. I invite you to join me for dinner. I have produced this for you as something more... dignified to wear."

His tone reminded me of the light nightgown I wore. Straightening, I said, "Is this man going to dress me or are you going to unbind my hands?"

"You will be unbound, for you are my guest. I am confident that you will not try to escape because this place is littered with janissaries who will catch you and return you to me within a moment."

I shuddered as I recalled the last time I heard that word, my heart wrenching at the thought of the European boys that grew up to serve the Ottoman army, leaving their families and never seeing them again. He handed the lantern to his servant and reached forward, untying me. Then the servant behind him held out a garment towards me. I glared at him and then at Cihangir Ali Bey before snatching it from his hands.

"We will give you time to make yourself..." he trailed off, his eyes sweeping down my body for a moment before continuing. It took everything to not slap him across the face right then and there. "Presentable. Then, we will return for dinner, Your Highness."

The folds of his robes swirled around him as he turned, exiting the tent. The moment he was gone, I released the breath I was holding, scrutinizing the predicament I was in. I was in a tent, an elaborate one that housed a cot and a table and two chairs. I held up the garment. It was similar to the robe the envoy wore but smaller. Not daring to think where this came from, I slipped it over my head, pulling it over my nightgown which was now to serve as my chemise. The voluminous sleeves hung past my wrists, forcing me to push them back in order to utilize my hands. It buttoned from my breast to the bottom of my waist but the front parted open to still reveal my nightgown underneath. It would have to do. My hair remained unbound, for I did not have anything to tether it, but nonetheless, I did my best to pat down the unruly tresses.

I went to the flap of the tent and lifted it to peer out. I was definitely in a Turkish camp, that was certain. It was littered with men all dressed similarly to the envoy but also different. Their robes were shorter with a tight vest over them and trousers underneath with thick leather boots encasing their feet. The most peculiar part of their uniform was their white hats. They were triangular, starting off more narrow near their heads, then fanning out with a pleat of fabric folded over and hanging down towards their backs. At the center was a metal piece attached to the hat. These must have been the janissaries that Cihangir Ali Bey had referred to. From what I could tell, I was imprisoned in the center of the camp, so there was no chance for escape. At least for now.

I lowered the flap, stepping back and sitting on the edge of the cot on which I had awoken. How did I get here?

I tried to remember what happened, but it was hazy. I was in my bedchamber, feeling dizzy and weak before ultimately collapsing to the floor. I had been fine before that. What changed?

It was an herbal drink that changed. I recalled the drink Helene had brought me. It had clearly been tampered with, but by whom? Certainly not Helene. She would sacrifice her life for my own in an instant without hesitation. Then who? Before my eyes fell shut, I saw leather boots approach me, standing over my body. I did not see the face belonging to them, but I recalled hearing laughter—the last thing I heard before slipping away.

The impaler prince.

Had he turned me over to the Ottomans? He hated them, though, so why would he turn me over to them? How had he done it? I remembered the looks of jealousy and fury Lacramioara had been giving me over the last few days with the attention I had been receiving for my upcoming birthday. Did she have a hand in it? Was she capable of such a thing? I recalled finding her in the suggestive embrace of the impaler prince. Had they been conspiring against me together? My head was just swimming with ideas. Well, it would seem for now that I would be spending my twentieth birthday with the Turks until I could find an opportunity to escape.

The tent flap opened violently and Cihangir Ali Bey came strolling in. At the sight of me, he grinned. "I have to admit that it looks very flattering on you. It's almost as if it was made for you." Behind him came servants shuffling in, bringing in platters and trays bearing goblets. Wordlessly, they laid the items out, sneaking peeks at me from the corners of their eyes all the while.

I did not know how to respond to the envoy. Instead, I just stared at him, keeping my distance. He took a seat at the table.

"Come," he bid me. "Come and sit. While I despise the Western way of sitting at a table, I thought you would find it more suitable."

Reluctantly, I came over and sat across from him, watching as the servant laid out unfamiliar foods. There were vegetables stuffed with meat, fluffy pastries oozing with chicken and onion, and finally, there was a dish I understood to be rice buried beneath more meat. Then, a servant came in wielding a sword, skewered with more meat. The servant propped the tip of the sword on the table, and using a dagger he pushed the meat off of the sword onto the platter beneath it.

While the servants disappeared, Cihangir Ali Bey reached forward and began to serve me himself, taking a little bit of each and loading it onto a plate. While he helped himself afterwards, I sat and stared at it for a moment, assessing the food.

"Go on," he said after noticing my reluctance. "It is not poisoned. You are far too valuable to do away with. Besides, if we wanted you dead, you would be dead already. Go on, eat."

As if to illustrate it was not tampered with, he took one of the meat-filled pastries and brought it to his mouth, his horse teeth chomping into it. My stomach gurgled rebelliously, and I had no choice but to give in, reaching for a piece of meat and placing it on my tongue gingerly.

"Rumor has it you are quite the musician," he said to me between bites. "Perhaps when we get to Istanbul, you can pay tribute to the sultan with your talents."

"*If* we get to *Constantinople*," I replied curtly. "I am sure Prince Vlad is aware that I am missing by now."

"Even if he is, we are dozens of miles ahead of the Voivode. Before he can gather the men and supplies, we will be too far ahead, and he will be unable to catch up to us." He tore a piece of bread and thrust it into his mouth, chewing loudly. "My men require very little sleep and can go for some time before needing rest."

Saying nothing, I popped another piece of meat into my mouth. I hardly listened as Cihangir Ali Bey continued to talk about the city of Istanbul—formerly known as Constantinople—and all of the changes that had happened to it since Bayezid's father, Mehmed the Second, conquered it. It had been a devastating moment in the Christian Western world. From what I heard, it had become the pinnacle of the Ottoman Empire, holding its arms open to all kinds, with Sultan Bayezid being a patron of both Western and Eastern culture. He boasted about how they welcomed in Spanish Jews and Muslims after the Spanish King and Queen expelled those people upon overtaking Granada.

I was surprised that he did not bind my wrists again when he left, clearly confident that I would not try to escape. He bid me goodnight after the servants cleared everything away, leaving me to ponder what I was going to do. I tossed and turned on the cot, having since removed the robe and draping it over myself to use as a blanket. The air was warm, but I still felt chilled as I tried not to succumb to despair. He said we were a long way from Târgoviște already, and even if I was to escape I did not have any navigational skills to get me back home. Having not traveled this far south before, I was wholly ignorant of the landscape. I would become utterly lost. As the hours crawled by, I played different escape scenarios in my head, trying to work out a plan until I eventually dozed off.

I was jolted awake by someone shouting at me. A janissary had made his way into my tent and was barking at me. I scrambled into the robe that Cihangir Ali Bey had provided me the night before, turning away for some decency as the janissary glared at me.

Once I was dressed, he stepped before me, grabbing roughly at my hands, jerking them forward so he could bind my wrists once more. Then, to my utter horror, he threw me over his shoulder and plucked me from the tent, tossing me into an open wagon. After having been imprisoned in darkness for so long, the light of the sun was blinding, disorienting me further.

"Once we are far from Romania, we will accommodate you with a horse," said a familiar voice. Cihangir Ali Bey. As my eyes adjusted, I could see him atop his own horse, grinning wildly. "We will surpass far beyond the border today, so rest assured, you will not be in that wagon too long."

I said nothing, only watched as the men continued to pack up the camp. Then, we departed and I was surrounded by the men in the ridiculous hats. The sun moved across the sky, indicating the progressing hours. The passing landscape filled me with dread as we moved further and further away from Târgoviște and closer to Constantinople. Reaching for the crucifix that still hung around my neck, I prayed that Prince Vlad was coming to my rescue. It was a bit ironic since I was doing my best to have my marriage to him declared null and void, but we had been on friendly terms, and I trusted he would do what was right. I did not think he would leave my fate in the hands of the Ottomans, in the very least seeing as it was clearly meant to insult him and he would not let such an insult go unaddressed.

Night fell, but we did not stop, and the bouncing rhythm of the wagon eventually rocked me to sleep until the sun came up the next day. It wasn't until night fell again that they stopped, looking to set up camp. By now, I was already long gone from Târgoviște and trying to keep track of the time. I observed the janissaries as they set up camp, trying to find some sort of pattern that could allow for my escape. It was interrupted, though, when that same rough janissary from before came to the wagon and hoisted me over his shoulder again. I squawked, which elicited some laughter from the others around him.

He whisked me to the same tent that had been previously erected, and Cihangir Ali Bey was there, seated at the table once more where dinner had been set.

"We are officially well beyond the border, Your Highness," he told me, his glee ever-present. "You will no longer have to ride in the wagon."

"How fortunate for me," I growled irritably. My skin felt grimy and unwashed and my legs were sore from remaining stagnant and unmoving for so long. As famished as I was, I did not wait for him to serve me, instead digging in right away and wolfing down food as quickly as I could.

"Sultan Bayezid likes a woman with an appetite," he said, his eyes glittering with amusement. That statement made my stomach churn and I set down my food. But that did not deter him from offering me something from another platter, his large garish ring glittering in the light of the lanterns. "Go on, try some of this. It's sweet—very delicious." It looked to be another pastry but glazed and dotted with nuts.

"No, thank you," I replied, flashing a sardonic smile. "My appetite has suddenly left me." I lowered my eyes and noticed one of the servants had dropped a serving knife on the ground without noticing. I slowly shifted my foot over it.

"What a shame, because you would truly enjoy it, I'm sure." He leaned in to grab one and took a bite. An avalanche of flaky pastry and nuts fell from his mouth as he continued to chew noisily. "Hopefully your prince isn't so foolish as to try to pursue us," he continued. "But we are not worried if he does—we are prepared to handle anything that the prince throws at us, should he attack. His troops will not stand a chance. Hopefully he has gotten wise and he will choose to negotiate your release instead."

He took another bite, and my foot practically throbbed knowing the knife lay underneath it. My heart pounded in my chest as my mind churned with continuous thoughts coursing through my head.

Part of me wondered if I had the courage to do it.

"You were sold to me by one of your own countrymen," Cihangir Ali Bey told me. "Very eagerly, I might add. It seems that your people still see you as a foreigner, an outsider that doesn't belong, and they do not want you as their princess consort. Do you know how much I paid for you?" When I did not reply, he smirked, his lips coated with glaze and small flakes like a greedy child. "Thirty pieces of silver. Just like Judas when he sold your so-called savior, Jesus Christ." He then burst out in a round of cackling. "Thirty pieces of silver!

That's all! The adequate price for a timeless betrayal." He threw his head back, still laughing.

Something took over me. A burst of courage rippled through me, and in one swift motion I swept the knife over with my foot, reaching down to catch it in my hand. I lunged across the table, my eyes centered on Cihangir Ali Bey's throat in a display I would have never thought myself capable of. The table crashed beneath me as I dove, the knife raised over my head. He was quicker than I was, and he caught me in his hands as we landed on the ground below, his chair overturning. We struggled, twisting and turning on the ground, my body contorting with his as I desperately tried to plunge the knife into his neck. Alas, it was no use, because he was far stronger than I, as he grasped my wrist and twisted it painfully, causing me to cry out and drop the knife. It clattered to the ground and he reached up, twisting a strand of my hair in his fingers and pulling hard. Tears sprang to my eyes as I cried out.

We twisted once more and my back crashed into the ground, forcing the air out of me. Cihangir Ali Bey was on top of me, then, his face contorted in a twist of rage. "You stupid foolish bitch!" he bellowed, spittle flying from his mouth. His hand gripped my wrists and he pressed them into my chest forcefully with his other hand raised. Before I knew it, his hand came crashing down onto my face, a white-hot heat searing me, blinding me. Then he did it again. "Did you really think that you would succeed?"

My lip throbbed, and the taste of blood rose on my tongue which told me my lip had split open. He wrenched my hands painfully, tying a coarse rope around them once again but tighter than before. The rough fibers of the rope cut into my skin. He stood over me, grabbing the rope and using it to pull me up towards him, the rope cutting deeper into my flesh with every movement.

He thrust his face into mine. "If you think you will escape, you are sorely mistaken. Should your prince show his face I will kill him myself, and I will make sure it is the last thing you see before you are locked away in the sultan's harem forever. You stupid, vile child!"

A wad of something thick and sticky suddenly landed on my cheek, just below my eye. *Spittle*, a faraway thought told me just before another blow landed across my face. Then, still holding onto the rope, he dragged me across the ground to the other side of the tent, throwing me down. He reached for the hem of the robe and he tore it off of me, tearing part of my nightgown in the process. Then, he bound my ankles together. Finally, before he left me there in a heap, his boot came crashing into my side, forcing the air out of me once more. He stormed away, shouting in his native language while I curled in a ball, trying to comfort myself while my head pounded, my lip throbbed, and my abdomen burned.

When I was finally able, I gasped for air, coughing. I had never been in so much pain in my life, nor had I been handled in such a way, ever.

Soft rustling and the clanging of metal made me wince and scramble backwards as best I could, being bound as I was. A couple of servants had come in and were cleaning up the mess I had caused. They wouldn't look at me and acted as if I wasn't there, but I didn't mind. My body was sore in a way I hadn't thought was possible. I don't know how much time passed while I lay there. At one point, I fell into a daze that was similar to slumber, eager to escape the pain that rippled through my body, if only for a moment.

XXXV

T HERE WAS A COMMOTION outside.

It sounded like thunder.

Then there was the sound of a horn lifting into the night sky followed by shouting. The thunder increased, though it wasn't thunder. It was the sound of horses charging towards us accompanied by war cries. My head throbbed, and I longed for a decent meal and a warm pillow under my head. I still lay curled on the ground, slowly coming to wakefulness, but at the comprehension of what was occurring I jolted up, alert.

The camp was being raided.

There was a fury of clashing metal outside along with the cries. Fear coursed through me at the thought of being caught in the middle of it. My wrists and ankles were still bound. I had to find a way to get them loose. The sounds outside grew louder, disorienting me as I tried to wriggle my hands free. It was no use, though, they were bound too tightly, penetrating violently into my flesh.

Just then, a janissary threw open the flap of the tent and came marching in, reaching towards me. I cried out, trying to maneuver away from him, but I could hardly get very far before he scooped me over his shoulder and carried me out of the tent.

Everything was smeared with crimson as flames surrounded us, the very sky itself seeming on fire. Dozens of tents were consumed with fire causing thick, black smoke to billow into the evening sky. Scattered around the flame-engulfed tents were bodies—mostly janissaries—and it was clear they had been caught by surprise. The air was pierced with screams and the continuous sounds of swords clashing, ringing amongst the cries. Arrows soared, whizzing past us in a whistled fury.

It was absolute chaos.

With my hair hanging over my face, I could not discern much else, and I could not tell who the men raiding the camp were. Another arrow went whizzing past me, screeching in my ear deafeningly, and it was met with a scream. Even through my disorientation, I realized at once that the arrow had struck the janissary holding me captive over his shoulder. He collapsed onto his knees and I came tumbling down with him, crying out myself. I landed painfully on the ground, and he landed on top of me.

I struggled beneath his weight, trying to toss my hair from my eyes with a flick of my head. He had drawn his sword at some point and it lay next to us, so I rocked my body back and forth as best as I could to get my arms out from underneath him. I was becoming glazed with sweat from my desperate exertions, but finally my arms became free and I reached for the sword. In the distance, there was the howl of a wolf accompanied by more screams. I used the blade to saw at the bindings around my wrists, trying to ignore the sounds of warfare around me. It was difficult, as the sword was still in my captor's hand. Since his grip on it had loosened, there was no force to keep it steady while I brushed the bindings against it. Finally, in my determination, it cut through the rope and my hands were free.

Without wasting a moment, I pushed the dead man off of me with all my strength. I wriggled out from underneath him, drawing myself up to remove the bindings from my ankles. Arrows went soaring over me in a hailstorm, raining down on the janissaries several paces behind me. They cried out as the arrows embedded into their bodies, furthering my determination to get out of there as soon as possible. I was covered in sweat and grime so my hands were slippery, making it challenging to get the rope off from around my ankles.

Over the sounds of the war cries, swords clashing, arrows soaring, chaos, and carnage came the intense sound of air being pushed.

I knew that sound all too well. No, it couldn't be!

The sound of large wings pushing through the atmosphere began to swell as whatever it was came closer. Screams intensified, and overhead, bursting from the flames and the tower of black smoke, came the figure of a man soaring over all of us. From behind him, bursting out from his back, were enormous wings that carried him through the midnight sky—wings that resembled those of a bat but far, far larger.

I stared, dumbfounded, unable to believe my eyes. I could not make out the man's identity, for he was too high up and the smoke obscured his features. I could only make out that his silhouette was male. Just then, his wings narrowed and he dove, reaching his hand out and grabbing at the throat of a janissary. His wings extended and then flapped, propelling him upward until he dropped the janissary, who came crashing down to the ground beneath, killing him instantly. The winged man did this again to another, but instead of dropping the janissary right away, he pulled the soldier towards him mid-air, bringing his mouth to his throat. The soldier screamed until his screams were silenced when his throat was torn out.

I cried out at the savagery as the winged man tore through the soldiers on the ground, tearing their throats out or breaking their necks in swift motions, all the while working desperately to get my ankles free. At last they were and I stumbled to my feet, running as fast as I could. I did not know what direction I ran, I was just determined to get as far away from this carnage as possible. I wove past soldiers fighting, jumping over those that had fallen, and dove under a wagon at one point to shield myself from another hailstorm of arrows. My chest became heavy as my heart pumped ravenously, and smoke filled my lungs.

Hiding under the wagon, I remained for a moment or two to catch my breath, and from underneath, I could finally see the edge of the camp and a line of trees that darkened into a heavy forest.

That is where I would run to.

Giving myself another moment to prepare, I took a deep breath and scrambled out from underneath the wagon.

The line of trees was growing larger as I got closer to it. A man fell down dead in front of me, and I stumbled backwards onto the ground to avoid him landing on top of me. I clambered onto my feet once more and took off running again when suddenly I was deafened by the noise of air being pushed over me.

"No!" I cried, willing myself to run faster. Tears mixed with sweat poured down my face in my desperation to get out of there. "No! Please!"

My feet were knocked out from underneath me and my vision whirled, disorienting me. The grass that had been under my feet was pulling away from me. The line of trees was falling away from me. I cried out, flinging my hands out to steady myself, to grasp onto anything, but it was futile, for there was nothing to grab but smoke. The sound of cries and swords clashing dimmed but the sound of flapping crescendoed. My hair covered my face until it was thrown aside from a gust of air as the ground continued to plummet away from me. Hands gripped my waist and underneath my knees. I was held captive. My freedom had fallen away from me.

I turned to face my captor.

I knew his face. I knew it all too well.

But the eyes. The eyes I did not know.

They burned bright crimson with the fires of Hell as they stared back at me. The eyes of a demon. Blood dripping within them. My throat burned as a scream burst through my chest.

The edges of my vision dimmed and the darkness swelled until it consumed me and I could see no more.

XXXVI

T HERE WAS DARKNESS.

Even when my eyes fluttered open, they were consumed by shadows. They closed again.

My throat burned. It burned horribly. My lips smacked, desperate for moisture. They were painfully dry. I winced, remembering that my lip had been split open. My hands shifted and I winced again. My wrists were sore, summoning memories of being bound. Then my ankles throbbed as if to remind me that they had been too.

My body felt broken. I groaned.

Then I remembered.

Flinging myself upwards, I remembered.

"You're awake," a soft voice lifted from the darkness.

The sound of it propelled me from the bed, and I scrambled backwards, my fear rushing in once again. A figure was seated in a chair across from me, against one of the stone walls encasing me. There was no light except for the light of the moon pouring in through a window, casting long shadows. The shadows shifted, and in the light of the moon, Prince Vlad was revealed. My fear faltered but did not diminish.

"Where are we?" I croaked.

My throat continued to burn.

"We are safe," he said reassuringly.

I was in a place I did not recognize. A bedchamber. I backed myself up against something hard and cool. A wooden door. I was in what remained of my nightgown, my pale legs glistening in the moon. My arms were bare. The torn sleeves had been removed entirely. A short sharp hiss emerged and then there was a flicker of flame which grew when it lapped at the candle on the table beside the Voivode. Its light was minimal, but between it and the moon, it made it easier to see.

My head throbbed and a wave of dizziness washed over me. In less than a second, Prince Vlad was at my side. I let him lead me back to the bed. His hand was cool on my back.

Then I remembered.

I flung forward, scrambling to the other side of the room and spinning on my heel to face him. I pressed against the cold stone wall as far away from him as I could get.

"Shoshana, please," he said in a tone I had never heard from his lips before. Nor had he ever referred to me by my name before. "You are safe. You need to rest."

"Where are we?" I croaked again, my own voice sounding strange to my ears.

"We are in Severin Fortress. There is no one here but us, you are safe."

I had no choice but to relent as the faintness was making itself known again. Prince Vlad did not touch me again but remained close. I sat on the edge of the bed and buried my head in my hands, waiting for the dizziness to subside. My body felt utterly broken. In the dim light, I could see black blotches on my legs. Bruises.

"Here." Prince Vlad knelt before me, handing me a waterskin to drink from. The water was refreshing as it passed my lips and soothed my aching throat. I set it aside and groaned, holding my face in my hands once more.

I had never felt so wretched in my life.

"It will be better after you have gotten some rest," Prince Vlad told me gently.

How could I rest? I pulled my hands away from my face and pierced him with my gaze. "What are you?"

He rose to his feet, resuming his place at the other side of the room. "I think you know already."

"How could this be? It was supposed to be your father, not you." Tears welled in my eyes, a mixture of sheer exhaustion, confusion, helplessness, and fear. "A s-stri..." I couldn't even bring myself to say it.

He sighed as if unsure where to begin. "He is one too. He is the reason for this, he is the reason for it all—this curse, your kidnapping. He possessed the curse and passed it onto me. Though ultimately, I am to blame, for I was struck by the power that came with it and insisted he pass it on to me. So, at my behest, he transformed me." My unshed tears poured over, then, and streamed down my face. "All this time, I needed to keep you at arm's length because I did not want you to know what I am. I was foolish to think that you would not catch on eventually—I underestimated your cleverness and determination."

I was reeling at his admission. He sat on the chair across the room, leaning forward. His elbows rested on his knees, his hands folded as if in prayer, fingertips touching and grazing the underside of his chin. This picture of him was far removed from his usual impenetrable and imposing stature.

The tears continued to stream down my face. I could not think straight. I was fortunate to be sitting down. My head was spinning.

"My first wife," he continued. "She did not know what I was. She was rather simple, lived in the moment. She was carefree, not keen or observant like you are. She... carried my child, and her body could not withstand the crossbreed infant; she could not sustain the life it needed, and it killed them both. So, you see? I could not give you a child even if you wanted me to. It would kill you. I could not allow that to happen, so it was best that I stayed away, letting you believe that I resented you or was using you for political gain. But then..." Another sigh escaped his lips. A weary one this time. "Now that you know the truth, I understand if you wish to return to your father. You had been searching for a cause to leave, well here you are. We can lie and say the marriage was never consummated, allowing room for an annulment. There is no reason to continue with this marriage. I will stand aside and comply with an annulment if that is what you desire."

I sat in stunned silence. How did he know this? "Ana-Maria..." I began, my voice barely above a whisper. "Her child. It killed her. It was deformed—I saw it... was it...? Did you..." My mind was flooded with that gruesome scene, and my eyes fluttered closed as grief bloomed in my chest once more.

"No, that was not my child. I have never laid a hand on Ana-Maria. That is another matter entirely."

"How did you know I was searching for a way to leave?" I asked, my voice still a mere whimper.

He paused before answering. "It has always been plain that you were unhappy," he said. "Though it is hardly surprising, as I said so myself, I have always kept you at arm's length. There is without question that I have contributed to your unhappiness. This entire time you suspected something was amiss and I allowed you to be tortured by the shadows that plagued you, instead of coming forward with the truth."

"And your father... he..."

"Yes." He seemed to already know what I was trying to ask. "He was the one who sold you to the Ottomans."

"Why?"

"I do not know for certain. I suspect it was to ignite a conflict between nations—Romania and the Ottoman Empire—to resume what he himself could not complete. He knew that there was no better way to do so than to stage your kidnapping and make it look like they had done it."

We fell into silence as my mind reeled, plagued by many thoughts at once. I gazed at him as he sat half-covered in shadows, half-blurred by the tears that continued to well in my eyes. I sensed his weariness rather than saw it as he watched me intently. My heart leapt in my chest.

Here he was, offering me the way out. A clean, simple way out. All I needed was to say so—that I wanted to leave, that I wanted to return home. And he would allow me to request an annulment, no questions asked, no resistance whatsoever, nothing in return. There would be no begging the Pope to grant it, no pressuring my father to influence him. At long last, I could finally be reunited with my beloved Austria, my beloved father, my home. Something I had desired deep down since I left Austria.

At least I thought that's what I desired.

There are times in life where you find yourself on a path that suddenly diverges. You find yourself completely halted, unsure which path to take, knowing that either choice will completely alter your life. Both are just as enticing yet equally daunting. The most intimidating part of it is that you are entirely aware of it as well—that the path you take will change the course of your life forever, but you *must* make the choice. There is no turning back. And the wrong choice could make all the more difference, yet you are blind to the repercussions that may befall you. Regret looms over you, silently pressuring you to make the right choice lest he swiftly springs upon you, ensnaring you in his trap for the rest of your life and making you wish that you had taken the other path. Soon, the anxiety swells, taking over, forcing you to close your eyes and take that first step...

The tears had ceased. My mind quieted, all thoughts receded. I found strength in my legs, rising from the edge of the bed and going to him. His face turned upward and he eyed me curiously. I leaned towards him and brushed my hand along the side of his face coated with stubble, and then I kissed him.

My other hand followed, grazing the other side of his face, guiding him closer to me. He returned my kisses eagerly, his hands sliding up the back of my tattered nightgown, moving me closer to him. A part of me wondered at myself, at the courage that welled within me, in awe of the sensations bubbling through my aching body as we continued kissing each other. His lips were soft and cool on my own tender and sore ones. An invigorating heat pooled in my belly and spread across my body, alleviating the aches and pains that had previously coursed through it, healing me. His hands traveled down, settling on the curve of my lower back and my own fingertips plunged into the curls of his hair, savoring its softness. All the tension of the past melted between us as our hands explored one another wonderingly for the first time, kissing all the while.

I had been ignorant of such things, not knowing such sensations were possible. It was though I had crossed the threshold of a new realm, a realm that enveloped me in heat, alerting all of my senses, almost as if they had woken up from a long, deep slumber. My body burned with this heat, but it was not painful. Instead, I relished it. I was not my own person anymore; I had become a slave to this, and I wanted *more*.

I pulled away from him and straightened. My hands traveled to the laces at my collarbone and my fingers plucked at the laces, the remnants of my nightgown falling away from me in a heap at my feet. There I stood before him, swathed in nothing but moonlight. He released a small breath, his emerald eyes combing every inch of my body. He stood, his fingertips grazing my shoulders, traveling down my back, his cool touch causing ripples across my skin. His hands traveled downward still, and he scooped me into his arms effortlessly, as if I weighed no more than a satchel of grain. He walked to the bed and laid me upon it gently, then lowered himself beside me, bringing his face to mine to kiss me again. His lips traveled downward, along my jaw, down the nape of my neck, to my collarbone.

His hands gently cupped my breasts and a little gasp escaped from my lips. I was undone. I was swept up in a current from which I did not want to escape. His lips traveled lower, replacing where his hands had been, and I thought I was going to die from his touch. The sensation was so marvelous that it couldn't have been earthly. I tugged at the hem of his shirt and he guided it over his head, tossing it aside, and my fingers explored his solid chest, covering every inch of it. My breath staggered as his hands continued to roam my body. Never before had my body and soul felt so united.

His hands pulled away for a moment, then he returned to me, enveloping me in his arms, our bodies pressing against one another. His knee pushed between my thighs, parting them, and he lowered closer to me. I gasped, my fingertips clawing at his back as we joined. He moved slowly at first, then rhythmically. I was flushed and covered in a sleek layer of sweat, crying out as the intensity increased, unable to contain myself. I was glowing, yearning, vibrating, ascending, soaring beyond my earthly being. There was no going back now. A part of me was dying away and something new and fresh was resurrecting in its place. I was falling, my chest heaving with air, carrying me back. He groaned in my ear as I floated back down like a feather, pulling away from me.

He was catching his own breath after his groans had subsided, enveloping me in his arms. Our bodies were sleek with sweat. I was beyond anything now. I was out of place and time. I had closed my eyes and taken that first step down that new path and it had made all the difference.

XXXVII

"YOUR EYES ARE SO silver," Vlad told me, "it's almost as if they contain the light of the moon within them. I have never seen anything like it."

This was the first thing either one of us said for hours. We laid together with me draped over him and one of his arms wrapped around me with the other reaching forward, grazing his fingertips through the ends of my hair. I was exhausted, but delightfully so. I expected my body to ache, but it did not, instead it seemed to have healed rather quickly. "Where did you acquire such disarming eyes?"

"It's an age-old mystery," I replied. My chin rested on my hands, which I had perched on his belly as I gazed up at him. His hair was tousled becomingly, and his emerald eyes molten as they peered down at me. "Many people have asked the same thing." There was a soft tentative knock at the door, making me stir. "I thought you said we were alone here."

"We are, mostly," he said, edging out from underneath me and reaching for his trousers. I wrapped the bed linens around me, unable to look away from the muscles on his back that rippled as slipped them on. "I sent Casimir ahead to prepare things here for our return. With this fortress being the closest to the border, we agreed to all meet here after the raid. In fact, it won't be long before the others arrive. Sometime this afternoon, I should think."

The knock sounded again. Vlad went to the door and opened it, slipping through it only to return with a small tray with food. I sat up, pulling the covers tight around me, suddenly feeling self-conscious of my nakedness. It was one thing to be shrouded in the cover of night, but another thing entirely when in the light of the sun, which poured through the windows in abundance. I had never been naked in front of any man before last night. Though, on the other hand, I had also never seen a naked man until last night.

"You will have to forgive my poor serving abilities," Vlad said, bringing the tray over and laying it on the bed next to me, "but I thought it better that I do it given your... current state." He grinned as he took the chair on the opposite side of the room while I assessed the food that was brought to me—a bowl of stew with a lump of bread. "I have sent him to the nearest village to acquire some clothes for you. They won't be the grandest or most fashionable but they should suffice until we can get you home. Much like that stew. I am afraid that is all that is available right now."

I took the bread and tore it into pieces, dipping them into the broth of the stew before popping them into my mouth. "I had never been so relieved to have stew before in my life," I told him. "Your manservant has done wonderfully. Would you like some as well?"

I had offered without thinking when he replied, "No, thank you. I am well sated after..." He trailed off, and the scenes from last night flashed through my memory, reminding me of him soaring through the sky picking off janissaries one by one. Those violent scenes almost made me shudder. I recalled what he was, my post-copulation reverie beginning to deflate.

"Is it true then?" I asked.

"Is what true?"

"That you... your kind—*strigoi*—only consume... blood?"

He sighed, his reluctance to have this conversation coming forward. "Blood is all that is needed to sustain me," he replied.

"But I have seen you eat at banquets before."

"Yes, but only to keep up appearances. You could only imagine what the reaction would be if it were to get out that I'm not exactly human. For a man in my position, that would be damaging. You can be assured that I would be at the mercy of a large mob. I am not terribly fond of eating food anymore as it can cause quite the discomfort, but again, sometimes I have no choice."

"I see," I said, contemplating as I took another bite. I pushed through any shyness that was coming forward, my curiosity getting the best of me. Apparently something about the shadows of night elicited a great courage that seemed to diminish in the light of day. "What is it like?"

"I am assuming you are asking what it is like to be a vampire. Or a *strigoi,* which is similar to the vampire but has more of the misled folklore that the people pass amongst themselves. Well, it's difficult to say. I do not remember much of what it was like before I changed, but from what I do recall, everything is more vivid now. My senses became sharper, such as my sight and hearing, and I became stronger—stronger than any mortal man, but only when night comes. I am somewhat equal to that of a normal man when the sun is out." When my eyes lowered and I fell silent, he continued. "I hope this does not make you think any less of me, Shana. I am no different now than you have ever known me, I assure you."

Now that it was the light of day, I found myself twisting with a hoard of different thoughts and feelings. I opened myself to him completely in the shadows the night before, but now I found my thoughts racing. "It is just a lot to comprehend. I had a very different understanding of what *strigoi* were before. And everything has happened so quickly—"

"I know. Ana-Maria had a different understanding, as well, but that is all right. How could she have known? She had grown up around all of the tales of the *strigoi* wandering the earth, as all Romanians are, and I guess what they say is true. All folklore is rooted in fact one way or another. But to her credit, she suspected something. I never knew her to be so clever and it is no wonder why you took such a shine to her." He then stood and moved towards me, taking my hands in his. "I can understand any reluctance you may have now, but I stand by what I said last night—if you wish, you are free to return to your father."

I looked into his eyes and saw earnestness in them but also a glimmer of hope. "I will think on it." That was all I could think of to say.

He gave me a half of a smile and let go of my hands gently.

"There is another thing I would like to ask you."

"Go ahead," he said, resuming the chair opposite me.

"Last night, you said it was your father that had sold me to the Ottomans. How did you come by this knowledge?"

"Cihangar Ali Bey's traveling companions delayed their departure, and we found them and questioned them. They were more than willing to divulge the information we sought, and their description of your mysterious captor matched that of my father."

I shivered, thinking of when I was in his captivity. "That name you called me," I said, a sudden memory flooding me. "I haven't been called that in years. My mother used to call me that—'Shana.' People tried to dissuade her from the name she gave me, saying that no follower of Christ should give their child a Hebrew name, but she insisted it remain for she had always loved it. My mother always went against the current. It's interesting that you should call me that."

"Considering it means 'beautiful,' it seemed fitting."

I laughed at his charm, unable to contain myself. It was meant to mask the blush that was rising to my cheeks. "You are too kind. I have one more question, then."

"Go on." His mirth shone through him, making my heart squeeze in my chest. He had never looked so handsome as he did now.

"Am I to take it that garlic does not repel the *strigoi*, then?" I recalled how he handled them in my bedchamber that one evening.

It was his turn to laugh then. "No, they do not. I don't mean to laugh at Ana-Maria's valiant attempts to keep you safe, but no. That is an old myth."

"Well," I said, taking the tray and rising to my feet, putting it on the table beside him. "Seeing as there doesn't seem to be any way to repel you, I suppose I have no choice but to keep you around then. At least for a little while longer." Standing in front of him, I let the bedcovers fall to the floor along with any shyness I had been feeling.

"Oh, *nevastă mea*," he said, his breath catching in his throat. My cheeks warmed at being referred to as his *nevastă*, his wife. "At one point, you might have thought me a beast, but you truly had no idea. You are about to find out what a beast I can truly be." He rose to his feet, coming closer to me, pulling at the front of his trousers.

"I am counting on it," I told him, my own voice becoming breathless.

Later that afternoon, Vlad's unit of men arrived at the fortress, just as he anticipated. By then, his manservant Casimir had returned with some clothes for me. It was the clothing of a Romanian peasant woman whom I was assured had been paid handsomely as this was most likely one of two ensembles she owned. It consisted of a loose linen shirt with wide sleeves that ended at my elbows. Along the upper arms of the sleeves was intricate floral embroidery of red and gold thread, the design traveling from the sleeves along the rounded collar and then down the front. Then the shirt was tucked into the plain cotton red skirt that wrapped around my waist a couple of times with the pleats reaching my ankles. Finally, my feet were encased in plain leather shoes. This had to have been the most simple ensemble I had ever worn, and yet I struggled to dress myself in it. Vlad had to help me tie the skirt in place.

Finally, when my hair was wrapped in the included head-scarf, he told me, "It suits you."

"I hope so, for there is no mirror for me to confirm as much. Still, it has to be the easiest I have ever moved in any garment I have worn." It was true, and it was probably the most comfortable thing I had ever donned.

Vlad had finished dressing long before me and he said, "I will have to greet my men and discuss with them what comes next. With your capture, our tentative peace with the Ottomans has surely fallen off the precarious precipice on which it stood, so we need to prepare. You may join me if you would like, otherwise you may stay here and rest."

"I will come with you, to give my thanks to the men who risked their lives to rescue me." My body still remained sore in the spots where I was struck by Cihangir Ali Bey, but my wrists and ankles no longer felt as sore from being bound except at the places where my flesh was rubbed raw. That would take some time to heal. Even still, I was well enough—invigorated, even—to show gratitude towards these brave men.

Vlad escorted me through the stone halls of the fortress and outside his battle-weathered men were dismounting from their horses. There were fewer than I had originally thought when I was escaping the camp, and I recognized many of the faces as they pulled their helmets off. The immensity of their mission dawned on me. It had been a near-suicide mission, as there had been far more janissaries than there were of them.

"My sovereigns." Lacramioara's husband, Răzvan, came forward. "The task was a success. We left no man alive, per your instructions." He bowed deeply before us and I reveled in the deep love and trust the men had in their Voivode.

"It was, indeed," Vlad agreed. "The princess consort is safe and in our hands again. What of their possessions?"

"We combed through their encampment thoroughly. There was no evidence that the princess' kidnapping was approved by Sultan Bayezid. It seems that this was entirely of Cihangir Ali Bey's own volition. Anything we could, we looted and brought with us."

"And what of Cihangir Ali Bey?"

"Dead, along with the rest of them, your Highness."

"Good. Rest and feed yourselves, you have all done more than enough, especially when we do not know what the next few weeks will bring."

I held out my hands to Răzvan, who took them eagerly. "You have my undying gratitude for everything that you and your men have done for me," I said.

He smiled warmly, and with another deep bow he said, "It is my utmost pleasure to bring my sovereign lady home."

Răzvan was a handsome man with his broad face, golden-brown hair, and deep set eyes, making me wonder why Lacramioara couldn't merely be satisfied with him. He had a good demeanor and was always ready with a smile. He departed with Vlad, leaving me alone to make my way through the rest of the men, expressing my gratitude to each and every one of them individually. There was one face among them that I was not expecting.

"Even dressed as a peasant girl, you are still a vision," Simon said, smiling weakly at me. He had lost all trace of his former gusto. His appearance was ragged, with eyes heavily ringed with dark circles. His skin was pale, his hair unkempt, and he was covered in dirt and grime. I noticed he was not dressed in armor like the rest of the men but wore plain linen clothes instead.

"Are you all right?" I asked him. "Are you wounded?"

"Yes, I'm fine, and no, I am not wounded. Do not fret over me when it was you that was captured by the Ottomans. Having been there myself, I know what they can be like."

He made an effort to pat his hair down, undoubtedly now realizing his appearance was in such disarray.

Forcing away any traces of anger and resentment I harbored—not only for myself but for Ana-Maria as well—I held out my hand and he took it, placing a kiss on the back of it. "You have my gratitude, Simon."

"No gratitude is required, Your Highness. If anything, I hope you will forgive me for everything. That night in Târgoviște—I was a fool, I was not myself, you see. I—"

"You are forgiven, Simon. You don't need to explain yourself any further," I told him, fully meaning it. "You partaking in my rescue and risking your skin to save mine makes us even."

"You are too kind," he said, planting another kiss on my hand before releasing it.

"Get some rest, Simon. Take care of yourself."

With that, I left him, turning my attention to the others who remained. Vlad summoned the rest of his military leaders into the fortress while the rest lingered outside, setting up camp and so on. I opted for a walk around the fortress campus, enjoying the warm air and my freedom from the Turks. The fortress was one large square made up of two compounds, one within the other. The outer compound consisted of a thick outer wall with watchtowers, while the inner compound housed additional watchtowers, a chapel, and the main residence. It was built for practicality rather than luxury, that much was certain.

As I walked, I contemplated the events of the last day and how much had been upended in such a short span of time. Only a day ago, I was in the custody of the Ottomans, then rescued by my husband who turned out to be a *strigoi*—or a "vampire" as he had called it—and now we might be facing a war with the Ottomans. Vlad had broken every under-standing I had of what I believed a *strigoi* to be, and now I wasn't even sure if I did understand anymore. I thought they were horrid bloodthirsty monsters, and yet Prince Vlad was everything but a monster. Even less so, as he had given me an opportunity to get out, away from all of this, leaving the door wide open for me to walk through. But I hadn't. In that moment, I felt I could not be without him—something tugged at my very soul, and with it came a great awakening, a torrent of foreign feelings and sensations stirring within me, some of which I could not make sense of even still. He had mentioned how he kept me at arm's length all this time in fear that I would learn what he was. Yet, simultaneously, I too had kept him at a distance. From the first day, I had hardly given him a chance, instead remaining so jaded by all of my past rejections, thinking my jadedness was a suit of armor when in reality it was only a shroud.

How foolish I had been.

I was left alone with my musings for the rest of the af-ternoon and into the night after returning to the bedcham-ber alone. Casimir appeared later with yet another bowl of stew and bread, serving me himself now that I was dressed. I was finishing my dinner when Vlad came in. I would have expected him to look weary, but he did not, instead looking vibrant and full of energy. The window told me the sun had nearly gone down, explaining his vigor, as I had recently learned.

"We expect retaliation from Bayezid and his men in the coming weeks," he told me as he came through the door. "I have already written to King Wladislas informing him of everything and urging him to be at the ready to send rein-forcements. I have also already written to your father, but for him to react would take even more time, and we cannot waste time. I am assigning men to be stationed here while we return to Târgoviște. Once we are there, you and your ladies will move on to Brașov where it is much safer. Unless you have decided to return to your father, that is..."

I did not reply to his last remark. "Are you certain of that? Will Bran truly be safer?"

"I cannot take any risks," he insisted. "The further you are from the Ottomans, the better, especially considering what has already occurred. And should the worst happen, from Brașov you can quickly travel to Hungary where you may seek refuge from your friend, Queen Beatrice."

It was all so ominous that it sent a chill down my spine. "But the worst won't happen, will it? You said so yourself, you are stronger than any mortal man. That must make a difference. You were unstoppable last night."

"Yes, but the fighting will not always be done in the evening hours. Besides, vampires may be stronger than that of a mortal man, and perhaps difficult to kill, but we *can* still be killed." He removed his light jerkin and draped it across the chair opposite the bed.

"It is no wonder why the village people tend to think vampires are unholy." I thought of the crucifix that still hung around my neck. "I take it crucifixes do not repel your lot either?"

"No. Despite my... condition, I still consider myself to be a man of God." Again, my thoughts were churning, and part of me was still in disbelief that this was all real. Then he continued, "it is all very real, I can assure you."

How peculiar. "You know something," I began, putting the bowl aside. "I have long felt since I have known you that you can read my thoughts. It has always unnerved me."

"That's because I can."

My mouth nearly fell open. "What do you mean you can?"

"I can't explain it, but sometimes your voice, or anyone's voice in close proximity, fills my mind. I have come to learn that it's your innermost thoughts. It happened after I changed. At first, I found it unbearable, but I have since learned to turn it off, only tapping into one's mind when it is most useful."

"Is that so?" I said, feeling indignant and more embarrassed about this than of my earlier nakedness. "So last night, when you said that you knew I was unhappy, that wasn't merely your observation, you truly did *know*... based on my thoughts."

Sensing my indignation and embarrassment—at least I hoped he was only sensing it—he turned to me and laughed. "Come now, I was not prowling your mind all that often, only the rare occasions when it mattered."

"Such as my consent for any further marital consummation," I replied, realization blossoming like a flower rapidly coming into bloom.

"Precisely. Can't you imagine how irksome it would be to listen to everyone's thoughts all the time? Especially when we have grand banquets like our wedding feast, or the one we held for the Hungarians? The chamber would be even noisier than they already tend to be at those events, and I would be absolutely bombarded." He leaned towards me and placed his hand over mine. "Now, seeing as the sun is down and the moon is coming out, let me show you just how real it all is."

We exited the bedchamber and Vlad led me to the top of the inner wall towards one of the watchtowers. Sure enough, the moon was out, a glowing orb in the dusky sky. In the not-so-far distance a wolf howled, something I had heard in abundance since arriving in Romania.

We reached the top of the tower and Vlad stood at the edge. A breeze blew through, lifting my skirt and hair, which had already been freed from the headscarf I wore throughout the day. Vlad eyed the ground below. Then, suddenly, his back contorted, twisting unnaturally. This lasted for a moment or so before great wings burst from his back—the very ones I had seen carry him through the night sky. Up close, they appeared even larger, and in a miraculous defiance of everything I thought I knew, they didn't tear though his linen shirt. Instead, they slipped through as though the fabric had its own set of sleeves for them. At the sight, I couldn't help but gasp in awe.

He turned, his arms reaching out for me. "Are you ready?"

"Ready for what?"

He gave me a mischievous smirk. Then, in one swift movement, I was in his arms. The wall below me fell away, and we were soaring towards the moon in the night sky, that all too familiar sound of air being pushed enveloping us. Instead of fear and panic, though, I was flooded with wonder and amazement. The night sky was so close I could almost touch it.

Such a marvelous thing that it was, I began to laugh, unable to control myself, and my laughter carried away into the night by the demure breeze. The sense of freedom that overcame me was unlike anything I had come across before as we soared further away from the fortress. It wasn't long before the Danube River was below us. Vlad's wings folded, drawing us closer to the river's surface, allowing me to reach out, my fingertips dipping into the black water. Then, his wings unfurled and flapped vigorously, carrying us higher into the dark cobalt sky dotted with stars to accompany the moon. He looped back and we started towards the fortress where he returned me to the watchtower.

"I must feed," he told me, "and while you are handling all of this far better than I could have expected, that is a sight that must wait. It isn't something you should see. Return to our bedchamber and wait for me there. I won't be long." With that, he planted a kiss on my forehead. He smiled at me once more as his great wings lifted him into the air, and I watched as he soared into the night, lingering until he disappeared into the horizon.

In the bedchamber, I lit the candle and removed my clothes more easily than it had been to put them on. First, the shoes came off and then the skirt as I recalled the thrill of soaring through the warm evening air, already eager for it to happen again. I threw the skirt aside before reaching for the hem of my shirt, peeling it off of me.

My skin rose in gooseflesh as memories of our copulating came flooding back—particularly when I had been so bold as to stand before Vlad in nothing but the light of the moon. The sorry state of what remained of my nightgown fell around me after I pulled it over my head once again. I was so giddy, so full of life and longing in that moment, I felt as though my skin was no longer my own, so foreign these feelings were to me. Even though my feet were planted firmly on the ground, I felt as though I was still soaring.

"Good evening," said a voice from behind me.

My skin rose again, but instead of gooseflesh, chills started at my scalp and spidered their way down my back.

XXXVIII

S LOWLY, I TURNED, FEAR gnawing at me. My heart throbbed in my neck, pumping the fear throughout the rest of my body and pulsing in my veins.

First, I saw the eyes. Green, almost like my husband's, but mossy, dark, and cruel, not captivating, warm, and enticing.

"How long have you been there?" I asked, struggling to keep the fear from my voice.

"Long enough," he replied, his eyes appraising my body knowingly, a sardonic grin pulling at his lips from beneath the mustache. His voice was pleasant, somewhere between a tenor and baritone, but the cruelty laced within it was unmistakable.

I was trapped. He was closer to the door than me as he sat, leaning back in Vlad's chair opposite the bed, the same chair where the truth had poured out—the chair that had served as my husband's confessional only the night before.

"What are you doing here?"

"It is about time I met my daughter-in-law," the impaler prince said. "You have been calling out to me for some time, searching for me, hoping to discover what you could about my history. In hopes, even, to destroy me—the garlic was an amusing touch. What you weren't expecting was my son being as I am—a monster. A vampire."

"No," I admitted, my voice coming out evenly. "I didn't." I sounded more brave than I felt as I was nearly drowning in fear.

"I have enjoyed watching you all this time," he continued. "You dance beautifully." His gaze coursed over my body once again. "It's a shame my son has not appreciated you as I would have had you been mine."

"He should be here any moment," I said, "you can tell him that yourself." I spoke with more bravery than I felt as I stood there, absolutely frozen in front of him.

"Ah yes, he is feeding. How considerate of him to take you out into the night sky, but it's really a shame you didn't get to witness him feed. Had you, would you be so forgiving, I wonder? That is when the real monster emerges."

"I know, I have seen it."

He laughed. "That night you stumbled upon him with the servant girl—that was nothing."

"No, I am not referring to that night. I speak of last night, when he rescued me from the Ottomans, to whom *you* sold me."

"I did sell you to the Ottomans," he said, quite pleased with himself. "And finally, it forced my son into action, to take up arms against them, something I spent all of my life doing. I could no longer stand idly by while my son refused to do what needed to be done, so I had to instigate him to take action at last.

"But even still, it is one thing to witness a vampire feasting upon the enemy, but a whole other thing when it is an innocent woman walking the streets of her village alone, or creeping into the bedroom of a child while he sleeps—preying on the innocent. Is that something you could forgive?"

When I did not answer, he laughed again. "My son has known you were aware of my existence all this time, and yet he let you walk the corridors drowning in fear, doing nothing to ease it. He left you alone in the shadows to ward off unseeable demons, slithering through the corridors observing you all the while. Once he heard the murmurs of your thoughts reveal a certain little note tucked in the Hungarian King's letter, he poured through your belongings like a thief in the night, and he stole the book from your sister warning you of my so-called 'atrocities,' detailing the monster within its pages, and destroying them both.

"You Habsburgs sit on your precipice casting judgment, yet you sit on your heels when it is time to raise arms and fight. What you call 'atrocities' are the vast measures I took to keep my people safe, though I needn't explain myself to you or your ilk. Your father has time and time again made promises to take up arms against the Ottomans, to fight for the West and all of Christendom, but falls through each time as he finds himself yet again in some sort of financial trouble, therefore branding him a liar. You Habsburgs bear no honor."

He shifted in the chair, his smirk returning once more. "Speaking of thieves and monsters... that thief even tried to alert you of his innocence. As it so happened, he *was* innocent, his words rang true. He was framed for a crime he did not commit. My son let him go to the gallows knowing full well that man didn't murder that girl—something even I have never done. So, tell me, is that something you could forgive my son for? Framing an innocent man to hide the identity of the real murderer?"

"If he did not murder Ioana," I said, my voice quavering, my facade of bravery faltering, "then who did?"

His mocking grin widened. "Why don't you ask my son? As you mentioned, he will be here soon."

The fear that gnawed at me churned in my stomach making me feel as though I might be sick.

His voice then softened. "You are beautiful... very beautiful. *That* I cannot deny." He then leaned forward in the chair and rose to his feet. I heard again the howl of a wolf off in the distance. "My son knew what he was doing in choosing a Habsburg bride, I will give him that, though even his marriage proves to be yet another one of his failures. He can't even beget an heir." He was coming towards me. Fear threatened to submerge me again, my heart pounding in my ears.

"I can hear your blood rushing through your veins," he said, falling into a whisper. "What a beautiful sound it makes." His eyelids fell heavily, hooding his cruel, moss-colored eyes. "Now it is time to do what my son has failed to do." Faster than the blink of an eye, he swept me up effortlessly, as if I weighed nothing, throwing me onto the bed. He threw himself on top of me. "My legacy must continue! I will do what my son has failed to do and that is to beget an heir!"

I struggled beneath his weight, crying out and thrashing my fists, but he was far too strong. He laughed as he grabbed my wrists, which were still sore from their bondage, pinning them down effortlessly with one hand. I wailed again, and his other hand wrenched at my breast, tugging at it rudely. I cried out again as he lowered his face towards mine, but my sounds were muted when he pressed his lips roughly to mine. His teeth nipped at my bottom lip, drawing blood, which sent his tongue flickering out and tracing alongside it.

"Your blood is sweet," he murmured into the flesh of my neck, "something I know not even my son has tasted. How fitting."

His hardness pressed demandingly against my leg before his knee thrust between my thighs. He withdrew his hand from my breast to pull up the edge of my nightgown.

Swifter than a crack of lightning, the impaler prince was torn off of me. He went soaring across the room, crashing into the stone wall on the other side. He landed on the table which collapsed and shattered beneath him. The sound of the shattering wood made me leap onto my feet and back into the stone wall furthest from him. Standing on the other side of the room was Vlad, his chest heaving as he crackled with rage.

"That is quite enough, Father," he said, keeping his voice steady. But I could hear the rage boiling within his tone.

Dracula cackled again as he stumbled onto his feet. "My son, how good it is to see you again. It has been too long."

"Get out." Vlad's voice rumbled deep in his chest, a growl containing his rage.

"We were having the most engaging conversation. I was telling your wife all about your schemes to cover a murder, to pin it on an innocent man, a conspiracy you yourself were in on." He straightened his coat and brushed the hair back that fell over his face.

"That is enough."

"Well, am I wrong? Is that a lie?"

Vlad lunged at his father, and Dracula braced himself as Vlad came crashing into him. I could only watch helplessly as they fought, throwing fists into one another and deflecting them where and when they could. They moved so swiftly it was hard to follow who struck who, and before me, I beheld the speed and might of vampires as they struggled. It was almost animalistic how they fought, like two wolves trying to tear out one another's throats.

Dracula parried an oncoming blow, dipping beneath Vlad's arm and lunging for me. Because of the small proximity of the chamber, it was easy for him to reach for me. His hand encircled my wrist, pulling me towards him. He whirled so that my arm was pinned behind me, and I was pressed against his chest. With the other hand, he cocked my head to one side, exposing my throat. I sensed the fangs extend in his mouth and hover over my bare flesh.

"You didn't answer my question, son," Dracula demanded, his chest heaving for air behind me as I was stuck pinned against him. "Was that a lie? I think for the sake of your wife, you really ought to answer."

Vlad straightened, his eyes refusing to meet mine. "No, it is not a lie."

"So, you did conspire to frame an innocent man of murder. Do you hear that, my dear?" His breath was warm on my neck. "Can you forgive that? It's a shame that you must learn what a monster my son truly is. He comes from my loins after all—the man you have long since dubbed a monster, when you have been married to one all along. Now tell me, son, who was it that murdered that servant girl?" His hand encircled my neck threateningly, tightening ever so slightly.

Vlad stiffened as he stared at us, his eyes wide. It was a moment before he spoke. Another confession. "It was Simon."

"Simon?" The name fell out of my mouth in a breath.

Vlad's eyes met mine. "What he says is true. Simon did murder her, and I assisted in preventing him from getting prosecuted. While I framed an innocent man and condemned him to death, I exiled Simon, sent him away so he could do no further damage. He is not well. There is another side to him, a side that you do not know, a side that no one can know. I could not let it be publicized. When I had understood that you were warned, I had to clear any evidence against him, including the letter you had hidden in your things, warning you."

For a moment, Vlad almost looked defeated, so far removed from how he always was and how I had always seen him.

"So, you see, dearest? There is a monster that resides in us all. No one is spared. Not even you," Dracula murmured menacingly in my ear.

There was an immense, piercing flash of pain that stemmed from my neck, nearly blinding me. Then my neck became tight. I struggled to breathe. Dracula released me. I was falling.

EPILOGUE

S HANA FELL TO THE *floor in a heap as Dracula released her, laughing. Vlad went to her, reaching for her, but Dracula lunged at him, his hands gripping his son tightly and throwing him into the wall.*

"You owe me everything, boy," he hissed, spittle spraying into Vlad's face. "I have made you what you are—without me you would have nothing."

Vlad threw his head forward, smashing into Dracula's aquiline nose. A loud, sickening crack echoed through the chamber. Dracula stumbled backward, blood gushing from his nostrils. His vision reeled from the impact, but the wound quickly healed, sealing the source of the blood, just as it would with all vampires. Dracula reached into his boot and, in a flash, a dagger went soaring through the air, landing in Vlad's upper arm. He cried out from the pain and pulled it from his flesh. The wound bled profusely, but the flesh swiftly knitted together, and the blood flow stopped. He threw the dagger at his father, embedding it in his belly.

Dracula cackled at the sight of it. "Spoiled boy! I was wrong to invest all of my efforts into you. Your brother Mihnea would have been far more suitable for the throne." He yanked the dagger from his flesh, the skin beneath his torn shirt fusing together. He tossed it into his other hand and lunged at Vlad, who procured a dagger from his own boot and parried the thrust of the incoming blade before it sank into his flesh again. The blades met, the sound of metal clashing reverberating throughout the room. "You were always weak, too immersed in your thoughts rather than taking action."

The blades continued to clash in an intricate weaving of both parties. Each fought to overcome the other, but their skills were equally matched.

Then, Dracula procured yet another blade, raising it over his head and bringing it down over Vlad's face. He saw it just in time and threw his head back. The edge of the blade nicked his cheekbone. With Dracula's arm raised, it allowed Vlad an entry point, and he raised his knee. When Dracula doubled over, Vlad raised his elbows and brought both down into Dracula's spine, bringing his knee back up and crashing it straight into his nose once more. Dracula reeled backwards, stumbling on the pile of wood from the broken table, and dropping the daggers which clattered loudly to the floor.

"It is true," Vlad told his father, grabbing him by the neck and hoisting him up, pinning him against the wall. Strength flooded through every corded muscle that rippled through his body. "I am not you, Father. I never have been and I never will be. You had no talent for diplomacy, you were brash, ruthless, and impatient—everything I am not. Those were the things that cost you your throne and your humanity. You call me a monster and that

may be true, but you... you are the Devil himself." He raised the dagger to his throat and held it there, their eyes boring into one another.

Dracula laughed again, his face coated in a macabre mask of dried blood from wounds that swiftly healed. "Go on, do it. Do it and prove that you are indeed my son. I fought for my throne. Prove that you deserve the throne you sit on, that you're willing to fight for it."

Vlad held the dagger, the temptation to drive it through his neck, to behead him weaving its way into his mind seductively. His chest heaved as the desire to—and the need to not—volleyed back and forth.

He lowered the dagger. "No. I stand by what I said, Father. I am not you, I refuse to fall in line with your methods. Instead, you are to be exiled. Should you show your nefarious face in my kingdom again, rest assured, my blade will be sweeping through your neck, and you will breathe your last breath."

Dracula's face fell and then he suddenly disappeared, nothing but mist left behind in his place. Then it dissolved, and Vlad knew for certain that he was gone.

Vlad threw himself onto his knees at Shana's side, cradling her head in his hand and assessing the damage done to her throat. She was growing pale, losing blood rapidly. Her chest was heaving, trying to grasp onto air to fill her lungs, but as her throat filled with blood, it was becoming increasingly difficult for her to breathe. Her eyes grew dull, the silver in them fading to a somber gray, a faraway look filling them. Then they flickered in his direction and she saw that the impenetrable mask he had always worn had been lifted, his face fallen, his emerald eyes filled with panic as she faded before him.

There, amongst the panic, she saw that his eyes were also brimming with love—stark, naked, unbridled love. A sight she was glad to take with her as she met her end. Her hand trembled as it lifted to caress his face one last time.

"Shana," he said to her, taking her delicate hand and bringing it to his lips. "There is a way... only if that is what you desire. I will never take anything from you that you do not wish to give."

Her eyes began to blink rapidly. Darkness was filling the corner of her eyes, and he was becoming blurred, difficult to see clearly.

"Shana," he urged her. "Tell me if it is what you desire." She was fading, leaving him quickly. Her breath was shuddering. He could hear her heartbeat slowing. It was nearly gone. Desperation consumed him and he leaned forward, pressing his lips to the wound at her throat. He drank deeply.

Her blood was the sweetest thing that had ever passed his lips.

He took only what was needed, then he tore his shirt at the neckline, exposing his chest. With his dagger, he sliced across his flesh, blood seeping from the wound. Then, cradling her in his arms, he lifted her, propping her against his chest. "Drink," he told her. "Drink, dragă mea. Stay with me."

He felt her soft breath on his chest, a tiny little wisp of air that was hardly noticeable. He held her closer, feeling her lips press onto the wound. He held her there for some time, letting the blood pour onto her lips. Then, he pulled her away. Her eyes were closed.

She was gone.

He stared at her, willing her to stir, but she did not. Her mouth was covered in his blood. The wound at her throat ceased to gurgle, and her heart had stopped. He could no longer hear it beating. Her porcelain skin went completely white tinted with blue. Her arms hung limply at her sides. Her raven hair spread around her like a h alo.

She was gone.

Rage burst through Vlad as a scream tore through his throat, pain coursing through his body, tearing at his chest. His scream *dwindled to a howl as he cradled Shana in his arms, pressing his forehead to hers, weeping. Regret came flooding through his body, an insidious companion to the pain. He regretted all the time he had wasted keeping her away from him, all the while unable to prevent himself from falling in love with her. He had not intended to, but he did. The moment he laid eyes on her that very first day in Bran Castle, where he came to her unannounced, finding her standing at her easel, her large silver eyes rounded in surprise. Then, his love for her had bloomed as he began to know her, learning how talented, kind, intelligent, and elegant she was. It had become harder to stay away from her. Her presence had awoken him from a reverie in which he had fallen into before she came into his life, going through the motions of life. But he forced himself to keep his distance. He thought by keeping her from him, he was doing a service to her—first out of necessity, then out of love. She was meant for him, and now he had lost her, and he was doomed to endure the rest of time without her. It was the hell he deserved.*

He continued to weep openly for her, cradling her against his chest. He did not notice the wound at her throat begin to knit together slowly. First, her fingers twitched once, then a second time. The stirring traveled up her arms and her body began to convulse. Vlad leaned back, shocked at the movement in her body. He held her through the convulsions, steadying her as her body slowly came back to life.

Then, she was still.

Everything was still.

Then, simultaneously, her chest flooded with air. She gasped loudly, and her eyes burst open, her irises a crimson red color at first, then fading into silver—the bright silver they had been before, containing the light of the moon.

Acknowledgements

If you have made it to this point, I am assuming you read the novel in its entirety, and I am eternally grateful. This novel has been a long, *long* process in which I have poured my everything into. However, bear in mind that this novel is heavily a work of fiction (I mean obviously, right? There are vampires, for crying out loud). But I say that in regards to the historic elements embedded in this work—yes, there are a lot of historic elements and events that are present, but many that I have played with immensely using my imagination. For example, Vlad Dracula did have three sons, and yes, Vlad was his second and middle child, though he never did end up reigning as voivode and instead lived a quiet life as a Hungarian noble as far as we can tell.

Maximilian the First did have a very happy but short-lived marriage with Mary of Burgundy, and they did have children, however they did not have an eldest daughter out of wedlock and instead had only two children, Philip and Margaret. Yes, our spunky main character was born of my imagination, I'm afraid. But, Maximilian's postal system did exist, though he was very careful to keep it within the borders of his own empire and certainly never would have extended it beyond.

Also, Constantinople wasn't named "Istanbul" until the twentieth century, but I felt it apt to provide the name change in my work to build the tension between the two kingdoms—to add insult to injury, as it were, as the Fall of Constantinople in 1453 tends to be regarded as a turning point in Europe today. So even though this novel takes place over forty years later, the effects still would have been felt by the people living in this time. I also tried to encapsulate some of the attitudes people would have felt about one another in their dialogue, such as the Romanian and Hungarian thoughts about the Ottomans and vice versa, attitudes that are outdated in our modern times. I also play with borders a lot in this novel; Romania wasn't a unified nation yet at this point and wouldn't be until much later. Instead, it was three separate principalities, though seeing as Bran Castle is always referred to as "Dracula's Castle" (even though he more than likely never resided there), I *had* to utilize it in my writing thus my reasoning for pushing borders in this area.

With all of this being said, I encourage you to review some of the extensive resources I have used that are listed in the bibliography, as Romania is full of rich and underappreciated history, and while I took many liberties, I hope I did it justice.

There are so many beautiful souls I have to thank. First and foremost, I would like to thank my husband, who served as not only an apt and attentive audience member, but as my inspiration. Not to mention the limitless patience he had when I became consumed by this thing, spending my every waking moment obsessing over it at times. Also, I can't fail to mention the amount of jokes we had at poor Helene's expense. My husband is a Godsend.

Next, I have to thank Svetlana Perović, that wonderful Serbian princess who came in hot to grace me with resources, reading the novel, feedback, glimpses into Eastern European culture, answers, marketing material, the back cover, and support. John D. Escu for tidbits of the Romanian language for that extra spice. Dr. Marijia Donovan Knežević, your kindness is beyond measure. My lovely parents deserve appreciation too for always believing in my writing capabilities. Then, I would like to thank my lovely readers Kathryn McKinnon, Ranie Glauner, Aleisha McQuown, Jillian Smith, Paige Fulford (who has also been an incredible source of love, kindness, and support too), Niko Blando, Liam McQuown, and Claire Pollock. Then, I would like to extend my gratitude to Sarah Waterman, my darling editor who came in to save the day, "trim the fat," and shower the pages with commas. I appreciate the wonderful folks of my street team for getting the word out about *Nocturne*—they were such a joy to work with and I am utterly beholden to them. Next, to all the generous donors who participated in the kickstarter campaign to help this thing get off the ground at long last. Finally, for those who I have failed to mention, thank you for all of your love and support.

I am eternally grateful.

Much love to you all—including you, dear reader.

Bibliography

Florescu, Radu, and Raymond T. McNally. Dracula, Prince of Many Faces: His Life and Times. Little, Brown, 2005.

Romanian history: A captivating guide to the history of Romania and Vlad the Impaler. (2021). Captivating History.

Blom, J. C. H.; Lamberts, E. (June 2006). History of the Low Countries. Berghahn Books. p. 253. ISBN 978-1-84545-272-8

Oppitz, Marcus; Tomsu, Peter (3 August 2017). Inventing the Cloud Century: How Cloudiness Keeps Changing Our Life, Economy and Technology. Springer. p. 27-29. ISBN 978-3-319-61161-7.

Pettegree, Andrew (1 February 2014). The Invention of News: How the World Came to Know About Itself. Yale University Press. p. 28-30. ISBN 978-0-300-20622-7.

Bauer, Conrad. Dracula: The Origins of the Myth and Legend. Maplewood Publishing, 2018.

Treptow, Kurt W. Vlad III Dracula: The Life and Times of the Historical Dracula. Histria Books, 2022.

McNally, Raymond T, and Radu Florescu. In Search of Dracula: The History of Dracula and Vampires. Houghton Mifflin, 1994.

Wellman, Billy. Enthralling History: The Ottoman Empire. 2022.

Rady, Martyn C. The Habsburgs: To Rule the World. Basic Books, 2022.

Terjanian, Pierre. The Last Knight: The Art, Armor, and Ambition of Maximilian I. The Metropolitan Museum of Art, 2019.

Fashion: The Definitive History of Costume and Style. DK Publishing, 2012.

Hernandez, Gabriela. Classic Beauty: The History of Makeup. Schiffer Publishing Ltd, 2017.

Groza, Adriana. Transylvanian Vampires: Folktales of the Living Dead Retold. McFarland & Company, 2014.

Ibrahim, Raymond. Defenders of the West: The Christian Heroes Who Stood Against Islam. Bombardier Books, 2022.

Pearson, Andrea (5 December 2016). Women and Portraits in Early Modern Europe: Gender, Agency, Identity. Routledge. pp. 79–87. ISBN 978-1-351-87226-3.

A History of the Roumanians. N.p., CUP Archive.

Winder, Simon. Danubia: A Personal History of Habsburg Europe. United States, Farrar, Straus and Giroux, 2014.

Seton-Watson, Robert. Maximilian I. Germany, Jovian Press, 2017.

Simon, Alexandru. In the World of Vlad: The Lives and Times of a Warlord. Germany, Frank & Timme, Verlag für wissenschaftliche Literatur, 2021.

Bain, Robert Nisbet. Slavonic Europe: A Political History of Poland and Russia from 1447 to 1796. United Kingdom, University Press, 1908.

Stollberg-Rilinger, Barbara. The Holy Roman Empire: A Short History. United States, Princeton University Press, 2021.

Văcărescu, Elena. Songs of the Valiant Voivode and Other Strange Folklore, for the First Time Collected from Roumanian Peasants and Set Forth in English,. United Kingdom, Harper & bros., 1905.

"1490-1499." *Fashion History Timeline*, 28 June 2021, fashionhistory.fitnyc.edu/1490-1499/.

The Princely Court from Targoviste, seating place for more than 30 voivodes. Romania Tour Store. (2023, August 28). https://romaniatourstore.com/blog/targoviste-princely-court/

Cârciumaru, Radu. "Historiographic Restitutions. Radu Gioglovan and His Studies on the Mediaeval City of Târgoviște." *Annales d'Université "Valahia" Târgovişte. Section d'Archéologie et d'Histoire*, vol. 22, no. 1, 2020, pp. 77–84. *www.persee.fr*, .

"Read About The Turkish Baths | A Historical Discovery." *Www.Turkish-Baths.Com*, .

The Origins of the Violin:The Birth of the Violin - Musical Instrument Guide - Yamaha Corporation.

Pittaway, Ian. "The Mysteries of the Medieval Fiddle: Lifting the Veil on the Vielle." *Early Music Muse*, 22 Nov. 2015, https://earlymusicmuse.com/lifting-the-veil-on-the-vielle/.

Album of Turkish Costume Paintings - NYPL Digital Collections.

Akbulut, Melisa, et al. *Chapter 6 Turkish Fashion: Ottoman Times Until Today.* 2018. *Ohiostate.pressbooks.pub*,

Clothing and Fashion in Istanbul (1453–1923) | History of Istanbul.

Ottoman, www.theottomans.org/english/art_culture/women.asp

International, Hektoen. *Eating and Drinking during the Renaissance - Hektoen International.* 6 Sept. 2018,

"Severin Medieval Fortress, Drobeta Turnu Severin » Audio Travel Guide." *Audio Travel Guide*, 6 June 2017,

Impact-Tour The Ruins of the Severin Fortress.

Istrate, Daniela Marcu, and Annamaria Diana. "The Black Church Cemetery: Interdisciplinary Approaches to the Study of a Medieval Urban Skeletal Assemblage (Braşov, Romania)." *Studies in Digital Heritage*, vol. 1, no. 2, Dec. 2017, pp. 364–79. *scholarworks.iu.edu*,

Medievalists.net. "Mary, Duchess of Burgundy." *Medieva lists.Net*, 17 Jan. 2014, https://www.medievalists.net/2014/0 1/mary-duchess-of-burgundy/

Overlaet, Kim. "The 'Joyous Entry' of Archduke Maximilian into Antwerp (13 January 1478): An Analysis of a 'Most Elegant and Dignified' Dialogue." *Journal of Medieval History*, vol. 44, no. 2, Mar. 2018, pp. 231–49. *DOI.org (Crossref)*,

The Early Renaissance C1445 – C1535 | Early Dance Circle. https://www.earlydancecircle.co.uk/resources/dance-t hrough-history/the-early-renaissance/

About the Author

K.G. Bolingbroke is a native of Wisconsin. She received her Bachelor's Fine Arts degree with an emphasis on acting. She is also a history nerd at heart, spending her free time not only showering her two dogs with attention, but researching and falling down the rabbit holes of history.

Nocturne is her debut novel.

kgbolingbroke.com
Instagram: @kgbolingbroke
X: @kgbolingbroke